I0596865

The Silver Crescent

By
Debby Grahl

First published by The Writer's Coffee Shop Publishing House, Australia, 2014

Paperback ISBN- 978-0-9994630-0-0

E-book ISBN- 978-0-9994630-1-7

A CIP catalogue record for this book is available from the US Congress Library.

Cover Images from ©konradbak / Depositphoto, ©FlexDreams / Adobe Stock and ©andreiuc88 / Depositphoto

Graphic Design: Niina Kokko

Dedication

With all my love to my parents, Jan and Dwain Paige. Thanks.

Cursed greed of gold, what crimes thy tyrant power has caused.
— Virgil

Prologue

Cedar Bend, Michigan, Circa 1900

The casement clock in the entry hall struck the hour. Cyrus Mosby, sitting behind the mahogany desk in his well-appointed library, read again the familiar handwriting upon the note he had received that afternoon:

> Cyrus, I will be at your home tonight at 8:00. I will be bringing someone associated with your past whom I am sure you will be pleased to finally meet. Trust me when I say it is in your best interest to keep this appointment.

Trepidation moistened Cyrus's hands as he refolded the paper. With trembling fingers, he took a small gold key from his weskit pocket and unlocked the bottom right-hand drawer of his desk, placing the slip safely inside.

At the sharp rap of the lion's head door knocker, Cyrus glanced at his beautiful wife's portrait hanging above the brick fireplace and whispered, "Virginia, my darling, I'm afraid the time may have come for me to pay the Devil his due."

As he had dismissed his small staff for the evening, Cyrus rose to let his visitors in. At fifty-two, his once thick, dark hair was thinning and now completely gray. Lines of age and sorrow creased his weathered face. His well-tailored, pinstriped suit fitted his slim frame to perfection. *It's been a long, hard road to get where I am today. And it all may have been for nothing.* Resigned to meet his fate head-on, he opened the front door.

Cyrus narrowed his eyes as he took in his fastidiously attired brother-in-law Garrison and the unkempt older man at his side.

Garrison smiled. "Good evening, Cyrus. How are you this fine night?"

It took everything Cyrus had not to slam the door in his face, but without a word, he stepped back and directed the two men into his library. Concealing his unease, he took what he hoped was an intimidating stance behind his desk.

"All right, Garrison, I'm here. Now would you be so kind as to explain what this is all about?"

The smug smile Garrison gave Cyrus didn't extend to his cold, green eyes. "Are you not at least going to give us the courtesy of inviting us to sit? Also, the offer of a glass of your excellent single malt would, I'm sure, be appreciated."

Cyrus wanted nothing more than to throw the young reprobate out on his ear, but in deference to the older man's frailty, he waved them into the two leather chairs facing his desk. He took his own seat, and with no attempt to disguise his disdain, addressed Garrison.

"I'm a very busy man. I don't appreciate getting mysterious notes demanding my presence, so I suggest you tell me what this is all about. Then kindly take your friend and leave."

Before Garrison could respond, a raspy voice said, "You don't know who I am, do ya', you son of a bitch?"

To Cyrus's disbelief, the old man lurched from his seat. Reaching across the desk, he grabbed Cyrus's coat by the lapels, bringing their faces inches apart, and said, through gritted teeth, "I've waited twenty years for this moment and here you sit in your fancy house, with your fancy new name, behind your fancy desk, wearin' your fancy clothes, and you ain't got a clue who I am, you lyin', cheatin', murderin', thievin' bastard."

Icy fingers of fear began to run up and down Cyrus's spine; his gut clenched with every word the old man spoke. He fought to maintain a haughty expression as he stared into those hate-filled eyes.

"Release me, sir, and control yourself," he said before Garrison spoke.

"Yes, my good man, this kind of behavior will gain you nothing. We're all civilized men here. I'm sure, after hearing what you have to say, our good friend Cyrus will be more than happy to atone for his past sins and give you your due."

"He damn well better." The old man sneered as he retook his seat.

In a gruff voice, throat gone dry, Cyrus demanded, "For the last time, what is this about?"

Garrison paused to light his thin cigar. "Well, Cyrus, it's about a Colorado silver mine and murder."

For a moment, silence filled the room.

Cyrus took a deep breath, and then forced his words to sound calm and steady. "I don't know what it is the two of you are trying to accuse me of, but I can assure you I know nothing of it."

The old man scowled. "You're a goddamned liar. You murdered two men then ran off, stealing their share from the silver mine, and after twenty years I'm here to get back what belongs to my family."

"Sir, I don't know who you are, but if this is some misguided attempt to extort money from me, trust me, it will not work."

"Perhaps, Cyrus, this will refresh your memory." Garrison tossed a document onto the desk. "Go ahead, read it. I'm sure you'll find the contents interesting."

Palms damp with sweat, Cyrus drew the creased document toward him. The first lines confirmed his worst fears: MINING DEED—Claimants Eli Wilkey, Nathan Hamilton and Clayton Hamilton —Signed the 5th day of April, 1879; Leadville, Colorado.

His entire body coated in a cold sweat, he looked at the old man and whispered, "Who the hell are you?"

"I'm the brother of the man you murdered. Did ya know he had a brother? You musta known he had a wife and baby girl back east. Since you seen to it they were left with nothin', I guess you didn't give a damn, did ya? I told his wife if it took me to my dyin' day to track down the no-account bastard who did this, that's just what I'd do. Now, by God's grace and the kindness of this young man, here I finally am."

Once again, a tense silence filled the room.

Then Garrison spoke. "In recounting your story to me, my good man, didn't you state there were two bodies found in that Colorado mine?"

"That's right," the old man spat. "Not only did this no-account bastard kill my brother, he killed his own."

Cyrus jumped to his feet. "I killed no one. If you've been searching for your brother's murderer for twenty years, I'm sorry to tell you you've been looking for the wrong man. For your information, your brother's murderer also died that day in the mine."

For a second, a bewildered expression filled the old man's face, replaced by one of doubt. "If you didn't kill them, why'd you run off with all their money?"

"You don't understand; I was given no choice." His anger spent, Cyrus slumped back into his chair. In a voice dead of emotion, he said, "Any wealth I gained from the sale of that accursed silver has been replaced. You are welcome to take it all."

Garrison leaned forward giving Cyrus a satisfied smirk. "Wait a minute. I want to make sure I understand this correctly, Cyrus. You're admitting to having the missing money from the mine?"

"Garrison, you're nothing but a worthless piece of horse dung. I don't know how you came to be a part of this, nor do I care. So let me be very clear. Whatever recompense I owe this gentleman and his brother's family is between us. This is none of your affair."

"Oh, but I'm going to make it my affair."

In one swift move, Garrison rose from his chair, snatched the deed from the desk, whipped out a pocket revolver, and shot the old man dead.

Stunned, Cyrus watched as disbelief filled the old man's face a moment before his limp body crumpled onto the Persian rug, blood darkening the front of his shirt.

A triumphant smile spread across Garrison's face as he pointed the gun at Cyrus. "All right, let's you and me have a little talk about where you've hidden the money from the sale of that silver. You know I never trusted you. I always thought you were concealing something and now, thanks to this gentleman here"—he kicked the prone figure with the toe of his shoe—"my suspicions have been confirmed."

Cyrus lunged toward him and cried, "You rotten little bastard!"

Garrison dodged, stepped out of Cyrus's reach, and laughed. "Temper, temper. I don't think you appreciate the position I have you in with this filth out of the way." He glared contemptuously at the dead man. "I'm the one holding all the cards." He waved the deed in the air and continued. "So you see, because of this little piece of paper and all it implies, you're going to give me the stolen money you've been hiding all these years."

His entire body shook with anger as Cyrus came slowly around the desk, his voice low and menacing. "You know nothing of the truth of what happened that dreadful day in that mine shaft, nor do I intend wasting my time trying to explain it to scum like you. One thing I will make perfectly clear." He jabbed his finger in Garrison's face. "You will never get your greedy hands on a single coin of that money. That silver is cursed. It's brought me nothing but personal grief and heartache. I'm sure that until it's in the hands of the one who is truly worthy, it will remain cursed. So it will stay where I put it."

"You're crazy." Garrison shoved the gun barrel against Cyrus's chest. "I don't give a damn if it's blessed or cursed. Tell me where it is."

As Cyrus stared into Garrison's eyes, another's eyes from long ago appeared in their place, eyes that mocked him, eyes filled with greed, eyes of another man who would kill to get what he wanted. He stood reliving the moment that had changed his life forever. Twenty years of rage erupted from deep inside—rage for the injustice, rage for twenty years of living with fear, rage for the loss of his beloved wife and children, rage toward the one who had turned his life into a living hell.

With a bellow that reverberated off the library walls, and with the strength of that rage, Cyrus snatched the gun from the younger man's hand.

At night, here in the library, the ghosts have voices.
— Alberto Manguel, The Library at Night

Chapter 1

Cedar Bend, Present Day

Majestic oaks, fields of corn, and rambling farmhouses flew past as Max Holt drove his black, '66 Mustang convertible down an unfamiliar rural road. Frustrated with his job and aggravated by his business meeting, Max had decided he needed a drive to clear his head. He turned his Bob Seger CD up and hit the gas.

Roaring along between the weathered fence lines, distracted by his thoughts, he barely registered the faded "For Sale" sign. As though an invisible force were pulling him back, he made a U-turn and drove up an overgrown, tree-lined drive to a three-story Victorian home surrounded by an unkempt lawn.

His pulse quickened as he stepped from the car. With childish delight, he stared at the house's crumbling gingerbread trim, peeling paint, and cracked windows.

Max smiled. His day may just have improved. He glanced around. The house seemed deserted. Should he go in? At worst, he'd get caught trespassing. He carefully walked up the rotted steps onto the long columned porch. At least the stained-glass fanlight above the front door was still intact. He tried the door. Finding it unlocked, he called, "Hel-lo, is anyone here?"

Not getting a reply, he stepped into the wide entry hall.

A strange sense of belonging came over him as he took in his surroundings. To his right, a curving mahogany staircase rose to an open landing on the second floor. Doorways lined the central hall to the rear of the house. It felt almost as if he'd been there before, but he knew that was impossible. Feeling somewhat foolish, he shook off the strange sensation and again called, "Hello?"

When the house remained silent, he began to wander through the spacious, empty rooms. Each step he took revealed intricate carved moldings, Adams fireplace mantels, and smiling cherub medallions above dusty crystal chandeliers.

His mind overflowing with ideas for restoring the house, Max didn't notice the growing cold until he paused in the library doorway. Turning to see where the draft was coming from, his eyes were caught by a portrait that hung above a brick fireplace—a beautiful woman, dressed in a long, dove-gray satin dress with a fitted jacket. As he stared into her blue-green eyes, they seemed to shift to look over his shoulder. An icy chill ran up his spine.

"What the hell?"

He spun around, but the hall was empty. He shook his head. *Come on, Max. Get a grip. You're alone in an old house, and your imagination is playing tricks. The portrait's eyes did not move.*

Yet, when he turned back, he could have sworn the woman made eye contact with him. He swallowed hard. *This is crazy. Paintings in old houses are always creepy.*

Still uneasy, he studied the room more closely. His forehead creased in puzzlement. The other rooms he'd gone through had been empty, but in here the ceiling-high shelves still held books. The Persian rug seemed almost new. The antique mahogany desk and other furnishings could have been there since the house was built but looked clean and cared for.

Again, he shook his head. *Weird.*

He crossed the room to look out a tall French window that flanked the fireplace. Max imagined the weed-choked yard as a pristine expanse of manicured lawn sloping down to a curving path through the trees, leading to the stream below, and thought of his architect friend, Jack Callaghan. *I'll bet Jack could design an outdoor terrace for summer dining.*

He smiled, thinking of the delight on Jack's wife, Kathy's, face when he asked her to do the interior decorating. His biggest challenge would be talking his friend Oliver into leaving his job as a sous-chef in Boston to come work for him.

Having a passion for restoring old houses, Max's dream had always been to open his own restaurant and inn. But after graduating with an MBA, he had taken a job as business manager for a small electronics company. Now a large corporation was buying the company and Max felt the time was right for him to leave and pursue his dream.

Max smiled. Fate had definitely intervened and led him to this house. Still gazing out the window, his mind bursting with ideas, a sound behind him made him jump. Turning, Max scanned the room. He saw no one, but the sense he wasn't alone had his palms growing damp.

He cocked his head, listening. The sound of his own breathing was all he heard. *I'm as jumpy as a bunch of little girls.*

Max tried to ignore the eerie sensation as he headed for the door. He'd only taken a few steps when he saw an object lying on the floor near the desk. He bent down to pick it up and frowned. Silver-gray in color, it was the shape of a crescent moon and made of heavy glass. *A paperweight, perhaps?*

As he placed it back on the desk, he noticed that the surface was polished to a glassy finish. The object must have fallen from the desk, and that had been the sound he'd heard, but how? Mystified, his attention was again drawn to the woman in the portrait. Her eyes seemed so real he could have sworn she was trying to tell him something.

Shaking off the sensation, he went to explore the rest of the house.

Upstairs, he found the master bedroom with an adjoining sitting room and a balcony that overlooked the stream. In the attached bath, the antiquated claw-foot tub and pedestal sink suited the house, but he'd replace them with a modern shower and whirlpool tub. There were six additional bedrooms and four more baths. *Plenty of room for paying guests.*

Back downstairs, he ended up in a small conservatory off the kitchen. The house needed some updates, but with the money he'd saved, and if he did most of the work himself, he could do it.

"Yes," he yelled, punching the air with his fist. "I've found the perfect house in the perfect setting and I'm not even sure where the hell I am." He laughed and hurried back out the front door.

Unable to contain his excitement, he sped down the drive, stopping long enough to write down the realtor's information. *Well, Miss Paula Reynolds with Cedar Bend Realty, I'm about to change my life, and hopefully, make your day.*

Max grinned at the prospect of telling his boss to shove it. He gunned the Mustang's engine and headed in the direction of town.

When Max entered the real estate office, he was greeted by an attractive woman in her early thirties with dark brown, shoulder-length hair, tortoise-shell designer glasses, and a navy blue business suit that showed off her trim body and long legs. *Very nice.*

"Hello, I'm Paula Reynolds. Can I help you?" she asked, flashing a brilliant smile as she walked toward him.

Max smiled back. "I certainly hope so, Ms. Reynolds. I'm Max Holt." He held out his hand. "And I was just trespassing on one of your property listings."

She shook his hand and asked, "Which property would that be?"

"An old Victorian about five miles out of town."

She hesitated. "You must mean the Mosby place. Was it a large house in need of repair?"

Max nodded. "I tried the door and it was unlocked, so I went on in and looked around. I know I shouldn't have done it without you being there, but I couldn't resist."

She narrowed her brows. "The house wasn't locked?"

Max shook his head.

"That's strange. I have the keys right here. In fact, I just showed that house a few hours ago, and I know I relocked the door. It didn't look as if it had been broken into, did it?"

"No, but it certainly needs some work. Has it been empty a long time?"

Again she hesitated. "Well, kind of."

Max cocked his head. "Is there a problem? The house is for sale, isn't it?"

"Yes, it's still for sale. In fact, I had an offer on it this morning."

"Damn. So I'm too late?"

"No, not exactly. The problem is that the person offered the asking price which means you'd have to go higher on a counteroffer."

"Great. Tell me what the asking price is, and we'll go from there."

She sighed. "Mr. Holt, before we go any further, I feel obligated to tell you that supposedly . . ."

"Supposedly what?" he asked when she didn't continue.

She lowered her voice to a whisper. "The Mosby house is supposed to be haunted."

Max couldn't help but chuckle. "Is that right?"

"I know that sounds crazy, but I grew up here and strange things have happened at that house."

"Like what?"

"Let me give you a little information first. Then perhaps it being haunted won't sound so bizarre." She pointed to a chair in front of her desk. "Why don't we sit down?"

Max sat where she indicated and propped a booted foot across his knee. "Okay, I'm all ears."

She took her seat behind her desk, folded her arms upon the shiny surface, and leaned forward. "The story remains Cedar Bend's biggest mystery. You see, more than a hundred years ago, the owner and two other men were found dead in the library—all of them shot. Why they were killed or who the killer was is still unknown." She shook her head. "People say images float past the windows, gunshots can be heard, and the lights blink off and on."

Max grinned. "I assure you, I don't believe in ghosts, but I am curious about one thing. Unlike the rest of the house, the library is still furnished and in surprisingly good condition."

Her cheeks paled. "You were in the library?"

Max nodded.

"Did anything strange happen?"

He paused, remembering the sensation of not being alone and the eerie portrait, then shrugged it off. "Miss Reynolds—"

"Please, call me Paula."

"Okay, Paula. Old empty houses always seem a little creepy. The thing I found strange about the library was that it looks as if someone still uses it. Not only is there some wonderful antique furniture, the shelves are full of books."

She nodded. "Cyrus willed the house to the town of Cedar Bend, as a historical monument to himself, I guess. Neither the house nor any of the contents could be sold or given away for a hundred years, so the city officials just hauled it all up into the attic and used the space for offices, meeting rooms and storage. Except for the stuff in the library. For some reason that was all left as it was. The town has also used the house for community functions and social activities, but the money Cyrus left for upkeep ran out, and rising costs have made it difficult to maintain the property. The city stopped using it years ago and finally decided to sell. People say that even while the house has been sitting vacant, whenever they have gone into the library, it's always clean and looks lived in."

Max shrugged. "Sorry, you still haven't convinced me ghosts are living in the library. But what an attraction for my guests that would be."

She frowned. "Guests?"

"My plan is to restore the house and open it as a restaurant and inn. So how do we get the ball rolling?"

"Mr. Holt—"

"It's Max."

She smiled. "If you're sure, Max, I'll put together the paperwork for your counteroffer and we'll see what happens. Are you from around here?"

"No, I was in Ann Arbor on business, and I just happened to be driving by and saw your sign."

Her dazzling smile back in place, she said, "Cedar Bend is a great town. I think you'll like it here."

Max smiled back. "Well, Paula, first I need to buy the house."

"Oh, I have a feeling you usually get what you want."

Back in the library of the old house, the woman in the portrait left her frame and gently floated to the carpet. "Honestly, Cyrus, did you have to play tricks with the boy? I couldn't believe it when you knocked the paperweight from the desk. The last thing we want to do is scare him off."

A shimmering shape materialized into the form of a man seated behind the desk. A look of satisfaction crossed his translucent face as he smiled at his wife. "I'm sorry, my dear. I couldn't resist planting our first clue."

"We've waited for over a century, and now he's here. Nothing must stop him from purchasing the house, especially Garrison. I was shocked to see him standing behind Max. I thought you had him under control."

"I managed to stop him from creating more mischief. But I'm afraid he may turn out to be our biggest problem."

Her still-vibrant blue-green eyes flashed. "Leave Garrison to me. I'll make certain history doesn't repeat itself. But what about the girl?"

"Thankfully Grace can communicate through the cheval mirror. When the time is right, she'll help Elise discover what she'll need. She's confident that is all it will take to send her our way. Grace is as anxious as we are to finally put this to rest. By the time Max restores our beautiful home, Elise will be here." He sighed. "Then, if everything goes according to plan, my debt to her family will finally be repaid and we can be at peace."

Virginia smiled at the man she'd loved through life and death. "Oh, love, our long journey may truly be at an end."

He rose and opened his arms to his wife. As their shimmering silver shapes merged into one, a collective sigh echoed through the house.

Because he is as greedy as the grave and like death is never satisfied.
— Habakkuk 2:5

Chapter 2

Standish, Pennsylvania
The familiar scent of lemon polish still hung in the air when Elise Baxter entered the empty house. She stood in the foyer blinking back tears as memories of childhood visits with her grandparents washed over her. She could almost smell the aroma of baking bread and oatmeal cookies as she remembered happier times. How could her grandmother have been alive three days ago and now be gone?

Elise took a calming breath. She needed to be strong to fulfill the promise she had made. Starting down the center hall, she paused at the door to the front parlor. Above the fireplace hung the portrait of her great-great-grandmother, Grace. If not for the Victorian clothing, the painting could have been of Elise herself. Grace's hair was a rich, dark auburn that fell past her shoulders in a cascade of curls. Her eyes were deep blue, set beneath delicately arched brows, her nose small and straight, her lips slightly full.

As a child, Elise had been drawn to this room. She'd gaze at the portrait and feel as if Grace were trying to speak to her—it had seemed so real. The first time it happened, it had scared her so much she'd run screaming to her grandparents. Her grandfather told her it was only childish imaginings, but her grandmother said that though sometimes things happened that couldn't be explained, she needn't be afraid. She told Elise there was a special bond between her and Grace and someday, when she was older, she'd tell her the story of Grace's lost treasure.

Her grandfather had angrily declared the tale was nonsense and best left alone. Her grandmother had ignored him, and once a few years had passed, told Elise how Grace's father had hit it big in a Colorado silver mine, but he and one of his partners were murdered. The other partner had vanished with all their money.

Elise walked into the room and stopped in front of the fireplace. "Okay, Grace, if there's a missing fortune, it's going to be up to you to lead me to it."

Had it just been a week ago when Elise had stood next to her grandmother's hospital bed as she tried desperately to speak? The stroke had rendered her bedridden and nearly incapable of speech. Elise had been able to decipher only a few words.

"You . . . find . . . Grace . . . trunk . . . attic . . . please." Her grandmother had become extremely agitated until she'd promised to do as she asked.

"So, Grace, I could use a little help here."

The room remained silent. Elise shrugged and made her way toward the back of the house and the attic staircase. When she reached the top and opened the door, she groaned. Grace and her husband Markus had built the house in the early part of the twentieth century, and it appeared that nothing had been discarded since.

Where to begin? As children, she and her cousins used to come up here and play dress up with clothes from the trunks, but if one had specifically belonged to Grace, she didn't know which. As she scanned the room, she saw a faint, shimmering light coming from the farthest corner. Sensing she wasn't alone, her heart sped up and she quickly glanced around.

Get a grip. There's no one here but you and the junk. But when she turned back toward where she'd seen the glow, the light was even brighter.

"O-kaay, if someone is there, you can come out now. The fun is over."

When the attic remained silent and the glow got even brighter, she eased her way back toward the steps. If this was one of her younger brothers' idea of a joke, she was going to throttle him. When she reached the top of the stairs, she paused. If she wasn't mistaken, her father and brothers were gone, meeting with her grandmother's attorney. So who else could it be?

"Hello. I know you're here. You might as well come out."

When there was still no response, she bit down on her lower lip. She was a journalist, wasn't she? Wasn't she supposed to investigate unusual happenings? Her curiosity stronger than her fear, she took a deep breath and began to make her way toward the glow.

As she wound her way around sheet-covered furniture, a child's wagon, a pedal sewing machine, and stacks of boxes, she realized that a jumbled pile of more of the same still barricaded the area she needed to reach. *Great, now what?* Hands on hips, she decided the best way was up and over. So she began to climb.

As she was about to come down the other side, a gasp lodged in her throat. A silver mist swirled around a large trunk nestled in the corner. The gold plate on the front blazed with the name GRACE WILKEY BAXTER.

"All right, whatever is going on, you're really beginning to freak me out."

The only sound was her own voice. She swallowed hard. She'd come this far, so she gathered her courage and made her descent.

As she knelt to open the trunk, the mist faded away, but a faint glow remained. Scents of lavender and cedar filled the air as she pushed back the heavy lid. "Oh," she cried in delight, seeing the trunk held colorful hatboxes. Since childhood, she'd had a passion for vintage hats and this was like finding a treasure chest.

With the thrill of her find, she forgot her unease and removed the first box. Across the top, written in silver script, were the words WILKEY MILLINERY, WILLOW GROVE.

Gingerly, she lifted the lid and sucked in her breath. Inside lay a wide-brimmed, black velvet hat trimmed in burgundy silk woven into a beautifully crafted rose. With excitement, she withdrew box after box until hats of every size and shape surrounded her.

When she reached for the last box, she realized it was heavier than the rest. Puzzled, she placed it on the floor in front of her. Her pulse quickened when she saw it wasn't another hat. Inside, tied up in red ribbons, were stacks of what seemed to be letters. Carefully, she untied the first stack and read the envelope's faded address:

> Emma Wilkey
> Willow Grove, Penna

She glanced at the return address:

> Eli Wilkey
> General Delivery
> Leadville, Col

With eager anticipation, she unfolded the thin, brittle paper and began to read.

> Leadville, Col
> July 12, 1879
>
> My dearest Emma,
>
> I am sending you wonderful news. After months of finding nothing but small amounts of silver ore, we've struck the main vein. Emma, my love, we may be rich beyond our imagining. My partners, Nathan and Clayton Hamilton,

believe the vein runs deep. Everyone said we were fools for buying the mine from Jake Potter, but now the joke is on them. This means I will not be home until spring. Even though I am not looking forward to spending the winter in these mountains, and I miss you and baby Grace terribly, I will be returning a wealthy man.

I am including a larger draft than usual this time. Hopefully, it will be enough to hold you until we are able to extract more ore. The silver strikes are bringing people in from all over. They even say we will have train service here by spring. The town is beginning to grow and is becoming more and more unruly. Knowing that you are safe and my brother Hank is looking after you both is what pushes me each day to go down into that hellish mine. Someday this will all be behind us, and my dear Emma, we will never have to worry about our survival again.

All my love to you both. Give Gracie a kiss from her papa.

Yours,

Eli

)

Leadville, 1879
Eli slipped the letter into the envelope.

"Come on, Eli. Nathan's got the team hitched to the wagon, and he's in a hurry to get to town and celebrate," Clayton Hamilton said from the open door of their one-room log cabin.

"I'm coming." Eli placed the letter in his pocket and reached for his hat.

Outside, the morning was warm and the sky a brilliant blue. At ten thousand feet, Leadville sat high in the Rocky Mountains. Though the terrain was rugged, with pine and aspen trees dotting the hillside, Eli was in awe of the beauty all around them.

"About time. Morning's almost over," Nathan said from the wagon seat as Eli climbed into the back. "I ain't never seen a man write to a woman as much as you."

Eli smiled. "I'm crazy about that girl. Besides, I had to tell her about the strike."

"What're you gonna do with your share, Eli?" Clayton asked from the seat next to his brother.

"I'm going to build Emma the biggest house in Willow Grove and take her to Philadelphia so she can buy all the fancy clothes she wants."

Nathan snorted. "No one but a damn fool spends all his money on a woman."

"Yeah, and what do you plan on doing with yours?" Eli asked. "Me, I'm going to own me a town, just like Mr. Horace Tabor owns Leadville. Then everyone will be bowing and yes-sirring to me like they do with him. I'll have me a fancy whore on each arm and a big old mansion right smack in the middle of town. No more will people look at me like I'm shit on their shoe."

Clayton shook his head. "You've always had big plans. Me, I'm heading for San Francisco."

"Why's that?" Eli asked.

Clayton shrugged. "I don't know. Guess because I saw one of those Daguerreotypes and always thought it seemed like a pretty place to live."

Again Nathan snorted. "It's a shame I have to split all that money with two dang fools."

As the wagon reached the outskirts of town, Clayton whistled. "I swear this place has doubled in size since the last time we were here."

Eli took in his surroundings, amazed at the number of businesses, hotels, saloons, and bawdy houses that now lined either side of the wide, dirt street. "What are they building over there?" He pointed at a large structure under construction.

"That's the new opry house," Nathan replied. "Ain't it something?"

"And the new bank is open," Clayton said. "Is that our first stop?"

Nathan nodded. "We'll deposit the silver then take the wagon to the livery. Then I plan on going to the barbershop for a bath and a shave. Then I'm getting something to eat, then going to Fanny's for a fancy lady and a bottle of whiskey. I'm thinking we should plan on staying in town tonight. Tomorrow's Sunday, and we weren't going to work anyways."

"Fine with me," Clayton said as he jumped down from the wagon. "How about you, Eli?"

"Sure. I'll go get us rooms at the hotel. I believe I'll also have a bath and some food."

"Don't suppose you'll be getting you a woman?" Nathan said.

Eli shook his head. "I have all the woman I want back home."

"Like she'd know if you got yourself a little. Damn it, man, it's only natural. No woman should expect a man to go without."

"But I'd know," Eli replied good-heartedly.

))

Leadville, Col
November 9, 1879

My Dearest Emma,

I can't tell you how much I enjoyed your letter. The nights here are long and lonely. It has been snowing up here, and getting to town is becoming almost impossible. We did purchase a wood stove, so at least the cabin is warm and we can cook. The mine is producing more silver than even we imagined. Clayton and I wanted to hire more men to help us, but Nathan will not hear of it. He is afraid if more know how rich our strike really is, we'll have trouble with thieves. There are many here who have not been as lucky, and desperate, hungry men will do desperate things. I understand Leadville's sheriff has his hands full. There are even rumors of outlaws in the area.

I miss you terribly and can't wait until spring when I can board a train and return to you and Grace. There's an old prospector with a sled who brings supplies to the camps. I'm giving this letter to him to mail.

All my love,

Eli

))

A blast of cold air filled the room as Clayton came through the door.

"Damn, it's snowing again." He stomped his boots and headed for the coffee pot they kept simmering on the stove. "I'm about half frozen. I told Nathan it was too damn cold to be in that mine, but he won't listen. I swear, Eli, all the man cares about is digging more silver. As for me, I'm not about to catch my death over something I don't need." He sipped the hot coffee. "I have more money now than I'll ever spend."

Eli nodded. "If it were spring, I'd take my share and head for home."

Clayton shook his head. "I don't know what's gotten into Nathan. He's determined to get every last drop of silver out of that mine." He glanced at the leather satchels full of silver bars. "He doesn't even want to keep the silver in the bank. He's afraid outlaws are going to rob it and we'll lose everything."

"As long as the snow keeps us pretty well isolated, we don't have to worry about thieves up here. But I know what you mean. I'm glad the mine account is in all of our names and the majority of the money is already there. That's a brand new bank with a Wells Fargo safe. I don't think we're in danger of having our money stolen."

)

THE COLORADO DISTRICT TELEGRAPH OFFICE
WESTERN UNION TELEGRAPH CO

MAY 5 1880
EMMA WILKEY
WILLOW GROVE PENNA

LEAVING LEADVILLE TOMORROW STOP
DEPOSITING OUR SHARE IN DENVER BANK THEN
TRANSFERING TO PHILADELPHIA BANK STOP
WILL SEND TELEGRAM FROM DENVER ONCE
COMPLETED STOP BE HOME SOON STOP
ELI WILKEY

)

Eli stood in the middle of the cabin staring at the stack of satchels bulging with silver certificates.

"It's quite something, ain't it?" Clayton remarked.

Eli nodded. They had just returned from town where they'd withdrawn their money and split their shares. "Too bad the money couldn't have been transferred from here. You best believe it won't leave my sight from here to Denver. What I don't understand is why Nathan wanted us to bring it all back here instead of staying in town? We're all leaving tomorrow and I thought we'd enjoy ourselves on the last night we'd be together."

Clayton shrugged. "He's been acting strange ever since that fever he took last winter. He said something about wanting to go back into the mine one last time before we split up."

Eli looked down and then back up at Clayton. "I'm going to miss you. If you ever find yourself in Willow Grove, stop in and see me. I'd like you to meet Emma and Grace."

Clayton smiled. "I'm gonna miss you, too, you old cuss. And if you find yourself in San Francisco, look me up."

Eli laughed. "Listen to us. A railroad runs the length of this country. And it's not as if we don't have enough money to take a trip and see each other as much as we like."

"That's right." Clayton slapped Eli on the back.

The door opened and Nathan stood there holding a bottle of whiskey. "You boys ready? Just for old time's sake, I figure we'll go have us a drink in the place that made us three of the richest sons of bitches in the West."

)

Standish, Present Day
Elise leafed through the stack of envelopes, but Eli's telegram must have been the last communication Emma received.

Damn it. The murders had to have occurred that night. But who murdered whom?

She looked back into the box and saw the bottom was layered with small books. Could they be diaries? She eagerly reached for the one on top. She withdrew the book and opened it to the first page:

May 16, 1887

This is the diary of Grace Wilkey.

As Elise began to read, a sudden stirring of the air made her look up. Fear sent her stomach plummeting and her heart pounding as a translucent image of a woman stood only a few feet away, smiling at her.

Elise opened and closed her mouth, a silent scream lodged in her throat.

"It's all right, my dear. I won't harm you," said the spirit in a soft, velvety voice.

"G-Grace?" Elise stammered.

The vision nodded. "The time is right for you to reclaim what was stolen from us."

Elise swallowed hard. "How?"

"You have my diaries. They will guide you. I wasn't able to continue the search, but as soon as you were born, I knew you were the one to carry on." She cocked her head to one side. "And Elise, remember, no matter what happens, always listen to your heart."

"But—"

Before Elise could say anything else, Grace blew her a kiss and disappeared.

Elise shook her head. Did she just have a conversation with a ghost? Or was it just her imagination? She began to page through the diary she still held, and a yellowed telegram fell into her lap.

> CEDAR BEND MICHIGAN
> JUNE 3 1900
> EMMA THINK THIS TIME I FOUND HIM FOR SURE STOP MET MAN WHO WILL TAKE ME TO HIM TONIGHT STOP IF ITS HIM WILL GET BACK WHATS YOURS AND GRACIES STOP MORE TOMORROW STOP HANK

Excited to begin reading, Elise emptied one of the hatboxes, filled it with the diaries, packed everything else back in the trunk, and headed downstairs.

$$\text{)}$$

Five weeks later, Elise zipped her last suitcase closed and with stoic determination, faced her father. "Dad, please try and understand. Getting this job on the *Cedar Bend Gazette* puts me one step closer to discovering what may have happened to the missing money."

"A wild goose chase is more like it," John Baxter replied, shaking his head in exasperation. "You should be staying here in Standish and working at the newspaper that's been in our family for over a hundred years. You could be a great journalist who's going to go nowhere at some small paper in some dinky town in Michigan, and you're too damn smart to waste your time looking for something that doesn't exist."

Elise sighed. "Dad, we've already been over this. You may not believe in Grace's diaries, but I do. I'm not going to be satisfied until I follow this lead. And if it turns out to be nothing, well, at least I tried."

"She's right, John," Fran Baxter said, placing a comforting hand on her husband's arm. "We have to let Elise do this."

John flung up his arms in disgust. "Don't you two think that over the past century, if there was a chance it still existed, someone in our family would have found it? Grace's money is long gone."

"I can't accept that." Elise hesitated. She could imagine what her father would say if she told him that Grace's ghost had led her to the diaries. Seeing the stubborn set to his jaw, she thought it best to keep this to herself.

"Fine," her father said through gritted teeth. "It's clear, no matter what I say, neither of you is willing to see reason. So Elise, go on your treasure hunt. And when you realize I was right, and you're ready to come home"—he swallowed hard—"your job will be here for you."

Elise grinned and wrapped her arms around her father's neck. "Thanks, Dad. I'm going to prove to you I was right and bring home Grace's lost treasure."

Lust is all GET—Love is all GIVE.

— Unknown

Chapter 3

Cedar Bend, Michigan

When Elise turned off US 23 and entered Cedar Bend, she was pleasantly surprised. The rural town looked well-kept and prosperous. Old-fashioned lampposts lined the main street with colorful spring flowers in full bloom around their bases. She waved back at a group of kids as she drove by a small park with brightly painted benches surrounding a fountain.

Anxious to find the newspaper office, she scanned the businesses as she passed. When she saw the sign for a diner, her stomach growled, reminding her it had been hours since she'd eaten. With thoughts of a cheeseburger and fries, she turned into the lot. She would grab a quick bite then do more exploring before it was time to meet with the realtor to look at apartments. She found an open parking spot next to a black convertible Mustang and pulled in.

When she stepped from her car, she decided it was warm enough that she didn't need her jacket. As she bent to place it on the backseat, she heard an angry male voice.

"Hey, watch it."

Elise turned to see a tawny haired guy standing about three feet away glowering at her. "Is there a problem?"

He pointed. "You just hit the side of my car with your door."

"Oh, I'm sorry." She quickly stepped back and closed her door. "I don't see any damage." She smiled. "By the way it's a great car. What year is it?"

"Sixty-six."

When he walked over and began to examine the Mustang, Elise rolled her eyes. "Honestly, I don't think I hit it hard enough to even leave a scratch."

He made a grunting sound and ran his fingers along the polished surface.

"Oh, for heaven's sake, I didn't damage your precious car."

When he turned his stormy eyes on her, she couldn't help but notice they were a smoky gray with thick dark lashes. Even though he was glowering at her, he was extremely handsome with a lean face, a straight nose, and a cleft in his chin below what looked to be very kissable lips.

"This is a 1966 Mustang that I restored to mint condition. I'd like to keep it that way."

Elise could feel her temper rising. "Then perhaps you shouldn't drive it. You aren't the only person on the road and accidents do happen."

As they stood between the closely parked cars glaring at one another, Elise was stunned to realize her anger was fading and sexual desire was taking its place. *Good grief, get a grip. He's gorgeous, but a jerk.* Hours seemed to pass as they stood staring into each other's eyes. Then abruptly he slipped on a dark pair of sunglasses and turned to leave.

"You should be more aware of your surroundings when you get out of your car."

The giddy sensation she'd been experiencing burst like a soap bubble. Her face burned with embarrassment. "And perhaps you should stop being such an ass."

When Elise heard a soft chuckle, she jumped. A short, slightly plump woman with curly dark hair was standing behind her smiling.

"I'm sorry, but I couldn't help overhear. What did you do to make him so mad?"

Elise watched as he pulled from the lot. "I barely tapped his precious car with my door."

The other woman shook her head. "Men and their cars. By the way, you wouldn't happen to be Elise Baxter would you?"

Surprised, Elise nodded. "How did you know?"

"You have Pennsylvania plates and I happen to be expecting a new reporter who's from Standish."

Elise grinned. "And I suppose you're Sandy Fitzpatrick, *The Gazette*'s assistant editor and my new boss?"

Sandy nodded and held out her hand. "That's me. Welcome to Cedar Bend and *The Gazette*."

Elise shook the offered hand. "Thanks. I'm looking forward to working on the paper."

Sandy gestured toward the diner. "Were you on your way in or out?"

"In. I'm starving."

"Me, too. Let's go get acquainted."

They found a booth next to a window and slid in. "For some reason, I'm dying for a burger. Are they good here?" Elise asked.

"The best in town. Nice and juicy and full of everything that is bad for you," Sandy replied wistfully. "As for me, I'm dieting again. Doc says I need to lose around twenty pounds."

"I'm usually pretty careful about what I eat, but for some reason I feel like being bad today," Elise said.

Sandy laughed. "I imagine being that close to Max Holt would make any girl want to be bad."

Elise cocked her head. "Who?"

"The hunky jerk with the Mustang. His name is Max Holt."

Elise made a sour face. "Is he a friend of yours?"

Sandy laughed. "I wish. No, he's new in town and we've never met. Besides, I'm sure he wouldn't look twice at me. Now with your looks, you'd probably have a chance."

Elise grimaced. "Thanks, but no thanks."

After the waitress took their order, Elise asked, "So did you grow up here in Cedar Bend?"

"Yep. I left long enough to go to college up in Lancing. Then about three months after I graduated, there was an opening on *The Gazette*. That was six years ago. If I remember correctly, your family owns the paper in Standish. If you don't mind me asking, why did you leave to work here?"

Not wanting anyone to know the true reason for her being in Cedar Bend, Elise said, "I needed the experience of working somewhere besides my family's paper to prove to myself I could make it on my own." As she said the words, she realized they were true. Finding Grace's lost silver wasn't the only reason she'd left.

Sandy nodded. "I can understand that. You'll have to remember Cedar Bend is a smaller town than Standish, and there isn't a lot happening here, but we do cover county events, along with news from Ann Arbor and Brighton. Unfortunately, being new you'll most likely be assigned the grunt jobs."

"That's fine. We all have to start at the bottom."

"Actually, the most interesting thing happening in town has to do with Max Holt and his inn."

Elise had to wait until the waitress served their food before she asked, "Oh really? What's that about?"

Sandy looked longingly from Elise's cheeseburger to her chef's salad and sighed. "I have a fantastic dress that I can't get into anymore. Every time I eat like a rabbit I think about how great I'll feel when I can get back into the damn thing."

Elise grinned. "Mine is a pair of jeans."

"Anyway, back to Max and his inn. He showed up about six months ago and bought the old Mosby place. Elise, are you all right?" she asked when Elise began to choke. "Here, drink some water." Sandy handed her the glass.

Elise sipped then motioned she was okay. Wasn't it just her luck the house that might hold the answer to the missing money belonged to that ass Max Holt? "Sorry, I swallowed wrong. Please go on."

"Well, there's not much more to tell. He's been working his butt off restoring it as an inn and restaurant. Brought in a couple of his friends to help with the remodeling and decorating, and supposedly his chef came from some high-end Boston restaurant."

"Sounds like he's pretty ambitious."

Sandy nodded. "According to those who've gotten a glimpse of the house, he's done an incredible job restoring the old place." She paused and her eyes filled with mischief. "You know, there's always been talk the house is haunted."

Recalling her encounter with Grace, Elise was intrigued.

"It's true. When I was a teenager, a group of us used to hang around there hoping to see the ghost, but we never did, although there are those who say they've seen lights flickering and shapes floating past the windows."

"No kidding? Does anyone know who these ghosts are supposed to be?"

Sandy shrugged. "Cyrus Mosby, I suppose. Over a hundred years ago, he and two other men were found dead in the library. Who committed the murders, or why, was never discovered."

Elise's pulse began to quicken. The house had to be the right one. She had to stay calm and not give anything away. "How interesting. I love a good ghost story. Is there somewhere I could get more information?"

"Check the library archives. They probably have the story on microfilm. As for the house, the paper is planning on doing a big spread on the inn when it opens."

Here was her chance to get into Cyrus Mosby's house. "Do you already know who's going to get the assignment?"

Sandy gave her an apologetic smile. "I can tell you'd like to be the one. Sorry, but I'm going to have to disappoint you. Gary Spreg has been covering the story since Max's plans were known."

Elise shrugged. "You can't blame a reporter for trying."

Sandy laughed. "Who knows, perhaps something bigger will come along and he'll happily turn the inn story over to you."

An attractive blonde in skin-tight black jeans and a low-cut crimson top walked up to their booth. "If it isn't Sandy Fitzpatrick," she said.

Elise saw distaste fill Sandy's face as she replied. "Hello, Constance."

Constance smiled, showing a row of tiny white teeth. "Have you heard the news?" Not waiting for Sandy to answer she continued. "Invitations for the Inn on the Bluff's grand opening have gone out. Being as he knows Max personally, Martin has received one, and he's asked me to go with him."

"Bully for you," Sandy replied.

Elise wasn't sure if Constance just didn't notice Sandy's sarcasm or chose to ignore it.

"So, Sandy, did you get your invitation?"

"I haven't checked today's mail yet."

"Well, I wouldn't be too hopeful if I were you. I understand the party is just a preview for the town's leading citizens."

Elise couldn't believe the woman's gall. Glancing at Sandy, she could see the suppressed anger in her eyes.

"Well, got to run. I'm meeting Martin for drinks at Pasquale's," Constance said as she gave Sandy one last smug smile and sashayed off.

"What a horrible person," Elise said. "Is she always like that?"

Sandy snorted. "That was nothing. You should see her when she's being a real bitch."

"I don't think I want to."

Sandy gave a dismissive wave. "I've been dealing with her since high school. Someday I'll tell you all the ugly details. Now, I have to run. What are your plans for the rest of the day?"

"I thought I'd do some more exploring. Then I'm meeting a realtor who's going to show me some apartments. That reminds me, where is *The Gazette* located?"

"Just a couple of blocks from here. It's Saturday, but there'll still be someone there. If you'd like to go over now, I'm sure they'd give you a tour. I'd take you myself, but I'm meeting my sister to look for a present for a baby shower." She made a face. "Don't you just hate going to those?"

Elise grinned. "Yes, actually I do. I'll wait until Monday and you can show me around."

"Sounds good. By the way, what realtor are you meeting with?"

Elise hesitated. "Paula?"

"Paula Reynolds?"

"That's it. Do you know her?"

Sandy nodded. "She's one of the top realtors in town. In fact, she sold the Mosby house to Max."

A few days later, Elise turned the key to lock the door of her small, furnished apartment located on the third floor of a Victorian house. She had to climb the fire escape to get to it, but she loved it. As in many such houses, hallways and stairs had been closed off to create apartments.

As she passed the second floor, she waved to her neighbor, Albert, a nice-seeming guy in his late thirties who worked from home. Her apartment was close enough to the newspaper office that she could walk, so she set out at a brisk pace. She liked everyone she'd met at the paper and was beginning to know her way around town. Everything was going according to plan except for one major obstacle, getting past Max Holt and into Cyrus Mosby's house.

She frowned. Max's grand opening was a little over a week away. If she could only be the one to do the interview and cover the party. That would give her a chance to do a little prying and snooping without raising suspicion. So far, her assignments had been a story on the ladies' garden society spring flower show and new playground equipment for the park. She couldn't help but smile. *Grunt work is right.*

She had dug up the newspaper articles on Cyrus Mosby's death. What she found strange was the lack of information. Supposedly, Cyrus was an influential person in town. Why so little on his murder? And what about the two other men? She was sure her ancestor Hank Wilkey was one of them, but who was this Garrison Hale? Her reporter's antennae quivered with curiosity.

The sound of screeching tires and a honking horn made Elise take an involuntary step back.

"What the hell is wrong with you? Don't you watch where you're going?"

Heart pounding, Elise found herself standing in the middle of a cross street looking past the hood of a black Mustang and into the angry face of Max Holt.

"Are you crazy or what? I almost hit you."

Slightly shaken, she opened her mouth, but nothing came out.

"If you're going to go around daydreaming, stay off the streets."

Elise could feel her cheeks turn hot with embarrassment. She was at fault for being lost in thought, but why did it have to be him seeing her make a fool out of herself?

"I'm sorry. I was thinking about something and wasn't paying attention."

"Obviously. Now if you don't mind getting out of my way, I have an appointment to keep in Ann Arbor."

Elise hurried to the curb and watched as Max drove away. Her mind began to race. Ann Arbor was more than a half hour away. Considering the time to get there, do whatever he needed to do, and get back, Max could be gone for at least a couple of hours. She bit her lower lip. Did she dare? If she were caught, not only could she get in trouble for trespassing, she might destroy any chance she'd have to talk Max into letting her explore his house.

And what if the house wasn't empty? Sandy had said his friends were helping him. Besides, she didn't even know where to look. She doubted Max had a fortune just lying around. *Damn,* what should she do? But as the question played through her mind, her decision had been made. She was reaching for her cell phone to ask Sandy if she could come in a little late, when it rang.

"Hey, Elise. Where are you?"

"Actually I'm . . ."

Without waiting for Elise to finish, Sandy said, "I need you to investigate a stolen pig."

"What?"

"We just heard Farmer Brown's prize pig from last year's fair is missing."

"This is a joke, right? Farmer Brown? Seriously?"

"No, sorry, it's true. He blames his neighbor for stealing it so we need you to go check it out."

"And where exactly would I find Farmer Brown? Next door to Old MacDonald?"

"Real funny. Welcome to life in rural America."

"Sorry. How do I get there?"

"He's located out on the state road. You can't miss it. He has signs for produce and Christmas trees. You go out past the Mosby place. You know where that is, don't you?"

"I think so."

"Good. I'll see you later."

Elise dropped her phone into her purse and headed back to get her car. Luck was certainly on her side. It wouldn't be unusual for someone new in town to get lost and have to ask for directions. She smiled. Cyrus Mosby's house just happened to be on her way.

Now I know what a ghost is. Unfinished business, that's what.
— Salman Rushdie

Chapter 4

Max glanced back through his rearview mirror to see the redhead just standing on the corner. The woman was a menace and shouldn't be allowed on the street. He headed out of town. Ever since his first encounter with her he hadn't been able to get her out of his mind. She was a knockout with a killer body and she was making him crazy.

On the outskirts of town, he pushed her from his thoughts and pulled into Todd's Granite.

"Hey, Max, how you doing?" Martin Todd asked.

"Great, thanks. I'm looking for some large stepping-stones for a path leading from the lawn to the stream behind my house. I thought I'd stop by and see what you have."

"No problem. Come on around back and I'll show you."

An inch or two taller than Max, with a muscular build, Martin had thick brown hair, a thin nose, and hazel eyes.

They passed what looked to Max like a pile of old tombstones. "Martin, are those what I think they are?"

He nodded. "They're from a small cemetery that the state moved in order to dam the area. They relocated the graves and we provided the new tombstones."

A name on one of the stones caught Max's eye and he walked closer. "I'll be damned, Martin. This one belonged to Cyrus Mosby."

"I saw that. It's quite the coincidence you bought his house and now I have his stone."

"How many do you have?"

Martin hesitated. "I'm not sure. At least a dozen or more. Why?"

"Because I just had a weird idea. My house is supposed to be haunted by Cyrus, so what if I bring his tombstone home?

"And do what with it?"

As the idea formed, Max couldn't take his eyes from Cyrus's name chiseled in the granite. "I was looking for paving stones to make a path, so why not make it out of these?"

"You want to make your path out of old tombstones?" Martin asked with incredulity in his voice.

Max shrugged. "Why not? It might be another unusual aspect of my inn to draw business. It'll certainly enhance the ghost stories. People love that nonsense."

Martin grinned. "Max, if you want them, they're yours."

"Great. How much?"

Martin shook his head. "I have no use for them, just take them."

"Well, I'm going to have to have them delivered and set. I insist on paying for that."

"It's a deal. When do you want them?"

"Whenever you have the time. I'll need to be there to show you where I'd like them placed."

"Actually right now would work best for me."

Max hesitated. He was going to drive into Ann Arbor and meet with a landscaper, but perhaps he could reschedule. "Give me a minute to make a call." He stepped away and took his cell phone from his pocket. After a brief conversation, he closed his phone and nodded to Martin. "Now will be fine."

"Great. Give me a couple minutes to load the stones and a few sacks of sand on the truck, and collect my tools."

"I'll go ahead to the inn and wait for you."

"I should be there within the hour."

$$\smile$$

Elise pulled into the inn's circular drive and parked her red Sable. She didn't see any other cars, but that didn't mean the house was empty. With nervous anticipation, she stepped from her car. An eerie silence surrounded her. She rubbed her arms.

Had the temperature dropped? There were a number of trees, but she stood in sunlight. She recalled her grandmother's attic and the cold she'd felt just before Grace's apparition had appeared. A twig snapped and she jumped. Turning quickly she saw a brown rabbit dart into the trees. She let out the breath she didn't know she'd been holding.

Get a grip, Elise. Walk up to the door and knock. If someone answers, act like you're lost and ask directions. And if no one answers, then what? She wasn't about to break into Max's house. As these thoughts went through her mind, she'd been walking toward the long columned porch and the double front door.

She took a deep breath and reached for the gleaming brass lion's head door knocker. When there was no response, she tried again. Deciding the house was empty, she walked to one of the bay windows and peered in. Through the filmy curtains she could make out what must be the front parlor. As she stood admiring the room's decor, the front door clicked open.

Elise let out an involuntary squeak. Her eyes glued to the door and her heart pounding, she waited, but she saw no one.

"Hello, is someone there?"

When she got no reply, she gathered her nerve and, her legs trembling, moved toward the door. When she reached the opening, she again called, "Hello?"

Still no response. *Come on, Elise, this is what you've been waiting for. Go in.*

Her stomach in knots, she took a deep breath and stepped into the entry hall. A curved staircase was to her right and to her left, the room she'd seen through the window. The wide hall led toward the back of the house.

In her grandmother's attic, Grace had led her to the diaries. Now that she was here, could Cyrus lead her to the silver? She swallowed the lump in her throat and said, "I'm Elise Baxter. I'm here to get back what was stolen from my family."

Without warning, something hard and cold slammed into her back knocking her to her knees.

"Never."

The single shouted word thundered off the walls. Whimpering in fear, she tried to gather her wits. Before she could get to her feet, the room filled with a flash of light and she thought she heard a woman's voice, high and shrill.

"Leave her be." Then silence.

Shaking uncontrollably and sobbing, Elise got to her feet, stumbled toward the door, and ran directly into Max Holt.

"What the hell?"

Elise felt his arms go around her. She clung to him and buried her face in his chest. "Oh, thank God you're here. Something just knocked me down."

"What? Who are you? I can't understand what you're saying."

Elise raised her tear-streaked face and saw the recognition and surprise in Max's eyes.

"You again." For a second he seemed speechless, then his eyes narrowed and he scowled. "What the hell are you doing in my house?"

Elise hiccupped. "I was lost and stopped for directions. The door was open so I came in. I didn't know this was your house." Elise prayed she sounded convincing. She hated lying to him, but she didn't dare tell him the truth.

"The door couldn't have been open. I know I locked it."

Still in his arms, she stammered, "I-I'm t-telling you it was open."

"Okay, say it was. What do you mean someone knocked you down? There's no one staying here right now but me."

"I was standing here and got hit from behind. When I fell I saw—"

Did she dare tell him she had seen a flash and heard a woman's voice? He already looked at her as if she was crazy. Better to keep it to herself.

"Nothing, it doesn't matter."

As she began to calm down, Elise noticed how nice it felt in his arms. A warm languid feeling came over her and she leaned in closer, wrapping her arms tighter around his neck. The sudden heat in his eyes had her body trembling, but this time not from fear.

Suddenly his lips were on hers, igniting a fiery passion she knew he also felt. With a low groan, she hungrily kissed him back. Lost in the kiss, she didn't realize they were moving until her back painfully connected with the newel post. Her eyes blinked open as he swore.

"Sorry, my aim was off," he said, giving her a grin that could melt ice. "The stairs are right behind you. Shall we go up?"

The realization of what he was suggesting hit her like a dunking in a cold stream. "No, I'm not here for—" God, she couldn't form a coherent word. "Please let me go. This has all been a terrible misunderstanding. I didn't mean to . . ."

He took a step back and did as she asked. "Didn't mean to do what? Break into my house? Or end up in my arms?"

Mortification fused her face. "Mr. Holt, I did not break into your house, nor intentionally fall into your arms."

He raised two tawny brows. "Then I'll ask again, what are you doing here?"

"I told you. I was lost and . . ." Seeing the disbelief on his face, she gave up. "Oh, the hell with it." She turned on her heel and fled out the door.

Max swore under his breath as he watched her drive away. He didn't buy her story about being lost, but what was she doing in his house? And what did she mean she was knocked down? He ran his hands through his hair. The woman had to be unbalanced and he was about to take her to his bed.

Christ, he didn't even know her name. He shook his head. *I've been alone too long if I'm attracted to a crazy woman.*

Max heard a truck come up the drive, and putting the girl out of his mind, went to meet Martin.

))

In the library, Virginia paced in fury.

"Cyrus, I thought you were going to keep an eye on Garrison? He came close to injuring the girl."

Cyrus, sitting behind his desk, opened his hands and let them fall. "My dear, I tried, but he got away from me. No harm was done. You were able to subdue him." Cyrus smiled. "Actually, Virginia, he's more afraid of you than me."

She narrowed her eyes. "He'd better be. I will not allow him to interfere with our plans. I hope once this matter is concluded we'll be rid of him for good."

Cyrus sighed. "So do I, but things are moving along nicely."

Virginia sat down in a Queen Anne chair and shook her head. "Cyrus, what in the world are you talking about? He thinks she belongs in Bedlam and she thinks he's some kind of . . . what is the word they use now? Jerk?"

Cyrus smiled. "I believe that is the correct term."

"We have to make sure Elise is the one sent to Max's opening. She must have a chance to convince him of the truth."

"Ah, well, I have an idea on how to accomplish that, but you may not approve," Cyrus stated.

"I'm listening." She shook her head when Cyrus had concluded. "You're right. I don't approve of using any kind of violence."

"Virginia, be sensible. I don't see any other way. Besides, it will only be a little push. Just enough to ensure he won't be attending the party."

"Well, I suppose we must. Now I see one other problem. There has to be total trust between those two. They each hold the knowledge to bring our plan to a satisfactory conclusion. Passion too early can create emotions which could lead to disaster."

"You can't stop desire, my dear. You of all people should know that."

Virginia cleared her throat. "Yes, well, that's neither here nor there."

The library door rattled in its frame as a dark gray mist emerged and took form as the apparition of a dapper young man in Victorian clothing. His eyes blazed with hatred and his teeth were bared. "The girl is a slut like you were, Virginia. She'll sell herself for the money just like you did."

At the same time, Cyrus and Virginia rose. Cyrus floated across his desk and roared. "You will not speak of my wife with such disrespect."

Virginia marched past Cyrus and planted herself directly in the newcomer's path. "Garrison, hear me well. I will not allow you to interfere. If you try, I will do all in my power to destroy you."

Garrison laughed. "Is that right? Well, you've been trying for over a hundred years and haven't succeeded yet. So, big sister, you must not be as powerful as you imagine."

Virginia's hands balled into fists and the room shook. "One thing you've forgotten, Garrison. I've been getting stronger while you've been getting weaker."

"Perhaps, but I have one on my side who's determined to own what should have been mine." His smile was pure evil. "That's right, sis. It seems you'll be up against more than just me." Deep rumbling laughter filled the room before Garrison disappeared.

Greed is sometimes seen as the root of all evil,
and the Doom by whose hand all of existence will eventually burn.
— Hetacomb

Chapter 5

Elise's emotions were spinning as she drove away from Max's house. How could she have gone from total fear to contented bliss in his arms? One thing she knew for sure, Max Holt was nothing but trouble, and she would have to be on her guard whenever she was around him. She knew as sure as the sun rose in the east, if nothing had stopped them, she wouldn't be on her way to find a missing pig—she'd be in Max's bed. The thought of it made her skin tingle. If he made love like he kissed, wow.

Stop it, stop it, stop it, she admonished herself. *Wipe thoughts like that from your mind. It isn't going to happen. The only thing you need from Max Holt is the missing money.*

That thought brought her mind back to the freakish happening in the house before Max's arrival. She knew damn well she hadn't imagined being hit from behind. Was Cyrus's ghost truly haunting the house? If so, who was the woman whose voice she heard? Goose bumps ran up her arms as she replayed the scene in her mind. She had no doubt Max Holt wasn't the only one occupying his house and she might find herself up against more than just him.

The afternoon of Max's pre-opening, Elise, frustrated that she wasn't the one covering the story, paused in Sandy's office doorway. "Hey, Sandy, since we're not going to the party, how about we treat ourselves to a pizza at Pasquale's?"

With a phone to her ear, Sandy held up her index finger then waved Elise to the chair across from her desk, mouthing there was a problem. Elise took the seat indicated and crossed her legs.

Sandy hung up the phone and smiled. "Well, this is your lucky day."

Elise laughed. "How's that?"

"You, my friend, have had your wish come true. You're going to get to interview Max Holt at his opening tonight."

Elise's heart did a little flip. "You're kidding? What happened to Gary?"

"That was him on the phone. Apparently, he was over at Max's getting some early shots when he tripped on a step. He's on his way to the hospital. He said he's not sure if his wrist is broken or just sprained, but he won't be going to any parties tonight."

"Why aren't you taking it? I know you're dying to meet Max and see the house."

"I'd go in a minute, but remember, my sister's baby shower is tonight, and she'd be really upset if I didn't show. Can you believe it? My chance to actually meet Max and instead I'll be playing stupid games and oohing over baby clothes." She grinned. "Maybe Max won't be the only one you get to interview. You might come upon Cyrus as well."

Elise's lips twitched. "I can't imagine he'll attend the party, but I'll keep an eye out for him."

"Seriously though, I'm sure you'll get to tour the entire house. Our female readers are going to want to know how a hunk like that decorates his bedroom, so take lots of pictures."

"Sure thing." Elise stood. "Thanks for giving this to me. I won't let you down."

Sandy nodded. "No problem. We'll get together and you can tell me all the details."

"Is it okay if I leave now? I'd like to see if I can get an appointment at Ellie's to get my nails done."

Sandy waved her hand. "Go on, make yourself gorgeous."

Elise paused. "What should I wear?"

"Put on that slinky blue dress you got in Ann Arbor and you'll knock Max Holt flat." She winked. "Who knows, you might get more out of tonight than a great interview."

"Don't count on it. I'll call you later and let you know how it went."

As she headed back to her apartment, Elise couldn't believe her luck. She hoped Gary was all right, but she couldn't help but be giddy with excitement. *Okay, you've gotten past the first obstacle. Now, all you have to do is persuade Max Holt to allow you to snoop around his house.*

Max stood on the outdoor terrace with his friends Jack Callaghan and Oliver Chandler as they surveyed Max's unusual addition to the landscape.

"Used tombstones? I've heard of grave robbing, but tombstone robbing? Max, buddy, I always thought you were a little strange, but this is even too weird for you," Jack said, gazing down at the tombstone path.

"Weird is right," Oliver added. "They give me the absolute creeps. I begged him not to ruin that fabulous garden walk with disgusting old tombstones. I mean, really. Are people supposed to sit out on this enchanting terrace, dining on my culinary masterpieces, and drinking fine wine while gazing down at tombstones? I ask you."

Max smiled at his two old college pals: studious Jack, with short brown hair and intelligent green eyes behind dark-framed glasses, and Oliver, with his blond hair and tan, who looked as if he should be selling surfboards, not creating mouthwatering dishes.

"Okay, okay. I get the point, but let me ask both of you, has my pre-opening of Inn on the Bluff been a colossal hit, or has it not?"

"I can't fault you there," Jack replied. "Not only is it a perfect spring evening, you have a great turnout. How did you manage to get all these people to show up?"

Oliver's face lit with triumph. "That was the easy part. Send out invitations promising free food and booze, and people will come from miles away."

"Hey, don't forget the added attraction of my ghost," Max said.

Oliver's smile faded. "Ghost? Maxwell, what's this about a ghost?"

Max feigned surprise. "Damn, didn't I mention him?"

Oliver lowered his voice, emphasizing each word. "No, Maxwell, you did not."

"So, Max, did he come with the inn or did you bring him home with one of the tombstones?"

Oliver frowned. "Oh, that's right, Jack, just egg him on."

Max looked from Jack to Oliver and smiled. God, it was great being together again.

"No, it seems Cyrus was already in residence." He paused. "Actually, it's an interesting story—"

"Stop right there, Maxwell. If I'm going to hear a story about how the house I just moved into is haunted, I'm going to need another drink. How about you, Jack?"

"Sure, why not?" Jack handed Oliver his empty glass. "I'll make sure Max doesn't say a thing until you get back."

"How kind of you."

Both Max and Jack chuckled as Oliver wove his way through the crowd. "Who would have ever guessed, when Oliver was making us eat all that horrible food he cooked up in the dorm, that someday he'd become such a great chef?" Jack reflected.

"No kidding. I'm just glad we've stayed in touch. I was surprised he agreed to come work for me. He said he was tired of the Boston scene and after his breakup, he was ready for a change."

Jack frowned. "Yeah, he told me the same thing."

"So maybe it's a new beginning for all of us. What do you think?"

"Wait a minute." Jack held up his hand. "Kathy and I were anxious to come and see the final results of all our hard work, but leave Chicago for rural Michigan? Buddy, not in a million years."

"Jack, Ann Arbor is only a little over a half-hour's drive."

"That's way too far for me. You know I'm a city boy."

Max needled him. "Kathy likes it here."

"For now, Kathy thinks it's a quaint little town. Trust me, the quaintness would wear off real fast. The Magnificent Mile it is not. And speaking of my lovely wife, who's that over there she's talking to?"

Max turned in the direction Jack was pointing and couldn't believe his eyes. The crazy redhead was in deep conversation with Jack's wife. He watched as a dazzling smile lit up her face.

"She's not at all hard on the eyes, is she? Buddy, if I were you, I'd go introduce myself."

"We've sort of met."

Jack cocked his head. "No kidding. Who is she?"

"I have no idea. It seems like every time I turn around, there she is. But I can tell you this, she's someone I plan on staying as far away from as possible."

"Why? She looks like someone worth getting to know."

"She's a menace and dating is the last thing on my mind. I plan on spending all of my energy on making this inn and restaurant the best around."

Jack sighed. "Max, I know your lack of interest in dating has to do with Teresa, but she's no longer a part of your life. Let it go. Your inn is finished. Now it's time for you to come back out into the real world and get on with your life."

Max narrowed his eyes. "My inn might be finished, but I still have a long way to go in making it a success. A relationship right now is the last thing I need. As for Teresa, I'm over her. It's just going to take me a while before I trust any woman again."

Oliver reappeared, drinks in hand. "What a crush at the bar." He smiled. "But I did have a brief conversation with a guy named Albert." He handed Jack his drink. "Can I dare to hope I've missed Maxwell's ghoulish story?" He hesitated, his eyes going from Jack to Max. "Maxwell, why do you look as if you've been sucking lemons?"

"It's my fault," Jack said. "I said the 'T' name and told him it was time he found another girl."

Oliver gave an exaggerated eye roll. "Never speak of the she-devil from hell, Jack. You know that. As for finding another girl, Maxwell would have to wash off the plaster dust and step outside this house."

Max gritted his teeth in annoyance. His friends were only trying to help, but damn it, neither of them had found his fiancée with another man. That kind of betrayal wasn't easy to forget. He sighed. It had been over a year since the breakup, so maybe Jack was right and he needed to try dating again. He glanced over his shoulder at the redhead who was still talking to Kathy. He had to admit she'd felt good in his arms and their kiss had aroused him to the point he wanted more. He frowned. The attraction might be nothing but sexual desire; his sex life was practically nonexistent. Something else he could thank Teresa for.

"Hel-lo, are you still with us?" Oliver waved his hand in front of Max.

"What?" Max shook his head, erasing the mental image of the girl wearing nothing but all that red hair. "Oliver, stop it." Max pushed his hand away. "If you two are done discussing my love life, I'll continue with Cyrus's story. That is, if you're still interested?"

Jack looked at Oliver and shrugged. "Sure buddy, we're dying to hear."

Still a little annoyed, Max led the way down the terrace steps onto a pristine lawn bordered by beds blooming with colorful spring flowers. "As I said, the little I've learned is rather interesting. A man named Cyrus Mosby built the house around 1882."

"Amazing, I had no idea the house was that old," Jack said.

Max nodded. "He was a wealthy stranger who showed up one day and later married the daughter of a local businessman. They had two children who both died tragically at a young age. One contracted some freakish fever, and the other one drowned."

"How horrible. That poor couple," a female voice said from behind them.

The three men turned to see Jack's petite wife, Kathy, and the pretty redhead.

"Max, I'm sorry. We didn't mean to interrupt," Kathy said. "I wanted to introduce you to Elise Baxter. She's here from *The Gazette* doing a story on the inn. Elise, this is Max Holt, my husband, Jack, and our friend Oliver."

"Hello. It's nice to meet all of you. Max and I have already met." She offered Max her hand. "It's nice to see you again. Your inn is great. I was hoping to get an interview when you have the time."

He automatically took her outstretched hand. When their palms touched, a warm tingling sensation went up his arm. *What the hell?* He dropped her hand and took a step back. From the surprise on her face, he thought she'd felt it, too. Trying to regain some sense of sanity, he said the first thing that came to mind. "You're a reporter?"

"That's right."

"I thought Gary was supposed to be here."

"I understand his wrist is sprained from his fall. So here I am instead. I hope you don't mind?"

The sexy smile she gave him was playing havoc with his emotions. Damn the woman.

"Hey, Max, are you ever going to finish telling us your heartwarming story?" Oliver asked. "You've left us on tenterhooks."

Max tore his eyes from Elise and took a deep breath. "The tragedy didn't end with the loss of the children. A few years after their deaths, Cyrus's wife died in a carriage accident." He lowered his voice for effect. "According to the local legend, Cyrus and two other men were found shot to death in his study. There's only speculation about what brought the men to this end, because no one lived to tell the story. But it's said that late at night you can hear a gunshot, followed by an inhuman scream which reverberates through the walls."

"Oh, good God." Oliver groaned. "That's it, Maxwell. I quit."

Jack chuckled. "Good story, Max. How much of it is true?"

Max's brow rose. "Why, all of it. And here we are at Cyrus Mosby's tombstone." As the little group looked down at the worn stone, Max noticed Elise's slight gasp. "So, out of respect for the old guy, and hoping his ghost won't scare off the inn's guests, I thought I'd place his tombstone here at the beginning of the garden walk,"

"Absolutely," replied a straight-faced Jack, nodding his head. "If I had a ghost living in my house shooting off guns and shrieking the walls down, I'd want to do all I could to make him as happy as possible."

Oliver threw up his hands and began to pace. "Oh, for God's sake, Jack, stop being a comedian and encouraging him."

They all laughed except for Elise who seemed to be transfixed by the name carved into the stone at her feet.

As they headed back toward the house, sounds of the party still in progress greeted them. Max turned in time to see Elise snap a picture of Cyrus Mosby's gravestone.

"She seems very nice, and I think you should ask her out," Kathy said halting next to Max.

Jack grinned. "Give it up, love. We've already tried and Max says he isn't interested."

"Sure, he's interested," Kathy replied with a knowing wink aimed at Max. "Men are always interested in a pretty girl."

Oliver laughed. "Not all men, sugar."

Ignoring his friends' banter, Max fixed his attention on Elise and the seemingly triumphant expression on her face as she turned from the gravestone. Curious, he slowed his pace to let her catch up.

"So, Miss Baxter, what do you think of my garden walk?" he asked as she approached.

"Unusual, to say the least. I'm curious to hear how you came to own old tombstones and why you decided to make a walk out of them. But please call me Elise. It's not like we haven't already met," she said, her cheeks turning slightly pink.

Memories of her in his arms and the taste of her kiss had Max's body responding in a way he tried to ignore. *Christ, I'm reacting like some horny teenager.*

Elise cocked her head. "Is something wrong? You have a strange look on your face."

Max ran his hand through his hair, giving himself a mental headshake. "No, sorry, I'm fine. I just have a lot on my mind." *Like getting you into bed.* "As I was about to say, being a reporter, you're most likely familiar with the story."

"What story would that be?"

"The hubbub over Cedar Bend building the dam and flooding the valley."

"I've only been here a short while, but I've heard there was quite a bit of controversy over it."

Max nodded. "There certainly was. An old cemetery sitting right along the river had to be moved. After a long dispute between preservationists and the state, the state won."

"What a surprise."

He smiled. "Now don't be too hard on those in power. The state offered to relocate the graves, at their expense, I might add."

She snorted derisively. "How kind of them."

"Hey, look at it this way, if they hadn't moved the cemetery, I wouldn't have my unique path."

"This is true."

"When I was looking for some stones for the path leading to the creek, I went to Todd's Granite to see what they had in stock. One of the owners, Martin Todd, had all these old tombstones. I guess when they relocated the graves, they were hired to design new stones, because some of them were in pretty bad shape."

"That was a nice gesture."

"I guess the state thought it was the least they could do since, after a hundred years, they were digging them up and disturbing their rest. Martin was telling me he was there while they were exhuming the caskets and remains. From what he said, decay had clearly taken its toll."

Elise shivered. "*Eww*. You know, Max, this entire story is giving me the creeps."

He grinned. "Sorry." He halted at the foot of the terrace steps. "Talking about giving you the creeps, I was coming back from Todd's Granite when I found you in my house. You never did explain what you meant when you said someone knocked you down. You were pretty freaked out when I found you. What actually happened?"

He watched as once again, pink suffused her cheeks and indecision flickered in her eyes.

Finally she said, "I honestly don't know. One minute I was standing there; the next I felt something hit my back and I fell."

"And?"

She shook her head. "Nothing." She sighed. "Look, Max, I know we didn't exactly hit it off when we first met, but I was telling you the truth when I said your front door was open. I know I shouldn't have gone in, but I thought someone was there."

Before he could press her further, Oliver appeared at the top of the steps.

"Come on and sit with us, Elise. We have a table in the corner. We'll all get drinks, and then Max can continue telling us his delightful bedtime story of ghosts, goblins, and gunfire."

Elise looked at him questioningly. "Do you mind? I still need to get the interview."

As he gazed into her bewitching blue eyes, every instinct in his body screaming for him to tread cautiously, he knew his unshakeable desire for her was going to win out.

"Go with Oliver. I'll be there shortly. I see Martin Todd with the mayor and his wife. I'd like to speak with them before they leave."

Monsters are real, and ghosts are real too.
They live inside us, and sometimes, they win.
— Stephen King

Chapter 6

"Hey, Max, congratulations on your opening," Martin said as Max walked up to him.

They clasped hands and Max said, "Glad you could make it."

Martin smiled as he glanced around the grounds. "You've done a great job with the house and out here. I have to tell you, when you told me your idea for those old tombstones, I thought it sounded pretty crazy, but seeing it finished, I think it's very cool."

"Thanks. If nothing else, it gives my guests something to talk about."

"Especially having the alleged resident ghost's stone at the head of the path."

Max smiled. "Yeah, it seems appropriate."

"You know, when I was laying the stones, I noticed the steps leading down to the creek are in pretty bad shape. If you'd like, I could remove them and pour new ones."

Max nodded. "That would be great. Could you have it done before I open for guests? I wouldn't want anyone going down there and falling."

Martin rubbed his chin. "I don't see why not. I could come by after work."

"If you wouldn't mind, I'd appreciate that."

"Sure, I'll drop by tomorrow and see exactly what needs to be done. So tell me, during the time you were restoring the house, did you encounter the famous ghost?"

"I'm sorry to say not one hair-raising howl or any bumps in the night. I wouldn't want my guests to hear me say this and ruin the inn's mystique, but as for ghosts, I'm a complete skeptic."

"I hear you. In all the years I've been in and out of cemeteries, I've never seen anything that came close to being a ghost."

"Yeah, I'm with you. But if the draw to my inn is coming to dine or sleep in a haunted house, that's fine with me."

"If tonight's turnout is any indication of the inn's future, you should do rather well."

"Thanks. I hope you're right. You know, it was weird, as soon as I saw this old house, I knew it was what I'd been looking for. It's almost like I was led here. And what's even more bizarre is the realtor told me that earlier that same day, she'd had another offer. Do you believe it? The house had been empty for a year, the city unable to get it off their hands, and they end up with two people interested at the same time. Let me tell you, they sure came out on top on this deal. I still can't believe what I ended up paying for a house that was in such bad repair. But it was like an obsession. I wanted this house so badly, it was almost like I was possessed," he said with a chuckle. "Maybe it was Cyrus Mosby's ghost pushing me on."

"It's amazing what you'll do to get what you want." Martin gazed up at the house. "You know, not only is the house supposed to be haunted, there are also tales that Cyrus hid some kind of treasure inside. When we were kids, we used to pretend we were pirates and spent hours searching for the treasure. I'll bet we explored every room. But to our disappointment, we never found anything, and we never did see the ghost."

"I wish I'd known about the treasure. I would have been on the lookout for it. God knows I could use it."

Martin smiled. "Yes, couldn't we all . . ."

"Here you are, Martin. I've been looking everywhere for you."

Their conversation was interrupted by the arrival of a pretty blonde in a low-cut, tight red dress.

"Well, hello Constance," Martin said, bending down to receive a quick peck on each cheek. "Max, let me introduce you to a friend of mine, Constance Poole."

Max smiled. "Hi, Constance. Welcome to Inn on the Bluff. I hope you've been enjoying yourself."

"Oh, yes, thank you," Constance replied in a sultry voice, smiling up at him and fluttering her long eyelashes. "You've done a fabulous job with the house. I especially love the bedrooms. Even though I live here in Cedar Bend, I wouldn't mind spending quite a bit of time in one of those beds."

When she gave him a sassy wink, Max couldn't hide his surprise. If he wasn't reading her wrong, the lady had just made him an offer. *Well, here's your chance to work off all those lustful thoughts you've been having about Elise Baxter.* But as his gaze traveled from Constance's honey-blond hair to her sky blue eyes and full lips, then to her voluptuous breasts beneath the silk of her clinging red dress, he didn't feel anything more than male appreciation for a beautiful woman.

He gave her a goodhearted smile. "I hope a number of people feel the same way and keep my guest rooms full. Now, if you'll both excuse me, I'd like to speak with the mayor and his wife before they leave. Please stay and enjoy yourselves."

After saying good-night to the last of his guests, Max rejoined his friends who were still discussing his tombstone path.

"Maxwell, this is all too bizarre," Oliver stated, shaking his head.

"Come on, Oliver, I thought the path was a pretty cool idea." Max took a seat next to Elise. "I mean, really, the stones are buried flat so people can walk on them, kind of like walking on the star's names on the sidewalks of Hollywood."

"Or like at Grauman's Chinese Theatre," Jack added.

Max nodded. "That's exactly right."

Oliver rolled his eyes. "*Au contraire*. I imagine most normal people would agree there might be a slight difference between, say, strolling down a beautiful street in Hollywood, reading the names of movie stars on the sidewalk, as compared to, say, walking on dead people's rotting, crumbling, dirty old tombstones in a backyard in Michigan."

Jack grinned. "He's got you there."

"I hate to burst your creative bubble, Max," Kathy said, "but I have to agree with Oliver. I think the tombstone path is creepy."

Max sighed. "Nowadays, inns and B&B's are springing up everywhere. So I thought perhaps the ghost story plus the tombstone path would draw the curious to come here instead of somewhere else."

Oliver leaned in close and pointed his finger. "I'm giving you fair warning right now, Maxwell. If I see something that could be a ghost or hear some weird ghostly shit, I don't care if the dining room is overflowing, I am so out of here."

Max laughed. "But Cyrus is supposed to be a friendly ghost."

"I don't give a shit if his fucking name is Casper. No ghosts."

Once they'd stopped laughing, Elise was the first to speak. "I have to admit I find the legend of the ghost fascinating. Maybe it's the reporter in me, but there's an unsolved mystery right here in front of us. I can't help but be curious as to why there might be a ghost hanging around. Or why Cyrus Mosby was found dead, along with two other men? Don't you want to know who they were and why they were all here that night?"

Max shrugged. "That story has been repeated for so long, no telling if it's even true."

"But that's my point," Elise said. "It's a story, a story which has been repeated for over a hundred years. If it's true, my first question is, were there police here at the time? Was there any kind of investigation? You know, I wonder . . . do you suppose there was a newspaper story? If so, I imagine it would have been in *The Gazette*."

Max took a sip of his beer. "Maybe the killings had something to do with the treasure."

"Treasure?" the rest of them exclaimed as one.

Max nodded. "Yeah. I just heard about it tonight. Martin Todd told me. Besides Cyrus's ghost haunting the place, treasure is supposedly hidden here. So, Elise, maybe that's your answer." Max smiled. "The two men were looking for Cyrus's treasure and he murdered them. Although I have to say," he continued, seeing the elation on Elise's face, "I believe in buried treasure about as much as I believe in Cyrus Mosby's ghost."

A cold wind suddenly whipped through the little group.

"What the hell?" Jack grabbed for the toppling glasses.

"Oh!" Elise cried as she stood to keep red wine from splashing her dress.

"Omigod," squeaked Kathy jumping to her feet.

Oliver covered his face. "For God's sake, Maxwell, tell him you believe."

"All right, everyone calm down," Max shouted. "It's only the wind picking up. There's probably a storm brewing."

"I hate to disagree, buddy, but there isn't a cloud in the sky." Jack pointed up into the star-strewn night.

Kathy shivered and her voice quavered. "And why is it so cold?"

"The temperature always drops before a storm. Come on, you guys," Max said with irritation. "It's just a storm."

"The temperature also drops when a ghost is near," Elise stated.

Max gave her an exasperated scowl. "Thanks."

Kathy was still shivering. "Storm or no storm, I'm not going to sleep a wink tonight."

"I'll protect you, love." Jack pulled her onto his lap. "Maybe I can take your mind off ghosts."

Standing with his hands on his hips, Oliver glowered at Max. "Even Barnabus Collins would get the heebie-jeebies in this place. The only way I'll get any sleep tonight here at Collinwood is to take a rather large sleeping pill and bolt my door. I'll see you in the morning, if we all manage to survive the night." Leaving them with that happy good-night thought, he fled through the open French windows.

"Well, I guess me and Kath will call it a night, too." Jack rose with Kathy still in his arms. "See you in the morning. Happy dreams."

Max sat heavily in his chair and gave Elise a slight smile. "Well, if that was Cyrus's ghost, he sure knows how to clear a room. I can't imagine what you'll write about the inn's opening."

She grinned. "Oh, that's easy. I plan on giving it four stars. The inn looks great, the food was superb, and the entertainment was . . . um . . . out of this world."

Max chuckled. "Can't knock a review like that."

Silence filled the warm night as they sat gazing into each other's eyes, until Max said, "You know, I haven't been able to get you off my mind since the first time we met."

She looked surprised then glanced down at her now empty wine glass and back up. "That wasn't exactly a pleasant encounter."

He smiled. "I've had better first meetings, but I'm still glad it was you the paper sent tonight."

She smiled back. "So am I."

He reached across the table and took her hand. "You have very pretty blue eyes."

"Thanks." Her reply was barely above a whisper. "Yours are quite"—she licked her lips—"nice, too."

When his attention traveled to her mouth, she withdrew her hand and looked away.

"It's getting late. I'd better be going," she said, a little breathlessly, as she stood to gather her camera and notebook. "I had a great time. Thanks." She swung the camera strap over her shoulder. "I'll definitely be recommending your inn."

"Wait. It's not that late. You don't have to go." He frantically tried to come up with a reason to see her again. His resolve not to date was quickly crumbling. "You know, you still didn't get your interview, and if you were serious about investigating Cyrus Mosby's story, you're welcome to come back." He inwardly smiled as her face lit with excitement.

"I do need to finish the article, and if you're serious, I'd love to do some investigating."

"I can't guarantee you'll find anything, but there're some old papers in the attic you can go through."

"That would be great, but if there was something worth finding, wouldn't you have come across it when you restored the house?"

"Trust me, Elise. All that was on my mind was getting this place ready to open. There are boxes and boxes of stuff in the attic. Who knows? Maybe you'll come across something that'll make even me believe in Cyrus's ghost."

As a breeze rattled the branches in an overhanging tree, she smiled. "Perhaps."

While walking her to her car, Max said impulsively, "If you'd like to begin looking tomorrow, Oliver makes one hell of a breakfast. Would you like to come?"

They'd reached her car and she hesitated before nodding. "All right, I'd love to. Thanks."

Again, they stood gazing into each other's eyes.

"I guess I should be going," Elise murmured.

Before he could stop himself, he had her in his arms, and his hungry lips were on hers. He felt her slight hesitation, then with a little sigh, she began to kiss him back. As the heat between them rose, Max moaned his pleasure while pulling her even closer and deepening their kiss. He felt the front of his jeans grow tight.

Her words came in shallow gasps when she broke away. "Max, we . . . have to . . . stop."

He held her close and whispered back, "Why?"

"This has the potential to get way out of hand."

"So, is that a problem?" He nuzzled her neck and smiled when she arched her back.

She put her hands on his chest and gave a little push.

"It's a problem because we just met and things are moving way too fast."

He moved from her neck and started nibbling at her left ear.

"Max! Stop doing that. I need to leave."

"You taste so good. Kiss me one more time. Then you can go."

As their tongues teased and explored, Max's hand traveled down her back to caress her bottom.

A low "oh" escaped her lips before she softly sighed, entangled her fingers in the hair at the base of his neck and tugged. He held her tight and began to move back toward the open front door.

"Come back into the house with me." As they reached the bottom step, a loud bang startled them and she jumped from his embrace.

"What the . . .?" Max turned to look at the now closed front door. When he turned back, Elise was down the walkway and headed for her car.

"Elise, wait." He hurried to intercept her.

"I'll see you in the morning," she called, closing and locking her car door. With a quick wave, she pulled out of the drive.

For God's sake, what do you think you're doing? Max asked himself, watching Elise's taillights disappear. No matter what his friends said, the last thing he needed was to get involved with Elise Baxter. He'd better get his horny ass upstairs and take a cold shower until she was washed clean out of his mind. And when she showed up tomorrow morning, he had better keep his distance.

As he made his way through the house straightening chairs and turning off lights, Max smiled with satisfaction, admiring how perfectly Kathy's decor complemented the old inn. He knew next to nothing about decorating, but he knew that the fabrics she'd chosen for the drapes—rich silks of blue, rose, and cream—were pleasing. He'd worked hard to refinish the dense heart-pine floors, but the vibrant, oriental rugs Kathy had placed around were perfect, giving the rooms a "finished" look. She had also found various Victorian furnishings which made the rooms seem elegant and inviting. He hoped guests would feel as if they'd stepped into the past.

Max went out onto the terrace to clear the table where they'd been sitting. A streak of silver light flashed across the garden path and he cursed.

What the hell?

When he turned to look in the direction of the light, the glasses slipped from his hands and shattered against the paving stones. His mouth agape, he stared in disbelief as a smoky, silvery shape rose from Cyrus Mosby's tombstone. The image wasn't clear, but it certainly looked like a man.

"Holy shit."

He closed his eyes and shook his head. When he reopened them, he saw nothing but the garden illuminated by tiny yard lights.

Whoa. He'd had a couple of beers, but he was far from being drunk. All this talk of ghosts must have had his imagination working overtime.

He stood there staring at the spot where he'd seen, or thought he'd seen, the ethereal figure. Then curiosity got the better of him. He stepped over the broken glass and began walking toward Cyrus's tombstone.

We are all born brave, trusting, and greedy, and most of us remain greedy.

— Mignon McLaughlin

Chapter 7

"Smells wonderful in here," Elise said as she came through the inn's front door the following morning.

At the sight of her, Max smiled. "You're right on time. Oliver's putting breakfast on the table."

"If it tastes as good as it smells, I'm glad you invited me."

When she walked past, the provocative fragrance of her perfume and the outline of her breasts beneath the soft fabric of her blouse sent Max's determination to ignore his desire for her flying right out the window. Damn the woman. She was making him crazy. He closed the front door a little harder than necessary.

"Everyone is back here in the dining room." He turned to lead the way.

"Max, is there something wrong?" She laid her hand on his arm, halting his progress. His skin prickled at her touch. "Did something happen? Was there another visit from Cyrus?"

Grateful to have something to think about other than how great she looked in her tight jeans, Max sighed.

"It's just Oliver. He swears he saw a flash of silver light outside his window last night. I told him he'd been watching too many reruns of *Dark Shadows*."

Elise smiled. "I love that show."

Max shook his head. "Whatever."

Elise pulled out a small digital voice recorder from her purse. "I need to take a few more notes for my article. Do you mind?"

"Be my guest," Max said with a sweep of his arm.

"Good morning everyone," Elise said as they entered the dining room. "Please excuse me for a minute." She switched on the recorder and began to dictate: "The dining room is spacious, with a mahogany Queen Anne table and twelve high-backed chairs that dominate the center of the room. A matching sideboard and glass-fronted cabinet displays elegant Royal Doulton china . . ."

"I'm impressed," Max said. "You seem to know your antiques."

"I grew up in Pennsylvania. A lot of the houses around there are historic."

Oliver smiled at Elise. "Help yourself to a plate. Everything is there on the sideboard." Vigorously buttering a slice of toast, Oliver gave Max a defiant glare. "I don't care what anyone says, I know what I saw."

"Oliver, Max didn't say he didn't believe you," Jack said as he poured hot maple syrup on a stack of blueberry pancakes. "He just said maybe you only dreamt what you thought you saw."

"Did I also dream that I got up and took a leak?"

Max grimaced. "God, I hope not."

Jack spluttered, spitting out orange juice.

"Jack, that's disgusting." Kathy handed him another napkin.

"That's what he gets for laughing with his mouth full. Sit here next to me, Elise darling, and ignore those two."

"Thanks, Oliver. My, everything looks delicious! You must have been up since the crack of dawn to have prepared all of this." Elise set her plate on the table and took the chair Oliver indicated.

"Well, the reason I was up so early is—"

"No, Oliver, not again," Max said. "I've already told Elise all about how you thought you saw a flash of silvery light."

Oliver smirked. "Yes, but did you tell her I also saw you checking out Cyrus Mosby's tombstone right afterward?" He nodded. "Uh-huh, uh-huh, that's right. Maxwell, you didn't give me a chance earlier to tell you the entire story before you so rudely interrupted to tell me I imagined the entire episode. Well, if I imagined it, what were you doing out there? Hmm?"

All eyes turned in Max's direction. Max racked his brain for a plausible response. He had no intention of telling them he'd also seen the silver light or telling them what he'd found when he got to the tombstone. He decided on the simplest explanation.

"I couldn't sleep, so I went for a walk. I guess I was just too wound up over the opening. Sorry it wasn't any more exciting than that."

Jack yawned. "Well, Oliver, there's your answer. I must say I didn't have any problem falling asleep."

"No, you didn't." Kathy frowned. "I was the one who couldn't sleep. I swear I kept hearing strange thumping and moaning sounds, like in some late-night horror flick. But I'm glad to say I didn't see any weird silver light."

Oliver folded his arms. "Well, I did. And I'll tell you what. If I have the misfortune to see any other strange happenings, I'm going to make sure I wake everyone up so I'm not accused of dreaming or imagining the entire event."

"I believe you, Oliver," Elise said quietly.

Oliver glanced at Max, a triumphant smile on his face. "Why thank you, sugar. It's so nice someone believes me, even though you're practically a stranger and not one of my so-called friends, whom I've known for years and years. But that's all right."

As Oliver droned on, Max stared into Elise's eyes. *She knows. She knows I'm hiding something. Shit.* Max broke eye contact and ran his hands through his hair. *Now, what the hell am I going to tell her? I'm not sure I believe it myself.* He looked up to find her steady blue gaze still locked on him.

"Well, what does everyone have planned for this sunny Sunday?" Jack interrupted Oliver's tirade, ignoring his scowl. "Kathy and I are going to take a drive into Ann Arbor and see the sights. Would anyone like to join us?"

"Yes, I believe I would." Oliver rose and began gathering dirty plates. "Let me put these in the dishwasher first."

"I'll help you," Kathy said. "I'm already ready."

"What about you two?" Jack asked Max.

"I told Elise if she's interested in finding out more about Cyrus, she's welcome to rummage around in some boxes in the attic. As for me, I have some paperwork I've been putting off."

"Oh, it's too pretty a day to spend indoors," Kathy said. "Our van will hold everyone, so why don't we all go for a drive. Then later, we can help Elise in the attic. I have to admit, I'm also becoming curious about Cyrus's story."

"Thanks, Kathy. A drive sounds like fun," Elise said. "But I have to turn in my article tomorrow. I'd like to finish my interview with Max and go through as many boxes today as I can."

"Why don't you three go ahead and go?" Max suggested. "Kathy, considering the jumbled mess the attic is in, I can guarantee there'll be plenty of boxes for you to help go through when you get back."

"Trust me, ladies. When Max says the attic is a jumbled mess, he's not exaggerating." Oliver scrunched up his face in disgust. "Not only are there boxes and trunks full of God-knows-what, but there are dust bunnies the size of schnauzers up there."

"Come on, Elise. I'll take you to the attic," Max said, seeing her eager anticipation to get started. "I don't think you'll let a few dust bunnies scare you away."

"Your friends are very nice," Elise said, as she followed Max down the hall toward the back of the house. "How long have you known each other?"

"We've all been together since college." Max opened the door to the attic steps and searched for the light switch. When he got it turned on, they began climbing the steep, dingy stairs.

"After graduation, Oliver went to culinary school in New York then ended up working for a four-star restaurant in Boston. When I got in touch with him, he had just broken up with his long-time partner, so he was ready for a change. I can't tell you how happy I was when he said he'd come work here."

"I can imagine." Elise brushed a cobweb from her face. "He's an excellent chef."

"Yes, and he's a great guy. He's had some tough times in his life, but he picks himself up and goes on. Kind of like the Energizer Bunny."

"I like him a lot. He seems to be full of fun."

Max laughed. "Oh, he's full of something, all right. I'm just not sure what to call it."

"Did Jack and Kathy meet in college?"

"Yeah, they got married right after we graduated. Then they moved to Chicago where Jack went to grad school. He's an architect and Kathy went into interior design. She's the one who helped me with the inn's decor."

"Yes, she mentioned that to me last night. When they reached the top of the steps, Elise glanced around and frowned. "Oliver wasn't kidding. This is a mess. Where should I begin?"

"How about back here?" Max headed for the far end of the attic. "There's a stack of boxes to get you started."

"Great."

Max thought this might be as good an opportunity as any to appease his curiosity. After his bizarre experience the night before, he was anxious to find out if her intense expression the previous day was caused by something she'd seen while taking the photograph of Cyrus's tombstone. He knew that by asking her, he'd be opening himself up to questions about his earlier behavior, but he needed to know. He decided to begin by asking about the pictures she'd taken at the grand opening, then he could lead up to the one of the tombstone.

"Elise, I saw you taking a number of pictures around the inn last night. How did they come out?"

"They came out great. In fact, I printed off a few I wanted to show you so you could choose the ones you'd like to appear with the article."

"Oh, really? Which ones are they?"

"Well, let me see." She pulled an old wooden chair in front of a stack of boxes and took a seat. "There's one of the front of the inn, the entry hall, the dining room, the terrace, a guest room, and a long shot of the tombstone path."

"Wow, it sounds like it's going to be hard to choose." Max tried to sound nonchalant when he asked, "What about Cyrus's tombstone? Didn't I see you taking a close-up of it?"

"Yes, actually, I did. You could add it to the grouping, if you'd like. But first, Max, why don't you sit down here and tell me what you saw last night." Patting a crate next to her, she gave him a reassuring smile. "Whatever it was, I gather you don't want the others to know about it."

Max knew a denial would be useless, so he took the seat she indicated. With a sigh, he began. "I didn't want to say anything to the others because I'm not sure if what I saw was real or just my overworked imagination. That's why I'm curious what's in your picture."

She gently placed her hand on his arm, eyes full of concern, and said, "Max, I know we just met and you don't know me very well. Believe me when I say you can trust me. Anything you tell me won't go further than this room."

He gave her a long, appraising look. "Before I answer your question, I'd like to ask one of my own."

"Okay, ask away."

"Yesterday, after you took the picture of Cyrus's tombstone, you had a strange expression on your face. What did you see to cause such a reaction?"

"What do you mean?"

"I mean you had an extremely intense expression on your face."

"Hmm." Seeming perplexed, she said, "Well, I remember taking the picture of Cyrus's tombstone. I thought you might want to include it in the article. Other than that, I'm not sure. I know a feeling of sorrow came over me when I saw his stone. Perhaps it was just hearing about all of the tragedies that beset the poor man."

I don't think so, Miss Baxter, he thought, gazing into her beguiling blue eyes. *There's something about Cyrus Mosby's gravestone you're not telling me, and I intend to find out what it is you're hiding.* He decided, for the time being, it would be in his best interests not to press her further.

"Would you mind showing me the picture of Cyrus's tombstone?"

"Sure, but I left the photos downstairs in a folder next to my purse. Would you like me to go get them?"

"Why don't I do that? You can start going through these boxes," he offered, wanting to look at the photo alone.

Elise hesitated slightly before agreeing, watching with growing unease as Max hurried down the stairs.

Relax. He just wants to see the picture. Damn, why didn't I hide my reaction better when I saw that tombstone? Keep cool. And keep your wits about you. He doesn't know the real reason you're here. Perhaps you'll be lucky enough to discover what Mr. Max Holt isn't telling.

Eagerly, she opened the first box and began sorting through the papers inside.

Downstairs, unnerved by Elise's photograph, Max now knew for certain that what he'd seen the night before had had nothing to do with alcohol consumption or his imagination. The crescent shape, which last night had glowed silver and was now carved into Cyrus Mosby's tombstone, wasn't visible in the picture taken earlier.

"Ooo-kay," he murmured. As much as he didn't want to believe it, clearly something weird was going on. That it had something to do with Cyrus Mosby's ghost was still too outrageous to believe.

So Max, old boy, what are you going to do about it? He slipped the photograph back in the folder. *I'd like to ignore it all, but something tells me that's not going to work.*

Up in the attic, Elise was working her way through the second box when Max rejoined her.

"How's it going?" He placed the folder on a stack of boxes.

"Nothing relating to Cyrus yet." Elise wiped perspiration from her brow, stood and stretched. "I'm afraid this is going to be a slow process. Are there any windows you can open? I could use some air."

"I'm not sure. That one over there behind all that stuff is the closest one. I'll see what I can do." Max worked his way around furniture covered with dusty sheets, old traveling trunks, lamps of every size and shape, a tin bathtub and a tall armoire. "Well, I'm finally here, but there's a bed blocking part of the window that I'm not sure I can move."

"Hang on, I'm coming. I can't believe all this stuff." She squeezed around a vanity table. "Oh, my!" She gasped as she saw the ornate carved headboard of the four-poster bed. "Max, this bed is gorgeous. Have you taken a close look? I'll bet it's solid cherry."

"What?" Distracted by his efforts to force open the painted-shut dormer window, he turned to see what had her so enthralled. "Yeah, it's pretty." He gave the bed a cursory glance and turned his attention back to the stuck window.

"Honestly, Max, I would think you, of all people, would appreciate antiques."

"I do appreciate antiques, but if you want this window open, that particular antique is in my way." He turned as Elise stepped up onto a short, rickety stool. "What are you doing?"

"The bed is too high for me, and I want to get a better look at the carving in the headboard."

The next moments seemed to pass in slow motion. Elise was standing on the stool one minute, and the next she was falling backward away from the bed, her head aimed directly for the sharp edge of the vanity table.

"Max!"

He had no idea how he managed to get around the bed in time to catch her flailing body. With Elise in his arms, he twisted them both away from the vanity, landing them half on and half off the bed.

"Oh, Max."

"It's all right. You're safe now. Just hang on to me." He rolled them both over until they lay together in the center of the bed, Elise clasped in his arms. As his body pressed her deeper into the mattress, he watched the fear leave her eyes and caution take its place.

"Max, we can't. Someone may come up"

His mouth stopped a breath away from hers. "It's okay. No one's here"

Their lips met. As the kiss deepened and their passion rose, Elise tightened her arms around his neck. He ran his hand down the front of her buttoned shirt, sliding his open palm over her full breast, gently squeezing and caressing her through the fabric.

Elise broke the kiss and gasped. "Max, we shouldn't. This isn't why we're up here."

He began to nibble her neck. "No, but it's a hell of a lot more fun than looking through old boxes."

"Yes-s, but there're a lot of boxes to go through. Max, quit that. I can't think."

"That's the idea. Stop thinking and let me do this." He kissed his way down her neck while unbuttoning her shirt until he'd exposed her pretty lace bra, her taut nipples clearly visible underneath. He ran his thumb gently back and forth across their hard peaks.

"Max, I don't have a lot of time to spend up here," she panted. "I need to get home and finish writing the article."

He chuckled. "Do you want to interview me now?" He nibbled her earlobe. "You can ask me what I like to do when I have a sexy woman beneath me in my bed." His erection strained against the zipper of his Levis and he pressed against her.

"I have a pretty good idea," she said breathlessly. "But I don't think we could print it."

"Hmm, you're probably right." He kissed her exposed skin above her bra, and then licked her nipples as they strained against the fabric.

"Oh, sweet heaven." Elise whimpered, arching her back to give him better access.

He unclasped the bra's center hook and released her soft breast into his palm. "Let me taste you."

"Oh, my," she said when his mouth closed around her nipple.

He began to suckle first one breast, then the other. He licked and sucked until he had her squirming beneath him. "You taste so damn good. I want all of you."

"I want you, too, but we should stop . . . before this goes . . . too far." Her words came in shallow gasps.

He'd unbuttoned her jeans, and he slid his hand down until he cupped her damp curls. He stared into her eyes, dark pools on the verge of release. In a voice raw with need he asked, "Do you really want me to stop?" He began to gently stroke her.

She dug her fingers into the fabric of his shirt. "Oh, Max, no, don't stop. I'm going to . . . Max!"

He stroked her faster and faster then smiled with male satisfaction as he felt the climax erupt throughout her body.

"Ohhh, God, Max, oh God."

"That's it, baby, let it come."

She clasped the back of his head and pulled his mouth to hers. She tugged the hair at the base of his neck while he plunged two fingers into her wet heat. Their kiss became a frenzied tangle of tongues as she moved against his hand.

"Mmm," Elise moaned into Max's mouth as the second climax slammed through her body.

"Elise, I can't wait any longer, I have to be inside you," he said in a hoarse whisper.

"I know." She tugged his shirt until it was free of his jeans and unsnapped his fly. She encircled his hard shaft with her hand. "Bring this to me."

"Stop what you're doing or I'm not going to make it," he said through gritted teeth. He'd managed to remove his shirt and was working on his jeans when a blinding flash of silver light above their heads made Elise scream.

There is no fire like passion, there is no shark like hatred,
there is no snare like folly, there is no torrent like greed.
— Buddha

Chapter 8

"Max, what was that?"

"It's all right, Elise. It's all right." Max burrowed them even deeper into the feather mattress.

"Something smells like burning wood."

"Don't worry. Just relax. I think it's only the bed."

"What? What do you mean 'it's only the bed'? Max, you're suffocating me. Let me up."

"For God's sake, ignore it," he whispered as he started nuzzling her neck again.

For the first time since the flash had scared the wits out of her, she became aware of her half-naked body and the spot where a certain well-endowed part of his anatomy was pressing.

"Max, not now. Stop that and let me up."

"If he weren't already dead, I'd kill that fucking ghost," Max mumbled as he rolled off Elise.

"What did you say?" she asked as she grabbed for the sheet to cover herself. "Do you think that flash had something to do with Cyrus? Oh, Max, look." She pointed, awestruck, at the window. It was open.

"If it is Cyrus, his timing fucking sucks," he grumbled as he swung his legs off the bed.

Elise stifled her laugh when she noticed the shock on his face as he focused his attention on the tall headboard behind her.

"What is it? What do you see?"

She scrambled to her knees and let out a soft '*oh*' when she saw the glowing silver crescent shape scorched into the headboard.

Max sighed. "Well, shit, not again."

" 'Not again'? Have you seen something like this before?" She fumbled around under the covers. "What have you done with my clothes?" She came up with her bra and blouse. "Turn around while I get dressed."

His white teeth flashed in a rakish grin as he leaned against the bedpost. "Isn't it a little late for modesty?"

Elise blushed and glared at him.

He threw his hands up in defeat and grabbed his shirt, weaving his way back around the jumble of furniture. "Okay, okay, I'm going."

For a second—just a second—watching the tall, gorgeous man with his muscular shoulders, a thatch of thick sandy hair covering his chest, knowing exactly what rested within his unsnapped jeans, she almost called him back. But she didn't. She thanked the sane part of her brain that kept her mouth shut.

Dressed, Elise knelt on the bed and examined the carved crescent shape.

"Max," she called. "Come here and see this."

"I saw it."

"Aren't you just a little curious, not to mention a little freaked out, about what just happened?"

Max walked up behind her. "Things started getting weird around here last night—and they seem to be getting weirder by the minute. First, a gust of cold wind blows up out of nowhere. Windows that were painted shut open by themselves." He slammed the window closed. "Streaks of silver light are flashing all over the place carving glowing crescent shapes wherever they strike. A smoky shape rises from the ground. Yes, Elise, I'd say I'm pretty freaked out. But what the hell am I supposed to do about it?"

Nonplussed, Max glowered at the offending silver crescent.

"And the bedding isn't even dusty," Elise whispered.

"What?" Turning, Max looked where she pointed.

"Everything up here is covered in dust, except for this bed and the bedding. Why would that be? Wait a minute." Narrowing her eyes, she pointed her finger into his now shirt-covered chest. "Max Holt, if you set this up in order to get me up here under the pretense of going through boxes, in order to get me into this bed, that's about as low as—"

"What did you just say?" he asked incredulously. "Elise, if I wanted to get you into my bed, I wouldn't have to trick you into some dusty attic to do so."

"What the hell is that supposed to mean?"

Max ran his hands through his hair. "Elise, I'm sorry. I've been bringing furniture down from up here as I needed it. I don't know why, but for some reason I was saving all of this old stuff for myself." He indicated the bed and adjacent furniture. "I've just recently finished the master suite. For God's sake, I only met you yesterday. When would I have had time to come up here and wash this bedding and dust off this bed?"

Elise shook her head. "No, I'm the one who should apologize. I guess I'm more shook up than I thought."

"Sorry enough to get back in bed?" he murmured, encircling her waist.

She chuckled. "No."

He grinned. "Well, as the saying goes, you can't blame a guy for trying. You know, I believe I could use a drink about now. How about you?"

"That's an excellent idea. A chilled glass of white wine sounds good."

"Then what do you say we leave all of this for now, go downstairs where we can be comfortable, and try to make some sense out of all this craziness?"

$$\smile$$

As they disappeared down the attic stairs, two shimmering shapes materialized and sat together on the rumpled bed.

"That was a bit dramatic of you, Cyrus. Don't you think?"

Cyrus chuckled. "You told me to interrupt them, and I did."

"I wanted you to stop them, not set fire to the bed."

"Well, it worked. But I don't know how long we'll be able to keep them apart. That is one frustrated young man." He sighed. "Perhaps, Virginia, as I said before, we should allow nature to take its course."

"You know as well as I that it's too soon. For their relationship to survive what's to come, they need to have honesty and trust between them before they become intimate. I'm afraid of the consequences if we don't discourage their passion." Virginia's mouth formed a thin line. "Max is just going to have to control his manly desires."

"That's not always so easy, my dear. Especially when a beautiful woman is involved."

Virginia placed her hand upon Cyrus's cheek. "I know, my love. It's also hard for a woman when there's a handsome man. But for the time being, we have to keep to our task. We waited too long to risk a misunderstanding ruining all our plans."

Cyrus took her hand in his and kissed her palm. "As usual, you're right, my dear. And your idea of using silver crescents to help them along is working famously." He chuckled again. "But I'm afraid they might be making poor Max about as distraught as his desire for Elise."

Virginia smiled. "At least he's beginning to believe there just might be ghosts living in his house."

Cyrus's hollow laugh filled the attic. "What an idea—ghosts." The laughter soon died away. "It's frustrating that our assistance must be so limited. I'd like to just tell them where the silver certificates are and be done with it."

Virginia stroked her fingers along his cheek. "Now, Cyrus, you must be patient. They must fall in love first. Passion isn't enough."

"I know, my dear. I just want this to finally be over." He gathered her into his arms. "But in the meantime . . ."

Virginia chuckled softly. "Yes, my love."

Max and Elise were seated side-by-side on an overstuffed sofa in the cozy library, drinks in hand.

"So, Oliver actually did see a flash of silver light?" Elise asked, nibbling on a cheese puff Max had found on a hors d'oeuvres tray in the refrigerator.

"Yeah, he must have seen it the same time I did. I felt bad acting as if he had been imagining things, but I wasn't ready to admit what I'd seen. Speaking of Oliver, these are great. I wonder if he was saving them for something?"

Elise laughed. "They were probably for when everyone gets back."

"Then it's a good thing they aren't here. Because we're going to do some real damage to this plate." Max popped another cheese puff into his mouth. "Sex always makes me hungry."

"We didn't have sex, remember?"

Max grinned. "Well, we got a damn good start. What do you say we continue where we left off?"

"Will you stop?" Elise rolled her eyes heavenward, trying to hide her smile, and took another sip of wine. She set her glass down on the old trunk Max used as a coffee table. "We need to decide what to do about Cyrus's ghost."

"But we don't know it's Cyrus who's responsible for all the weird shit that's been going on." He stood and went over to the long French window that overlooked the lawn and the tombstone path. "Listen to me. I sound as if it's possible my inn may be haunted by a century-old ghost, who for some reason, has chosen me to . . . to what?" He turned and gave Elise a bewildered look. "Communicate with me? I just can't believe that."

"I know it all sounds outrageous, but you yourself listed all the strange things that have happened. I think Cyrus's story is worth pursuing. What if he's trying to communicate with you in order to lead you to something?"

"Don't tell me you're referring to the supposed hidden treasure Martin Todd was talking about?" He shook his head in disbelief and sat back down on the sofa. "Elise, it was a game children used to play. There isn't any treasure."

"You don't know that. What would it hurt to see what information we can gather on Cyrus and his background?"

"If there is hidden treasure, and if this is Cyrus, why would he wait until now to try contacting someone? Don't you think that when the town took over, someone would have reported strange occurrences?"

"But they did. Everyone I've talked to has said the house was supposed to be haunted." Agitated, she began pacing in front of the brick fireplace. "What if, for decades, Cyrus has been trying to contact someone and no one would listen?"

Max snorted. "If people thought there was a chance there was buried treasure in this house, someone would have torn it apart board by board. I can't imagine people haven't inspected every inch. Besides, what kind of treasure are we talking about? Martin wasn't specific. He just used the word *treasure*. That could mean anything from gold, to jewels, to cash money."

Her downcast expression made Max hesitate. The little voice in his head reminded him of his earlier apprehension over what she might be hiding. *Just take it slow. Let it play itself out. It can't hurt to let her do some investigating, as long as you stay alert.*

"Okay, I guess you're right," he said. "A little investigation won't hurt. Feel free to go through the house searching for hidden clues. Hopefully, your snooping won't result in any more ghostly light shows."

"Max, are you afraid of Cyrus's ghost?" she teased.

"Well, Nancy Drew, if you saw a smoky silver shape coming out of a tombstone, I think you'd be a little leery yourself." In one swift move, he pulled Elise onto his lap and covered her mouth with his.

"Silver shapes coming out of tombstones?" Oliver exclaimed. "Maxwell, perhaps you could come up for air long enough to explain."

"Shit," Max said, releasing his hold on Elise.

"Oh!" Elise cried, quickly standing, her face turning as red as her hair.

"Um, hmm," Jack cleared his throat. "Sorry, we didn't mean to . . . ah . . . interrupt."

"No problem," Max said, smiling around gritted teeth.

"Oh, my God," said Oliver. "What have you done? You've eaten most of tonight's hors d'oeuvres."

"Sorry," Elise said. "We were starving, and they looked so good."

"Don't worry about it, sugar." Oliver picked up the half-eaten tray. "We happened to come across this fabulous wine and cheese shop in the city. We bought oodles of stuff I can put together for us. So why don't I go do that while Jack makes us all cocktails? Then you two can fill us in on the latest ghoulish episode here at Collinwood."

"That's a great idea." Elise headed for the door. "I'll be back in a minute."

"I'll go see if Oliver needs any help," Kathy said, giving Max a big smile.

"Well, old buddy, how was your afternoon?" Jack asked with raised brows as he headed for the drinks cabinet. "Did you accomplish all you hoped to?"

"No," Max replied curtly. "Between ghosts and friends with lousy timing, I didn't accomplish a damn thing."

"Sorry about that. Next time, maybe, you should at least close the library door."

"I'll be lucky if there is a next time," Max sighed, taking the drink Jack handed him.

"You mentioned ghosts and friends. Don't tell me there was another unearthly visitation," Jack said jovially, taking a seat across from Max.

Max shook his head. "I don't know what the hell is going on around here, but there have been too many unexplained events to ignore."

"Such as?"

"Let's wait for everyone to get back. I don't want to have to tell this twice. You know, I'm beginning to wonder if this is all just someone's idea of a practical joke. The problem is, I can't figure out how they're doing it."

"Doing what?"

"Sorry, I'm just thinking out loud. You'll understand once I explain. Good, here they come." Max stood to help Kathy with the tray. He then turned and faced the little group. "Okay, first, Oliver, I owe you an apology. You didn't imagine seeing that silver flash. I saw it, too."

"I knew it." Oliver beamed in vindication. "And, Maxwell, I appreciate your apology."

"So you both saw a flash of silver light," Jack said. "Couldn't it have just been a streak of lightning?"

Max nodded. "That was my first reaction. But when I looked toward the garden walk . . ." He glanced at Elise who gave him a "go on" smile. "I thought I saw a smoky shape rising from Cyrus's tombstone."

Oliver jumped to his feet. "What did you just say?"

Kathy's eyes opened wide. "Oh, my God."

Jack looked amused. "No shit?"

" 'No shit' is right," Max said. "At first, I tried to convince myself I had too much to drink and was seeing things, but curiosity got the best of me, so I went to investigate. Oliver, that must be when you saw me heading toward the tombstone path."

"That's right, but I sure as hell didn't see any shapes coming out of the ground," Oliver said with a shiver. "If I had, I can tell you I would have expired on the spot."

Kathy rubbed her arms. "You and me both. I'm sure I don't want to know the answer to this, but what did you find when you got to the tombstone?"

"Actually, it would be easier to show you," Max said. "Shall we go for a walk?"

Oliver shook his head vehemently. "Maxwell, are you nuts? I'm not stepping a foot outside of this house."

"Come on, Oliver," Elise coaxed. "We'll all go. It will be fine. Besides, the house isn't out of Cyrus's reach either."

"What? What's that supposed to mean? No, no, don't answer that. I don't want to know." Oliver put his hands over his ears and began to hum loudly. "*Hmm, hmm, la-la-la,* I'm not listening. *Hmm, hmm, la-la-la.*"

Elise laughed. "It's all right. Honestly, it will be fine." She put her arm through Oliver's, and guided him along as the others headed toward the dining room and the terrace that led to the back lawn.

As the little group stood by Cyrus's tombstone, the shadows of dusk fell and a cold wind wrapped its icy fingers around them. They shivered from the sudden chill and huddled closer together.

"I don't like this," Kathy said. "It's creepy."

"That makes two of us," Oliver replied. "Maxwell, please remind us why we're standing here reliving your horror hallucination?"

"I wanted to show you what I found here last night. Look, there it is." Max pointed.

Carved into the stone, a silvery crescent shape was visible.

"What is it supposed to be?" Jack asked.

"It looks like a crescent moon," Kathy replied.

"I don't know what it means," Max said. "I just know it wasn't there when I placed the stone."

"Are you sure?" Jack ran his finger along the curve of the crescent.

"Yes. Elise has a photograph she took yesterday of the tombstone and the crescent isn't there. Besides, when I saw it last night after the flash, it looked freshly carved and it was glowing silver."

"Like the bed," Elise whispered.

"Whose bed?" Oliver asked.

"Oops." Elise bit her lower lip and gazed at Max.

"Ah, w-well," Max stuttered. "It was while we were in the attic and, well, you see . . ."

"We came across a bed with the same kind of symbol," Elise added.

Moments passed in silence as three pairs of eyes studied Max and Elise, then Jack cleared his throat and said, "I think we've seen all there is to see out here. So I say we all go back in."

"Great idea," Kathy said. "It's getting colder, and where did this fog come from?"

Oliver pointed. "What the fuck is that?"

Their mouths agape, they watched, rooted to the spot, as the fog formed into a black mass, began to swirl, then headed directly toward them.

"Everyone get down," Max called as he grabbed Elise and rolled with her onto the ground. As rain that felt like shards of ice pummeled his back, he tried to protect her with his body.

> *Greed is a fat demon with a small mouth,*
> *and whatever you feed it is never enough.*
> — Jan Willem van de Wetering

Chapter 9

"Is everyone okay?" Martin Todd asked as he hurried to where they all lay.

The fog had lifted as quickly as it had come and the sky was now clear. Max got to his feet and helped Elise to rise.

"What the hell happened?" Martin asked. "I was coming up from the stream and one minute I could see all of you, the next you disappeared into some weird squall or something."

More shaken than he wanted to let on, Max shrugged. "I don't know. It came out of nowhere."

He turned to the rest of the group. Kathy was in Jack's arms, her eyes huge and frightened. Oliver still lay face down on the ground, his arms over his head.

Max went and knelt next to him. "Oliver, are you all right?"

He peered at Max from under one arm. "Maxwell, I don't know what kind of fucking freak show you've gotten us into, but I quit."

"Come on, Oliver, it was only a little rain and wind, we're all fine."

"Fine." Oliver sat up. "You, Maxwell, may be fine, but I certainly am not. I'm not sure I'll ever be fine again."

"I agree," Kathy said, her teeth chattering. "Max, that was awful."

"Oh, for Christ's sake, let's just go into the house and get dry. Oliver can make us some hot toddies and we'll all feel better."

Oliver got to his feet. "Maxwell, that's the best idea you've had yet."

Max watched the little group head back toward the terrace, and turned to Martin. "Sorry about all the drama. What brings you out this way?"

"I came to look at the steps you want repaired. I knocked earlier, but there wasn't any answer. I know it's Sunday, but this was a good time for me to come by."

"Sure, it's fine. In all the commotion, I forgot all about it."

"If you don't mind me asking, when I came up the path I saw all of you staring at something. What was it that had you so enthralled?"

"Come over here and I'll show you." Max led him back to Cyrus's stone and pointed. "I noticed this marking and I wanted to see if anyone knew what it might be. Have you ever seen anything like that?"

Martin knelt down to get a closer look. "No, and I don't recall seeing this on the stone when I set it in the path. You know, it almost seems like a fresh cut." He stood and brushed the dirt from his pants. "It's certainly unusual. How do you think it got there?"

Not about to tell Martin what he'd seen, Max shrugged. "I have no idea. The only logical answer is that it was there and we didn't notice it."

Martin studied the stone then nodded. "I suppose you're right."

"Why don't you come up to the house and tell me what needs to be done about the steps. That's if you have the time."

"Sure, that would be fine. Thanks."

When Max and Martin entered the library, Oliver had just set down a tray of delicious smelling hot drinks. After introducing Martin to the group, Max took a mug and dropped onto the couch.

"I'm going to the kitchen where I'm going to begin stringing garlic," Oliver declared. "So don't expect a lot of garlic in the pasta cream sauce, because it's all going to be around my neck."

Jack laughed. "Who's going to tell him that garlic only works to ward off vampires?"

"I'll go see if he needs any help," Kathy said. "Elise, you're going to join us for dinner, aren't you?"

"Well . . ."

Max nodded, ignoring Elise's frown. "Of course, she is." Before she could protest, Max continued. "Martin, would you also like to join us? When Oliver cooks, there's usually enough for ten people."

"I wouldn't want to impose," Martin said hesitantly.

"You wouldn't be imposing," Max replied. "Kathy, would you please tell Oliver that Martin will be staying as well?"

"I'll go and see if I can also help," Elise said, following Kathy.

"Well, Martin, have a seat and help yourself to a toddy. I have beer if you'd prefer?"

"Thanks. Actually, a cold beer sounds good."

"I'll go get it," Jack said. "I'd like one myself."

"So back to our discussion of the steps," Max said. "I assume you'll be able to replace what's there?"

Martin nodded. "It should just be a matter of digging up the old and pouring the new. Although due to my other commitments, the job may take a while to finish. Either myself or my brother, Mike, will come by in the evenings after work."

"Whenever either of you can fit it into your schedule will be fine."

"Sorry it's taken me so long," Jack said, coming back into the library, handing Martin his beer. "I've been trying to convince Oliver garlic won't work against ghosts."

Max saw the quizzical expression that came over Martin's face and reluctantly explained. "Oliver is a little jumpy over this nonsense of the house being haunted." His next words died on his lips as the house was plunged into darkness. From the direction of the kitchen came a loud crash, followed by a scream.

Max swore. "Don't anyone move. I have a flashlight here in the desk. You two stay here. I'll go see what happened. Oliver probably blew a fuse." As he made his way down the hall, Oliver's voice could be heard coming from the kitchen.

"I cannot understand how someone could take advantage of a friend by not informing him, when he asks that friend to come work for him, that the place he'll be working in, and living in as well, will be crawling with ghosts. Everyone knows how much I care for Maxwell, and I want him to make a success of this place, but this is asking too much."

"Everyone calm down," Max shouted. "I'm sure it's only a blown fuse. Give me a minute and I'll have it fixed."

But before he could reach the fuse box, the lights came back on. Max wasn't sure whether to laugh or cry at the scene that met his eyes.

Oliver, Elise, and Kathy were all standing around the kitchen's center island, their eyes wide as saucers. A large quantity of cooked pasta was hanging from just about every part of their bodies, especially Oliver's, whose head seemed to have caught the most.

Unable to control himself, Max began to chuckle. "Oliver, I love what you've done with your hair." He leaned back against the counter and roared with laughter.

"I'm so glad you're amused, Maxwell," Oliver said, delicately peeling the sticky mess from his head and slamming it to the floor. "Perhaps you won't find it so funny when I tell you I quit."

"What's going on in here?" Jack asked, stopping in his tracks as he came through the kitchen door. "What the hell happened to you three?" Jack began to laugh uncontrollably. "Is this a new way of testing pasta to see if it's done?"

The other three looked at one another trying to contain their mirth. One by one, they gave up and joined in, including Oliver, whose laughter was the loudest of all.

"Ah, I, ah . . ." Martin entered the room glancing from face to face, his mouth open in shock. "I, ah, came to see what was wrong."

Max grinned. "It looks as if Oliver had a little mishap with the pasta."

Still chuckling, Kathy said, "The lights went out the second Oliver began to toss the pasta. The next thing we knew, we were all wearing it."

"Well, why don't all of you get yourselves cleaned up and we'll order pizza or something," Max said.

Oliver shook his head. "That's not necessary. I have plenty of pasta. I'll just cook some more. Maxwell, you and Jack take Martin back to the library and we'll get everything cleaned up in here. If you're starving, there're some cocktail nuts in the cupboard."

Max grinned. "So I guess you're not quitting?"

"Just go. Get out of my kitchen," Oliver said, waving his hand in dismissal.

)

Back in the library, munching on nuts, Max said, "At least the pasta mess has taken Oliver's mind off ghosts."

"For the time being," Jack said.

"Does the legend of the ghost actually have Oliver spooked?" Martin asked. "I mean, has something happened?"

"No," Max replied. Having had all the ghostly encounters he could stand for one day, he dismissed the entire subject of ghosts with a shrug. "It's just Oliver's vivid imagination working overtime. That reminds me, Martin, perhaps you can help me with a small problem."

"Sure, if I can."

"I'm looking for someone to fill a managerial position here at the inn. I'd need this person to oversee the staff, such as housekeeping and the dining room. Also, I'd expect them to work the front desk, checking people in and making sure the guests have whatever they require. I'd like to hire someone local. I thought, since you're from here, you might know of someone who would be qualified for the position?"

"*Hmm*, let me think."

"You don't have to come up with a name right now. Just let me know if someone comes to mind. I'm going to be putting the ad in the paper for staff next week."

"Sure, I'll let you know."

"Dinner is served," Elise announced, standing in the doorway, all traces of spaghetti removed from her hair and clothes.

As the three men stood, Max noticed the portrait hanging over the fireplace had caught Martin's attention.

"She's beautiful, isn't she?" Max said.

"Yes. I've always thought so," Martin replied.

"Do you know who she is?"

Martin shrugged. "Judging by her clothes, I'd say she was painted in the late nineteenth century, and I assume she was Cyrus's wife, Virginia."

"You could be right. The portrait was here when I bought the house."

"Her eyes are her most striking feature. If you study them long enough, they almost seem to glitter."

"They're definitely an unusual color," Max replied. "In fact, when I first went through the house, I could have sworn they moved."

"God, that must have been eerie."

"It was, but you know how old houses can mess with your imagination."

Martin nodded. "She looks as if she could step right out of that portrait. Did you happen to try and take it down?"

"No, why?"

"Because I've heard it can't be removed from that spot."

Max grinned. "Come on, you can't believe that."

Martin gave him a challenging grin in return. "Give it a try."

While Max stared at the portrait, the woman's eyes seemed to bore into his, making the hair on the back of his neck rise. Swallowing his unease, he forced a chuckle. "It's too heavy to lift down. I'll have to get a ladder."

Martin smiled. "Well, let me know what happens."

Once the men had left the library, Virginia did as Martin had suggested and sailed down from the painting. With narrowed eyes and her mouth a thin line, she turned to face Cyrus, now seated behind his desk.

"That was a close call. I didn't know if Max would feel my warning."

"By the look on his face, I'd say you got through loud and clear."

"What shall I do if he tries to remove my portrait?"

Cyrus shook his head. "I don't think he will. And if he does, we'll have to stop him."

Virginia rubbed her temples. "And what about the outdoor display Garrison put on?"

Cyrus frowned. "I'm surprised he's strong enough to conjure something like that."

"I'm afraid if he keeps scaring them, they'll leave, and our future will be doomed."

He shook his head. "I have a feeling they're tougher than that. We'll just have to double our effort to subdue him."

At that moment, one of the long French windows blew open and Garrison strolled in.

"Did I hear my name?" He sat down in one of the high-backed chairs, propped his foot across his knee, and smirked.

Cyrus leaned forward and folded his arms on his desk. "You may be enjoying yourself with your little games, but your amusement will be short-lived. Trust me, you will not win."

Garrison's smirk turned to a grin as he reached into his pocket, removed a phantom cigar and lit it. "Are you sure about that, Cyrus old man?" His eyes glowed with hatred. "Who holds the power may soon change." He let out a stream of tobacco smoke and disappeared.

Her face stricken with fear, Virginia turned to Cyrus.

He floated across his desk and took her in his arms. "It will be all right, my dear, don't worry."

She laid her head on his shoulder. "Cyrus, he can't have meant what I think. If so, it's too horrible to imagine."

He stroked her back. "Hush, now. We must do the best we can to help them along."

"Yes, and we must keep them safe."

Cyrus nodded.

"Perhaps we need something besides the crescents?" Virginia asked.

"Let's give them a little longer. If they don't figure it out, I have another idea."

When they heard voices in the hallway, Virginia gave Cyrus a quick kiss and reentered her portrait, and Cyrus vanished.

After saying good-bye to Martin, the others returned to the library to discuss how to begin their research into Cyrus Mosby's history and mysterious death.

"What's that smell?" Kathy asked.

Jack sniffed the air. "It smells like cigar smoke."

Max nodded. "It does."

"Where did it come from?" Kathy asked.

Elise pointed. "Look, the window is open."

"Could someone have come in?" Kathy asked.

"To do what, sit down and smoke a cigar?" Jack asked with amusement.

"Nothing that happens in this house would surprise me," Oliver stated.

Max went over to the window and peered into the darkness. "I can't imagine anyone just walking in. The wind must have blown it open." He closed and latched the window.

"And the smell of cigar smoke?" Elise asked.

"Just some smell from outside."

Elise gave him a skeptical frown and took a seat on the couch. "Okay, well, if we want to get back to Cyrus, I'll find out if *The Gazette* was in business during the latter part of the nineteenth century. If so, maybe their archives will have the paper with the story of the three deaths."

"You may have to research those at the library," Kathy said. "Max, does this town have a library?"

"As far as I know," Max replied a little testily. "We're not that far out in the sticks."

Oliver snorted. "You could have fooled me. Nothing around for miles but trees and streams. No wonder the ghosts amuse themselves by scaring the pants off people; they're bored to death."

"Speaking of ghosts, how did searching through the boxes in the attic go?" Jack asked. "Did you come up with anything interesting?"

"Elise, when we were outside you mentioned something about seeing that symbol on a bed in the attic. What did you mean?" Kathy asked.

When she gave him a pleading look, Max jumped in. "There's an antique bedroom set I've been saving for the master suite. While I was showing it to Elise, we noticed the crescent carved in the headboard."

Elise smiled gratefully at Max, "It's a beautiful bed. It looks like solid cherry. The workmanship is outstanding. Max, I didn't notice the other pieces. Are they just as nice?"

Max gave her a conspiratorial wink. "Yeah, they are. If you'd like, we could go back up and you can take a closer look."

Elise rolled her eyes. "That's quite all right. I'll take your word on it."

"Max, have you noticed that crescent anywhere else in the house?" Kathy asked.

"No, but until I saw it last night on Cyrus's tombstone, it would have been meaningless to me." He shrugged. "As far as that goes, it still means nothing to me."

"As bizarre as it seems, that crescent has appeared twice now. I think we need to try and figure out its significance," Elise said.

"Could it be a symbol for something?" Kathy asked.

Jack nodded in agreement. "That could be. This library is quite extensive. I could start looking through the books."

"Be my guest," Max said. "I was surprised to find out of all the rooms needing rehabbing, this library was in remarkably good condition. In fact, the majority of the books in here came with the house. Whoever the previous owners were made sure the books were kept in pristine condition."

Elise stood. "It sounds as if we have a plan, then. And if I'm going to get up for work tomorrow, I should be leaving. Oliver, thank you for a delicious breakfast and dinner."

Oliver smiled. "Anytime, sugar."

"I'll walk you to your car," Max said.

"Good-night, everyone. I'll let you know how my investigations go tomorrow."

"If you'd like, I could help out by going through more boxes in the attic?" Kathy offered.

Elise nodded. "That would be great."

"Max, we must have left the folder of photographs up there," Elise said, noticing its absence while gathering her purse in the entry hall.

"I'll go get them after I walk you out. That's if you don't mind leaving them here?"

She hesitated. "Well, I was hoping to do the layout for the story tomorrow. I do need you to pick which ones you'd like me to use."

Max gave her a wicked grin. "No problem. We could go back up now and get the folder and continue the interview."

"You know, the more I think about it, I have enough information to begin the article. Waiting until tomorrow for the photos will be fine." She headed toward the door. "Just call me at the paper and let me know which ones you choose."

"Hey, not so fast." Max hurried out the door after her. He caught up with her as she fumbled with her car keys. He swung her around and pinned her between him and the car.

"Max, what are you doing?"

He caressed the back of her neck with one hand and wrapped the other around her waist. His lips inches from hers, he whispered, "Don't I get a good-night kiss?"

Not waiting for a reply, he covered her mouth with his. Her lips trembled as he felt her surrender to his deepening kiss. He shifted his weight and pressed his increasing arousal against the juncture between her legs.

She moaned deep in her throat dend wrapped her arms around his neck.

Thoughts of taking her right there against the car flitted through Max's fevered brain before some semblance of sanity took over. *Okay, I need to get us horizontal.* He tried to think. *The backseat? No, too small. The lawn? Well, maybe. The grass would be soft.*

As her arms tightened around his neck, he made his decision. The grass it would be. Without breaking their kiss, he lifted her into his arms and took only two steps before . . .

Honk . . . honk . . . honk . . . honk.

"Fuck. Not again."

Elise tried to hold back her laughter. She held up the remote, still clutched in her hand. "Must have hit the alarm."

Honk . . . honk . . . honk . . . honk.

"Turn it off," Max yelled. "Elise, turn the damned thing off."

Honk . . . honk . . . honk . . . honk.

She was still laughing as she hit the off button. Once again, the night was blessedly silent—until the front door of the house was flung open and Oliver, Jack, and Kathy all came running out.

Max ground his teeth as he set her back on her feet.

"What's going on?" Kathy called as they hurried down the steps.

"Is everyone all right?" Jack asked.

"Don't tell me our resident ghost has decided it would be fun to play with car horns?" said a frazzled-looking Oliver.

"I don't think this time it has anything to do with the ghost," Jack remarked with a grin.

Max glowered.

"Perhaps we should all go back in," Kathy said.

"Good idea," Max agreed.

"That's okay. I was just leaving. Max, I'll talk to you tomorrow," Elise said as she hurried into her car. "Good-night again."

She slammed the car door and sped down the drive.

Max's gaze moved from Elise's disappearing taillights to the questioning looks on his friends' faces.

"What?"

"Nothing, nothing at all," Jack said as he tried to hold back a laugh. "We just wondered what happened to cause her to race out of here as if the hounds of Hell were on her heels."

"Hounds of Hell is right," Oliver stated, arms akimbo. "I'll bet spending the day here at Motel Hell has the poor girl's nerves in a tizzy. I know mine are."

"She's in a tizzy all right," Jack replied. "But I don't think it has anything to do with ghosts."

"If everyone is through putting sin their unwelcome two cents," Max said through gritted teeth, "I have some business to take care of in the attic."

Jack grinned. "I thought your 'unfinished business' just drove out the driveway."

Max flipped him the bird, then turned and stomped toward the house, not slowing his pace until he reached the top of the attic steps. In utter frustration, he kicked the first object in his path, which turned out to be a rather solid trunk. Cursing colorfully, he collapsed into a chair.

Damn the woman. He rubbed his throbbing toe.

You can run, Miss Elise Baxter, but soon, I'm going to catch you. And when I do . . . I'm not going to let you go.

A grin of pure devilment spread across his face as he pictured what he planned for Elise. Scenes from their earlier encounter played before his eyes, turning his smug smile into a frown as he thought about how close he'd come to fulfilling his fantasy.

Max glared in the direction of the bed, and his eye fell upon a photograph lying on the dusty floor. Puzzled, knowing he'd placed the folder on a stack of boxes, he got up and walked over to the spot where it lay. As he bent to pick up the photograph, his hand froze inches above the paper.

The lusts and greeds of the body scandalize the Soul;
but it has to come to heel.

— Logan Pearsall Smith

Chapter 10

"All right, all right, all right, Cyrus. I get it," Max shouted impatiently as he snatched up the photograph of the tombstone, a scorched crescent shape now visible in its center. "You're obsessed with fucking crescents."

He returned to the chair and sat studying the picture.

"Okay, Cyrus, if this is your handiwork and you're trying to tell me something, I'm going to need a little more information."

As he'd expected, several minutes passed without any ghostly response. He stood and made his way back through the attic's jumble toward the ornate bed, wanting to get a closer look at the crescent on the headboard. He cursed the insufficient light, deciding he'd ask Jack to help him move the bed downstairs the following day. As he retraced his steps, he retrieved the folder with the remaining photographs.

After the day he'd had, he headed to his bathroom, intending to take a long, hot shower. But with the thought of Elise lying beneath him on that damned bed filling his mind, a cold shower seemed more appropriate.

A short time later, his mind still on Elise, Max paced. If he didn't stop thinking about getting her into bed, he was going to drive himself mad.

This is what happens when a healthy, thirty-year-old man goes without sex for too long. You become a sex-starved maniac.

It was all Teresa's fault. If she hadn't screwed him over, leaving him gun shy when it came to having relationships with other women, he could have been having a normal sex life. He ran his hand through his damp hair. After he'd purchased the house, he and Paula Reynolds had spent a couple of hot nights together, but other than a physical attraction, he'd been more interested in renovating his house than dating her.

Now here he was, practically forcing himself onto a woman he hardly knew.

God, has it only been a couple of weeks since she turned my life into chaos?

After a few more futile minutes of pacing, he threw up his hands in defeat. Knowing he wouldn't sleep until he'd heard her voice, he reached for the phone.

I'll call and tell her about the photograph.

"This is so pathetic," he murmured as he dialed her number.

In her small one-bedroom apartment across town, unable to sleep, Elise also paced the floor.

It was bad enough I almost let Max Holt make love to me in that attic; we almost ended up doing it on the damn front lawn.

She had to get a grip on her emotions and stop thinking about him, but as hard as she tried, visions of Max lying on top of her kissing her senseless kept floating through her mind. Elise groaned remembering the feel of his hands as they brought her body to heights she'd never before experienced.

Stop it. Concentrate on why you're here and your final objective, which doesn't include getting yourself entangled in a relationship with Max Holt.

So far, luck had been on her side and everything was falling into place. Now all she had to do was make sure Max allowed her to continue searching through his inn. The thought of Max and his inn brought back visions of the two of them together in that bed, and sweet anticipation of their bodies becoming one.

She sat down with her head in her hands. *Great timing. The last man you need to be attracted to is Max Holt. Even if he has the means to help you unravel a century-old family mystery, you can't let your emotions cloud your judgment.*

She knew nothing about Max or how he'd react if he discovered her secret. *Remember how well you thought you knew Jason and what a creep he turned out to be.*

Her mind a jumble of thoughts, she decided a relaxing cup of herbal tea was what she needed. Kettle in hand, she was startled by the ringing phone. Curious as to who would call this late, she set the kettle down and with trepidation answered the phone.

"Hello."

"Hi, Elise, it's Max."

"Oh, hi, Max."

"Sorry to be calling so late. Did I wake you?"

"No, it's okay. What's up?"

"I found something I thought you'd want to know about."

"Really? What?"

"When I went to the attic to get the folder of photos I found the picture of Cyrus's tombstone lying by itself on the floor."

"But Max, I saw you put that folder on a stack of boxes."

"Yes, I know."

"And?"

"The picture now has a crescent burned right into the middle of Cyrus's tombstone."

"What?"

"Somehow, the picture of Cyrus's tombstone now has a scorched crescent shape," Max repeated.

"How can that be possible?"

"I don't know, but it's true. I have it right here in front of me."

"Okay, I believe you. How do you think it got there?"

"Hell if I know. Cyrus's ghost, I suppose."

"Why do you sound so angry? Did something else happen?"

"Elise, I don't believe in ghosts. All of this creepy bullshit is beginning to make me fucking nuts."

"Well, Max, you may have to start believing."

There was a long pause before he replied. "Okay, let's say Cyrus's ghost is hanging around. What is he trying to tell us by leaving these crescent shapes?"

"That's the first thing we have to discover. Once we know what the symbol means, I'm sure we'll be on the right track."

"You're not talking about that so-called treasure, are you?"

"Max, you did agree to let me do some investigating."

He let out a long sigh. "If you want to waste your time searching for buried treasure, go right ahead. As for me, I'm about to chalk all this ghost bullshit up to someone's idea of a bad joke."

"If so, who's doing it? No one, other than people you know, has been in the house. And I can't imagine Kathy, Jack, or Oliver is behind it."

Again, there was silence. Then he said, "Elise, it's late. I think we both could use some sleep."

Elise narrowed her eyes at the brusque tone of his voice. "You're absolutely right, Max. It's late, and I'm tired."

"Well, good-night then."

"Good-night."

It took everything she had not to slam the phone down in his ear.

Well, thank you, Max Holt, for being such an incredible ass. You've managed to take my mind off you and sexual fantasies and onto this interesting development with the photograph.

Could Cyrus's ghost actually be trying to contact them? The appearance of Grace when she'd discovered the diaries had put to rest any doubts she may have had about the existence of the supernatural. She bit her lower lip. However, seeing one ghost was nerve-racking enough; she truly didn't want to see another.

She carried her cup of tea back to her bedroom and positioned herself comfortably against the pillows. From the top drawer of her bedside table she withdrew three well-thumbed diaries knowing each word as if she'd written them herself. She opened the top book to the first page and read the young girl's handwriting.

This is the diary of Grace Wilkey

Willow Grove, Pennsylvania
May 16, 1887

Today is my tenth birthday and Mommy says I'm a big girl now, so she gave me this diary. She said I could use it to write down all my secrets and special wishes. My first special wish is for my Uncle Hank to find the mean man who killed my daddy and stole all our money. Uncle Hank has been looking for this man called Clayton Hamilton for a long time and can't find him. Sometimes my mommy cries because she still misses my daddy. I was a baby when my daddy died and I didn't know him. My mommy says he was a fine man and even though he didn't see me grow up, she knows he would have loved me a lot. Uncle Hank wasn't here for my birthday but he sent me a pretty, new doll he said came from a place called Independence. She's real pretty. Uncle Hank said she looks like me. She has red hair and blue eyes. I love Uncle Hank a lot. Mommy says he's all we have. Uncle Hank helped Mommy get her job working in Mrs. Peabody's millinery shop. Mommy and I live above the shop. Mrs. Peabody is real nice. She gave me a pretty blue ribbon for my hair for my birthday. I hear Mommy calling me. I will write more tomorrow.

Elise smiled as she set the diary aside and opened the next book on her lap to its first page.

May 16, 1895

Dear Diary,

I've turned eighteen today. Mother has given me my traditional diary, along with a beautiful bonnet she made. Sadly, Mrs. Peabody passed away a month ago, but she generously left the millinery shop to Mother. The shop has been doing very well. Mother says that perhaps we may even be able to afford a small house. Oh, how wonderful that would be! The rooms above the shop have been adequate, but it would be so nice to have a house with a porch swing.

Oh, how I'd love to sit and swing on a warm summer's night with Mr. Markus Baxter. He's so handsome, with his thick, dark hair and his unique gray eyes. When he gazes into my eyes, I get rather fluttery inside. Markus's father owns the general store and is hoping someday Markus will take over the business.

But yesterday at the church picnic, Markus confided in me his true ambition and dream was to start up his own newspaper. That would mean Markus would have to leave and go elsewhere, since here in Willow Grove we already have our own paper. I truly want Markus to have his dream, but I find myself becoming quite fond of him.

I cannot bear the thought of him going away and leaving me here, but dear diary, my fears may be for naught. I'm beginning to believe Markus has the same affectionate feelings for me as I do for him, for something simply wicked occurred yesterday at the church picnic to reinforce this belief. Markus and I went for a walk. He led me into a small copse of trees, and oh, my dear diary, he kissed me! Not just a quick peck on my cheek, as he's done in the past. This time, he held me tight in his arms and kissed me passionately.

Just recalling the experience has my pulse racing. The sensations I felt when his tongue touched mine had me weak in the knees to the point I had to cling to him ever so tightly in order to remain on my feet. It was during this kiss that Markus did something quite scandalous. He put his hand on my breast then began to stroke me, ever so gently. I know I should have stopped him, but oh, it felt too deliciously wonderful.

"Damn." Elise slammed the book closed.

I've read these diaries a million times. How could I have forgotten about Grace and Markus and all their scandalous behavior?

She recalled her shock the first time she'd read Grace's words. She had found it hard to believe anyone could become so besotted with another person that they would totally disregard all conventions and let passion take over.

Is history repeating itself? asked a little voice in her head. *Certainly not,* she mentally replied.

Markus and Grace had found themselves hopelessly in love. They married, moved to Standish, Pennsylvania, where Markus eventually ran his own newspaper, raised three children, and spent a happy life together.

That kind of love story isn't in the cards for me. I'm here for one reason, and it's not to fall in love with Max Holt.

Recalling that this particular volume continued with more of the premarital escapades of Grace and Markus, which for once she couldn't bring herself to read, Elise reached for the third and final diary.

Standish, Pennsylvania
May 16, 1900

Dear Diary,

Today, my twenty-third birthday, finds me both happy and sad. Markus and I are doing well here in Standish. Thanks to Markus's father bestowing upon us a generous gift of money for our marriage, we were able to purchase a small house. We now have one son and another baby on the way. Markus is happy with his job as assistant editor on our local paper. He believes that when Mr. Price, the paper's current owner and editor, retires he'll offer the ownership of the paper to Markus.

I also have a heavy heart. I lost Mother a little over a week ago. Mercifully, she didn't linger long with her illness. I'm so glad that when Markus and I moved here to Standish she agreed to come with us. The incredible, sad irony is that on the day before she died, I received a telegram from Uncle

Hank informing us he thought, after twenty years of searching, he'd finally found Clayton Hamilton. I told mother this, but I'm not sure she understood what I was saying.

In a previous telegram, Uncle Hank had said he'd traced Clayton to Detroit, Michigan, but lost his trail after that. This telegram from Uncle Hank was rather vague about how he had come to think that this time he'd found the right man. The day after Mother died, I sent a telegram back to Uncle Hank asking him if he'd truly found Clayton and informing him of Mother's death. This I sent to a place called Cedar Bend, Michigan. I find it strange that I haven't received any other communication from him.

June 26, 1900

Dear Diary,

I find myself in fear that some tragedy has befallen Uncle Hank. Still not having any further communication from him, I asked Markus to see if he could discover his whereabouts. Markus was able to contact the authorities in Cedar Bend. He was told an unbelievable story of the deaths of three men. The authorities told Markus the bodies were found in the home of a wealthy man named Cyrus Mosby. They also told him they believed robbery was the motive.

Markus explained we'd received a telegram from my uncle and hadn't heard from him since. Markus was given the descriptions of two men. I haven't seen Uncle Hank in years, but the description given Markus of one of the men could easily fit Uncle Hank. Markus was willing to take me to Cedar Bend to see if this man was Uncle Hank, but we were informed that, due to his unkempt appearance and lack of identification, as well as the circumstances in which the man was found, he was assumed to be a vagrant and was put to rest. So, unless I hear from him, I'll assume this man was Uncle Hank.

I guess I'll never know if the man calling himself Cyrus

Mosby truly was Clayton Hamilton, or what tragedy befell Uncle Hank that fatal night. Markus asked if I wanted to continue the search for the missing silver. After long thought, I told him no. I imagine the silver stolen from my father twenty years ago has to have been long spent. I told Markus that as long as Mother and Uncle Hank were alive, I still had hope. But now, I'm happy to live my life as I am, here in Standish, with Markus and our children. I'll keep these diaries and perhaps someday one of my descendants will once again take up the quest for the missing silver. But for me, the mystery of my father's death and the whereabouts of his stolen silver will remain buried with him in a mine in Leadville, Colorado.

Elise pulled the yellowed telegram from the back of the diary. Opening it, she reread it:

CEDAR BEND MICHIGAN
JUNE 3 1900

EMMA THINK THIS TIME I FOUND HIM FOR SURE STOP MET MAN WHO WILL TAKE ME TO HIM TONIGHT STOP IF ITS HIM WILL GET BACK WHATS YOURS AND GRACIES STOP MORE TOMORROW STOP HANK

"Well, Grace, I'm one step closer." She refolded the telegram. *And like Uncle Hank, I intend on searching until I retrieve what rightfully belongs to our family. No matter the growing attraction I may have for Max Holt, neither he nor anyone else is going to stand in my way.*

*Greed is a bottomless pit which exhausts the person in an endless effort
to satisfy the need without ever reaching satisfaction.*
— Erich Fromm

Chapter 11

"It's silver," Jack exclaimed early the next morning.

"What?" Max glanced up from his bookkeeping ledger to see a triumphant Jack standing in his office doorway, book in hand.

"I found it. The crescent. It could stand for silver."

"No kidding? Let me see."

"It's right here."

Jack placed the book on the desk in front of Max. There, on a page listing alchemy symbols, was a crescent moon shape, indicating silver.

"Well, I'll be damned," Max said. "Jack, you did it."

"Yeah, but what does it mean?"

Max shrugged. "How the hell would I know? I guess whatever Cyrus is trying to tell us must have something to do with silver."

"So you're ready to admit Cyrus's ghost has been leaving all these crescents?" Jack teased.

"Well . . ." Max frowned, running his hands through his hair. "It's beginning to seem as if I'm not going to have any choice. Look at what I found last night when I went back into the attic." He handed Jack the tombstone photograph with the scorched crescent.

"Wow, Max, this is pretty weird stuff. Are you telling me you think Cyrus's ghost did this?"

"I can't come up with any other explanation."

"Max, buddy, you do realize how unlikely it is that a ghost burned a crescent in this photograph?"

Max sighed. "I hear you, but there have been so many unexplained happenings around here in the past two days, I can't help but think something supernatural may have caused them. It hardly seems physically possible it could all be part of some complex practical joke. So it might as well be Cyrus." He shook his head. "God, I can't believe I'm saying this."

"I can't either," Jack replied.

"Okay, there's something else I want to show you." Max rose and headed for the library door. "Come on, it's up in the attic."

"Good grief, what is all this stuff?" Jack asked as they reached the top of the attic stairs.

"It's quite an impressive variety of junk, isn't it? And believe it or not, I've already taken some stuff out of here."

"I don't see how Elise and Kathy expect to find anything in all this mess."

"Well, most of the boxes Elise began going through are stacked over there." Max indicated the far corner. "They're all she's interested in. What I want you to see is over here."

They made their way through the cluttered maze toward the antique bed. "Look." Max pointed, indicating the silver crescent carved into the headboard. "Yesterday there was a silver flash, then that appeared right over our heads while we were in the bed."

Jack looked from the rumpled bed back to Max. His eyebrows rose and he asked, "Whose heads?"

Max threw up his hands in exasperation. "Elise's and mine. Who the hell else would I mean? But that's not the point." He gestured at the silver crescent. "Out of nowhere, that appeared right over our heads."

Jack smiled. "For someone who the day before didn't want anything to do with the lady, you seem to have passed Go and gone straight to Park Place."

"Well, I may have passed Go, but thanks to untimely interruptions, I haven't reached Park Place," Max retorted. "I only got as far as Community Chest. So if we could get this conversation off of my nonexistent sex life and back onto the subject of crescent shapes and Cyrus's ghost, I'd appreciate it."

"Whoa." Palms up, Jack laughed, "Sorry, buddy, I didn't realize. You mean to tell me you got as far as having the lovely lady in this bed and didn't . . ." At Max's glare, Jack's sentence trailed off. "You poor guy. No wonder you're like a cork ready to pop."

Max exhaled a long breath and leaned back against the armoire. "The woman is making me crazy. I can't stop thinking about anything else except how I'm going to get her back into this bed."

"Gee, buddy, I wish I could help."

"You can by helping me get this damn bed downstairs. The lady seems to have a fondness for it, so let's get it where it's in a more accessible place."

Jack put his hands on his hips and glanced around, taking in the large bed and all the furniture surrounding it. "You're kidding, right?"

"I know," Max said, grimacing. "We'll have to move some of this other furniture out of the way first. Actually, I wanted to put some of these pieces in the master suite, so we'll take them down. That'll make room for us to get to the bed."

Oliver's raised voice came from the top of the stairs. "Omigod, it looks worse than I remembered. This is a fucking nightmare."

"Hello, are you two up here?" Kathy called.

Oliver snorted. "If they are, sugar, we may never see them again."

"We're over here," Max yelled.

"Did you drop bread crumbs?" Oliver called back.

Kathy giggled. "Come on, Oliver. Follow me. I think they're this way."

"Oh, it is gorgeous." Kathy gasped upon seeing the antique four-poster bed. "I can see why Elise fell in love with it. Oh, and there's the crescent shape you were telling us about. And you're right; it's identical to the one on Cyrus's tombstone."

"And Jack may have found out what it means," Max said.

"Really? What?"

"It's the alchemical symbol for silver," Jack replied. "That's only a guess. We don't know for sure that's what it's supposed to mean."

Kathy looked thoughtful. "But if it stands for silver, couldn't that be referring to the hidden treasure?"

"Oh, for Christ's sake, not you, too?" Max sighed. "Kathy, the chance of there being treasure hidden in this house is about as likely as you being hit by lightning."

A flash lit up the attic, followed by a loud bang.

"Hit the deck," Oliver screamed, throwing himself to the floor.

Kathy cried out and leaped into Jack's arms, burying her face in his shoulder.

Jack's eyes opened wide as he stared at the antique bed. "Holy shit."

Max looked where Jack was pointing and swore. The crescent on the headboard was glowing bright silver.

"See what I mean, Jack? No matter how outrageous it seems, I think we're going to have to admit that for some reason, Cyrus Mosby is trying to tell us something."

Oliver, a little disheveled, picked himself up from the floor. "What it's telling me, Maxwell, is that I am so fucking out of here. I quit."

"You can't quit," Kathy said, wiggling out of Jack's arms. "As scared as I am, I don't want to miss out on finding the lost treasure, do you?"

"If there's anything buried in this house, sugar, I'm not about to help dig it up."

Ignoring Oliver, Max said, "I'm as freaked out about what's been happening as all of you are. When I bought the house and was told it was haunted, I sure as hell didn't believe it. So I guess you need to decide if you want to stay. This is my dream, not yours, and I wouldn't blame you if you left, but I'm staying right here. I have no idea what this is all about, but I'll be damned if I'm going to be run off by some ghost. Besides, my curiosity is piqued to the point I have to see it through."

Without hesitation Jack said, "I'm more intrigued than freaked, and I still have a few days before I have to get back to work, so I'm in."

"I'm scared to death, but I already said I'm not going anywhere," Kathy stated.

All eyes turned to Oliver.

He stiffened his spine and glowered back. "I've never been one to desert a friend, even if that friend has asked me to work in the Victorian version of the Bates Motel. So unless the creepy bullshit around here gets out of control, I'm staying."

Kathy hugged Oliver's neck. "I knew you'd stay. Think how exciting it will be when we find the hidden silver."

Oliver rolled his eyes. "That's if we live to tell about it."

"Okay, everyone, can we get back to the reason why we're up here? I'd like to get this bed and some of this furniture down to the master suite."

Oliver shook his head in disbelief. "Maxwell, how in God's name do you intend on doing that? In case you haven't noticed, there's at least an acre of junk between this bed and the stairs."

Max threw up his hands in exasperation. "Well, first, I guess we're going to have to move some of this stuff out of the way."

"We can help by moving the smaller items," Kathy said. "Come on, Oliver, you and I can start over here. This will be fun. Who knows what we might find?"

Frowning, Oliver followed Kathy. "Sugar, the only thing we're going to find in this mess is dirt. And there had better not be any mice. I don't do mice."

"This is unbelievable," Jack said, stepping closer to the bed to get a better look at the glowing crescent. "Max, come here. I may have found something."

Max peered where Jack indicated and saw an ornately carved flower with a raised center. "What is it?"

"Look where the lower half of the crescent is pointing. Do you see any other flowers with a raised center like that?"

Max stepped back and scanned the bed's headboard. "You're right. It's the only one. Jack, how in the hell did you spot that?"

Jack smiled. "Must be the architect in me—and the architect is telling me that's not an ordinary flower." He reached out and lightly touched its raised center, then gave it a gentle turn. They heard a soft click.

Max stared in astonishment. "A secret compartment?"

"Could we have actually found hidden treasure?"

"Could be. Let's open it and see."

"Be my guest." Jack stepped back to give Max more room. "If so, it's your treasure."

Max opened the small panel and peered in. "Well, if there's anything in here, I don't think it'll be enough to make us all rich."

"Is it empty?"

"I think so. No, wait. There is something." Max reached in and removed a small red velvet pouch. He untied the tiny silk ribbon and dumped the contents into his palm.

Jack let out a long whistle when he saw what fell into Max's hand. "You may have been mistaken, old buddy. That might be worth enough to allow all of us to take early retirement."

Max stood there gaping at the largest diamond ring he'd ever seen. "Jesus, Jack, what do you think it's worth?"

"I haven't any idea, but I'd suggest you get it appraised then lock it away somewhere safe."

"No kidding." Still awestruck at finding the ring, he noticed a thin silver band lying next to the diamond. "There's also a wedding band." He held the small ring up for Jack to see.

"You'd better check and make sure there isn't anything else in the pouch."

"I don't think so." Max handed Jack the rings and checked the bag. "Wait, there is something." He withdrew a handwritten card yellowed with age that read: *With love, to my beautiful wife, Virginia, on our wedding day, April 30, 1882.*

"That was yesterday," Jack noted.

"Yeah, so?"

"Max, you and Elise were in this bed yesterday when the crescent appeared pointing you to the secret compartment where Cyrus's wife's wedding ring was hidden. Yesterday was April thirtieth."

Max stared open-mouthed, from the two rings on Jack's palm to the pristine bedding, replaying in his mind Elise's words of the day before, *"Everything up here is covered in dust except for this bed and the bedding. Why would that be?"*

He shook his head and vehemently said, "Oh, no, Jack. That idea is way too crazy."

Jack shrugged. "If you're ready to believe that all this strange shit has been caused by Cyrus, well, I don't see that this is any stranger than anything else that's occurred. I also think Cyrus wants you to give these rings to Elise." He handed Max back the two rings. "And I wouldn't be surprised if we find out this was their marriage bed." He chuckled. "Buddy, you should see the look on your face."

"Hey, we have a problem over here," Kathy called from the top of the stairs.

"What is it?" Max asked.

"I can't open the door at the bottom of the steps," she replied. "It seems to be locked."

"It can't be. There is no lock."

"And I'm telling you it won't open."

Max gritted his teeth and headed for the stairs. At the bottom he turned the knob and pushed. When nothing happened, he cursed colorfully and hit it hard with his shoulder. Still it didn't budge.

Jack joined him. "Could it just be stuck?"

"This is nuts, but it almost feels like it's being pushed back from the other side."

"Oh, my God," Oliver cried. "Something's locked us in up here. What if we're never found among all this junk?"

Jack studied the door and the stairway. "The steps aren't wide enough for the both of us to hit it together."

Oliver placed his hands on his hips. "I knew it. Whatever freakish thing is living in this house has trapped us up here. How long do you think we can survive without food or water?" he said with dismay. "God, I don't even have my cell phone."

"Does anyone have their phone?" Jack asked.

Max shook his head. "No, why would I? I came up here to move furniture."

"Should I stick my head out the window and call for help?" Kathy asked.

"No one would hear you, sugar, but rabbits and squirrels," Oliver said.

"You know, Max, I think it slammed shut when that flash filled the attic," Jack said.

"That's right," Kathy agreed. "I heard a loud bang."

Angrily, Max once again hit the door, then cursed as pain shot up his shoulder. "Damn it to hell."

"Hello? Is anyone here?" A woman's voice came from the other side of the door.

"In here," Max called. When the door swung open, Max was surprised to see Paula Reynolds. "Hey, thanks."

Looking perplexed, she stood back to allow Jack, Kathy and Oliver to pass. "No problem. What's going on?"

"We couldn't get the damn thing open," Max replied.

"But it wasn't locked."

Aggravated with the entire incident, Max shrugged. "I don't know.

Maybe it was stuck or something."

"Well, anyway, I'm sorry to have just walked in, but the front door was ajar," Paula said.

Max opened his mouth to tell her the door had been locked, but thought, *the hell with it*, and said, "So what brings you out here?"

She tilted her head and smiled. "I wasn't in town for your pre-opening party, so I was hoping for a private tour. You did promise I'd get to see the house when you'd finished."

Max hesitated. He wanted to get the furniture moved, but she was right, he'd promised to show her around. When he had begun the restoration, she'd been extremely helpful in introducing him to painters, plumbers, and electricians. They'd even gone out a few times, but his mind had been focused on the inn, not her.

"Sure, but it will have to be quick. I'm in the middle of moving some furniture down from the attic."

"Oh, I don't want to interrupt you while you're working. Is there any way I can help?"

Max took in her trim business suit, silk blouse, and heels and grinned. "I appreciate the offer, but I don't think you're dressed for moving furniture."

She laughed. "I had a meeting this morning. But honestly, I can come back another time."

"I'd be happy to take her through the house while you boys finish," Kathy said, coming back into the hall. She turned to Paula. "Hi, I'm Kathy Callaghan, a friend of Max's."

Seeming a little flustered, Paula recovered quickly. "That's awfully nice of you, but I wouldn't want to impose. I'll just wait until Max isn't so busy." She turned to Max. "Call me when you're free. I can see the house, and then perhaps we could go to a new Asian restaurant in Ann Arbor I heard about. It's supposed to be fabulous."

Damn, now what was he supposed to say? He liked Paula well enough, but she'd never made his blood race the way Elise did. Feeling a little uncomfortable, he had to come up with a nice way to tell her he wasn't interested. He looked at Kathy, who glowered back. Then inspiration hit and he smiled.

"You know, that sounds like fun. We'll get a group together and go."

Annoyance flashed in Paula's eyes before she smiled and said, "Sure, that would be great."

Max took her arm. "Come on. I'll walk you to the door."

Out on the porch, Paula placed her palm on Max's chest and leaned close. "After we have dinner, perhaps we can come back here and try out that new whirlpool tub of yours." She kissed him lightly. "Call me." She smiled and walked down the steps.

Rather taken aback by her persistence, Max watched her gently swaying backside as she headed for her car. She certainly was attractive, but as his gaze moved to her legs, another pair of legs filled his mind, silky and smooth as they wrapped around him . . .

"Max?"

The mental image of Elise naked in his bed burst and he jumped. Max could feel the blush creep up his cheeks as he turned to see Kathy standing in the doorway.

"Um, s-sorry," she stammered. "Jack wanted to know if you still wanted to tackle trying to bring that furniture down."

"Yeah, sure, I'll be right there." *Damn it,* he had to get his mind off Elise, and off getting her into bed, but as he walked back into the house, he knew that was about as likely as finding a fortune of silver buried in his house.

)

"Whew," Oliver said hours later. "I'm in need of an icy cold beverage and then a hot shower. Look at us. We are all so nasty." He scrunched up his nose in disgust. "Maxwell, I don't recall heavy manual labor being part of my job description."

"Oh, but see how beautifully this bedroom is coming along," Kathy exclaimed. "I can't believe how perfect the cream-colored walls look with these furnishings. Max, I'm so glad you decided to have the hardwood floor refinished. Now that the furnishings are in place, we'll have to order the perfect rug and we'll need new draperies and a number of throw pillows for the bed. It's wonderful that this exquisite, handmade coverlet is still in mint condition. Then, we'll need new towels and accessories for the master bath and—"

"Stop," Max groaned.

Jack smiled with amusement. "Honey, take a breath. You're overwhelming Max."

"Kathy, I appreciate all your help and your enthusiasm, but I'm too exhausted to deal with all of that now."

"Saved by the bell," Jack said as the phone began to ring.

A forlorn expression filled Kathy's face. Oliver took her by the arm. "Come with, sugar. We'll go get us a drink. Then you can tell me all about draperies and rugs."

Max glanced at the clock and cursed. "Damn, Jack, I was supposed to call Elise hours ago . . . hello," he said.

"See you later," mouthed Jack as he left the room.

"Hello, Max. It's Elise."

"Yeah, hi, Elise. I'm sorry I didn't call you earlier, but we've been working in the attic all day, and we just finished."

"It's okay. Don't worry about it," she replied. "I've been busy, as well. What have you been doing in the attic?"

"Jack, Kathy, and Oliver helped me bring down some furniture for the master bedroom, including the antique bed you're so fond of. You'll have to come over and see it. Kathy says it looks great in here."

Elise cleared her throat. "Did you come across anything interesting while moving the furniture?"

Max thought about everything that had happened and decided for now to keep it to himself. Instead, he said, "No, nothing but a lot of junk. I'm going to have to figure out some way to get rid of most of that stuff."

"Well, I had a somewhat productive day at the library going through the newspaper archives. Would you like to hear what I found?"

"Sure, but would you mind telling me over dinner? I need a shower, and I'm starving. We missed lunch."

She hesitated. "I'm pretty tired. I didn't sleep very well last night."

"That's funny. Neither did I, although I know what my mind was on that kept me awake. What about you?"

"Why, Max, I was thinking about Cyrus Mosby. Weren't you?"

Touché, he thought. "If you have dinner with me, I'll tell you what Jack found while researching the crescent."

"Did he discover what it means?"

"Have dinner with me and find out."

"Max, that isn't fair."

"Those are my terms. Take 'em or leave 'em."

"Fine. But I want to go somewhere casual. I'm not in the mood to get dressed up."

"How does pizza sound? Pasquale's is close to the newspaper office and they make the best pizza."

"All right, Max. I'll meet you there in an hour." Not waiting for a response, Elise slammed down the phone. "Incredible, arrogant ass."

"Pleasant conversation?" Sandy asked, standing in the entrance to Elise's cubical.

Elise smiled. "Hi, Sandy. Come on in. That was Max Holt insisting I have dinner with him."

Sandy's brows rose. "By your reaction, I take it you're not enamored with our resident hunk."

"The man is making me insane." Elise waved her into a chair.

"This is getting better by the minute." Sandy made herself comfortable. "This is the first opportunity I've had to ask you how the opening went. Obviously you became better acquainted with Max. So, in just two days, what could he have done to have you calling him an incredible ass?"

Elise closed her eyes and held her head in her hands. "Oh, Sandy, you have no idea what's happened since I left your office."

"Don't keep me in suspense. Are you about to tell me more went on between you and Max Holt than just getting a great interview?"

With her head still in her hands, she nodded then shook her head.

"Elise, so tell me. If Max has asked you to dinner, whatever it is that's got you wound up can't be all that bad."

Elise looked up into her friend's warm, friendly eyes and exhaled a long breath. "I'm supposed to meet Max at Pasquale's for pizza. Why don't we both walk over and I'll tell you along the way. Then you can stay, meet Max and have dinner with us."

"I'll be happy to walk over with you, but after I meet Max, I'm out of there."

"Why?"

"Because, Elise my friend, he didn't ask me to dinner. He asked you. So let's get going. I'm dying to hear why you feel the necessity of having me stay and be a buffer between the two of you." She rose. "I'll get my purse and meet you out front in five minutes."

$$)$$

"Do you have any idea how outrageous all of this sounds?" Sandy asked as they slid into one of the restaurant's red vinyl booths across from one another. "Hidden treasure, glowing silver crescents, and a ghost? I've heard the stories of Cyrus Mosby's ghost supposedly haunting his house, but I've never heard anything about hidden treasure. Nor have I ever heard anyone seeing flashes of silver light or glowing crescents. This is all too unbelievable."

"I know." Elise shrugged. "But it's true. That is, the flashes of light and the crescent shapes. As for the hidden treasure, well . . ." Again, she shrugged.

"Where did you say you saw the silver crescents?"

"Well, one was on Cyrus's tombstone and the other was, ah—" She hesitated.

"Yes?"

"Um, the other appeared over our heads in the headboard of an absolutely gorgeous old four-poster. Oh, Sandy, the headboard is intricately carved with flowers, and it's cherry—"

"Wait a minute. Back up."

"I'm sorry. What?"

"I said, 'back up'. Back up to the part where this happened above your heads. You used the word 'heads', meaning two. Am I correct in thinking Max Holt's head was the other one in this fabulous bed?"

Elise took a long sip of her soda. "Well, ah, yes."

"And?"

"And what?"

Sandy leaned across the table, lowered her voice and asked, "Did you or did you not make love with Max Holt?"

"Well, kind of."

She lowered her voice even more. "Kind of? Can you elaborate a little? Details, Elise, I want details. Is he as good in bed as he looks like he'd be?"

"Sandy—"

She gave a dismissive wave. "You don't have to give me intimate details, just generalize."

"Well, we were . . . I mean he was . . . then, j-just as we were about to . . . well, that's when we were interrupted by Cyrus's ghost."

"Are you telling me that at the critical moment, you were stopped by a ghost?"

"It's true. There was a flash of light and a silver crescent appeared above our heads."

Open-mouthed, Sandy could only stare.

Then a deep voice from behind them said, "Hello, ladies. May I join you?"

Love is blind, and greed insatiable.

— Anonymous

Chapter 12

The two women, intent on their conversation, jumped at Max's sudden appearance.

"Sorry, I didn't mean to startle you," Max said, sliding into the booth next to Elise, trapping her between him and the wall. He held out his hand to Sandy. "Hi, I'm Max Holt."

"Um, h-hi, I'm Sandy Fitzpatrick." Sandy shook Max's outstretched hand. "I work with Elise. It's nice to meet you."

"Hi, Max. Sandy is going to join us for pizza," Elise said, giving Sandy a "don't-you-dare-say-no" look. An unnerving spark of desire shot through Elise when Max's thigh rubbed against hers. This, combined with the scent of his spicy aftershave, set a kaleidoscope of sexual fantasies whirling through her mind.

"Elise?"

"What?" Elise blinked away the image of a bare-chested Max. "I'm sorry, Sandy, what did you say?"

Sandy laughed. "Where were you? The waitress asked if you'd like another soda and what we'd like to have on the pizza."

"Oh, sorry, I was just . . ." Elise saw the humor in Max's eyes, knowing he knew exactly what she'd been thinking. Damn the man. He was turning her into a babbling idiot. She took a deep breath, hoping her next words would sound more coherent. "Oh, I'm not picky. That is, well, I like anything—except anchovies. And I'd like a glass of wine. How about you, Sandy? Would you like some wine?"

"Sure, a glass of wine sounds fine," Sandy replied, visibly holding back a smile. "On the other hand, maybe we should order a bottle."

Max gave Elise one of his most infuriating grins and then turned to the young waitress. "A bottle is an excellent idea, so please bring us a bottle of

Chianti and three glasses. As for the pizza, we'll have an extra-large with the works."

After giving her their order, Max leaned back, laying his arm along the back of the booth, playing with a strand of Elise's hair. "So, Sandy, how long have you worked at *The Gazette*?"

"I was lucky enough to be hired right out of college," she replied. "I grew up here and when I heard there was an opening, I jumped at the chance. I've never been interested in working on a big city paper. Small towns like this suit me just fine. How about you? What brought you to Cedar Bend?"

"To be honest, I didn't know the name of the town until I went to talk with the realtor," Max said. "I was in Ann Arbor on business and decided to go for a drive. I found the house and here I am."

"Did you always have the desire to own an inn? From what I've heard, you've done wonders with the house."

"Well, yes and no. I have a degree in business, but I enjoy restoring old homes." Max paused to pour them each a glass of wine. "My being here running an inn can be blamed on my parents."

"Really, Max? What do they do?" Elise asked, realizing she knew near to nothing of this man to whom she found herself increasingly attracted.

"They're the proud owners and proprietors of a small hotel they restored in Leadville, Colorado. That's where I grew up."

Elise, taking a sip of her wine, began to choke.

"Max, do something!" Sandy cried.

Max patted Elise's back until she managed to gain control. "Are you all right?"

"I'm fine," she gasped, her throat raspy. "It just went down the wrong way. Max, will you please excuse me? I'd like to go to the ladies' room."

When Elise entered the restroom, she was relieved to find it empty. She dampened a paper towel with cold water and dabbed her flushed face with trembling hands. *This can't be happening.* She gazed unseeing into the bathroom mirror. What were the chances of meeting a man from the same town where her great-great-great-grandfather had owned a silver mine? She held the damp towel against her forehead and tried to think clearly, but as all that had occurred since she'd first stepped into Cyrus Mosby's house flickered through her mind, the color drained from her flushed cheeks.

This can't all be mere coincidence.

She tossed the wet towel in the trash and began to dry her face.

She knew, deep in her heart, there could only be one answer. As fantastical as it all sounded, nothing could be that coincidental. A chain of events had been put into motion, and all she could do was wait and see what would happen next.

"What you need to decide," she said to her reflection, "is how much you dare tell Max about your family's history and the real reason you came to Cedar Bend." She squared her shoulders and returned to the table.

"I was about to come looking for you," Sandy said as Elise rejoined them.

"Sorry, there was a line. But I'm just in time. Here's the pizza."

Sandy opened her mouth to respond when Martin Todd suddenly appeared.

"Well, hello, everyone. Didn't mean to interrupt your dinner," Martin said. "I came in and saw you sitting here and thought I'd stop by and say hello."

"No problem. It's good to see you. Would you like to join us?" Max asked.

Elise noticed how Sandy's face lit up with pleasure upon seeing Martin. She'd recalled her friend telling her she'd had a crush on him since high school. She smiled and repeated the invitation. "Yes, Martin, please join us. The pizza just arrived and as you can see, there's plenty."

"Well, if you're sure?" He hesitated, glancing at Sandy.

"Oh, yes, please do. Here, I'll scoot over."

"Martin, I'd offer you a glass of wine, but it seems we've finished the bottle," Max said. "Should I order another?" Max directed his question to the table at large.

Elise stiffened as Max's hand began to caress her knee beneath the red-checkered tablecloth. She felt her temperature rise.

"Sure, why not?" Sandy laughed. "Martin?"

"I'm game, and this one's on me."

"You three go right ahead," Elise said, gritting her teeth, surreptitiously lifting Max's wandering hand as it eased its way up her thigh under her dress. "I'm afraid if I have any more I'll fall asleep."

"I'll be happy to take you home and put you to bed," Max whispered while the other two were distracted with ordering the wine.

"Stop it," Elise hissed.

"Max, I'm glad I ran into you," Martin said. "I may know of someone who would suit the managerial position you were telling me about."

Still chuckling, Max turned from Elise and gave his attention to Martin. "That's great. Who is it?"

"Actually, you met her briefly the night of your party. Her name is Constance Poole. She's local, but has been working in Ann Arbor as the manager of a large restaurant. She's taking care of an elderly aunt here, and working closer to home would be more convenient for her."

Elise saw Sandy's mouth tighten at the mention of Constance's name and recalled the blonde she'd seen in the diner the day she'd arrived. When she realized Max was considering hiring the woman, she stared at Sandy with disbelief. Sandy gave her a slight shake of the head and mouthed, "Not now."

Max nodded. "I remember meeting her and she sounds perfect. Give me her phone number. I'll call and set up an interview."

"Great. I know she'll look forward to hearing from you," Martin said. "Also, Mike or I will come by in the evenings throughout this week to begin work on the stairs."

"I saw pictures of your garden path made out of old tombstones," Sandy said. "I have to admit, it's certainly unusual."

Martin nodded. "At first I thought he was crazy." He smiled over at Max. "But they definitely add to the mystique of the place."

"Well, when I saw that one of them belonged to the ghost who is supposed to haunt the house . . ." Max spread his hands. "What else could I do but bring the old guy's stone home?"

The rest of their dinner passed humorously. Martin and Sandy regaled them with stories of childhood pranks played around the allegedly haunted house.

"Well, in all of those years, I never saw the ghost," Sandy said. "If I had, I would have died of a heart attack."

Elise smiled. "This has been fun, but it's getting late. I'm afraid I need to get home."

"Oh come on, it's not that late," Sandy said. "Stay for a little longer."

"Elise, I'll be happy to give you a ride home." Max motioned for the check. "I'm ready to go as well. It's been a long day."

"They have a jazz band that plays during the week," Martin said, smiling at Sandy. "Would you like to stay?"

"Sure, why not? I love jazz," Sandy said. "Are you sure you two won't join us?"

"No, sorry. I'm going to have to pass," Elise replied. "You'll have to tell me all about it tomorrow." Elise slid from the booth, flashing Max her sweetest smile. "You don't have to drive me home. I can walk. It isn't far."

"That's okay, it's getting dark. I'll walk you."

Max said good-night to Sandy and Martin, took Elise's elbow, and guided her out the door.

"You're not getting rid of me that easily," Max said as they stepped onto the sidewalk. "Besides, I thought you wanted to know what Jack found out about the crescent."

Damn, Elise thought, seeing the triumphant gleam in his eyes. The revelation that Max was from Leadville, and the complications that might ensue had unnerved her to the point she'd forgotten the original reason she'd agreed to have dinner with him. Determined to keep control of the situation, she headed briskly toward home.

"I live a few blocks this way. It's close enough that I can walk to work.

So what did Jack find?"

"Silver."

Elise stopped so suddenly, Max almost ran into her. "Whoa, Elise, what's wrong?"

Heart pounding, she turned to face him. "What did you just say?"

"I said silver. Are you all right? You look as if you're going to faint or something."

"No, I'm fine." She brushed away the arm he'd placed around her shoulders. "Max, what do you mean by 'silver'?"

He regarded her with curiosity and stepped back.

She reached out her hand. "I'm sorry, Max. I didn't mean to react like that. It, well, you surprised me. All I could think of is the hidden treasure."

Max put his arm back around her shoulders and they continued on. "Well, it does have to do with silver, but we didn't find the treasure. Jack found a book which listed alchemy symbols, and the crescent was there. It's the symbol for silver."

"No kidding," she exclaimed, again coming to an abrupt halt, the thrill of impending success lighting her face. "This is terrific news." She brushed a kiss across his cheek. "Don't you see? Cyrus is trying to tell us the hidden treasure is silver."

"Elise." Max sighed, as they resumed their walk. "I know you want to believe there's treasure hidden in my house, but do you realize what the likelihood of that would be?"

But you don't know what I know. She smiled to herself.

"Oh, here we are. This is where I live."

He nodded appreciatively at the pretty, three-story house set mid-block on a treelined street.

"It's nice, isn't it? I live on the third floor. Come on, my entrance is around back."

"Who else lives here?" he asked.

"An older couple who owns the house lives on the first floor, and a great guy named Albert lives on the second." She paused at the foot of the tall fire escape. "You know what, Max? I should introduce him to Oliver. I bet they'd hit it off." She smiled as she began climbing the stairs.

"That's a good idea. Might take Oliver's mind off ghosts."

She put her key in the lock and they entered her small apartment.

"Kathy was right when she said I'd have to go to the library for the newspaper account of Cyrus's death. Fortunately, it had been put on microfilm. I also came across the article on Cyrus's marriage. I have everything right here with me." She placed her large bag on the kitchen counter. "And here they are."

She turned, triumphant, photocopies in her hand, and then froze, her mouth suddenly dry at the sight of Max slowly coming toward her looking as a predator must when it's just cornered its prey. Unable to speak, the papers slipping from her numb fingers, she watched as he gave her the wickedest grin she'd ever seen.

Step by step, he came closer, halting just inches in front of her, backing her into the counter, placing first one hand, then the other on either side of her, securely trapping her between his arms.

He bent down until their lips were a fraction of an inch apart and whispered, "Did I tell you how much I like that little dress you have on?"

Her pulse quickening, she managed a breathless "no".

"Do you know what I'd like even better?"

"Nooo."

"I'd like you to take it off." He gently ran his tongue along her lower lip, setting her mouth on fire. "Then, I'd like to . . ." Leaving her mouth, his tongue trailed slowly along her neck. Stopping at her ear, he whispered, ". . . kiss and caress my way down your body, until I have you so hot and so wet that when I reach the sweetness between your legs, I can taste you when you come."

"Oh, sweet heaven."

He let out a low chuckle. "It will be. I promise." Again he whispered, his mouth so close she could feel his warm breath. "Unless you'd like me to pleasure you right here against the counter, I suggest you take me to your bed." He pressed his lips against hers, ravishing her with his kiss.

Her emotions whirling, Elise abandoned all rational thought, thinking only of Max and the pleasure his words and kiss promised. Mistake or not, she wanted this man and to hell with the consequences.

"My bedroom is down the hall," she said as he lifted her into his arms.

When her feet once again touched the floor, a soft "no" escaped her lips at the loss of contact with his warm mouth. As her eyes fluttered open, gazing into his, dark as smoke and filled with passion, she said the words she knew he'd been longing to hear.

"Make love to me, Max."

Twilight cast dim shadows across the room. Max, his eyes never leaving hers, reached around her and began to ease the dress's zipper down. As the thin cotton slid from her body, Max caught his breath.

"God, Elise, you're so beautiful," he murmured huskily, watching in wonder as her full breasts were revealed, spilling out of her lacy strapless bra. His gaze followed the dress as it slid over her flat stomach, tiny waist, and gently rounded hips. A slip of lace concealed the thatch of delicate red curls nestled between her creamy thighs. Two frilly garters held up her sheer stockings.

"Good God, Elise, I'm not going to make it."

She gave him a tentative smile.

As the dress pooled at her feet, his voice was harsh with desire. "Loosen your hair."

With trembling hands, she reached for the silver clip securing her hair behind her neck. A cascade of dark red tresses tumbled down her back.

"Elise, I've never wanted any woman as much as I want you." He took her into his arms, gently laying her on the bed. Slowly, ever so slowly, running his hands down each leg, he removed her stockings, leaving the slip of lace that was her panties.

He tossed a packet of condoms on the nightstand and removed his own clothing. He lay down beside her and took her in his arms. "I want to touch and kiss every inch of you and watch you come over and over again," he said, his words a soft caress as his mouth covered hers.

The heat of his kiss ignited a passion in her she didn't know she possessed. She moaned deep in her throat as she returned the bold strokes of his tongue. She wanted more. Max broke their kiss.

"I've never tasted anything as sweet as you."

He kissed his way to her swollen nipple, suckling slowly as he ran his tongue back and forth across the hardened peak. Elise was mindless of anything except the excruciating pleasure he was giving her.

As the heat built inside her, she wound her fingers in the hair at the base of his neck and tugged, whispering his name.

"What, love? Do you want more?"

"Oh . . . yes." Each word was a tiny gasp.

"How about this?" His warm mouth traced kisses down her stomach. "Let's see what else I can find that tastes sweet."

Inch by inch, Max drew her panties over her hips and down her legs.

Lost in a haze of erotic desire, she cried out when his mouth gave her the most intimate of kisses. The exquisite sensations from his masterful caresses had her body screaming for release. Her soft whimpers turned into frantic sounds of pleasure as the full force of her climax consumed her body. She dug her hands into his thick hair.

"Max, oh God, Max, I'm . . ."

"Oh yeah, baby, come for me." He plunged two fingers into her and once again, he brought her over the edge.

"Maaax."

"Hang on, sweet."

Max quickly slipped on the condom and in one swift move buried himself deep inside her. As her body adjusted to him, Elise couldn't suppress her gasp of surprise. She saw the confusion that filled his fevered eyes.

Oh, please don't let this go badly, she silently prayed.

"Elise?"

"I'm all right. I wasn't expecting you to feel so . . . " He began to move inside her. She sighed. "Good."

He slowly increased his thrusts until she was squirming beneath him. She dug her nails into his back, and with a low groan, he covered her mouth with a fevered kiss. Claiming her body as his, he once again brought her to an earth-shattering climax, joining her as he tumbled them both into satiated bliss.

Lust and greed are more gullible than innocence.
— Mason Cooley

Chapter 13

Elise lay smiling languidly, gently stroking the back of the man who had just taken her to sexual heights she'd never thought possible. She chuckled.

You are as good in bed as you look.

"What's so funny?" Max murmured next to her ear.

"Oh, nothing. I just feel deliciously wicked."

Max rose, bracing himself on both arms, and smiled down into her content face. "You are deliciously wicked," he whispered, placing a light kiss on her lips. "But, my sweet, there is something we need to discuss."

"Hmm."

"Elise, open your eyes and look at me."

"Why are you so serious?" she purred, trailing one finger down the side of his face. "I think you should kiss me again."

"Kissing you is what led us to be where we are right now."

She licked her lips. "That's right."

He glanced away and then back. "Elise, if you were uncomfortable making love, you could have told me."

She sighed. "I've only been with one other man and, well, let me just say those sexual encounters didn't go nearly as well as this." She grinned. "I had no idea sex could be such fun. I have a feeling there's a lot more you can show me."

She ran her fingers through his thick chest hair.

The grin he gave her made her toes curl. "Sweetheart, it will be my pleasure."

With Max still inside her, she began to move her hips.

"Elise, stop that."

"Why? Is it too soon? Ohh."

"As you can tell, the answer to your question is 'no', but this time we'll take it a little slower.”

She pulled his mouth to hers. “Then stop talking.”

“How’s this?”

“Oh, yesss . . . that’s nice.”

))

The next morning, scooping coffee into the automatic coffee maker, Elise marveled at the changes in her life since she’d left Standish. Suddenly, she felt a hand on her bottom and jumped.

“Max!”

“You’ve been saying that a lot since last night.” He chuckled and began to nibble on the back of her neck.

“You startled me. Stop that. I have to get ready for work.”

“Mmm, you smell great. Now, aren’t you glad you let me show you how much fun we could have in the shower?”

“Yes, but we’ve had enough fun for now.” She pushed his wandering hands away.

“Oh no, my sweet.” Nibbling his way to her ear, he said, “Our fun has just begun.”

“Max, I’m not kidding. I have to get ready for work.” She stepped from his encircling arms and opened the refrigerator. “Are you hungry?”

His white teeth flashed. “I’m starving. I worked up quite an appetite. What do you have in there?”

“Bagels and yogurt.”

“What? I need real food. Don’t you have any bacon and eggs? Maybe some sausage, and how about frying up some potatoes?”

Elise lifted her head from inside the refrigerator. “Oh, you’re in luck; look what I found. This should help fill you up.”

She smiled warmly as she handed him a container of cream cheese, and laughed at the dismay that filled his face. She kissed him and went to get dressed. As she walked around the counter, she noticed the microfilm printouts still lying on the floor where she’d dropped them. She bent down and picked them up.

“Max, I didn’t get a chance to show you what I discovered at the library.” She placed the papers on the kitchen counter. “I found articles on Cyrus’s death and his marriage.”

“What?”

“You didn’t hear anything I said last night, did you?”

He shook his head. “My mind was focused on getting you into bed. So tell me now what you said.”

He began to smear a heaping mound of cream cheese on a bagel.

"Max, that's disgusting."

"I'm hungry."

Even with a mouth full of cream cheese, he looked sexy as hell, she thought, standing there with damp, tousled hair, wearing nothing but jeans which fit him like a second skin.

"If you keep looking at me like that, sweet, I'm going to have to show you how much fun we can have with this cream cheese while you sit on the kitchen counter."

Erotic images of what he might have in mind made her cheeks turn pink. Clearing her throat, she began to read aloud:

" 'Cedar Bend Businessman Found Dead.' "

"Late yesterday evening, June sixth, Mr. Cyrus Mosby, his brother-in-law, Mr. Garrison Hale, and one unidentified older man were found shot to death in Mr. Mosby's home. The authorities are investigating. Mr. Mosby resided in Cedar Bend for twenty years. Throughout those years, he was an upstanding member of his church and community. He was preceded in death by his wife, Virginia, and their two children. The community sincerely mourns Mr. Mosby's tragic and untimely passing."

"That's it?"

"I found one other reference to the deaths." She read:

" 'Death of Local Businessman a Mystery.' "

"The deaths of Mr. Cyrus Mosby, Mr. Garrison Hale, and another man, tentatively identified as Hank Wilkey of Willow Grove, Pennsylvania, all of whom were found shot to death a week ago in the library of Mr. Mosby's home, has the local authorities baffled. Due to a lack of evidence to the contrary, an attempted robbery is thought to have led to the killings. Authorities believe Mr. Mosby fought heroically to defend himself and Mr. Hale and was able to kill the thief, but that he and Mr. Hale were themselves mortally wounded in the course of the struggle. Authorities suspect Mr. Wilkey was the perpetrator but this has not yet been verified. Authorities state that unless other evidence is found, the verdict of self-defense will stand. They do not believe anyone else was involved or in the house at the time."

"I can't believe the authorities would just let it drop like that," Max said incredulously. "I mean, can you imagine if today a prominent businessman were found shot in his home and the police dropped the investigation after only a week? And what about the newspaper? Wouldn't you think they'd be all over this? That had to have been the most newsworthy event ever to happen in Cedar Bend."

"As far as the authorities are concerned, the time period and the rural location have to be taken into consideration. Forensics weren't a big deal then. As for the newspaper, they can't print what they don't know."

Max laughed. "Elise, you've got to be kidding. You're a reporter. Can you imagine letting a hot story like that die? Why, if that were to happen today, the press would be all over it like ham on rye. Speaking of ham on rye, don't you have anything else in here to eat?" He stuck his head in the refrigerator. "Yes." Triumphant, he stood holding a package of bologna, then made a face when he saw it was turkey bologna. "Take that guy. What was his name? Wilkey?" He munched on a slice. "Who was he and why was he there?"

Okay, here's my opening. I can't wait any longer. I have to take a chance and tell him who I am and what I know.

Gathering her courage, she took a deep breath. "Max—"

He ignored her, absorbed in his thoughts. "You know, this might be the explanation of why Cyrus is still hanging around. If it was me, and I was found dead in my library, and after only a week the investigation was dropped, I'd be pretty pissed off."

"Max, there's something I have to tell—" Startled by the small cuckoo clock in the kitchen, Elise stopped mid-sentence. "Oh, my, look what time it is. I'm going to be late for work. I've got to call Sandy and let her know. Where did I put my phone?"

"Did you look on the coffee table?"

"Thanks. That's funny, the red message light is flashing, but I don't recall hearing it ring." Puzzled, phone in hand, she headed for the bathroom. "Max, I have to tell you something, and it's important. I'll come by tonight, and we'll talk." As Max entered her bedroom, Elise closed the bathroom door and dialed Sandy's office number.

"Sandy, it's Elise. I'm going to be a little late. I'll explain when I get there. Okay?"

"Sure. Am I right in thinking Max Holt has something to do with why you're going to be late?" Sandy teased.

"Ah, yes."

"This is going to be good," Sandy said with a chuckle. "I can't wait."

"Okay, I'll be there as soon as I can."

Elise put on a light coat of makeup and had just finished spraying her hair when the bathroom door burst open. Confused at the sight of Max's utter fury, she took a step back.

"Who the hell are you, Elise, and what the hell is this?" Max demanded, waving a small book in his hand.

Elise's mouth went dry at the sight of what he held.

Oh, no. I must have left them on my nightstand.

She reached out a tentative hand. "Max, I can explain."

"Explain what, Elise? Explain how you've used me, taking me for a fool?

You know, you really need to be more careful keeping your secrets hidden, especially from the man you're screwing over. You shouldn't leave things like this lying around." He held up Hank Wilkey's yellowed telegram. "Then there's this." Grace's diary was inches from her nose. "Obviously, I haven't had a chance to read much of this interesting little book, but what I did read told me enough to know you've been feeding me a bullshit story ever since you walked through my front door."

"Max, if you'd stop yelling—"

"Stop yelling? Elise, I haven't begun to fucking yell."

He turned and stomped into the bedroom, tossed the diary onto the bed, and finished buttoning his shirt. "You know what's ironic? If I hadn't knocked your little book off the nightstand looking for my shirt, I would have never known the truth. How long did you plan on stringing me along, Elise? And what the hell else are you hiding from me?"

He put on his sneakers and headed down the hall, grabbing his keys off the kitchen counter.

"Max, no. Please wait. I wanted to tell you, but—"

"Wanted to tell me? Wanted to tell me when, Elise? When you acted as if you'd never heard of Cyrus Mosby and his past? Or would it have been when you were trying to convince me that searching for hidden treasure was just for fun, knowing all along there was a real chance there's silver hidden in my house? Or, perhaps, you were going to tell me . . ." He stood with his face inches from hers. "When you were lying beneath me screaming my name?"

"Max, please listen to me," she cried, unable to keep her tears from flowing freely.

"God damn it, I knew better. Why did I ever think I could trust another woman?"

He strode angrily to the front door, yanked it open, and turned. "I'll tell you what, Miss Baxter, or whatever the hell your real name is, all you had to do was be honest with me from the start about who you were and what you were looking for. I would have been more than willing to let you do whatever you needed. God, I probably would have helped, but—"

Pausing, he dropped his voice very low. "If, by some remote chance I do find silver hidden in my house, I'll be damned if you'll ever know about it now." Max raked her body with eyes that were stormy dark and full of hurt.

He smiled contemptuously before adding, "By the way, thanks for the good time."

Tears blinding her eyes, Elise stumbled toward the door Max had just exited, his last words like ice piercing her heart. As his tread on the stairs grew fainter, Elise collapsed on the top step, head in her hands, and sobbed.

"Elise, are you all right?" asked a hesitant voice.

Elise looked up through her tears and saw her downstairs neighbor, Albert, standing below, an expression of concern filling his craggy face.

"Oh, Albert." She hiccupped. "I'm sorry if you heard all that. My friend and I, ah, well, had a little . . ."

"No problem. You don't have to explain. I just wanted to make sure you were okay."

"Thanks, I appreciate you asking, but I'm . . ." Her voice cracked on a sob and she ran back into the house. Not knowing what else to do, she stumbled back into the bathroom and picked up the phone where she'd left it laying on the sink. With hands that shook, she dialed Sandy's number.

"Sandy?" she gasped when the phone was answered.

"Elise, is that you? Are you all right?"

"Please come," was all she could manage before the tears began again.

"I'm on my way. I'll be there in a few minutes. Christ, Elise, what has he done?"

"It wasn't him. It was me. Sandy, hurry."

))

As Max reached the front sidewalk, he angrily looked for his car. When he remembered he'd left it parked at the restaurant, he swore. With long strides, he began to walk, replaying in his mind the scene he'd just had with Elise, hearing her plead for him to let her explain. He increased his speed. As he pictured her tear-streaked face, he walked even faster. When he began to wonder if he should go back, he ran.

"Fuck the car," he growled and turned in the direction of home.

))

"But, Jack, we can't leave," Kathy exclaimed, sitting on a tall stool at the large kitchen island. "Now that Max has the furniture in his bedroom, I have to choose draperies and rugs and towels and—"

"Okay." He held up his hands in surrender. "We'll stay for a few more days, but I do have to go back to work."

"You have your laptop with you and your cell phone, so I don't see why you can't do some work this morning from right here." She turned her attention to Oliver, who was busily beating eggs for an omelet. "Besides, Oliver and I are planning on driving into Ann Arbor later to do some shopping."

"That's right. Sugar here wants to surprise Maxwell with the *fait accompli*. I told her perhaps before she goes out choosing accessories for Max's bedroom, she might want to check with Elise first and see what colors she'd like." He winked. "I'm assuming, since Maxwell didn't come home last night, Elise must have stopped running."

Oliver was happily grinning as he poured the egg concoction into a sizzling skillet. A loud bang made him jump.

"What the hell was that?" Jack asked.

"It sounded like someone slammed the front door," Kathy replied.

A minute later, the three friends stared slack-jawed at an out-of-breath, sweat-soaked Max. Eyes blazing, he looked as though he would hit the first person who spoke.

"I'm going to take a goddamned shower, then I need someone to drive me into town so I can get my fucking car." Max turned, and without another word, stomped up the stairs.

"Well, sugar, perhaps you don't need to concern yourself with what colors Elise prefers after all."

$$\text{☽}$$

"So where did you leave your car?" Jack asked.

Not looking as though his shower had cooled his temper in the least, Max slammed the passenger door of Jack's van and sat back in the seat.

"In town, at a restaurant called Pasquale's."

Jack pulled out onto the road. "Okay, I guess you can show me when we get there." He gave Max a sideways glance. "Do you want to tell me what happened between you and the lovely Elise? I can't imagine you're this pissed because the lady didn't succumb to your charms."

Max's laugh was without humor. "No, Jack, that's definitely not the problem."

"I'm listening."

"What is it with me and women, Jack? Why are they always screwing me over? Do I have a sign on my back that says, 'Hey, look at me! I'm a nice guy; come fuck with me'?" Not waiting for a reply, he continued his rant. "First, there was Teresa and that rich asshole she met in California. Now I've managed to get mixed up with a liar and a sneak."

"Elise?"

"Yes, Jack, Elise. Who the hell else would I mean?"

"Sorry, I just wouldn't have thought of her in those terms."

Max laughed sardonically. "Well, Jack, until this morning, neither would I. Pull into that diner. I'm starving. Maybe food will help cool me down."

Seated at a booth in the crowded restaurant, Max ordered more food than he could possibly eat. He took a sip of hot, strong coffee, sat back, and told Jack what had happened that morning.

"Wait a minute," Jack said when Max had finished. "I'm not sure I'm following all of this. You found an old diary written by someone named Grace. She talks about Cyrus Mosby and someone named . . ."

"Clayton Hamilton," prompted Max.

"Yeah, and a guy named Hank Willey—"

"Wilkey."

"Who sent a telegram from Cedar Bend, and then there's also an old silver mine in Leadville, Colorado. Do I have all of that right?"

"Pretty much." Max scooped up a mound of fried potatoes. "No wonder Elise choked on her wine last night when I mentioned I was from Leadville."

"But what does it all mean? I'm sorry, but I don't get the connection with Elise."

"I don't know how it all fits together, but I'm guessing Elise is related to Grace and Hank Wilkey, and somehow they're connected with Cyrus Mosby. Did I tell you Hank Wilkey was one of the men found dead with Cyrus?"

"No. How do you know that?"

"Elise found the newspaper story of the deaths and read it to me this morning. Damn it, Jack, she stood there and read that story as if she didn't know who Hank Wilkey was."

"Well, what was her explanation for all of this?"

Max concentrated on his food.

"Max?"

When he still didn't reply, Jack sighed. "You didn't let her explain, did you? You lost your temper and stormed out. Right?"

"Jack, she had the perfect opportunity to tell me her entire story the first night we met. We were sitting on the terrace after everyone had left, discussing Cyrus and his death, but she didn't say a thing." Angrily, he threw down his napkin and poured himself more coffee. "Instead, she acted as if it was all news to her. Then she had the nerve to talk about how interesting it would be to investigate Cyrus's death. Oh, and while we're doing that, why not search my house for hidden treasure as well."

"I agree it all sounds questionable, but maybe you should hear her side of the story."

"Hell, I don't know. The way I feel right now, I'm tempted to chalk the night up to a good time and let it go." He drained his coffee cup and glanced around the full diner. "Do you see our waitress? I'm ready for the check."

"My advice, for what it's worth," Jack said, as they got back into his car, "is first off, you need to remember that Elise isn't Teresa. Second, you should at least give her a chance to explain. Max, we've been friends long enough for me to know you must have feelings for the lady, otherwise you would have walked away and been done with it. You wouldn't be sitting here hours later, still pissed off."

"There's more to it than just the diaries." Anger spent, Max laid his head against the backrest and closed his eyes. "She was practically a virgin, Jack."

"What?"

"I know. Trust me. I was a little taken aback myself. I sure as hell wasn't expecting that." Max turned and stared out the passenger window. "And I was so pissed, I said some really ugly things before I left."

"And what are you going to do about it?"

"Hell if I know. That's what's wrong with being a nice guy. You just can't walk away. But you know what? Sometimes I get tired of being such a nice guy. There's my car."

Jack pulled to the curb and Max got out. "Thanks a lot for the ride and for listening to me bitch. I'll see you later. I need to drive and think this bullshit through."

Max gave Jack a wave and headed for his car. He slid onto the Mustang's leather seat and punched the button to put the top down. He turned onto the two-lane road leading out of town and, with Bob Seger singing "Against the Wind," hit the gas.

It is greedy to do all the talking but not to want to listen at all.
— Democritus

Chapter 14

"Here," Sandy said, handing Elise another tissue. "I want you to blow your nose and drink this hot cup of coffee. Eat one of these fattening doughnuts I brought. Then, when you're calm, you can start from the beginning and tell me what's going on."

Elise, not holding anything back, told Sandy everything—from the silver mine in Colorado to all that had happened between her and Max since they'd met, ending with "the most wonderful night I've ever had—and I probably won't ever see him again."

For a minute, Sandy was speechless. Then she said, "Tell you what. Go wash your face and get dressed. By that time, I should have a plan."

Elise sniffed. "Truly?"

Sandy shrugged. "Well, I'm not guaranteeing it will be a great plan, but I'll do my best. Obviously, finding a way to get Max to listen to you is our first priority. We can deal with missing silver later."

Elise smiled for the first time since Max had walked out. She gave Sandy a hug and went to do as she had been told.

"Make sure you put on something that will make Max Holt drool," Sandy called.

"Okay, I think I look presentable. Hand me one of those doughnuts, then tell me what to do next," Elise said, coming back into the room.

Sandy gave her an appreciative nod and smiled. "You'll do."

"So you think he'll like it?" She turned to give her the full effect of her strappy navy heels, short pleated navy skirt and clinging white camisole covered by a little navy jacket.

Sandy grinned. "Oh, yes. He'll like it."

Elise slumped back down on the kitchen chair looking dejected, the happiness she'd felt punctured like a balloon.

"What if he won't even talk to me? He was furious when he left."

"Listen to me. This is how I see the situation. Considering all you've told me about Max and how he's been acting toward you since you met, I believe the guy honestly cares about you. So I wouldn't be surprised if, after he's had time to cool off, you hear from him."

A spark of anger began to replace Elise's hurt as she recalled Max's final cutting words.

"Does he actually care for me, Sandy? Or did he just want to get me into bed?"

"We'd be pretty naïve if we didn't admit sex had to be one of his motivations, but I saw the way he looked at you last night at the restaurant, and I'm sure it wasn't all about sex."

Elise placed her hand on Sandy's arm. "Here I've been going on about myself and I haven't even asked you how it went with Martin after we left?"

"Oh, well, it was fun. I had a nice time and I think he did, too."

Sandy stood and began to busy herself with clearing up the coffee cups and napkins from the table.

"Is there something wrong?" Elise took the cups from her hands and carried them to the sink.

Sandy sighed. "No, I most likely read more into the evening than I should have. And Martin might be seeing someone. He probably only asked me to stay because we've been friends for so long. So that's where the love life of Sandy Fitzpatrick stands."

Elise saw the hurt in Sandy's eyes as she tried to shrug it off.

"Do you have any idea who he's involved with?"

Sandy rolled her eyes. "Are you ready for this? It could be Paula Reynolds, the realtor who sold Max his house."

"No kidding. Are you sure?"

Sandy shrugged. "She's recently divorced, and I've been seeing her and Martin around together. Paula grew up here with the rest of us and I think, like me, she's always been attracted to him."

"What about Constance? I thought Martin was seeing her?"

Sandy snorted. "Who knows? If he's good looking and might have money, Constance is interested."

"Hopefully you're wrong and Martin and Paula are just friends." She gave Sandy a hug. "You truly are a dear friend, and if there's ever anything I can do for you, please ask."

Sandy hugged her back and sniffed. "We'd better get out of here or we'll both be a mess. Are you up to going in to work? I told the boss you weren't feeling well and I was coming to check on you, but if you're not up to it, I'll tell him you're still sick."

"I'm okay. I don't want to sit around here by myself. Besides, I can't waste this killer outfit. Who knows? I might run into Max. I'll get my bag."

In her bedroom, the sight of the rumpled bedding and the thought of how wonderful her night with Max had been almost had her crying again. Instead, she took a deep breath, stiffened her spine, grabbed her handbag and left.

"I can't get over your story about the stolen silver and the chance it might still be hidden in Cyrus's house," Sandy said as the two got into her car.

"I know it seems too fantastic, especially if it is Cyrus's ghost trying to tell us where it is, but what else could those silver crescents mean?"

"I have to admit that in a weird, creepy way it makes sense. But a ghost?" Sandy shook her head.

"Well, ghost or no ghost, unless Max forgives me, I'll never know if it's true or not."

Hours later, as she and Sandy were leaving the newspaper building, Elise's heart did a flip, for sitting there at the curb in his black convertible was Max.

"Sandy, look."

"I see him."

"What should I do?"

"Go see what he wants. I told you he'd be back." She gave Elise a gentle push toward the glass door. "Now go."

"Do you see his expression? He doesn't look too happy."

Sandy frowned as Max impatiently tapped his steering wheel.

"Well, perhaps not, but he's here. So go."

"Okay. Wish me luck." Elise gathered her courage and walked toward the car.

Behind his Ray-Bans, Max's eyes narrowed as Elise strolled toward him. How the hell was he supposed to stay pissed when one look at those long legs beneath that short skirt had him wanting nothing more than to find the closest bed and throw her in it? He'd been driving around for hours, replaying his reaction to her betrayal. He'd fluctuated between telling her to get the hell out of his life and wanting to hear her explanation. Curiosity and his better nature finally won out, and now here he sat.

When she reached the curb, she gave him a tentative smile.

Max nodded. "Get in."

"What?"

"I said, 'Get in.' "

She visibly bristled. "Why?"

"Because I want to talk to you. That's why."

"Is that right?"

"Yes, that's right."

"Considering the tone of your voice, what makes you think I want to get into this car with you?"

Max sighed. "Elise, please just get in the car."

She gave him a long look before she bent to stash her bag on the floor behind the seat and slipped in next to him. "All you had to do was say please."

Max gritted his teeth, trying to tamp down the jolt of lust that shot through him when she'd bent over giving him the full impact of her cleavage. "Do you always dress like that to go to work?"

She seemed surprised. "Why? Is there something wrong with what I'm wearing?"

"Not if you're going to dance on a bar for tips."

She unbuckled her seatbelt, grabbed her purse, and reached for the door handle. "Obviously, Max, you're still pissed. So I'm leaving."

She had the door partially open when he reached across and slammed it shut.

"You're not going anywhere. I said I wanted to talk to you."

"As long as you're going to be hateful, I'm not staying. So let me out."

"I'm not being hateful."

"You could have fooled me."

"Elise, I'm sorry I said that. I came back here to get you so we can talk." He put the car into gear and pulled away from the curb.

"Can I at least know where we're going?"

Max didn't trust himself to speak until he'd driven through town and they were out on the two-lane. How could someone he'd known for such a short time have his emotions in such chaos? He took a deep breath.

"Okay, this is what's going to happen. I'm going to drive this car. While I'm driving this car, I want you to start at the beginning and tell me all. I mean everything, starting with the silver mine in Colorado, up until your arrival in Cedar Bend. I'm going to keep driving until I'm satisfied you've told me every last detail." He hesitated. "And I don't give a shit if I have to drive all the way to Standish, fucking Pennsylvania, to hear it."

"Are you always such a domineering, arrogant, pompous ass?"

Max glowered. There was a temper to go with that red hair. Well, he didn't give a shit if he was pissing her off. He was tired of women using him.

"Elise, I don't like being lied to and taken for a fool."

Elise took a calming breath. "Max, I never intended to lie to you or make a fool out of you. I'll be happy to explain everything. I told you this morning I had something important to talk to you about, but you wouldn't listen."

"The less said about this morning the better. I'm still not real happy with you."

"Then why am I here?"

Because I haven't been able to get the smell of you or the taste of you or the feel of you out of my mind. All I've wanted to do is take you home to my bed.

Max pushed away those unwelcome thoughts.

"You're here because I think I deserve an explanation."

"You deserve an explanation? You know what, Max? I want you to stop this car and let me out."

"Exactly where do you suggest I do that? Along the side of the road?"

Elise's blue eyes flared. "At this point, Max, I don't really give a damn. Just do it."

He hit the gas, controlling the urge to do as she asked. "How about if I say I'd like to hear your explanation? Is that better?"

"Yes, much."

"Then, I'm listening."

She sat, seeming to gather her thoughts. "Max, everything I'm about to tell you I know from reading my great-great-grandmother's diaries. They're quite detailed, but not complete, so I don't want to be accused of holding information back or being a liar."

"As I said, I'm listening. Just tell me."

"Okay, this is what I know. In 1878, a man named Eli Wilkey was a partner in a silver mine in Leadville, Colorado, with Clayton and Nathan Hamilton. They worked their mine for a year before it played out. Eli wrote to his wife, Emma, telling her they'd hit it big, but he thought they had about exhausted their mine's silver load and he'd probably be home soon.

"Now, this is where the story becomes vague. Emma, back in Pennsylvania, had a young daughter who was my great-great-grandmother, Grace. While Eli was in Colorado, he would send letters containing small amounts of money home on a regular basis. When a couple of months went by without hearing from Eli, Emma became worried. So his younger brother, Hank Wilkey, went out west to see what was going on."

"The same Hank Wilkey who was supposedly killed in my house?"

"That's right. Anyway, when Hank arrived in Leadville, he found the mine deserted and was told that both Eli and Nathan had been murdered in the mine. The night before the bodies were discovered, Clayton had been seen boarding a train. Hank found their cabin had been stripped bare. He then went to the bank where he was told that all three men had closed out their accounts. The sheriff in Leadville told Hank that Clayton was a wanted man, suspected of murdering both Eli and Nathan and stealing the money. Hank went back to Willow Grove and stayed with Emma until he was able to get her a job working in a millinery shop. All of Emma's family was dead and Hank was the last of the Wilkeys. Hank decided he was going to track Clayton Hamilton down and get his brother's share of the silver back for Emma and Grace. Hank was gone for twenty years."

"Twenty years?"

Elise nodded. "In that time, he sent letters and telegrams back to Emma, letting her know where he was and what progress he was making. Then he sent Emma a letter telling her he'd tracked Clayton to Detroit. The next time Emma heard from Hank, she was on her deathbed. Grace read her Hank's telegram from Cedar Bend telling them he'd met a man who was going to take him to Clayton Hamilton that night."

"Wow." Max shook his head. "So Cyrus Mosby was actually Clayton Hamilton?"

"I'm assuming so." Elise shrugged. "Grace never heard from Hank again. Her husband, Markus, contacted the authorities in Cedar Bend and was told about Cyrus and the two other men found dead in his house. From the description of one of the men, Grace concluded he was Hank. By the time Grace found all this out, Hank had been buried. Who knows? Hank might have been buried in one of the graves you were telling me were removed from that old cemetery."

Max looked thoughtful. "I'll bet you're right. Wonder if I have his tombstone?"

"Do you have any marked John Doe? Remember, nobody knew who he was until after he was buried."

"Don't know. I'll have to look," Max said.

"All right. So with both Emma and Hank dead, Grace decided that after such a long time, the silver must be gone, and I guess she just didn't have the ambition to continue the search. Grace had three sons, her youngest being my great-grandfather, who had two sons and a daughter. My grandfather was the oldest of the three. Even though the story of the silver and speculation on what might have happened to it has been passed down throughout the generations, no one in my family, until me, has been interested enough to pursue the search. I found Grace's diaries after my grandmother died, and I've been fascinated with the story ever since."

Max heard the hesitation in her voice and glanced her way. "And?"

And I saw Grace's ghost, she thought.

Deciding not to bring that up right now, she shook her head. "It's hard to explain. It's almost as if I have this uncontrollable need to discover who Cyrus Mosby was and what might have happened to the missing silver. I managed to get a job on the Cedar Bend paper in order to be close enough to do some investigating. So, Max, that brings us up to right now, this minute, in this car."

He scowled. "I don't think sarcasm is going to help this situation. Why in the hell didn't you just tell me all of this from the start?"

"First, how did I know you'd believe me? You might have thought I was some nut. Secondly, you were a stranger I knew nothing about. How would I have known how you'd react? I mean, how could I know you wouldn't search for the silver on your own?"

"Okay, I'll give you that, but after you realized what a nice, honest guy I am, to the extent that you took me to your bed, why in the hell didn't you tell me then?"

She took a deep breath. "I tried to tell you this morning, but you wouldn't listen. Some of us do have to work, Max, and are expected to be on time. So I told you I had something important to talk to you about and I'd see you tonight. As for not telling you last night, when exactly would you have had me tell you? If I remember correctly, talking wasn't really what you were interested in doing. For God's sake, Max, it's only been three days since I walked into your house. What was I supposed to say? 'Hi, I'm Elise Baxter and my great-great-great-grandfather's stolen silver might be hidden in your house, so would you mind awfully if I look for it?' "

Long minutes of silence filled the car.

"You know what, Max? Obviously, you're still pissed. So why don't you just turn this car around and take me home?"

"Elise, I still think you had plenty of opportunities between 'hello' and us ending up in your bed for you to have told me. No, wait. Hear me out." He held his hand up to stall the retort he saw forming on her lips. "But I can also see where you would have been hesitant to do so."

"How kind of you," she said dryly. "So what happens now?"

Max smiled. "We go home." He slowed enough to do a U-turn and then headed back the way they'd come. "I'm starving. How about you? I saw a restaurant not too far back. We'll stop there."

She stared at him with amazement. "Your mood swings are enough to make a person crazy. You know that?"

Max turned into the restaurant parking lot and hit the button to put the top up. Reaching for Elise, he brought his mouth close to hers. "I know other ways to make you crazy."

A few minutes later, he broke the kiss. "I'm so sorry for the ugly things I said to you this morning," he whispered, their lips only an inch or two apart.

She sighed. "I'm also to blame. I should have made more of an effort to tell you. Let's just forget about it."

Max leaned back in the seat and ran his hands over his face. "I'd like to explain, then perhaps you'll understand why I reacted the way I did."

She touched his arm. "If I had to guess, I'd say it involved someone you cared deeply about."

He laughed without humor. "Yeah, I'd say so. We'd just finished college and were about to get married. Teresa was pretty and bright and we had a lot of the same interests, except for lifestyle. She came from a small town in Georgia and dreamed about living in a fancy condo in some big city. She loved designer clothes and swore someday she'd drive a Porsche. I was so stupid in love with her I thought I could give her what she wanted even though none of that meant anything to me. She was a sales rep for a cosmetics company, and a month before the wedding, she went out to California to some conference.

"I thought I'd surprise her and meet her there. But she wasn't registered at the hotel where the conference was. I found out where she was staying only because a woman she worked with, who was also at the conference, didn't like her and was more than happy to tell me. Teresa had met some guy when they'd all gone out on a chartered boat." He paused and stared out the window before continuing in a low voice. "I found her in his arms lying half naked on the deck of his yacht."

Elise took his hand in hers. "Oh, Max, I'm so sorry."

He squeezed her hand back. "Yeah, well, at least I found out before I married her."

"If you don't mind me asking, what did she say to you?"

"Not a damn thing. She saw me standing there and she just smiled and took her engagement ring off and tossed it at me."

"My God, what a . . ." She hesitated.

"The word is 'bitch.' "

Elise shook her head. "I can't imagine the pain you felt."

"I flew back to Chicago and stayed drunk for about two weeks. Jack, Kathy, and Oliver finally sobered me up and a few months afterward, I found myself in Cedar Bend and discovered my dream house and my inn." He turned to her. "And you."

She smiled and fell into his arms.

He held her tight and kissed her. "How hungry are you?"

"Not very," she replied breathlessly.

"Good, neither am I."

Kathy ran into the library where Jack and Oliver were sitting. "You'll never guess who just came through the front door."

"If they came through without opening it, sugar, I don't want to know," Oliver stated.

A wide smile spread across Kathy's face. "Oh, they opened it all right. It was Max and Elise."

Jack set aside his paper. "Well, that didn't take too long."

"Was Elise kicking and screaming?" Oliver asked.

Kathy giggled. "Ah, no, I don't even think they saw me. He had her by the hand and was practically dragging her up the stairs."

They all glanced up at the ceiling as they heard Max's bedroom door bang shut.

"Well, I'm glad Maxwell came to his senses," Oliver said. "I like Elise. She's perfect for him. Not like that bitch, Teresa. I told Maxwell she was a slut, but did he listen? No, and we all know how that turned out, don't we?"

"Max, Kathy was in the hall."

"So?" He had her jacket off and was working on her skirt.

"Max, they're right downstairs."

"Again, 'so'? Where's the zipper on this thing?"

"Max—"

"Elise, those are three adults sitting downstairs who know exactly what we're going to be doing up here. Unless your screams of delight penetrate through the floor, trust me, they're not interested."

He managed to loosen her skirt so it fell at her feet, leaving her in nothing but her camisole, skimpy panties, stockings and heels.

The look Max gave her was pure heat. "I'm going to do what I've wanted to do since you got into my car." He picked her up and tossed her into the middle of his bed.

"Max . . ."

"We've got some unfinished business in this bed."

As he unbuttoned his shirt, the expression in his eyes had her breath coming in shallow little gasps. He knelt on the bed between her legs.

"Well, sweetheart, it seems we're right back where we started." He stretched out to his full length, his hardness pressing against the silk of her damp panties. "The only difference this time," he whispered, his mouth inches from hers, "is that I intend on finishing all that I begin."

Elise chuckled and wound her arms around his neck. "Is that a promise?"

"Oh, yes."

Greed is all right; by the way, I think greed is healthy.
You can be greedy and still feel good about yourself.
— Ivan F. Boesky

Chapter 15

"You're serious?" Oliver exclaimed. "This isn't a joke?"

After dropping Elise off at her apartment that morning, Max was back home, and over a breakfast of French toast and bacon, was filling the other three in on what Elise had told him the day before. "No, I'm not kidding. Kathy, would you please pass me the syrup?"

Kathy handed him the bottle.

"Thanks," Max said as he smothered his French toast in syrup. "According to Elise, there's a real chance either silver or a large amount of money could be hidden somewhere in this house."

Looking and sounding skeptical, Jack asked, "Just how do you plan to go about finding this so-called lost treasure?"

Max shrugged. "I haven't the slightest idea. Maybe Cyrus will help us out."

Oliver grimaced. "Oh, great, just what I want to hear; we're going to play 'find-the-treasure' with a ghost."

"Actually, Elise is coming over tonight. I thought we could all put our heads together and see if we can come up with some ideas. In the meantime, since I didn't accomplish anything yesterday, I need to get some work done around here today. Martin Todd gave me the name of someone who might be interested in the managerial position. I plan to give her a call. And Elise wrote such a complimentary article on the inn that I have phone messages from people who weren't able to make the opening asking for private tours."

Oliver's brows rose. "Well, Maxwell, just whose fault is it that you didn't accomplish anything yesterday? That is, except for driving all over hell and back putting unnecessary mileage on your car. All I can say is I'm glad you finally came to your senses. When Jack told us what had happened between you two, I said right then that Elise probably had a perfectly reasonable explanation—and I was right."

Max glared. "I don't know that I'd go as far as saying her explanation was reasonable."

"The good news is that you two made up and we're all glad," Kathy said. "Max, I didn't get a chance to tell you about the window coverings and rug I ordered yesterday. They're going to be perfect. Jack and I were planning to stay for a few more days so I could finish your bedroom, but now that we're seriously going to begin looking for hidden treasure, I'm not going anywhere until it's found. This is really exciting, isn't it?"

Jack's brows rose in surprise. "Kathy, I have work I need to get back to. Do you have any idea how long it could take to find this supposed treasure?"

Her mouth formed a thin line. "Jack, you're a junior partner who is entitled to some time off, which you never take. Besides, you can work from here as easily as you can in Chicago. If you feel obligated to leave, that's fine, but I'm staying. I'm not missing out on finding the treasure."

Jack looked rather taken aback by his wife's vehemence. "Okay, I'll see what arrangements I can make to work from here, but I can't be away for weeks. So if this treasure isn't found in a reasonable amount of time, I guess I'll be going back to Chicago alone."

Kathy kissed his cheek. "Oh, don't act so grumpy. I'm sure we'll find it in no time."

"Sugar, consider the size of this house." Oliver ticked each room off on his fingers. "Two parlors, the library, the dining room, kitchen, conservatory, Max's office, six bedrooms and baths, not to mention numerous storage closets, the basement, and that disastrous attic. Why, by the time we search all those places, we'll be so old that if we did find the treasure, we wouldn't have the energy to spend it."

Max glanced at Jack. "Maybe, but we have the perfect person sitting right here to come up with some ideas to get us started."

"Me?"

"Yes, you, Jack. Who else could be better than an architect to puzzle out where the treasure might be hidden. Remember, it was you who discovered the secret compartment in the headboard. We know Cyrus built the house. So, Jack, if you had designed this house, where would you have stashed the loot?"

Jack rolled his eyes in amusement. "Do you even know what kind of loot we're going after? I seriously doubt there's a large quantity of silver ore stashed in this house. The first step would be to do some research on how one would have gone about exchanging silver after it was mined into some form of cash, such as gold coins or dollar bills. What time period are we talking about?"

"1879 to 1880," Max replied. "Who knows, there might be a book in my library on silver mining. If not, maybe you could try the Internet."

"Excellent idea," Kathy said enthusiastically. "And I'll help by searching through more of the boxes in the attic. I suppose any reference to Cyrus could be useful."

Max nodded. "Okay, you two, that sounds like a good start. As for me, I'll go call these people back and try to come up with a time they can come tour the inn. I wouldn't be so concerned, but they could be influential residents who could bring us business. I'll also give Constance Poole a call. I'm hoping she'll be able to meet with me this afternoon. Oliver, I'm going to be working on the employment ad for the paper next week. You'll have to let me know how much kitchen staff you're going to need and what their duties will be. If Constance works out, she'll oversee the dining room staff so you won't have to worry about that aspect."

"Will I be interviewing the applicants?" Oliver asked.

"Sure. They're going to be your staff."

"Do I have to tell them they might be coming to work in this house of horrors?"

"Only if the pots and pans begin to levitate," Max called as he left the room.

"So tell me everything," Sandy said, as she and Elise sat down in a booth at the local diner. "I've been on pins and needles since you left with Max last night."

"Well, I guess you could say we made up. What sounds good to you for lunch?"

"Elise, for God's sake, put that menu down and tell me what you mean by 'I guess.' Either you made up or you didn't."

Elise placed her menu on the table, looked at her friend, and sighed. "Sandy, I'm not sure how I feel about the way the evening ended. We went for a long drive. He informed me, in no uncertain terms, what he expected me to tell him. I did as he asked. He sort of accepted my explanation, and we ended up in his bed."

"That sounds to me like you made up."

"Sandy, the man is making me insane. He can be such an arrogant, pompous, authoritative ass that I just want to tell him to go to hell and walk away."

"And? What stops you?"

"Then he starts kissing me and I lose all my reason. And you can wipe that smile off your face. It's not funny."

"God, Elise, I would think losing one's sanity while being kissed by Max Holt isn't something most women would complain about." Unable to stop herself, she laughed harder.

Elise rolled her eyes. "Well, I'm not exactly complaining about his kisses. It's the way he takes control of a situation and maneuvers me to his will that I don't like."

"Are you talking about him maneuvering you into his bed? Again, Elise, what are you complaining about?" she said, breaking into a fit of giggles.

"Sandy, stop. You know what I'm trying to say."

"I'm sorry." She dabbed tears from her eyes. "I understand what your concerns are, but do you realize the number of women who would love to be in your shoes?"

"Evidently, all of those other women don't realize there's more to being with Max than a good time in bed." Elise frowned and began shredding a paper napkin. "Did I mention he can have an awful temper, and he can be stubborn to the point you want to scream?" Her litany of Max's faults trailed away as she closed her eyes and began to massage her temples. "He can be thoughtful, extremely sweet, and considerate. He has a great sense of humor, and he makes me feel incredible, and I'm crazy about him—and I don't know how to deal with all of this."

Sandy put a comforting hand on Elise's arm. "I know you're confused and your emotions are whirling. One problem might be that the relationship between you and Max has moved too quickly."

"That's definitely an understatement. If anyone had told me I'd fall into bed with a man practically the day after we met, I'd have told them they were crazy, but here I am."

"Well, obviously you have strong feelings for Max or that wouldn't have happened. You told me the reason you came here was to find your family's missing silver. You didn't plan to fall for the man whose house the silver might be hidden in."

"And that's what is scaring me to death: falling too hard and too fast for Max Holt. I told you about my last boyfriend and how that relationship turned out, didn't I?"

Sandy nodded.

"I don't want to be hurt like that again." She shuddered and hugged herself before continuing. "I dated Jason for months before I even considered going to bed with him, and when I finally decided to, well, I was told I was nothing but a frigid tease and a total disappointment. Needless to say, it was a disastrous evening, best forgotten."

"Oh, honey, I'm so sorry."

Elise sighed. "But do I learn from my mistakes? No. What do I do but rush right into bed with Max. Honestly, Sandy, when his hand first touched mine, I felt such an instant spark of desire I'm not sure I wouldn't have rolled around in the grass that first night with him if he'd asked."

"Oh, dear, you do have it bad."

She nodded, her tears threatening to spill.

Sandy handed her some tissues.

"He must have strong feelings for you as well. I can't imagine he'd have taken the time to come back yesterday and wait for you to get off work to give you a chance to explain if he didn't care."

"I guess. But he wasn't exactly nice about it."

Sandy chuckled. "Elise, he's a man, and men usually have very big and very fragile egos. Oh, damn. Not both of them."

Elise glanced up to see what had caught Sandy's attention. Two women were coming through the door. She recognized the blonde in the short, black dress as Constance Poole and the tall brunette with tortoise-shell glasses as the realtor Paula Reynolds.

She whispered, "They know each other?"

Sandy nodded and leaned in close. "We all grew up together. Remember I told you I thought Paula was seeing Martin? The latest gossip at Ellie's is he might not be the only one she's seeing. As for Constance, she's been a royal pain in my ass since high school, and I hate her guts."

"What did she do?"

"Her mission in life seems to be to try and take every man I'm interested in away from me, and throughout the years, she's done a pretty good job of it."

"Why does she dislike you so?"

"Because all she has going for her is her looks. She's basically as dumb as a bag of rocks. I got better grades. I was the head of the debate team, class president, and valedictorian. She was head cheerleader and homecoming queen. Boys would fall at her feet, and I assume men are doing the same, but she always envied my smarts."

"Constance sees us. Here she comes," Elise said.

"Well, Sandy, we meet again. Long time, no see."

Sandy forced a smile. "Hello, Constance."

When Constance glanced at Elise, Sandy made the introductions.

"This is my coworker, Elise Baxter. Elise, this is Constance Poole."

Constance dismissed Elise with a nod and turned her attention back to Sandy.

"We just dropped in for a quick bite. I have a personal interview this afternoon with Max Holt." Her low, husky voice seemed to purr Max's name. "He wants to hire a manager to help out in that fabulous inn of his. Have you seen it?" Not waiting for a reply, she smirked. "Although on your salary, Sandy, I doubt you'd ever be able to afford to dine at Inn on the Bluff."

"That's okay, Constance. I'd take a bag of White Castles any day," Sandy retorted.

Constance ignored Sandy's remark. "You know, Sandy, it was Martin who was kind enough to set up this interview for me." She smiled. "Martin said Max already sounded as if he thought I'd be perfect for the job. I met him, you know, while I was at his fabulous pre-opening party. Oh, that's right, Sandy, you weren't there, were you? Too bad. It was such a terrific party. Only the important people were invited." Constance looked extremely pleased with herself. "I understand I'll be working very, very, closely with Max. Well, I'd better hurry and eat. I wouldn't want to be late. Why, just one look is enough to tell you a girl would have to be crazy to keep Max Holt waiting for anything."

She gave Elise and Sandy a dazzling smile and sashayed off.

Temporarily speechless at the woman's audacity, Elise finally spoke. "Sandy, are you going to beat her face to a pulp, or am I?"

☽

"Hello, Constance. It's nice to see you again. Please come in." Max stood and went around his desk, holding out his hand. "Please have a seat." He indicated a chair facing his office desk. "Can I offer you a beverage?"

She sat down and crossed her legs. Giving Max a bright smile, she nodded. "Sure, I'd love a glass of red wine. Thanks."

Max turned to Oliver who stood in the doorway. "Oliver, would you mind getting Constance her wine?"

Oliver let out a snort, turned and without a word walked away.

Max, not certain Oliver would return, cleared his throat, smiled, and addressed Constance. "I assume Martin gave you a description of what this job entails?"

"Yes, he did, and I believe I'd be very happy working here. You can be assured that if you hire me, satisfaction is guaranteed. I sincerely hope we can come to an equitable agreement."

Max nodded. "Well, Constance, so do I."

Oliver came back in and, without a word, handed Constance her wine, gave Max a look that said, 'you've got to be kidding,' and left.

"Max, once again I have to tell you what a fabulous job you've done with this house," Constance said, sipping her wine.

"Thanks, it was a lot of work, but I'm happy with the results."

She leaned forward to place her glass on his desk and gave him a nice view of her cleavage.

Max cleared his throat. "Yes, well, I understand you've been working at a restaurant in Ann Arbor. What exactly were your duties?"

Constance sat back in her seat and crossed her legs. "Besides being the head hostess, I took the reservations, and oversaw the dining room, which included scheduling the workers. On occasion, I ordered supplies, such as damaged linens or broken crystal and china."

Max nodded. "You duties here would be similar. You'd be in charge of the front desk, housekeeping, and the dining room staff."

"Will my hours be strictly daytime or would I work some nights?"

"Until I see how busy the dining room is going to be, the hours may vary. Will that be a problem?"

She shook her head. "Not really. I may need to run home occasionally and check on my aunt. Martin did tell you I take care of her?"

Max nodded. "That's fine. This is not a strictly nine-to-five job. Your hours can be as flexible as you need."

Again, she gave him a dazzling smile. "Sounds perfect. And, Max, if you ever need me to work late, well, that wouldn't be a problem."

"Great. Then, Constance, welcome to Inn on The Bluff. How about if I show you around? We can begin with the upstairs."

"Oliver, who was that you took into Max's office?" Kathy asked, as she came into the kitchen.

"That, sugar, was a viper in drag."

Oh, the jealousy, the greed is the unraveling.
It's the unraveling and it undoes all the joy that could be.
— Joni Mitchell

Chapter 16

Elise had a light afternoon at the office, so she arrived at the inn earlier than she'd planned. Now that everything was out in the open, she could hardly contain her excitement. When she rang the bell, it was Kathy who answered.

"Hi, Elise, come in."

"Hi, I got off work a little early and thought I'd come on over. I hope that's okay?"

"Sure. Come on back to the kitchen. I'm helping Oliver with dinner prep. Jack's still closeted in the library looking for information on silver mining."

"Really? Why?"

"Max told us the story of your family history and the missing silver. I have to tell you, hunting for the missing treasure is going to be so exciting."

Elise smiled. "I think so, too. But Max insists we need to be practical and realize that the chance of it still being here is probably pretty remote."

"Oh, poo. Max and Jack can be too practical. Let's not be like them. Let's be positive."

Elise's smile widened. "Okay, it's a deal."

"Jack thought a good place for us to begin would be by finding out what would have happened with the silver after it was mined. So, he's doing what he loves to do." She grinned. "Research. Honestly, the man should have been a historian instead of an architect."

The sound of laughter floated down from upstairs. Elise paused in the entry hall and gave Kathy a questioning look.

She scrunched up her nose and whispered, "Max's new manager."

Elise, feeling as if someone had just doused her with cold water, watched as Max and a very satisfied looking Constance came down the stairs.

"Well, Max, the bedrooms are all just as sumptuous as I remembered,"

Constance gushed. "I can imagine lying in one of those beds and never wanting to get out."

Max chuckled. "That's the idea. Keep the guests comfortable and satisfied."

"Oh, I'm sure anyone staying in one of your beds couldn't be anything but satisfied."

Elise couldn't move. Her entire body went rigid. When they reached the bottom step, Max glanced her way.

"Elise, hi. I didn't know you were here."

"Obviously."

His smile faltered and he hesitated. "Let me introduce you. This is Constance Poole. She's going to be my new inn manager. Constance, this is Kathy Callaghan and Elise Baxter."

Constance narrowed her eyes in recognition. Recovering quickly, she pasted a false smile on her face.

"Why, I met Elise earlier with Sandy Fitzpatrick. It's nice to see you again. And it's nice to meet you, Kathy."

Kathy gave her a quick nod of acknowledgement.

Elise didn't even bother to speak. When Max gave her a reproachful look, she gritted her teeth.

Is the man so stupid he can't tell the woman is nothing but a slut who's after him?

Max shrugged, took Constance by the arm, and guided her toward the front door.

"I'll see you the day after tomorrow. Ten o'clock would work well for me."

"That will be perfect. I'll let my boss at the restaurant know I'll be leaving. He's aware I've been trying to find a job closer to home, so he's having me train someone for my position. Again, Max, I know you won't be disappointed in my performance."

Elise fumed as she followed Kathy down the hall. At the door to the kitchen, she turned in time to see Constance give her a satisfied smirk.

"Oh, no. Don't tell me he's gone and hired Miss Thang," Oliver exclaimed as Elise and Kathy stormed through the door.

Kathy made a sour face. "It's true, all right."

She picked up a knife and began to chop vegetables.

Elise paced back and forth in front of the counter. "How could he have hired that woman? Can't he see what she is?"

"Elise, he's a man. They can't see past tits and ass."

"You'd better give me that knife, sugar," Oliver said. "You're supposed to be slicing those carrots, not hacking them to death."

Hearing approaching footsteps, the three turned their attention toward the kitchen door as Max strolled in.

He stopped at the sight of three pairs of disapproving eyes. "Would someone like to tell me why you're all glaring at me as if I've been outside torturing puppies?"

As no one spoke, he looked directly at Elise. "What's wrong? What did I do?"

"Did you actually hire that woman?"

"If you're referring to Constance, the answer is yes. Why? Is that a problem?"

"Yes, it's a problem, because she's mean and spiteful and will do nothing but cause trouble."

"Now, wait a minute. How in the hell can you say that? As far as I know, you just met her."

Elise snorted. "When it comes to women like that, all it takes is five minutes in their company to see what they are."

"And just what exactly is she?" Max demanded.

"A trouble-making little tramp whose goal is to land herself in your bed, and if you can't see that, Max, perhaps you should listen to someone besides me."

"You know what, Elise? I'm perfectly capable of hiring my own employees. In fact, it isn't anyone else's business who I hire."

She headed for the door. "You're absolutely right, Max. If you want a scheming little bitch working for you and sleeping in your bed, go right ahead."

"Where the hell are you going?"

"Home."

"No, you're not. We're not done with this." Reaching the front door a step ahead of her, Max blocked her exit.

"Max, get out of my way."

"I'm not moving until you tell me what this is all about."

"I don't want to discuss this. I want to go home."

"Well, that's too damn bad. I'm not going to spend the rest of the night wondering what the hell I did and why you're so pissed off. And why you think I'm going to have Constance in my bed. So we're going to finish this."

"I'm not going to stand here in this entry hall and have this conversation with you. Do you understand me?"

"Fine, we'll go into the library and have this conversation."

"Max, put me down," Elise cried as he unceremoniously tossed her over his shoulder.

As they reached the library door, it was opened by a startled Jack. "What's going on?"

"Elise and I are having a slight disagreement. Are you through in here?"

"Well, yes. I found some information on silver mining that would be of help. I was just coming to tell you."

"Great, we'll be there as soon as we work this out." Max shut the library door and turned the key.

Elise pummeled his back. "Max, if you don't put me down this minute I'm going to scream."

He set her on her feet. "Then scream. It sure as hell won't be the first time."

She spoke through gritted teeth. "I don't appreciate being manhandled like that. Don't ever do it again."

"Well I don't appreciate having someone pissed off at me when I've done nothing to deserve it. Suppose you tell me why you're so mad."

Her next words caught in her throat. "You and that woman seemed awfully pleased with yourselves when you came down the stairs. What had you two been doing up there?"

"What the hell are you talking about?"

When tears began to fill her eyes, realization dawned.

"Elise, she's going to be working for me. I was just showing her around. Come here, sweetheart, please don't do that." Cradling her face between his hands, he began kissing away her tears. "Sweetheart, I can't get my fill of you. You're all I think about. What would make you think I'd be interested in anyone else? Besides, she's not my type. Can't you tell I prefer redheads?"

The entire time he was talking, he'd been walking her backward until she came up against the library's large desk. Before she realized his intention, he had her sitting on the edge of the desk, positioning himself between her legs.

"I've been fantasizing about doing this all day, and now I've got you right where I want you."

He grinned wickedly seconds before his mouth claimed hers.

As she battled the emotional roller coaster Max seemed to keep her on, the meaning behind his words didn't penetrate her muddled brain until she felt her panties slip down her legs.

"God, Elise, I love these little dresses you wear. They make getting to you so nice and easy." He nibbled on her earlobe.

"Max, stop that. We can't. Not here on the desk."

He chuckled low. "Oh, yes we can. Just sit there and let me show you what I can do."

"Would one of you like to tell me what's going on?" Jack asked as he entered the kitchen. "I just had the library door slammed in my face by Max, who, by the way, had a kicking and screaming Elise thrown over his shoulder."

"It's all because of the inn's new resident black widow," Oliver replied.

"What?" Jack glanced over at Kathy for clarification.

She sighed. "It's Max and his new inn manager, a woman named Constance Poole, who none of us like, especially Elise. And I can't say I blame her in the least."

Jack smiled. "Okay, I'll bite. What could Constance have done in such a short amount of time to have all of you disliking her so much?"

"Jack, if you could have seen the way that woman was gushing all over Max. It was pretty obvious what she's all about and it isn't good. Poor Elise looked as if someone had just ripped her heart out."

"That was until Maxwell pissed her off," Oliver said. "Elise told him exactly how she felt about his choice in managers then stormed out."

"Well, he caught her," Jack said, "because both of them are now locked in the library."

Oliver grinned. "I wonder if they're killing each other or making up?"

"Hopefully, they're making up," Kathy said. "I'd hate to see that woman come between them."

"The chicken cordon bleu is almost ready. What should we do?" Oliver asked, with uncharacteristic annoyance. "I have to say, sometimes Maxwell's tirades are a bit much."

"What smells so good?" Max asked, striding into the kitchen. "I'm starving, Oliver. Is it ready to eat?"

"It looks as if they made up," Jack murmured, seeing the satiated expression on Max's face.

"Oliver narrowed his eyes and peered past Max's shoulder. "Yes, Maxwell, dinner is ready. What have you done with Elise?"

"Max," Jack cautioned as a mischievous grin creased Max's face.

"Oh, Elise is just fine. She's in the powder room. She'll be right along. So, Oliver, let's eat."

After dinner, they all eagerly settled down in the library with coffee to hear what Jack had discovered in researching silver mining. Elise cuddled up next to Max on the sofa.

"Okay, here's what I found out, but I want to warn you ahead of time, it isn't much. We're going to have to take what little I know and surmise the rest," Jack began. "I felt there were three key questions we needed to answer. First: What happened to the silver after it was brought out of the mine? In 1879, there were already smelters in Leadville, so the miners could have taken the silver ore there, where I suppose an assayer would have paid them for it.

"This leads to our second question: What type of currency would they have been paid in? During that time, Leadville was growing into a prosperous town. With the considerable amount of silver coming out of the mines, the probability of there being a local bank is high. So a miner could have either been paid with cash or maybe a bank draft, which he then would have deposited in the bank.

"So the final question: When Clayton Hamilton-slash-Cyrus Mosby left Leadville, what was he carrying? Did he have a trunk full of cash? Did he go into the bank and have them issue him a bank draft? Which brings up another question maybe Elise can answer: Whose names were on the deed, and do you know if each man had his own bank account?"

"I do know Eli Wilkey sent his copy of the deed back east," Elise replied. "In one of Grace's earlier diaries, she talks about how her mother would occasionally open a metal box she kept hidden and cry over a piece of paper. Later, when Hank decided to go looking for Clayton, her mother was reluctant to give Hank the deed, though in the end she did. As to where the deed is now, I haven't any idea. Do you think it could be of importance?"

"In the unlikelihood we do find this money, considering what the total amount could be, being able to prove your family has or *had* ownership might be necessary."

"Necessary for whom, Jack?" Max asked. "If we find the money, it belongs to Elise."

Jack smiled. "Oh, I was thinking of, say, someone like the IRS. According to my research, the mines in Leadville were producing extraordinary amounts of silver. If the money still exists, we could be talking about millions of dollars."

Max watched the color drain from Elise's face. "Oh, my God. Jack, are you serious?"

He shrugged. "Well, it's a possibility. I feel the answer to that depends on my earlier question: What form of money, and how much, did Clayton leave Leadville with? Was it cash or a bank draft?"

"What would be the difference?" Kathy asked.

"Well, either he left with a trunk full of cash or a single bank draft. If it was me, and I needed to leave in a hurry, I'd want the draft. But here's where I ran into trouble in my research. I'm having difficulty finding out if, in 1879, a bank in Leadville would be issuing drafts. If they were, would Clayton have been able to cash it, oh, let's say, in Denver? Were this the case, he could have easily slipped out of Leadville with the draft, cashed it in Denver, changed his name and disappeared. No one would have thought anything of a man boarding a train in Denver with a number of trunks, whereas in Leadville it would have been pretty conspicuous."

"I can be of some help with the question of bank accounts," Elise said. "I know Hank was told the account for the mine was closed out by all three men."

Max looked thoughtful. "I guess the next question is: Were they each issued individual drafts or just one draft which they were planning on dividing among the three of them?"

Jack nodded. "That's an excellent question. We have to remember, Leadville is up in the Rocky Mountains. Even though there was train service, there were also bandits, including Jesse James and the Ford brothers. I doubt Eli Wilkey and the Hamilton's would have taken a chance leaving Leadville carrying trunks full of money. Let's say the bank issued the three men a bank draft in the mine's name, in which all three were equal partners. Their plan must have been to leave Leadville by train, cash the draft in Denver, divide the money and go their separate ways."

"But we know that's not what happened," Elise said. "Clayton Hamilton got on a train alone."

"Yes, but it could explain how he was able to steal all the money," Max suggested. "If they'd each been issued individual drafts he wouldn't have been able to cash them."

"But how do we know a bank in Denver would have given just Clayton the money when the draft was made out in the company's name?" Kathy asked.

"An excellent point. But as I said, this is all speculation," Jack reminded them. "We don't know how particular banks back then would have worked."

"So we're right back where we started," Oliver stated.

"I agree," Kathy said. "What conclusion can we draw from all of this?"

Jack paged through his notes.

"Let's see. We know for certain that silver mines in Leadville during that time were flourishing. Therefore the story of the three men striking it big is most likely true. We know they all withdrew their savings from the bank at the same time. And we know Clayton Hamilton left Leadville by train alone, either with a trunk full of cash or a bank draft. So I'd say, one way or another, he managed to disappear with a hell of a lot of money which could be hidden right here under our noses." Jack finished with a grin.

"People, you're making this all more complicated than it need be," Oliver said.

"How's that?" Elise asked.

"Does anyone know what the highest denomination of currency would have been back then? I mean, why fool around with bank drafts if it wasn't necessary? If the bank could have given them their money in, say, thousand-dollar bills, well, you could cram a shit load of those in a normal-sized trunk."

"Or a leather satchel," Kathy said, excitedly. "That's true,"

Max said. "Jack, what do you think?"

"Oliver may be on to something. Since you can't get them any longer, I wasn't considering bills in large denominations. That gives me something to look into tomorrow."

"So the bottom line is we need to start searching in places where a large, but not too large, amount of bills could be hidden?" Kathy asked.

"I suppose," Max replied. "In this house, that's still a tall order."

"I would also assume it would have to be somewhere that could have remained dry and sealed for all these years," Jack added.

Oliver grimaced. "Well then, as much as I'm not looking forward to rummaging around in hidey-holes, I guess we'd better get our tushes in gear. The inn will officially be opening for business soon. I can't imagine Maxwell will want us excusing ourselves to the guests while we crawl around under their beds. You know, Maxwell, I don't understand why your ghost friend doesn't make this easier for us by just making one of those crescents appear showing us where the money is."

"What the hell?" Jack yelled.

O accursed hunger of gold, to what dost thou not compel human hearts?
— Virgil

Chapter 17

A book flew from the bookcase, spun in the air, and ping-ponged back and forth over their heads.

"Oliver, look out!" Elise cried.

"Shit, are you all right?" Max asked, leaning over a prone Oliver.

"What the hell happened?" Oliver asked, his voice muffled by the Oriental carpet.

"You were hit on the head by a book," Elise gasped with astonishment.

"Poe, to be exact." Jack picked up the leather bound book from the rug.

Kathy stared wide-eyed. "Did everyone see what just happened? That book came flying off the bookcase, flew around the room, then headed right toward Oliver."

Jack put his arm around his wife. "It's all right. He's fine."

"Maxwell."

"I know, Oliver. You quit. Here, let me help you up."

"Fucking-A, I quit." Sitting up, Oliver glared at Max.

Elise's eyes were huge in her pale face. "Oliver, I'm so s-sorry."

"You didn't do anything, sugar. It's Maxwell who has us all living in the House of a Hundred Horrors."

"But I started all of it with this treasure business. I don't want anyone to get hurt."

Oliver smiled. "It would take more than some crazy old ghost to take me down. Trust me, I've been attacked by worse."

"I don't think Cyrus was trying to hurt Oliver," Max said. He turned the book so everyone could read the title, *The Gold Bug and Other Tales and Poems*. "Perhaps he was trying to tell us something."

"I think he was just being an ass," Oliver said, hands on hips. "I don't know about the rest of you, but I've had enough of 'Ghosty' for one evening. I'm making myself a double and going to bed."

"I'm right behind you," Kathy said. "Jack, fix us each a large brandy before you come up, then lock the bedroom door after you. Elise, I'll see you tomorrow. Perhaps we can go through more stuff in the attic."

"Sure, Kathy, that would be great."

"Well, Max, old buddy, you might have to consider raising your rates to include the additional entertainment," Jack said. Brandy decanter in hand, he left the room.

Sitting back down on the sofa, Max took Elise into his arms. "Are you okay? You still look shaken."

"Max, that was the scariest thing I've ever seen."

"It was pretty wild, that's for sure."

"That book hit Oliver in the head. It could have really hurt him."

"I doubt it was meant to hurt anyone. Cyrus had probably been listening to our conversation, and that was his only way of communicating with us."

"What?" She glanced nervously around. "Do you think he's in this room?"

"Could be. Why?"

"Because I don't actually like the idea of being in the room with a ghost." Her eyes opened wide. "Could he have been in here earlier?"

"Again, I don't know." When he realized what she was thinking, he laughed.

"What's wrong? Are you afraid he may have seen what I was doing to you on the desk? I have a feeling that desk belonged to him. Maybe he was envious, knowing he isn't able to do that anymore." He kissed her lips. "I love the way you blush when I talk about sex. After everything we've done, you should be used to it. We could lie here on the sofa and see if we can get Cyrus riled up again."

"Max, stop. I have to go home."

As he lay her down, the French window next to the fireplace blew open, admitting a swirling black mass.

Elise screamed.

Max wrapped his arms around her and rolled to the floor until he covered her with his body.

"Max!" Again Elise screamed as books were hurled from their shelves, glasses and decanters toppled from a table, and lamps crashed to the floor.

"Leave this house," a guttural voice demanded.

Elise buried her face in Max's chest and sobbed.

Not sure if he was more pissed than scared, Max held her tight. "I'm here, baby, I'm here."

A barrage of silver flashes filled the room, followed by a long unearthly wail, then silence. After a few minutes, Max took a deep breath and lifted his head, glanced around, and frowned.

"Max, I don't want to open my eyes. How bad is it?"

He sat up. "It's okay, look."

Elise peeked from under her lashes, then opened her eyes in surprise. "Nothing's out of place."

"I know."

"Max, we didn't just imagine what happened."

"No, we didn't."

Elise shivered. "Whatever it was wants us to leave. Do you think it was Cyrus?"

Max shook his head. "It was different from anything Cyrus has done. So far, he hasn't been violent, and that sure as hell wasn't friendly."

Elise got to her feet and shakily walked to the couch. "Do you realize what you're saying?"

Max sat next to her and ran his fingers through his hair. "What, that there's another spirit here besides Cyrus? Elise, I honestly don't know what to believe." He frowned. "I wonder . . ."

"Wonder what?"

"If whatever it was is trying to scare us off, then that proves it's not Cyrus. He's been dropping clues all over the place."

"Max, I'm really scared. This is getting out of control." She placed her hand on his arm. "Perhaps we should stop this right now."

"Stop what?"

"Digging into Cyrus's past and looking for the silver. None of this craziness happened before I showed up, did it?"

He started to shake his head, then remembered the strange feelings he'd had when he first entered the house. "Actually, there were a few things the day I found the house." He told her about the portrait's eyes that seemed to move and the cold draft that came from nowhere. "So, you see, none of this is your fault. Besides, I'm too curious and in too deep to stop now."

Elise sighed. "If we're right and there is something evil here, I'm not sure that I want to provoke it."

"We don't know that there's another spirit here. Maybe it was Cyrus, but either way we weren't actually harmed—scared shitless—but not hurt. So I say we continue, but this is your family's treasure so the final decision is yours."

She bit her lower lip. "It's not just us we're talking about. There're the others to consider. Max, I couldn't live with myself if they were injured."

"We can tell them what happened and see what they say, but I have no doubt they'll want to go on. Actually, if they knew about this, it might make them even more determined."

"They're not easy to scare off, are they?"

Max smiled. "No."

Elise's mouth formed a thin line. "Then I say let's keep going."

Max kissed her. "Good."

))

After walking Elise to her car, Max went back to the library, sat in a soft old leather wingback chair, and thumbed through *The Gold Bug*. He glanced at the mantel clock and frowned at the amount of time that had passed since she had left. As his gaze shifted to the portrait above the clock, an icy fear clenched his gut. The woman's unusual, blue-green eyes seemed to be pleading with him. Suddenly, he knew that Elise was in trouble.

Dropping the book, he reached for the phone, but before he could pick it up, it rang.

"Hello?"

"Max." Elise's voice shook.

"Elise, what's wrong? Are you all right?"

"No. Yes. Well, I am now. But, Max, there was someone in my apartment when I got home, and he knocked me down."

Max's heart was pounding so hard he could hardly breathe. "Elise, where are you now?"

"I'm downstairs at Albert's. He heard me scream and came to help."

"I'm on my way." Max slammed down the phone and ran.

))

Eyes flashing, Virginia floated down from her portrait and stood next to Cyrus in front of the fireplace.

"It's begun."

Cyrus nodded.

Virginia began to pace, her shimmering dress swirling around her feet. "I will not let this happen. Garrison, appear to me at once," she demanded.

Cyrus shook his head. "He won't come. He's done his damage."

"At least Max and Elise aren't easily frightened. For a minute, I was afraid all was lost."

Cyrus smiled. "I was pretty sure the boy wouldn't be scared away. Plus he was smart enough to realize it wasn't me."

"My concern is with Elise. We cannot protect her if she isn't here."

"I know."

Virginia balled her hands into fists. "If we could only leave the house and grounds."

Cyrus sighed. "Well, my love, we can't. Not until this is resolved."

"Then Max must get her under this roof because I'm more convinced than ever that there's an outside force in league with Garrison. This time Elise was lucky. The next, she may not be."

Cyrus rubbed his chin in thought. "She's not going to readily agree."

Virginia shook her head. "No, she will not. It will be up to Max to convince her she'd be safer here."

"Yes, but what about Garrison?"

"We managed to put a halt to his tirade tonight. We can do it again."

"We can only hope Max's thoughts regarding Elise's safety move in the same direction as ours."

Virginia smiled. "I have a feeling that's one thing we don't have to worry about." She looked down to where Max had dropped *The Gold Bug.* "Cyrus, you have to stop frightening the Chandler boy."

Cyrus stiffened. "I only wanted to land the book at his feet. It wasn't I who aimed it at his head. If you recall, Virginia, I tried to deflect the book."

She glided over and kissed his cheek. "Yes, I know, but you do have a fondness for pulling pranks."

Cyrus grinned. "Clues, my dear, they're clues. Such as showing them the hidden compartment in the bed."

"That was very clever of you." She frowned. "Then Garrison had to play his nasty joke."

He sighed. "I'm afraid, my dear, our troubles have only just begun."

"Elise, drink this." Albert handed Elise a steaming mug. "Is Max on his way?"

"Yes, he's coming. What is this?"

"Just some hot tea with honey and a little rum. It will help calm you down."

"Thanks, Albert. I really appreciate you helping me."

"Not a problem. I'm just glad I was home. Are you going to call the police?"

"I'll wait until Max gets here and can go through the apartment with me so I can see if anything is missing."

The sound of screeching tires filled the room. "He's here."

Albert held the door open as Max barreled past.

Gathering Elise in his arms, he held her tight. "Are you sure you're not hurt?"

"I'm okay, just a little shaken. Max, I'd like you to meet my neighbor, Albert. He was kind enough to come to my rescue."

For the first time, Max took notice of the tall man standing by the door. "Hi, it's nice to meet you." With one arm still around Elise, he shook Albert's hand. "I can't thank you enough for helping her."

"I wish I could have done more, but I was working at my desk." He gestured toward the back of the apartment. "I use the smaller bedroom as an office. Anyway, I heard a loud thump on the ceiling, then Elise screamed. By the time I got to my door, whoever it was had gone. I ran upstairs to find her lying on her living room floor. I'm sorry, that's all I know."

"I'm just glad you were here," Max said. "Thanks again."

"You know, a break-in around here surprises me," Albert said.

"Why is that?" Max asked.

Albert shrugged. "It's a nice, quiet neighborhood whose residents are mainly older couples. I'll bet Elise and I are the youngest for blocks. It's just not the type of place I would expect something like this. But I guess the times they are a-changing."

Elise nodded. "Albert's right. That's why I chose this apartment. Speaking of which, Max, we'd better go see if anything's missing. If I'm going to call the police, I probably shouldn't wait too long."

Elise gave Albert a hug and kissed his cheek. "Thanks again."

"Sure. Let me know if there's anything I can do."

"Elise, how did they get in?" Max asked, as they reached her landing.

"Through the door, I guess."

"Wasn't it locked?"

"I think so."

"What do you mean, 'I think so'? Don't you check after you close the door?"

"Not necessarily."

Max shook his head before examining the lock. "It doesn't look as if it's been fooled with. So, due to the fact you live on the third floor and there isn't any other way in, I'd say they either skillfully picked the lock or you didn't lock it."

She narrowed her eyes in irritation and brushed past him into the apartment. "At this point, Max, what does it matter?"

"So where were you standing when you first saw him?"

"I didn't see him clearly. I was here at the kitchen counter taking papers from my bag when I caught a movement from the corner of my eye. The next thing I knew, I was on the floor."

"That brings up my next question. Don't you leave any lights on when you go out?"

"Yes." She pointed to the low wattage light above the stove.

"Oh, that's a lot of help. No wonder you couldn't see anything."

"You seem to be forgetting I wasn't expecting company. If I had been, I would have left every light in the place on."

Impatiently, he hit the kitchen light switch. "That's better. At least now, we can see. Okay, can you recall anything at all about this guy? Was he tall, short, heavy, thin?"

"I'm not even sure it was a man. It all happened so fast. They knocked me down and ran out the door."

"Did you lock the door behind you when you came in?"

"I shut it. I normally go back and lock it after I put down whatever I'm carrying. And before you start in on me again, as Albert told you, this is a neighborhood where I felt safe."

"Well, it looks like you're going to have to start being a little more alert to your surroundings." The thought of someone hurting her still had his stomach in knots. Running his hands through his hair, he sighed. "Okay, I guess we'd better see if anything is missing. If he came at you from the side, he was coming from your bedroom. Let's start in there."

"Max, Grace's diaries!" She ran to where the contents of the nightstand drawer had been dumped out on her bed.

"Is that it?" He pointed.

She hurried to where the corner of a book was just visible. "There're only two. Where's the third? And where's Hank's telegram?" Frantically, she searched through the pile of notepads, pens, tissues, an aspirin bottle, Chap Stick, a romance novel, letters, and a chocolate bar. "Max, they're gone."

"Are you sure the diary and the telegram were in the drawer?"

She nodded. "It was the one you read and threw on my bed when you were yelling at me. I remember putting them in the drawer when I changed the sheets." Tears began to flow down her cheeks. "Max, why would anyone want that diary?"

When he recalled the harsh words he'd said to her the morning he'd discovered the diaries, he took her into his arms. "Before you get yourself all upset, let's look around. It might still be here."

A short time later, heartsick at the loss, Elise dropped onto the sofa. "We've looked everywhere, and it just isn't here. Nothing else is missing. Why would someone break in and steal that diary?"

Max sat down next to her and put his arm around her shoulder. "I don't know. It doesn't make any sense. It would mean nothing to anyone except us."

"That diary has been in my family for over a hundred years. I feel like someone's just stolen a part of me." Crying softly, she buried her face in his chest.

"I know." He held her close and tried to comfort her.

Wanting to beat the shit out of whoever did this to her, he looked toward the front door. An indistinct object lying on the floor in a dark corner between the wall and a potted plant caught his attention.

"Elise, I think I see it."

She sat up and wiped the tears from her face. "Where?"

He pointed. "Over there."

Jumping to her feet, she hurried to where he'd indicated. "Max, it is! It's the diary. But I don't see Hank's telegram. Wait a minute, here it is." Relieved, she held them to her chest and beamed.

"Is there any reason you would have put those behind that plant?"

"Of course not. Why would I do that?"

"For them to end up in that spot, they had to be thrown. I'm guessing you interrupted your intruder going through your things. In their hurry to leave, they tossed them in the corner."

She sat back down on the sofa and laid the diary and telegram on the coffee table. "Someone broke in specifically to steal Grace's diaries? But why? No one is aware they exist except you and me, Oliver, Kathy, and Jack. Oh, and I told Sandy. Max, we know none of them broke in here. Besides, in order to have any interest in the diaries and their meaning, you'd have to know the story of the missing silver. No one besides my family and those I just mentioned know."

Max leaned his head back on the sofa and ran his hands through his hair. "Damn, Elise, it's probably all my fault."

"How could that be?"

"Because when I left here the other morning, I hadn't gotten over being pissed. Jack drove me into town to pick up my car. We stopped at the diner where I proceeded to tell him all about Grace, her diaries, Clayton, Cyrus, and the missing silver. The place was packed and anyone could have overheard me."

"But even if you were overheard, there's nothing in them to help someone find the silver."

"We know that, but others wouldn't."

"Max, you're scaring me. A group of friends having fun hunting for buried treasure is one thing; breaking into someone's apartment is downright creepy."

"I'm sorry. Like it or not, there's someone out there who broke in believing either you or those diaries could lead them to a hidden treasure.

And I have a bad feeling we haven't seen the last of whoever it is."

"Should we still call the police?"

Max hesitated. "That's up to you. However, you'd have to tell them about the diaries and the silver. Do you want to go into all that? Besides, a break-in where nothing is stolen won't exactly be high priority."

She sighed. "You're right. It probably wouldn't accomplish anything. And I really don't want anyone else to know about the silver. I'll just have to be more cautious." She glanced around the apartment. "Though I have to admit I'm not crazy about staying here alone."

Max took her into his arms. "I'll be here. Nothing's going to hurt you as long as I'm around."

*It is preoccupation with possessions, more than anything else,
that prevents us from living freely and nobly.*
— Henry David Thoreau

Chapter 18

As the predawn light filtered through the bedroom curtains, Max lay awake replaying all that had occurred in his life since he'd first laid eyes on the woman sleeping peacefully in his arms, her soft, naked body pressed against his. What had begun for him as nothing more than extreme sexual desire had evolved into emotions, which, if examined too closely, would scare the hell out of him.

His sexual attraction to her hadn't diminished in the least. If anything, it was stronger than ever. The more he had her the more he wanted her. The intense raw fear he'd felt when he'd heard she'd been attacked and the desire to always be there to protect her from any kind of hurt were so strong that he tightened his arm around her waist, pulling her closer until her bottom rested against his growing arousal.

"Max?" Her voice was sleepy.

"Hush, sweet, it's okay," he murmured into her ear.

"Well, good morning." Elise wiggled her bottom against him. "I see you're fully awake."

"Oh, I'm awake all right." Reaching his hand around, he began to gently squeeze her breast while kissing the back of her neck.

"Max, you can't want more—"

"Oh, yes I can. Do you want me to stop?"

"No." She moaned.

He chuckled. "I wasn't planning on it. Roll over onto your stomach, sweet."

"What?"

"Trust me." He turned her so she'd lie flat. "I haven't disappointed you yet, have I?"

"No, Max, but—"

"It's all right, sweet, just relax." He brushed her long hair to the side and began kissing the back of her neck. His hand moved languidly down her spine, stopping to caress her firm bottom. "You have the sweetest ass. Did you know that?"

She gasped her pleasure when his hand slipped between her legs, stroking her.

"And the tightest little—"

"Max."

He trailed warm kisses down her spine while his fingers worked their magic between her legs. "Raise up, sweetheart." He slid a pillow beneath her stomach.

"Max."

"Yes, sweet." Sliding one finger into her heat, he stroked faster. "Just let it come."

She dug her fingers into the mattress, crying his name. As wave after wave of release shuddered through her body, he slid his hard shaft deep into her warmth. With every thrust, he sent their passion spinning higher and higher.

He watched her back arch to meet his thrusts and gritted his teeth for control. She tightened around him as her climax took her. He gave way to the unrestrained lust building inside him.

Deep in his throat, he growled. "That's it, sweetheart. Let me feel you come . . . oh, sweet . . . I'm glad you're enjoying this . . . because I'm gonna take us for one hell of a ride."

$$\smile$$

"Max, I'm perfectly capable of walking to work on my own."

Elise had just shut her apartment door and they were on their way down the stairs.

"I know you're perfectly capable of walking to work, but I'm driving you, so get over it. Are you sure you checked the lock?"

"For the tenth time, yes."

"Don't roll your eyes at me like that, Elise." Max unlocked the Mustang. "You were the one who couldn't remember last night if you'd locked your door. Which reminds me, give me your keys. I'm going to come back and replace your lock with a better one."

"What for?"

"Because, if by chance your door was locked last night, obviously the lock you have is useless." Slipping his sunglasses on, he put the top down and popped the Mustang into gear.

"What time will you be getting off?" he asked a few minutes later when he stopped in front of the newspaper building.

"I'm not sure. Why?"

"I'm going to pick you up."

"That isn't necessary. I can go home, get my car, and drive myself to your place."

"No, you can't."

"And just why can't I?"

"Because I have your keys." Grinning, he reached for her and gave her such a passionate good-bye kiss that two women who were walking by stopped to watch.

$$\big)$$

"I see you and Max are getting along fine today," Sandy said with a smile as Elise came through the lobby door.

Elise chuckled. "For the time being, I guess. But with us, you never know from day to day." She fell into step next to her friend. "You're not going to believe what happened last night. But before I say anything, you have to promise to keep it to yourself."

"Sure, no problem."

As they walked up the stairs to their offices, Elise began with the book flying off the shelf and hitting Oliver, described the terrifying experience when the window blew open, and ended with the intruder in her apartment.

"Oh my god," Sandy exclaimed. "How horrible for you. I don't know which must have been worse, some ghost making things fly around the library or an intruder knocking you down."

"The ghost thing was pretty awful, but honestly I was more afraid in my apartment. At least Max was with me in the library."

"This entire ghost business is like something out of a movie. I still can't believe it's real."

Elise shook her head. "Tell me about it. If I hadn't actually witnessed it with my own eyes, I'd have a hard time believing it myself."

"Do you think Max is right and there's more than one ghost? And the nasty one is trying to keep you from finding the silver?"

They'd reached Elise's cubical and she slumped down in her chair. "I don't know. When I began all this, I thought it would be fun, but now . . ." She shook her head. "I'm not sure it's worth it."

Sandy placed a comforting hand on her arm. "I'm actually more concerned with the flesh and blood person who broke into your apartment.

It sounds as if you may have scared them as much as they scared you."

"I suppose so." Elise shuddered, involuntarily reliving the fear she'd felt when she'd realized she hadn't been alone. "Max thinks someone may have overheard him talking to Jack about the missing silver while they were in the diner, then broke into my apartment looking for Grace's diaries, hoping they would lead them to the treasure."

"Considering nothing else was tampered with, I'd have to agree with him. What time did the break-in happen?"

"I'm not sure. It was kind of late. Why?"

"I'm wondering how they knew you weren't at home."

Elise cocked her head. "What do you mean?"

"To know you weren't home, they'd have to know what your car looks like. Also, that backyard and the steps going up to your apartment are well lit. No one would want to spend a lot of time standing there knocking on the door if they were up to no good."

"Are you saying they went to my house knowing I was with Max?"

"Not necessarily knowing you were with Max, but knowing you weren't at home."

"That would mean they were watching either me or Max."

"I know, and I'm not trying to scare you. I just want you to consider all possibilities."

"Maybe I should put a sign on my back saying: 'We don't know where the missing silver is, so leave us alone.' "

"Just please be careful. I don't think that, for the time being, you should stay in your apartment alone."

Elise grimaced. "God, Sandy, don't let Max hear you say that. He'd have me moved in with him quicker than you could blink. Now, wait until you hear about Constance, or as Oliver calls her, The Black Widow."

"I'm not sure about this, Max," Kathy said as they entered Elise's apartment. "Elise may not appreciate you taking it upon yourself to move her in with you."

"It's the only thing that makes sense." Max put down his small toolbox and a new door lock. "You'll know what she'd want to bring, so while I'm changing this lock, you can pack what she'll need. Then you can drive her car back to my place."

"I don't know. I'm not at all comfortable doing this. Maybe we should call her and ask her if it's okay."

"If we call her, she'll say no. Then she and I will get into an argument, which will eventually end with her agreeing to move in. By doing it for her, we'll save time and avoid all of that."

"Max, I love you like a brother, but I have to say I don't know how Elise puts up with your 'me Tarzan, you Jane' attitude."

"Kathy, someone broke in here last night and Elise could have been hurt. Until we solve the issue of the missing money, I don't want to have to worry about her being alone in this apartment. I have a business to run, so it wouldn't be practical for me to move in here. This makes more sense."

"I don't want her to get hurt either, but I'm going to make sure she knows I did this under duress."

"Think about it this way, she'll be right there in the house. You two can snoop around to your hearts' content. Don't forget to pack everything she has in her nightstand," he called. "Especially the diaries. I'm going to put those in the safe in my office."

$$\smile$$

"Hi, Max, I love your car," Sandy said as Max pulled up to the curb.

"Thanks, Sandy. I'm kind of fond of her myself. Is Elise still working?"

"She should be done. She was meeting with Carson Ames at Pasquale's, but that was a couple of hours ago."

"Who's that?"

Sandy made a sour expression. "Some would-be politician. He's running for county commissioner and he's a total idiot. Poor Elise got stuck with the interview.

"Thanks. I'll drive over and see if she's still there."

"Elise told me what happened at her apartment last night. You two, please be careful."

Max grinned. "I took care of that. You don't have to worry about Elise."

Sandy lifted her brows. "What did you do?"

"I've moved her in with me."

She stifled a laugh. "Does she know?"

"Nope."

"Then, I wish you luck. Because, trust me, you're going to need it."

$$\smile$$

Max entered the dimly lit restaurant and spotted Elise seated at a booth. As he made his way to the bar, he saw a distinguished-looking, silver-haired man sitting across from her take her hand. Frowning, Max took a seat and ordered a beer. He watched Elise smile sweetly at something the old asshole said. Downing his beer, Max ordered another and wished he could hear what they were saying.

"Mr. Ames, please let go of my hand," Elise demanded. "I'm flattered by your dinner invitation, but as I told you earlier, I'm seeing someone. Besides, aren't you a little too old for me?" She withdrew her hand and began to gather her things. "I appreciate the interview, but I have to go. My friend will be wondering where I am."

"Does the man in question have light brown hair, and maybe needs a haircut?"

She stared at him in surprise. "Why, yes."

"Could he be wearing a black T-shirt and blue jeans?"

"What?"

"Does he scowl a lot?"

"Mr. Ames, what is this all about?"

"A gentleman fitting that description is sitting at the bar to your right, and he doesn't look pleased."

Elise turned to see Max scowling at her.

Carson Ames stood. "It must be time for me to leave. It's been extremely nice meeting you, Miss Baxter. I thoroughly enjoyed our talk. Please remember me in November." He took her hand one last time, whispering, "If you change your mind, call me. Trust me, I'm not too old."

Shaking her head at the man's audacity, Elise reached for her purse.

"Having fun?"

She glanced up to see a steely eyed Max slide into the seat across from her.

"Max, hi. Sorry to keep you waiting, I got held up interviewing Carson Ames."

"So I saw." He gave her a brittle smile. "You two seemed real cozy. You must give one hell of an interview. You had that poor sucker looking at you as if he could eat you for dinner."

"You can be a real ass. You know that?" She headed for the door with Max right on her heels.

"My car is over here."

"Good for your car."

"Elise, you can't walk home."

"Watch me."

"You don't have any keys."

"Albert has a spare."

"It won't work."

"Why not?"

"Because I changed your lock today."

She stopped, turned, and glared. "Give me the key."

"I don't have it with me."

"Then I'll go home, get my car, and drive to your house where you'll give me the key to my apartment."

"No, you won't. Your car isn't there."

"What? Where's my car?"

"Elise, just come with me and I'll explain."

"I don't want to come with you."

"What are we going to do, stand here on the sidewalk all night?"

"You can for all I care. I'm going home. I'll have Albert break my door in."

"I moved some of your clothes to my house," he called to her retreating back.

She turned and stomped back until she was inches from him, punching her finger into his chest, enunciating each word. "What . . . did . . . you . . . just . . . say?"

"People are beginning to stare. Let's get into my car and I'll explain."

"Fine." She walked to where the Mustang was parked, slid onto the seat and slammed the door, satisfied when she saw him wince. "All right, Max, I'm in the damn car. Explain."

"Sweetheart, will you please calm down?"

She narrowed her eyes. "Don't you 'sweetheart' me, you . . . you overbearing, bossy, pushy, arrogant, pompous ass. Ahhh!" She pounded her fists on her knees. "You're making me crazy."

He glanced at her, shook his head, started the car, and pulled away from the curb.

"Elise, I'm sorry. I saw you sitting there with that guy holding your hand and I overreacted." Silence filled the car. "What was he doing, anyway?" More silence.

Max pulled into the inn's circle drive and shut off the engine.

"We're not going to work this out if you don't talk to me."

She turned to him and glowered. "I don't recall saying I wanted to work this out with you."

"Well, at least you're talking to me. That's a start."

She took a deep breath. "Why did you move my clothes?"

"Until this business of the missing money is solved, I thought it would make more sense for you to stay with me. I took Kathy along when I went to change your lock and asked her to pack a few of your things."

"You took it upon yourself to move me into your house without asking me?"

Max sighed. "Elise, this isn't a joke. Someone broke into your apartment. You're not safe staying there alone, and I can't stay there with you. We have no idea if last night they got scared off and won't try again, but what if they come back thinking you know something about the silver and come after you? I thought it would be safer and quicker if I got your things while I was there."

"And it never entered your mind to talk to me about this first, before you decided to take charge of my life?"

"Damn it to hell. I'm not trying to take charge of your life. I happen to care deeply for you, and I'm just trying to keep you safe."

Silence again filled the car as his words settled over both of them, Elise staring at him with wide-eyed surprise.

"What are you two doing at that window?" Jack asked as he entered the front parlor. "And why don't you have any lights on?"

"Don't touch that switch," Kathy whispered. "We're watching Max and Elise."

"What?"

"They're sitting out front in his car," Oliver replied in a stage whisper.

Jack shook his head. "For heaven's sake, come away from there."

"Damn," Kathy swore. "Max just put the top up."

"It looked like Maxwell was yelling again." Oliver moved away from the window. "Honestly, I'm beginning to wonder if he needs some kind of pill or something."

"Why are you two spying on them?" Jack asked.

"Sugar's worried Elise is going to be furious with her for helping Maxwell relocate her things without her permission," Oliver stated. "She wanted to get a heads-up on her mood before she comes in."

"Uh-oh, here they come and neither one looks happy." Kathy hurried from the window. "Come on. We'll wait in the library."

"It smells good in here. I wonder what Oliver is cooking for dinner?" Max said, trying to lighten the mood as they entered the house. Getting no response, he tried again. "I imagine everyone's in the library. Should we join them? I could use a drink. How about you?"

"I'm going to the powder room, then to your office. We're not through with this. You can get us both a drink and join me there."

"Yes, Ma'am," he mouthed to her retreating back.

Oliver poked his head from around the library door. "Is it safe to come out? I heard a bang, and I need to check on the pork tenderloin." He peered up and down the hall. "I thought Cyrus was out here doing his ghostly bullshit."

Max glowered in the direction of the powder room. "For the moment, you're safe. It wasn't Cyrus. It seems Elise has a passion for slamming doors."

Kathy poked her head out under Oliver's. "Does she know about my part in all of this?"

Max shook his head. "I told her I did it all." Kathy and Oliver moved aside to let him pass. "I've been summoned to my office, and I was told to bring drinks."

"How pissed is she?" Jack asked.

"On a scale from one to ten, I'd give it about a nine."

"That bad? Buddy, I'm glad I'm not in your shoes."

Kathy put her hands on her hips. "I told Max that Elise wouldn't like him moving her in here without talking to her about it first, and I was right."

Max grimaced. "I thought once I had her things here, she'd be more agreeable to the move than if I were to discuss it with her first."

"Well, I guess you were wrong, weren't you?"

Yet it isn't the gold that I'm wanting, so much as just finding the gold.
— Robert W. Service

Chapter 19

"Elise, sugar, hello. You'll have to excuse me," Oliver said in a rush as he scooted past Elise who was standing in the library doorway. "I have to check my pork."

"Hi, Elise. I have to help Oliver," Kathy called as she hurried past.

Following the other two, Jack bent down and whispered in her ear. "Max can be a real shit sometimes, but he means well."

"Elise, come on in and close the door," Max said. "We've managed to clear everyone out."

"I prefer the door open." She took a seat in a high-backed chair. "I'll have a glass of red wine."

"Sure thing." Max gave her a sidelong glance and headed for the small liquor cabinet. "I believe I'll have a martini."

"Thanks." She took the glass he offered and took a sip.

While she watched him make his drink, his words *I happen to care deeply for you* still played through her mind. Judging by the expression on his face, she didn't think he'd meant to say them aloud. She took another sip of her wine. Was she reading more meaning into them than she should? Was she fooling herself into believing Max's interest in her went further than sexual desire? She frowned. And what about her own feelings? Did she want more from this relationship than a means to find the silver? She couldn't deny her own sexual attraction toward Max, but did her feelings go deeper? When he wasn't being a jerk, she had to admit she enjoyed his company. Now he wanted her to move in with him. Things were complicated enough. Staying here would only make matters worse.

"Elise, are you just going to sit there staring at me?"

Startled out of her musings, she jumped.

He grinned. "Sorry."

A spark of anger shot through her. There he sat, acting all nonchalant with a martini glass in hand, his ankle resting upon his knee, and smiling at her as if they'd just sat down to have a friendly chat. Her fingers tightened around her wine glass.

"Max, are you always used to having your own way?"

He straightened and smacked his now empty glass down.

"No, Elise, I don't always get my own way. Nor do I expect to. What I do expect is for intelligent people to respond to potential danger reasonably, not to act as though I've intentionally gone out of my way to mess with their lives." His volume rose with every word.

"I understand what you're saying, and if I were being honest, the thought of being alone in my apartment gives me the creeps. So staying here would probably make sense, but what I find unacceptable is the way you just took it upon yourself to move me in here without asking. Damn it, Max, who made you my keeper?"

As soon as the words left her lips, she wished she could bring them back, for now there was hurt mingled with the anger in his stormy eyes.

She sighed. "I know you thought you were doing what was best, but I've always been pretty independent. I'm not used to someone else making my decisions. My mother wanted me to stay at home and attend a local college, and I didn't. My father insisted I stay in Standish and go to work for the family paper, but here I am. Now do you understand why I was upset?"

A myriad of emotions flickered in his eyes before he said, "Maybe you're right. I guess I was being a little high-handed—"

She rolled her eyes. "A little high-handed? Yeah, I'd say so."

He frowned. "But you didn't let me finish."

"Okay, I'm listening."

Max leaned forward and folded his arms on his knees. "I admit I should have talked to you first before moving your things, but I was afraid you'd say no, and we'd end up arguing about it."

"Which we did anyway."

He nodded, then grinned. "Yes, but your things are already here."

Her mouth formed a thin line. "Max, I don't like being manipulated like that."

Max sighed. "Last night you told me that the thought of staying alone in the apartment scared you. So I took you seriously." He spread his hands. "Elise, I'm sorry. I honestly only wanted to keep you safe."

Her anger spent, Elise rubbed her temples. "All right, Max. I can see your point, but don't ever do anything like that again."

"Can we kiss and make up?"

She couldn't help but laugh. "Oh, what am I going to do with you?"

His grin widened. "Come over here and I'll show you."

)

"Phew, I'm glad that's over," Kathy said, hurrying back into the kitchen. "They're sitting on the sofa, and Elise is laughing."

"I didn't know I married a Peeping Thomasina," Jack said, sitting at the kitchen island drinking his beer.

"I'm not," she said indignantly. "It isn't my fault they left the door open and anyone could hear. Besides, I had a part in why Elise is upset. I just wanted to make sure she'd calmed down."

Jack grinned. "Sure, love, whatever you say."

"I'm beginning to think it isn't just an inn that Maxwell's opened," said Oliver. "It's more like *Desperate Inn-Keepers*."

)

"Max, stop that. The door is open."

"And whose fault is that? I told you to close it." He eased her down on the couch.

"Stop it. Let me up."

He kissed his way down her neck. "You know, Elise, I love arguing with you."

"Why is that?"

He chuckled. "Because we have so much fun making up. You know, we could continue this upstairs."

"What about dinner?"

"They can eat without us."

"But I'm hungry."

"I'll take your mind off food."

"Well, I suppose we—Max!"

"Christ, what's the matter with you? You just screamed in my ear."

She shoved against his chest. "Max, there's someone outside the window behind you."

He rose from his position on top of her and turned. "I don't see anything."

"I'm telling you, someone was standing right out there." She sat up and pointed at one of the long French windows flanking the fireplace.

Max crossed the room, pushed open the window, and stepped out. "There's nobody here."

She went over to stand beside him. "I know what I saw."

"Well, there's no one there now." He stepped back in and closed the window. "You know what? I'll bet it was Martin Todd."

She gave him an exasperated look. "Why would Martin be standing outside the window?"

"He's been coming over in the evenings to work on the steps leading down to the creek. Maybe you just saw him walk past."

"Then where is he now?"

He shrugged. "I don't know. I can't see all the way down the path from here, but if it will make you feel better, I'll go take a look. Wait here."

A few minutes later, he returned shaking his head. "I didn't see anyone. It must have been some weird trick of the light."

A loud gong sounded, reverberating through the hallways.

Elise flinched. "What was that?"

"Oliver's new toy. Come on. I'll show you." Smiling, he put his arm around her shoulders and led her through the library door.

"Isn't it just too fun?" Oliver beamed, standing next to an antique brass gong, padded mallet in his hand. "Kathy found it while she was ransacking the attic today. We thought it would add a bit of atmosphere."

Kathy nodded. "Like being at an Agatha Christie country-house party."

"Didn't someone end up getting murdered at those?" Jack asked, coming into the entry hall.

"Jack, that's not funny."

"Kathy, it was a joke."

"Don't pay any attention to him," Oliver said as he led the way to the dining room. "Who'd want to kill any of us?"

After dinner they gathered in the library, and Jack filled them in on what he'd been able to discover.

"I've learned a lot about early US currency, but not specifically for the time period we're talking about." He smiled apologetically. "Now, all I've used is the Internet. A library might have more in-depth information. So, if I had to make a guess using the information I found, I'd say the bank of Leadville most likely would have paid the three men in silver certificates, which could have come in denominations of up to one thousand dollars."

"No kidding?" Max said. "You could probably stack those pretty tight. I mean, how many do you think you could get, say, stacked like a deck of cards?"

"It seems that in 1929, the treasury department shrank the size of a greenback—better known as a dollar bill—by twenty-five to thirty percent, compared to what they are today. So a stack of thousand-dollar silver certificates would take up a little more room than a stack of today's dollar bills."

"I wonder what their value would be now?" Kathy asked.

Jack shrugged. "I don't know. I tried to find that out as well, but I didn't have any luck. If we do happen to find this money and it is in silver certificates, Elise will have to get in touch with someone who's an expert in old currency."

"Well, tomorrow's Friday. I have Constance coming over in the morning." Max ignored the scowl Elise gave him. "She's going to begin by organizing the linen closets that housekeeping will be using, so she'll be here for most of the day. We don't want any more people than necessary knowing we're going to be searching the house for a stash of hidden money, so I suggest we wait until tomorrow night to begin our treasure hunt."

"Constance won't think there's anything strange about me rummaging around in the attic," Kathy said. "I can just say I'm trying to find additional items to add to the inn's decor."

"I don't have anything scheduled for tomorrow," Elise said, "so I'll help Kathy in the attic."

Max nodded. "That's fine. We'll just go about our day as usual. We can begin tomorrow night."

"We need to have some kind of system for searching," Jack said. "How about if we each take a part of the house and make a list of everywhere we've searched? Then we won't waste time looking where someone else has already been."

"Great idea," Max said. "Since I know more about the layout of the house, I'll break it up into sections, and we can each begin in our assigned area."

"Just so you know, Maxwell, I don't have any intention of going spelunking in that dark, nasty basement, nor will I be climbing around all of that junk in that disgusting attic."

"Oh, come on, Oliver, where's your spirit of adventure?"

Oliver snorted. "You may look upon this as an adventure, but I see it as nothing more than a way to further piss off an already pissed-off ghost."

"Speaking of ghosts, I wish Cyrus would have at least left a few clues to where he hid the money," Kathy said.

"I don't think he was expecting to die when he did," Elise said. "Perhaps he'd planned on leaving a letter or something and never had the chance."

Jack rubbed his chin. "I don't understand why he wouldn't have just put the money in the bank. He was a stranger when he got here. I can't imagine anyone would have questioned where he came by his money."

"The answer to that lies in whatever happened in Leadville the day he took off with it," Max said.

"He must have known he was a wanted man," Elise added. "He did change his name. Perhaps he thought it would be safer not to deposit a large sum in the local bank. If he just hid it, who would know?"

"And not only did he take off with the money, he was suspected of killing Elise's great-great-great-grandfather and his own brother," Kathy stated.

"That reminds me," Elise said, "I reread the newspaper article on Cyrus's death, and I can't believe I missed the fact that the other man found dead was Virginia's brother Garrison."

"No kidding," Kathy said.

Elise nodded. "All Hank's telegram said was that he met a man who was going to take him to meet Cyrus, I wonder if Garrison was that man?"

"He didn't say anything else?" Jack asked.

Elise shook her head. "Only that he met him here in Cedar Bend."

Max looked thoughtful. "I didn't make the connection either. And if I recall, the newspaper account of the deaths didn't say much at all about Garrison."

"Don't you think that's a little strange?" Elise asked. "I also find it strange that there were only two newspaper articles on the deaths. It's almost as if the entire incident was hushed up."

"But why would that be?" Jack asked.

"If the third man was someone who lived here, maybe there was a reason to keep his identity out of the newspaper," Max replied. "Especially if they'd really come here to rob Cyrus."

"I don't believe Hank would have stooped to robbery," Elise said. "Confront him and demand his brother's share of the money, yes, but rob him at gun point? No."

"I understand Hank was a distant relative of yours, Elise, but you didn't know him," Max said. "All you can go by is what Grace wrote in her diaries, and to her he was this heroic man who spent twenty years of his life trying to get back what belonged to her and her mother. After twenty years of roaming the country, by the time he did find Cyrus, he could have become a dangerous man."

Elise shrugged. "Perhaps. I just have a strong feeling that's not what happened."

"But since all three men died, we'll probably never know the truth," Kathy said.

"Maxwell, I don't recall, from your delightful retelling of the ghastly events of that night, exactly where the shootings took place."

"Why, Oliver, I believe it happened on the very spot where you're sitting."

Take care, and be on your guard against all kinds of greed;
for one's life does not consist in the abundance of his possessions.
— Luke 12:15

Chapter 20

"Where are you two going with Cyrus's desk?" Elise asked, watching from the stairs as Max and Jack maneuvered the mahogany monstrosity through the library door.

"Kathy woke up this morning with the great idea that it would be perfect as a reception desk here in the entry hall," Jack said with a grunt. "So, before we've even had our breakfast, she wanted us to get it moved."

"She was barking orders like some kind of miniature general," Max added.

Kathy appeared behind the two men. "I heard that. Don't feel sorry for them, Elise. Oliver hadn't even started breakfast when I very nicely," she said, smiling sweetly, "asked them to move the desk."

"Damn, I can't believe how heavy it still is after we took the drawers out," Max groaned.

"Kathy, tell us where you want this before we drop it," Jack said through gritted teeth.

"Right there by that empty wall," she said pointing. "That's perfect. It's convenient for when guests come in, but it's not in the way. Elise, what do you think?"

She nodded. "It looks great. Now, we need something to hang on the wall above it."

"I thought while we were in the attic today we'd see what we could find."

"Good idea." Elise continued down the stairs and stopped when she reached the desk. "This is a heavy piece of furniture, but I wonder . . ."

"Wonder what?" Max asked.

"Some of these old desks had secret compartments or a hidden drawer. I thought perhaps . . ."

"No." Max shook his head. "It couldn't be that easy."

Jack laughed. "Wouldn't that be something? Talk about right under our noses."

Gong.

"Damn," Max swore as they all jumped. "Kathy, I'm not so sure that gong was such a great idea."

"I guess breakfast is ready," Jack said.

Kathy giggled. "Oh, Max, don't be such a grump."

"Did you get that enormous desk moved?" Oliver asked while serving them eggs Benedict.

Max winked at Elise. "Yes, but I'm going to miss having it in the library."

Kathy gave Max a puzzled frown. "Why? You don't use that desk for business. You have another one in your office."

When Max opened his mouth to reply, Elise cried, "No, Max."

Oliver covered his ears. "For God's sake, Maxwell, TMI."

Bewildered, Kathy turned to Jack.

He grinned. "I'll explain later."

Elise cleared her throat. "Oliver, this is delicious."

"Thanks. I'm experimenting with different breakfast ideas. When I worked in Boston, I was strictly a dinner chef."

Elise dabbed her mouth with her napkin. "You can experiment on me anytime. I have a feeling that while I'm staying here eating your fabulous meals, I'll have to exercise twice as hard as I normally do."

"Do you like to run?" Max asked.

"Yes, I do. Do you?"

"Yes. We'll have to get up and go for one. Tomorrow morning?"

"Sure, as long as it's not too early."

"Well, that takes care of tomorrow morning. What about today?" Jack asked. "Max, I know we're going to wait until later on this afternoon to begin our search, but is there anything we can do this morning?"

"I thought you and I could take a look at that desk before Kathy puts the drawers back. Who knows? Elise might be on to something."

"Kathy and I are going to hit the attic," Elise said, "but first, I have a bigger problem to tackle."

"What's that?" Max asked.

"Calling my parents and letting them know I'm staying here. How I'm going to explain this to my father is beyond me." She shook her head. "He's not going to like it one bit."

"I thought you told me you pretty much did as you pleased? Besides, you're a big girl."

Kathy snorted. "Spoken like a man, Max. Don't you remember how your father reacted when your younger sister took off for Europe with that ski instructor?"

Max's frown deepened. "That was different. She had just finished college and we hardly knew the guy. For God's sake, she was only in her twenties. She had no business leaving home that young, running off with some stranger."

Kathy smiled at Elise. "If you don't mind me asking, how old are you?"

"Twenty-four."

"It's not the same thing." Max tossed his napkin on the table and rose. "Come on, Jack. Are you ready to check out that desk?"

"Sure, why not?"

"What are you going to tell your parents?" Kathy asked Elise as they finished their coffee. Oliver had excused himself, mumbling something about a recipe for she-crab soup.

Elise took a deep breath. "Since they know why I'm here in Cedar Bend, I'll tell them the partial truth, which is that there's a chance the silver or money could be hidden here, and the owner has graciously invited me to stay while we search for it. How does that sound?"

Kathy gave her a conspiratorial grin. "That should work. As long as they don't know the man who invited you to stay is thirty, an absolute hunk and that you're sleeping with him, you should be fine."

Elise laughed. "I have a feeling my mother would take one look at him and think he was trouble waiting to happen."

"And she'd be right. You go make your call. I'll get my old clothes on, and then I'll meet you in the attic."

"Speaking of clothes, thanks for helping Max pack my things. I can't imagine what I would have ended up with if he'd done it on his own."

"I'm so sorry about all of that. I told him it wasn't a good idea. Did he tell you he coerced me into helping?"

"I figured he pressured you until you agreed. It's fine, truly." Elise gave her new friend's hand a reassuring squeeze. "Honestly, I don't blame you in the slightest."

"Boy, I'm glad to hear that. What is it about Max? No matter how much you want to, you can't tell him no."

Elise laughed. "Tell me about it."

"I don't know, Max. I don't see anything that could be a release for a hidden compartment," Jack said, flashlight in hand.

"You're not having any luck?" Elise asked as she and Kathy approached them.

Max shook his head. "Doesn't look that way. Jack's been crawling around, under and over the desk, and he hasn't found anything yet."

"Well, it was worth a try," Kathy said. "I'll go ahead and put the drawers back in."

"I'll help you. Where are they?" Elise asked.

"They're in the library," Jack said. "We can all help. There're like nine of them."

"Max, did you notice this bottom right hand one has a lock?" Elise, seated on the floor, asked as she tried to slide the drawer into place.

"Yeah, but it doesn't work," Max said. "Well, at least I don't think it does. I don't have the key."

Bong . . . bang . . . bong . . . bang.

"Damn it to hell," Max swore as the casement clock in the entry started to rock back and forth.

"Ahhh," Kathy cried when the chandelier began to swing wildly.

"Holy shit," Jack exclaimed when the desk tilted up on its side toward Elise who was still sitting on the floor.

"Max!" Elise screamed, her foot wedged under the desk.

Reaching the antique clock as it was about to tumble to the floor, Max turned.

Jack braced himself against the desk. "I can't hold it up," he yelled.

"Shit, shit, shit." Oliver raced past Max and grabbed Elise, pulling her out of the way just as she untangled her foot.

Howling like a banshee, a mass of dark smoke slid down the banister then spun crazily over their heads.

"Max, do something," Elise sobbed.

Max reached into the drawer Kathy still held and grabbed the first hard object he found. "Get the fuck away from us!" he hollered as he threw it into the black whirlwind.

Low guttural laughter filled the room as the mass spun faster and faster.

"I'm not looking, I'm not looking, I'm not looking," Oliver chanted, wrapping his arms over his head.

Suddenly a silver flash pierced the smoke. A hollow scream filled the room, then silence.

For a few seconds, they were all motionless then Oliver, now seated on the floor next to Elise, cried, "What the fuck was that?"

Max ran unsteady hands through his hair. "I think our other visitor was back."

"Oh, sweet heaven," Kathy said, shakily sinking down into a chair. "I've never been so scared in my life."

"What other visitor?" Jack asked.

"Max, you'd better tell them," Elise said.

"Maxwell, are you telling us there're two ghosts living in this house?" Oliver asked incredulously after Max had concluded.

He nodded. "I'm afraid so."

"I guess you've made a believer out of me now," Jack said. "Damn, I wish I still smoked."

Oliver got to his feet. "I'm making us all coffee heavily laced with brandy, then I'm fucking calling *Ghostbusters*." He turned to Max. "And, Maxwell, I want a raise."

"I'll see what I can do, as long as you aren't quitting again." Max walked over to where Elise still sat on the floor. "Are you all right?"

She nodded. "Somehow I got my foot caught behind one of the desk legs and couldn't get it out."

He helped her to her feet.

"I didn't know Oliver could move that fast," she said.

Max grinned. "All those years of running track." His face sobered and he glanced around the entry hall. "That was one hell of a performance. I wonder if it has something to do with us moving the desk?"

"But I don't think it was Cyrus who was upset," Elise said. "He's been trying to help us."

Max nodded. "Maybe whoever that other thing is was trying to distract us."

"From what?" Jack asked.

"From whatever is in this desk."

Jack looked thoughtful. "Okay, say you're right, what were we doing when it started?"

"I was trying to slide in that drawer." Elise pointed to the empty drawer next to the desk.

"Dare we try it again?" Jack asked.

"We've come this far. Besides, I doubt our friend will be back," Max said.

Kathy covered her eyes. "I can't watch."

Max turned to Elise. "Do you want to do it, or do you want me to?"

Elise gathered her courage. "I'll do it." She picked up the drawer and, once again seated on the floor, started to slide it in. She paused and studied the interior. Her pulse quickened. "Max, I found something."

"What?" Bending down, he watched as she pressed a tiny black button barely visible in the mahogany wood.

"Will you look at that," Kathy said excitedly when the bottom of the drawer popped up, revealing a shallow compartment below. "Is there anything in there?"

Elise held her breath and peered into the darkened space. "Yes, there is." She reached in and extracted two folded pieces of yellowed paper.

"What is it?" Max asked impatiently.

She carefully unfolded the smaller of the two pages, her eyes opening wide as she read the faded words.

"Elise, what is it?" the three asked as one.

Without a word, she handed Max the note.

He read aloud: "Cyrus, I will be at your home tonight at eight o'clock. I will be bringing someone associated with your past whom I am sure you will be pleased to finally meet. Trust me when I say it is in your best interest to keep this appointment."

"Holy shit," Jack exclaimed.

"Max, do you think it's from the man who was bringing Hank to meet Cyrus?" Elise asked excitedly.

"It sure sounds as if it could be. What else do you have there?"

Unfolding the second, thicker sheet, Elise caught her breath.

"Max, it's Clayton Hamilton's copy of the deed to the Leadville silver mine."

"No kidding? Let me see." He took the document. "Well, I'll be damned. It is." Smiling, Max showed Jack and Kathy. "Well, sweetheart, you did it." Helping her to her feet, he gave her a long kiss.

"What's happened now?" Oliver asked as he came into the entry hall carrying a tray of coffee cups.

"Oh, Oliver, look what Elise found in the desk drawer." Kathy hurried to show him the two papers.

He set the tray down on a side table. "Well, this explains Ghosty's obsession with those crescents," he said, reading the deed.

"What do you mean?" Max asked, releasing Elise.

Oliver turned the paper so they could all see.

"It's right here." He pointed at the faded calligraphy. "It's the name of the mine."

They all gathered close. At the bottom, they could just make out: *For the claim known as the Silver Crescent Mine.*

Eyes narrowed, Max took the deed from Oliver's hand. With skepticism in each word he asked, "Elise there've been silver crescents appearing all over the place, and you didn't know that was the name of the mine?"

"No, Max, I did not. Grace never mentioned the name in her diaries."

His brows rose. "Really? I find that rather hard to believe."

Elise clenched her jaw and fought back tears. "Yes, Max, really. And you can find it hard to believe all you want; it's the truth."

Caught up in the moment, none of the little group noticed the front door open.

"Hello."

Startled, they all turned to see Constance Poole standing just inside the door.

She hesitated. "I'm sorry. Have I done something wrong? I thought, since I'm going to be working here, I could just let myself in."

Max recovered first and smiled. "Constance, you're fine. Come on in. I'm sorry. I lost track of time." Refolding the deed, he handed it to Elise. In a low voice he said, "Put this and the note away somewhere. Later, I'll put them in my safe." He turned back to Constance and continued in a normal voice. "Come on back to my office. I have some paperwork I need you to fill out. Then I'll get you started on those linen closets."

Devastated by Max's distrust, Elise refolded the papers in stony silence. Through blurry eyes, she watched Constance put her arm through Max's as they walked toward the back of the house.

Turning to Kathy, in a slightly quavering voice, she said, "I'll take these upstairs, call my parents, then meet you in the attic."

Before Kathy could reply, Elise hurried away.

))

"Sometimes I'd like to shake Max until his teeth rattle," Kathy said once Elise was gone. "How can he hurt her like that? It was obvious she'd never heard the name of that mine."

"Sugar, I think Maxwell's blockheaded behavior can be laid at the feet of that tramp Teresa. She fucked him up bad."

"That was over a year ago. It's time Max got over it. If he doesn't start watching what he says, Elise just might tell him to stuff it and walk out of his life. Then where will he be? She's perfect for him."

"Calm down, Kathy." Jack put his arm around his wife. "They'll work it out."

"What worries me," Oliver said, narrowing his eyes in the direction of Max's office, "is the fact that that black widow will be scurrying around here waiting to pounce. Maxwell needs to realize she's the one he shouldn't trust." In a mockery of Constance's voice, he purred, " 'Will you come into my parlor?' said the spider to the fly."

))

Upstairs in the bedroom she now shared with Max, Elise slipped the two pieces of paper into a drawer then spoke briefly with her mother on the phone, trying as she did so to hold back the tears that had threatened to spill since Max's hurtful words.

"Damn the man." She sat down on the bed, brushing away the tears she couldn't stop from flowing. She reached for a tissue.

If you were smart, you'd say good-bye to Max Holt and leave this town, said the sensible voice in her head. *But you haven't found the money yet,* said the headstrong voice which had gotten her into this mess in the first place. *Damn it,* she thought, hearing the bedroom door open.

Hoping Max hadn't seen her tears, she headed for the attached bathroom.

Before she could close the door, he was right behind her.

"Max, do you mind? I'd like some privacy."

"What the hell is going on? I just saw Kathy, who gave me a dirty look and walked away. Now I find you up here crying."

"Nothing's wrong. Go away so I can change my clothes and go help Kathy."

"I don't want to go away. I want to know what's wrong."

"Max, let it go."

"This isn't over Constance again, is it?"

"No, it isn't over Constance." Frustrated, she brushed past him back into the bedroom. "It's about the fact that you still don't trust me."

"What? What are you talking about? Elise, come back here."

"Max, I don't want to be around you right now so leave me alone."

"What did I do?" he yelled as she left the room.

"Kathy," Elise called, when she'd reached the attic.

"I'm over here."

Elise found her up to her elbows in a trunk of old clothes.

"I think I might have found Virginia's wedding dress." She lifted out a dress of ivory satin, lace and pearls with long, fitted sleeves and a bustle with a draped, tiered train that had been carefully packed in unbleached muslin and sprinkled with dried sprigs of lavender. "It's in remarkably good condition, isn't it?"

Elise gasped and reached for the dress. "Oh, it's exquisite. Look at the detailed workmanship of the lace . . . and the tiny rosebuds down the front . . . and . . . oh . . . they're also along the hem."

Kathy smiled. "It would look wonderful on you. You have to try it on."

"Oh no, I couldn't." Her eyes glowing, Elise shook out the gorgeous dress and gazed at it.

"Why not? Come on. Please try it on? Here, I'll help you."

"Oh, okay."

They quickly had her in the dress. Kathy fastened the tiny row of pearl buttons down the back and attached the bustle and train.

"A perfect fit." Kathy laughed with delight. "Turn around and let me see. Oh, Elise, you're beautiful. Where's a mirror? There has to be one up here." Standing on an old wooden chair, she scanned the attic.

"There's one. Wait here. I'll see if I can drag it over."

"Kathy, be careful. That looks heavy."

"It's okay. It's on rollers." She placed the cheval glass in front of Elise.

"Now, see how enchanting you are."

They stared at Elise's reflection and froze.

Any so-called material thing that you want is merely a symbol:
You want it not for itself, but because it will content your spirit for the
moment.

— Mark Twain

Chapter 21

"Oh, sweet heaven, not another one," Kathy said, her voice barely above a whisper. "Elise, do you see what I see?"

Elise opened and closed her mouth twice before she was able to respond. "Yes."

"She looks like the lady in the library portrait."

Elise nodded.

"I think I'm going to faint."

"Kathy, don't you dare."

"Did you happen to notice she's also wearing the wedding dress?"

"I see that."

"She's smiling. I hope that means she's not upset that you have it on."

"She doesn't seem to be."

"Do you think she can hear what we're saying?"

"I think so."

"Omigod, she's nodding and pointing at the dress. What is she trying to say?"

"I don't know."

Taking a deep breath, Elise spoke softly to the shimmering figure in the glass. "Virginia, I'm sorry. I don't understand. Are you trying to tell me this is your dress?"

"She nodded 'yes'. She's pointing from her to you."

"Yes, I see. Virginia, are you saying you want me to have this dress?"

"She's nodding again," exclaimed Kathy. "Ask her about the silver."

"Virginia, is the silver in this house? Can you tell us where it's hidden?"

"Oh no, she's fading away."

Elise stepped toward the glass. "Virginia, please don't leave. We need your help."

"She's gone. Now I can faint." Kathy collapsed onto a wooden chair.

"Before you faint, help me get out of this dress."

"I'll try, but my hands are still shaking."

"Why would Virginia appear to us if she wasn't going to tell us where the silver is hidden?"

"I don't know if the silver had anything to do with why she appeared. Maybe she wants you to wear her dress for your wedding to Max."

"Why would she think I'm going to marry Max?"

"I don't know. Elise, do you realize we're trying to figure out a message from a ghost?" She put her face in her hands. "I have to tell you, I'm still freaked out over what happened earlier. Now this."

Elise gave her a hug. "So am I. But wait until you hear how I found Grace's diaries."

"Oh my God, Grace actually appeared and spoke to you? I would have died on the spot."

Elise grinned. "I was so scared, I couldn't move. But, Kathy, I honestly believe Grace, Cyrus, and Virginia are trying to help us, not harm us."

"I agree, but what about that other thing?" Kathy gave an involuntary shudder. "It was awful. I don't want to see it again."

Elise ran her hands up and down her arms. "Neither do I. Hopefully Cyrus can keep it away." She shook her head. "Listen to me talking nonchalantly about a ghost."

Kathy laughed. "Tell me about it. And I can hardly wait 'til Oliver hears there's another ghost in the house." She folded the wedding dress across her arm. "Okay, now what should we do with this?"

"I don't know. It's so beautiful; I hate to put it back in the trunk."

"You could hang it in your closet," Kathy suggested, "or maybe we should take it and have it professionally cleaned."

"What for?"

She smiled. "Oh, I don't know. If we had it cleaned, well, then it would be ready to wear."

Cocking her head, Elise studied her friend. "Are you thinking Virginia's right and I might have a use for this dress?"

"Well, maybe."

"Yeah, a really big maybe. As you noticed earlier, Max still doesn't trust me. I can't imagine he's going to ask me to marry him."

"If he has any sense, he will. It's not you he doesn't trust; it's Teresa and what she did."

Elise nodded. "Max told me what happened. I can't imagine the hurt he felt and I can see why he's leery about trusting, but he has to realize I'm not her. Yes, I kept my knowledge about Cyrus and the silver from him, but even before he discovered the diary, I had every intention of telling him the truth. You know, he didn't tell me what he did after Teresa tossed her ring. I've seen him mad; I can't imagine what he'd do in a situation like that."

"But that's the problem, he didn't do anything, he just walked away."

"He didn't do anything? He just left? Kathy, that's hard to believe."

"I know, but I think that's what's wrong with him. He's held the hurt in for too long. He probably would have been better off if he'd pounded the guy."

"Could he still be in love with her?"

"No, not at all." Kathy shook her head vigorously. "I think he's afraid of being hurt again. You care for him, don't you?"

Elise sat down on a crate next to Kathy and nodded. "There's been a spark between us since we met. The question is, is it love or is it lust? One minute I don't care if I ever see him again, and the next minute I'm in his arms. I can't help but wonder if he's using me to get over Teresa, or just keeping me around until we find the treasure. What if I find I'm truly in love with him? Am I setting myself up for a fall?" Tears welled in her eyes.

"Ahh, honey. Don't cry," Kathy said, giving her a hug.

Elise hugged her back. "I don't know what to do. My plan was to come here, find the silver and go back to Standish to work on the paper with my dad. Falling in love with Max Holt was definitely not in my plans." She reached up to wipe away the tears streaming from her eyes. "Damn, here I go again. Do you have any tissues? Honestly, I swear I spend more time crying over that man than I do smiling."

"Here." Kathy handed her a tissue. "Elise, please don't give up on him. I truly feel he cares for you. Just give him some time to learn how to trust again. In the meantime, enjoy being with him, and try to ignore it when he acts like an ass."

Laughing, Elise dried her eyes. "But I have to tell you, ignoring him when he's acting like an ass is becoming harder to do. Like earlier; he hadn't a clue why I was upset with him."

"I know. Remember, he's a man and sometimes they can act like they're brain-dead."

Elise chuckled. "Yes, they can, can't they? Now, enough about my problems." She looked at the dress Kathy still held. "What should we do with it? I don't think I should hang it in my closet. Max might see it and wonder what it's doing there."

"But aren't we going to tell the others about seeing Virginia?"

"Yes, but I feel foolish telling them I tried on her wedding dress."

"Then we'll just say we came across some old clothes and tried some of them on for fun."

Elise nodded. "Good idea, and while we were doing that, Virginia appeared.”

“You know, now that she’s gone, seeing her wasn’t all that creepy.”

“Perhaps it’s because she didn’t look scary. It’s almost like she had more of a calming effect.”

“Did Max tell you he swears Virginia’s portrait was trying to tell him you were in trouble the other night?”

“No. He didn’t say anything to me.”

“He told us this morning before you came down.”

“That’s incredible.”

“I think she likes you and is trying to look after you. That’s why she wants you to have the dress. How about if I put it in my closet? I can guarantee Jack won’t notice.”

“That’s a great idea. Thanks. Would it seem too strange of me to ask Max to bring the mirror down to our bedroom? If Virginia appeared once, perhaps she might do it again.”

“It makes sense, really. I’m sure when we tell the others about Virginia, they’ll be anxious to check it out. Now, I suppose we should get to work going through the rest of these boxes, although if Cyrus were putting important papers in that hidden compartment in his desk, I doubt we’ll find anything up here to lead us to the money.”

Elise grinned. “No, but we’ll have fun going through all this junk.”

In the hall below, Max and Constance stepped from his office. “I have to say, Max, that, even in the brief time I’ve known you, I can tell that you’ll make Inn on the Bluff not only the premier place to dine for miles around, but to come and stay as well.”

“Thanks, Constance. I appreciate your confidence in me. I hope your predictions come true. I’ve put a lot of hard work into this place, but a business doesn’t run smoothly without a great staff.”

She smiled. “Well, I’m going to try my best never to disappoint you in any way, or let you down.”

“I’m going to count on that.”

“Hello again,” Jack said, as he came through the library door into the entry hall. “Max hurried you off so quickly this morning we didn’t have a chance to be introduced.”

“By all means, let me correct my mistake,” Max said with a grin. “Constance, this is my good friend Jack Callaghan.”

“It’s nice to meet you, Jack. I believe I met your wife the other day.”

“Yes, that’s right. You did,” Max said. “Jack and Kathy are going to be staying here with me for a while. Actually, we have her to thank for doing such a great job with the decorating. Now she's busy completing the master suite."

"I'd love to see it when she's done. I'll bet it will be as scrumptious as the other bedrooms. I assume it was Kathy's idea to place this beautiful desk out here?"

"She thought it would make a nicer reception area than putting in a counter. Since it will mostly be you checking in the guests, I'll leave it to you to organize the desk with the necessary paperwork."

"That will be fine." Constance moved closer to the desk. "It's in remarkably good condition. How old do you think it is?"

"I'd guess late nineteenth century."

"So it could be original to the house?" She ran a well-manicured finger along the polished wood. "It could have belonged to Cyrus Mosby?"

Max and Jack exchanged an uneasy glance before Max replied, "I'd say there was a good chance. I take it you've heard the stories of Cyrus haunting this house?"

Constance nodded. "When we were teenagers we'd hang around the house hoping to encounter the ghost, but needless to say, we never did." Anxiety filled her eyes as she looked from Max to Jack. "Don't tell me you have—"

"No," they replied in unison.

Chuckling, Max continued. "Oh, there've been a few bumps and bangs, but this is an old house where there's bound to be weird noises. I can assure you, there isn't any ghost."

She looked relieved. "Actually, I'm glad to hear that. To tell you the truth, even when we were kids I never wanted to be the one to come face-to-face with Cyrus, and I feel the same way as an adult."

"You and Oliver both," Jack said.

"Who's Oliver?" she asked.

"Oliver is another good friend of mine and my chef. You met him briefly when you were here the other day. He showed you in to my office."

"Oh, yes. Now I remember. He seemed very nice."

"Yes, he's usually a perfectly nice guy. But I have to warn you, he can have a strange sense of humor and can sometimes come across sounding like a smart-ass. The best thing to do when he gets like that is to ignore him."

She grinned. "I'll keep that in mind."

"Also, don't forget Oliver is in charge of the kitchen staff," Max added. "So there won't be any need for you to concern yourself with any part of the kitchen."

"Sure, I wouldn't want to step on any toes."

"Great, I'm sure you and Oliver will get along just fine."

"And what about Elise? Does she work here as well?"

"No, Elise is my girlfriend. She's staying with me for a while."

"Oh, I see. So she doesn't live here permanently?"

Max shook his head. "Not at the moment. Why?"

"No reason. I just want to make sure I know who everyone is, so I don't make any mistakes."

"Great, then if you don't have any more questions, I'll show you where the housekeeping linen closets are located. I have to apologize for the disarray. When the linens arrived, I just piled everything in the closets, so they're not in any kind of order. If you have time, the guest beds need to be made up and the bathrooms filled with towels and toiletries. But I don't expect you to get all of this done today."

"Max," Jack said, "when you're through, I'd like to talk to you."

"Sure, I'll meet you in the library in a few minutes."

"She should feel right at home hanging around in a dark, musty closet, shouldn't she?" Oliver said, coming up behind Jack.

Jack chuckled. "Now, Oliver, Max told Constance he thought you and she would get along just fine."

"Maxwell also believes a ghost is going to lead him to a fortune in buried silver, doesn't he? *Hmm.*"

"I'm beginning to believe that's not as far-fetched as we think."

"Oh, do tell. What's happened now?"

"Come into the library and I'll show you. I was going through the stuff from the desk, which Kathy had put in a box, and this is what I found." Jack held out an oddly shaped black lump.

Oliver looked at the object with distaste. "Lovely. What is it? The world's ugliest paperweight?"

"More likely an extremely valuable paperweight."

"What is that thing you're holding, Jack?" Max asked.

He handed him the object. "What's it look like to you?"

"Holy crap, Jack. Where did you find this?"

"It was in one of the desk drawers."

"You mean to tell me this has been sitting in that desk all this time?"

"Hello, remember me?" Oliver waved his arms to get their attention. "Perhaps you two would be so kind as to fill me in on why that has the both of you grinning like idiots?"

"It's the proof we've needed." Max grabbed Oliver and began to swing him around.

"Maxwell. Have you totally lost your mind? Let go of me."

"You'd better stop," Jack warned. "He's turning green."

"Sorry, Oliver."

Oliver gratefully collapsed into a chair.

"Jack, wait until I show this to Elise. Are they still in the attic?"

"As far as I know. Did you go through the desk when you moved in?"

"I glanced through the drawers, but since I wasn't planning on using it, I didn't pay much attention to the contents. Besides, even if I had noticed this at the time, I don't think I would have realized what it was. Why would I?"

"You grew up in Leadville. I would have thought you'd have known what that was as soon as you laid eyes on it."

"Well, maybe." He frowned down at the dark lump in his hand. "Jack, are you sure it came from the desk?"

"I assumed it did since it was with the rest of the stuff Kathy put in this box." He indicated a cardboard box sitting on the floor. "I guess we'll have to wait and ask her."

"Stop." Oliver jumped to his feet. "What the fuck is that thing?"

"What is what?" Kathy asked coming through the library door, followed by Elise. "And why is Oliver shouting?"

"I'm shouting, sugar, because these two won't tell me what's so exciting about Jack finding this." Oliver snatched the object from Max's hand and held it up. "Whatever this ugly thing is, it has the two of them about to piss their pants with excitement. It looks like a petrified turd to me."

"Let me see that," Kathy said. "Oliver's right, it's awful. What's it supposed to be?"

She directed her question to both Jack and Max.

"You've never seen it before?" Jack asked.

"No, why?"

"You're sure you didn't put it in this box of stuff you emptied from the desk?" Max asked.

Kathy gritted her teeth. "Yes, I'm sure I've never seen this thing before. I can see why Oliver is about to throttle the both of you."

"No kidding, Max," Elise said. "You're making all of us crazy. Tell us what that thing is."

Max smiled. "Why, it's a very nice chunk of silver ore."

Three great forces rule the world: stupidity, fear and greed.
— Albert Einstein

Chapter 22

"Max, are you sure?" Elise asked.

He pulled her into his arms. "Oh, yes, I'm sure. While growing up, I saw chunks like this either in school or at museums." He kissed her soundly. "So, my sweet, this is the final proof I needed to be convinced there's buried treasure somewhere in my house, and," he said, kissing her again, "we're going to find it."

"Wait a minute. Let's back up a little," Jack said. "Max, are you suggesting Cyrus put the silver ore in the box?"

Oliver rolled his eyes. "He'll have to stop trying to remove Elise's tonsils with his tongue before he can answer you."

"Don't move away from in front of me," Max murmured into Elise's mouth. "I can't turn around right now."

"Max!" She gasped as she felt what pressed against her jeans. "Stop that."

"I'm trying."

"This is embarrassing."

"We could just ask them to leave."

She managed to pull herself from his embrace. When she faced the others, she blushed to her roots.

Oliver smiled. "It's all right, sugar. We've all been around Maxwell long enough to know he has a problem controlling himself."

"Okay, everyone, let's get back to my question," Jack said. "Am I correct in surmising that your thought is that if none of us put the silver ore in the box, Cyrus did?"

"Can anyone think of anyone else?" Max asked.

"There's Virginia," Kathy said, her eyes locking with Elise's.

"Virginia?" Max looked from Kathy to Elise. "Is there something you two would like to tell us?"

"Actually, there is. That's one of the reasons we came down," Elise replied.

"That and lunch," Kathy said.

"Wait a fucking minute. Are you two about to tell us that not only do we have two lunatic ghosts to contend with, we now have another one as well?" Oliver asked.

"It's okay," Elise said reassuringly. "She's harmless. In fact, she's really nice."

"Oh, sweet Jesus. 'She's really nice'? Have you all lost your minds?" Arms waving, eyes popping, Oliver yelled, "These are dead people we're talking about. Haven't any of you ever seen *Night of the Living Dead*?"

"Oliver, will you calm down?" Max said. "Let's hear what the girls have to say."

Elise described the clothes they had found and that they'd seen Virginia in the mirror.

"Then she just faded away," Kathy concluded.

"That's it," Oliver cried. "I'll never be able to look in another mirror in this house. God knows what might be looking back."

"That's incredible," Jack said. "Kathy, I can't believe how calm you are. I would have expected you two to come running down screaming."

Kathy snorted. "We saw Virginia hours ago. And, no, we weren't scared in the least. She wasn't at all like that other thing."

Max turned to Elise. "Are you really convinced she was trying to communicate with you?"

"I think so. She kept pointing at me."

"Elise asked her where the silver was hidden," Kathy said, "but that's when she faded away."

"How do you know it was Virginia?" Max asked.

"Isn't that her?" Elise pointed to the portrait above the fireplace, where all eyes turned.

"*Ahhh*—" Oliver screamed and collapsed onto the floor.

"He's fainted." Kathy hurried to where Oliver lay on the rug.

"Max, did you see that?" Elise exclaimed.

"See what? I didn't see anything."

"Neither did I," Jack said.

Kathy patted Oliver's cheek. "The portrait, Jack. Virginia. You didn't see her wink?"

"Oh, come on," Jack protested. "Neither Max nor I saw anything. All this ghost business has your imaginations running wild."

"I know what I saw," Kathy stated. "How about you, Elise?"

She nodded. "Sorry, Jack, but I saw it, too. And obviously, so did Oliver. Kathy, is he all right?"

Oliver sat up, appearing slightly dazed. "I'm fine, thanks. Maxwell, I—"

"Is there a problem?"

Startled, they all turned to see Constance standing in the doorway.

Recovering his voice first, Max replied, "No, everything's fine. Oliver just had a little accident. Here, Oliver, let me help you up."

Constance looked from face to face before she spoke. "Max, I finished organizing the closets. If there's anything you don't like, tell me, and I'll rearrange things."

"No, no, I imagine it's fine."

"I was wondering if it would be okay if I went to lunch before I began making up the beds?"

"No problem. You go right ahead. In fact, you don't have to worry about those beds today. You can do them on Monday when you come back."

"I don't mind doing them this afternoon. I thought, while I was out, I'd run over to The Powder Puff and see what kind of little baskets they have for us to put the complimentary toiletries in, if that's all right with you."

"Yeah, sure. If you find something, have them bill me directly." Realizing he still held the chunk of silver ore, he placed it on a side table.

"All right then, I'll be back in an hour or so." She stepped farther into the room. "Before I leave, Kathy, I wanted to tell you what a beautiful job you've done with the inn's décor."

"Why, thank you. I enjoyed doing it."

Constance pointed at the chunk of ore. "That's quite an unusual piece. What's it supposed to be?"

Jack laughed. "According to Oliver, it's the world's ugliest paperweight." He shrugged. "It's just something we found in a box. We haven't a clue what it actually is."

Constance smiled up at Oliver. "I agree with you. It's ugly, all right." Getting no response, she turned her attention to Max. "Well, I guess I'll be going. If you need me to pick up anything else while I'm out, you have my cell number."

Max smiled. "Thanks, I'll do that. Here, I'll walk out with you."

"That was close," Kathy said, collapsing into a chair. "How much do you think she could have overheard?"

Elise glanced toward the now empty doorway and frowned. "It depends on how long she'd been standing there."

Oliver scowled. "If I had to guess, sugar, Little Miss Latrodectus had been dangling in the hall for quite a while before she made her presence known."

Jack sighed with exasperation. "We don't know she was out there listening at all. You three have to give the poor girl a break. Come on, Kathy, there's no reason to be glaring at me like that. What has she done that's so bad?"

Kathy's glare turned icier. "She's in this house, and she's a man-eater. I wouldn't be surprised if she turns her sights on you the same way she's after Max, so you'd better be on your guard."

Jack rolled his eyes. "Oh, for heaven's sake, she's not after Max. She's only trying to be friendly and fit in."

"What? Jack, you need the prescription for your glasses increased if you can't see what's right under your nose."

"What's all the yelling about?" Max asked, coming back into the room.

"Nothing. Kathy's imagination is working overtime," Jack said, giving his wife an annoyed glance.

"Max, has Constance left?" Elise asked.

"Yes. Do you think she overheard our conversation?"

"We were just discussing that," Elise said. "If she heard anything, it wasn't much."

"Well, even if she didn't hear anything, our behavior was strange enough to pique anyone's interest," Jack said.

Kathy shook her head. "Her timing is uncanny. First she walks in on us this morning, then again just now. It's too bad she wouldn't just go home when Max told her to. Obviously, we'll have to be more careful when she's in the house."

"Well, this afternoon she'll be busy upstairs," Max said. "We can do a little snooping around down here until she leaves."

"If we're lucky, by Monday we'll have already found the money and won't have to worry about her being here," Kathy said.

Elise narrowed her eyes. "As long as that woman is in this house, we'd better be on our toes."

Max frowned with irritation. "I thought we'd gotten beyond this problem with Constance."

"Until she's no longer working in this house, there'll be a problem," Elise said.

Max threw up his hands. "Fine, but she does work here, and until she gives me a reason to fire her, she'll continue to work here." Max narrowed his eyes at Elise. "Or does this have more to do with why you were angry at me this morning? If so, I can't do anything about it unless you tell me what I did."

"Before Elise explains to you why you're being an incredible ass, Maxwell, I'm going to go make myself a strong drink," Oliver said, "because I know I saw that woman in that picture wink at me. I'll prepare us a late lunch, but don't expect to have much for dinner. I'll most likely be passed out by then."

"Oliver, you can't get drunk," Kathy said. "We're going to begin looking for the treasure tonight."

"Sugar, I've had enough excitement for one day. Wake me if you find anything."

"I'm going to wash up a little before lunch," Kathy said, following Oliver from the room.

"I'm going to get a beer," Jack said, following Kathy.

"Okay, Elise, tell me the truth. Did you really see Virginia's portrait wink?" Max asked.

"Yes, Max, whether you believe me or not, I did." She turned to leave. "I need to get cleaned up as well."

"Hey, come on, I believe you." He pulled her into his arms. "Tell me why you're still mad at me and why I'm an incredible ass?"

"You really haven't a clue why you upset me earlier, do you?"

He shook his head. "If it's all about Constance, I told you I'm not interested in anyone but you."

"No, it isn't all about Constance." She stepped from his arms. "Tell me something, Max, do you trust me?"

Her question seemed to surprise him. "What do you mean? Of course I trust you."

She shook her head. "Earlier today you questioned my honesty when you saw the name of the mine. I told you I didn't know it was called The Silver Crescent, and you didn't believe me."

He frowned. "Is that why I found you crying?"

"You hurt me, Max. I thought that once I told you everything I knew about the silver, you would realize I wasn't holding anything back."

He ran his hands through his hair. "I'm sorry, Elise. I didn't mean to hurt you. I think questioning you was an automatic response." He lifted his hands and let them fall. "I didn't realize how bad Teresa messed me up." He reached for her hand and drew her back into his arms. "Please believe me when I tell you I trust you."

She laid her head on his shoulder. "I've never experienced the kind of pain you must have felt when Teresa did that to you, and I can understand you being a little wary of trusting another, but Max, I'm not her and I'm not going to hurt you like that. Nor am I going to hold back information about the silver."

He kissed the top of her head. "I know, sweet. Just bear with me."

She heard the truth in the tenderness of his voice, but when she raised her head and gazed into his eyes, she could see traces of his past hurt still lingering in their depths. She brought his lips to hers and whispered, "I won't hurt you, I promise."

After a long and satisfying kiss, Elise lifted her mouth from his. "We'd better stop. The others are going to wonder what happened to us."

"Let them wonder." He kissed her again.

"Max, stop it. I wanted to run an idea past you in regards to Cyrus."

He nuzzled her neck. "Why do you always smell so good?"

She laughed. "Stop and listen to me." She stepped from arms reluctant to release her. "I wonder if, by leaving the chunk of silver ore, either Virginia or Cyrus is trying to help us out?"

"If so, I wish they'd just show us where the damn money is instead of dropping clues left and right."

"Perhaps there's a reason they don't want to make it easy for us. I wonder if we're supposed to prove ourselves first? I wish there was a way for us to know if we're the only ones Cyrus has ever tried to contact."

"Why would that matter?"

"Well, if we are, wouldn't that tell us that, for some reason, we're the ones he's chosen to find the money?"

"I guess, but what would make us different from anyone else?"

"First off, there's the fact that it was my ancestor he stole the money from, and you and he had both lived in Leadville. You don't have any connection to the Hamilton brothers. Do you?"

"Not as far as I know. I could call my parents and ask them how far back in our family tree their knowledge goes. If I do have a connection, I'd say it would have to be on my father's side. He's from Leadville, but my mother isn't. They met in college."

"And I don't know if the Hamiltons were originally from the area or if they went west, like Eli Wilkey did."

"Cyrus died without heirs, but how about Nathan? Did he leave anyone behind?"

"I doubt it. Max, don't you think, if Nathan had any family other than Cyrus, they would have tried to track him down like Uncle Hank did?"

"I suppose. Well, then, I can't see any connection between Cyrus and me." He shrugged. "Except the fact that I come from Leadville."

"Maybe that's all that was needed. While I was working in the attic I was going over all that's happened to us since we've met. I know what brought me to Cedar Bend, but you didn't have any connection here at all. You just happened upon the town and found this house. But what if it isn't that simple? What if we were both meant to come here?"

"Are you saying Cyrus brought us together, here in this house, so we could find his hidden silver?" He smiled indulgently. "I'll concede that all the weird happenings around here might be caused by Cyrus, but the idea he somehow orchestrated our meeting . . . I'm sorry, but that's too much."

Elise hesitated then sighed. "Max, I have something to tell you. And before you jump all over me for keeping things from you, until now I didn't think it was important."

He folded his arms and leaned against the bookcase. "I'm listening."

She told him about finding the trunk and the hidden diaries and the appearance of Grace's ghost.

"So you see, it was the right time for me to find the diaries. For years, my cousins and I used to play in that attic and I didn't even know that trunk was there. Then I'm able to get a job on a small paper where openings are few and far between. Next, the night of your pre-opening party, I wasn't the reporter who was supposed to cover the story. That person fell and was hurt. I happened to be in Sandy's office when the call came in so she sent me instead, and I get here to find you've made a garden walk out of old tombstones.

"You have to admit that's all a little peculiar. You, yourself, admitted you went to buy normal stepping-stones and changed your mind when you got to Todd's Granite. What changed your mind? Whose tombstone was the first one you saw? This all just can't be coincidental."

As she spoke, his mind went back to his overwhelming desire to have this house from the minute he'd laid eyes on it, the way the idea came to him to bring Cyrus's tombstone home and place it at the head of a garden walk, and how none of the weirdness had begun until after Elise had entered his life. Then there was Elise herself and his fervent desire for her. He'd been instantly attracted to women in the past, but never as intensely as with her. He had to admit that his feelings for Elise from the start were deeper than just sexual satisfaction.

These thoughts brought his mind back full circle to the present, back to a place where no matter how deeply he cared for her, he still couldn't totally open his heart to this beautiful, loving girl smiling up at him.

"Sweetheart, please don't give up on me," he choked out, the words barely audible before his mouth claimed hers.

"What did you say? I didn't hear you," she whispered when their lips parted.

"Sorry, nothing. I was thinking about something else."

"Well, that's nice." Again, she stepped from his arms. "I'm trying to figure out what's going on here, and you're not even listening."

"I've been listening. And believe it or not, as outrageous as your theory sounds, I'm beginning to think you might be somewhat right."

"You mean that?"

"Yes, but that brings us right back to our original question: Why doesn't Cyrus just show us where the money or silver or whatever is hidden?"

"Maybe once we begin searching in earnest, if we get close, they'll help us along."

Max chuckled. "What? Like kids playing 'you're hot, you're cold'?"

"Don't laugh. You never know."

*An object in possession seldom retains the same charm
that it had in pursuit.*

— Pliny the Younger

Chapter 23

"Okay, Constance has left for the day and we can begin our search," Max said as the little group settled themselves in the library. "Here are my thoughts on how we should go about this. Let me know if you have any suggestions, okay?

"I've narrowed the rooms down to those I feel are the most likely hiding places for Cyrus's stash. Since it's already late afternoon, I don't expect we'll accomplish much today, but at least we'll get a start. If we don't find anything in these rooms, we'll start on the next group. The first are the library, my office, the cellar, and the master bedroom. I don't think we need to spend any more time in the attic. Elise and Kathy have done a pretty good job up there. Besides looking inside pieces of furniture, there aren't that many places left to search."

"That reminds me, Max," Elise said. "Would you mind if we brought the cheval mirror down and put it in your bedroom? I thought if we had it close, Virginia might appear to me again."

"Sure, as long as you wouldn't be too freaked out if she does appear. But we'd better be careful which direction the mirror faces," he said teasingly. "I doubt you'd want an audience—although mirrors can be fun."

Kathy rolled her eyes. "Honestly, Max, behave yourself. Look how you've embarrassed Elise."

"Sorry, sweet." He gave Elise an impish grin. "I couldn't resist."

"Maybe we should get back to why we're here," Jack said. "I'm afraid if we don't get moving, Oliver is going to lose his nerve."

All eyes turned toward Oliver sitting upright with his back to the portrait, looking as if he'd bolt at any minute.

"I'll be fine," Oliver stated through stiff lips. "I've come to the conclusion that the longer it takes us to find the hidden money, the longer the spectral freak show in this house will continue. I, personally, have had enough of being used as a source of amusement by people who are dead and should be acting like dead people are supposed to act, which is to go wherever dead people are supposed to go and stay there."

Max's lips twitched. "That's great, Oliver. I'm glad you're getting into the, ah, spirit of the hunt." He turned back to the others. "Here's how I thought we'd split up. Jack, I'd like you to begin in here. Take down each book, shake it, and maybe we'll get lucky and find a treasure map hidden inside. Check the wall behind the bookcase as you work your way along. I know this is a big job. Oliver, would you be willing to help Jack?"

"I think I can handle it in here," Jack replied. "Put Oliver somewhere he'd feel more at ease. If I find I need help, I'll let you know."

Oliver smiled. "I don't believe Ghosty hid his treasure in my car. And since that's the only place here at Bates Motel on the Bluff that I feel safe, I might as well help Jack."

Max nodded. "Then we'll move on. Kathy, I thought you could begin in my office. I don't know what the room was used for during Cyrus's day, but considering it's a smaller version of this"—Max waved his arm to indicate the library—"there's a chance he would have used it for a study or office as well. Again, take down each book and tap the wall behind. I guess, for that matter, maybe we should all tap the walls along the baseboards in each room as we go along, although I hope we don't have to start tearing out walls or floorboards." Max frowned, thinking of his pristine paint and newly sanded floors.

"What are we listening for by tapping walls?" Elise asked.

"I'm not sure, but they're always doing that in books and movies when they're looking for secret passages."

"Actually, that's not a bad idea," Jack spoke up. "It's possible that when Cyrus had the house built, he designed an area where he could conceal a safe or maybe just a large space behind a wall. If so, it should sound hollow."

"Or behind a bookcase," Kathy added excitedly. "People in books are always finding some kind of hidden lever which causes a section of a bookcase to swing open, revealing a hidden room. Or sometimes there's a door which leads into passages that wind all through the interior walls of the house."

Elise jumped to her feet. "That's right. Max, there're floor-to-ceiling bookcases covering two walls in here. Perhaps this is where we should begin the search."

Max turned to Jack. "What do you think?"

"Oliver and I can handle this room. I'm afraid if we're all in here, we'll only get in each other's way and not accomplish anything."

"You're probably right. I'll leave this room for you two and I'll take the cellar. Elise, how about you start in the master bedroom?"

"Isn't the basement area huge?" she asked. "Wouldn't it be more productive if we both began down there?"

"Sure, if you'd like. I have to warn you, though, other than the wine cellar, the rest of the basement is pretty dark and dirty."

"Believe me, sugar," Oliver said. "Nasty doesn't begin to describe the conditions down there." He shuddered with distaste. "Maxwell, that's where you should have your new manager work. She'd probably feel right at home. I'll even bet she'd find some of her relatives hanging around in the corners."

Max ignored Oliver. "Okay, let's get started. How about if we work for a couple of hours and then meet back here?"

"Sounds good," Jack said. "Maybe one of us will have good news to report by then."

☾

"Wow, Max, this wine cellar is quite impressive," Elise said when they turned into a long, low room near the bottom of the steps. "Did you put all of this in?"

"No, the cellar area and the wine racks were already here. I just cleaned everything up and, believe it or not, while I was working in here I found a number of bottles of excellent wine stored in crates."

"You're kidding? How old? I mean did it date back to Cyrus's time?"

He nodded. "A few bottles did. Most were from the twenties and thirties. Maybe it was hidden away during prohibition."

"I'd assume some of it would be worth a great deal of money. What did you do with them?"

"I had a wine expert come out to take a look. Some of the bottles ended up being worth quite a bit. Those I sold." He shrugged. "I couldn't bring myself to drink wine that was worth that kind of money. Nor did I feel comfortable offering such extravagantly expensive wine to my guests, but the majority I kept. I'll have to bring a bottle up to our room one night." He smiled. "We can get into the whirlpool tub and I'll show you how to—"

"Stop right there."

Max had been edging closer until he'd backed her into one of the wine racks.

"That all sounds very nice, but right now we have a job to do. So put that intriguing idea on hold and let's get to work."

"Are you sure?" he whispered, taking her open hand and kissing each finger. "We could begin right here."

"Stop it." She pulled her hand from his, stepping out of reach. "The sooner we begin, the sooner we can go upstairs."

"Okay, sweet. You win, for now. Since this room is the cleanest and best lit, why don't you begin in here. Go along the wall looking for any irregularities in the positioning of the stones. Or a crack, either in the stones or running along their edges, that seems out of place. I'll be over in the next area, if you need me."

))

A few hours later, a dejected group sat around the dining room table eating omelets Oliver had hastily whipped up.

"I don't suppose we actually thought we'd be so lucky as to find the money on our first attempt," Jack said, breaking the silence.

"No, but I was so psyched up," Kathy said. "I hoped we'd at least find another clue."

"I know," Elise said. "I thought, for sure, when I showed Max those loose stones in the basement wall, I'd found something."

Max frowned. "She found something all right, something that's probably going to cost me a fortune to have fixed."

"What's that?" Jack asked.

"There's a part of the exterior basement wall that looks as if the stones have shifted. I'm just hoping it doesn't mean the foundation is beginning to crumble."

"And you're sure that's all it is?" Jack questioned. "There couldn't be a space behind there that's collapsed?"

"I doubt it." Max's frown deepened. "Maybe after we eat, Jack, you should take a look."

"Sure, I'd be happy to."

"Perhaps you found the treasure after all, Elise," Kathy said excitedly.

"Don't get yourself all worked up. I imagine Max is right, and it's nothing more than a structural problem," Jack said.

"Well, I think we should all go down and see," Kathy said. "If it's a secret room, I want to be there."

"Count me out," Oliver said. "I plan on taking a shower and then getting into bed with this great book I found while going through the bookcase."

"Really, what did you find?" Elise asked.

Oliver displayed a pristine copy of *The Castle of Otranto*.

Elise gaped with surprise. "Oliver, that's a horror novel."

"Well, I know that."

Elise looked confused. "But I thought you hated spooky stuff?"

"Only real life spooky stuff, sugar. Spooky stuff in books is okay."

Max shook his head. "Good grief, Oliver, just don't come screaming through the house in the middle of the night after reading that."

Kathy got to her feet. "If everyone's finished, let's go downstairs. I'm dying to find out if Elise discovered something."

))

"The good news is the problem isn't structural," said Jack a little while later as the four again sat together in the library, "but it was worth taking a second look."

"It was worth taking a second look because in Jack's professional opinion my entire foundation is not collapsing," Max said with evident relief.

"I thought, for sure, when Jack found that chunk of silver ore, Cyrus was going to help lead us to the treasure." Kathy glanced at the table where the ore had been. "Jack, what did you do with it?"

"Do with what?"

"That chunk of ore that was sitting on that table." She pointed.

"I didn't do anything with it."

"Well, it's not there. Max, did you move it?"

"No. It was right there the last time I saw it."

"Elise?"

"No, I didn't touch it."

"It must have been Oliver," Max said.

Jack shook his head. "I don't think so. He was working through those bookcases over there." He indicated the far wall. "I didn't see him go near that table."

"Then where is it?" Kathy asked.

"Let's look around on the floor," Elise suggested. "Perhaps it got knocked off the table."

"I don't see it anywhere." Kathy stood and brushed off her knees.

"Okay, everyone, it has to be here," Jack said.

"We've looked all over, and it's just disappeared," Kathy replied.

Jack sighed with exasperation. "It didn't leave on its own."

"I'm going to go see if Oliver's still awake, and if he knows anything about it," Kathy said, leaving the room.

"Max, I have a bad feeling," Elise said. "All I can think about is the night someone broke into my apartment."

"Yes, but you weren't at home when they broke in. We've been in this house all evening."

"Not in this room," she pointed out. "We were all in the dining room, then downstairs. There was plenty of time for someone to come in."

"Someone like whom?"

Elise narrowed her eyes. "Someone who knew about the chunk of ore. Someone like Constance."

"Oh, for God's sake, Elise. I know you don't like Constance, but why in the hell would she want to steal that silver ore? She didn't know what it was or its significance."

"You don't know that."

"Wait a minute, you two," Jack interrupted. "Let's try and figure this out rationally."

"Oliver doesn't know anything about it," Kathy said, coming back into the room. She paused. "What's going on?"

"Elise believes Constance might have had something to do with the missing ore," Max said.

"I agree with Elise," Kathy said. "She did seem interested in knowing what it was when she was here earlier."

Jack shook his head. "Kathy, stay out of it."

"I don't care. I think Elise has a valid point. Who, other than Constance, knew about the ore?"

Elise gritted her teeth. "Well, do either of you skeptics have a better solution? Max, have you even bothered to check to see if the window locks in here have been tampered with?"

"No, but if it will make you happy, I'll do that right now." He strode purposefully across the room to the French windows.

"Well, I'll be damned."

"What is it?" Jack asked.

"This window isn't locked, and I normally keep them latched." He pushed it open and stuck his head out.

"Do you see anything?" Elise asked.

"No, it's too dark."

"Maybe there are footprints," Kathy suggested. "Max, where's a flashlight?"

"We haven't had any rain lately, and the ground is pretty dry," Jack said. "I doubt there would be any visible prints."

"Max, what do you think?" Elise asked.

"Jack's right. There won't be any footprints." He went to check the other French window. "There's also a real possibility someone came in here and took that chunk of ore." Max saw the triumphant look on Elise's face. "But I'm not convinced that person was Constance."

Kathy put her hands on her hips. "Then who?"

"If I had to guess, the same person who broke into Elise's apartment."

"Whoever took the ore had to know it was here," Elise said.

"I agree," Max said. "Anyone standing by one of those windows could have seen it sitting there."

"Wait a minute," Jack said. "Are you seriously thinking someone was outside listening earlier when we found the ore?"

Max shrugged. "It's the only thing that makes any sense. The other night, Elise thought she saw someone standing out there looking in. I just assumed she saw Martin Todd go by, but maybe it wasn't him."

"Perhaps it was Martin that I saw, and he's also the one who took the ore," Elise suggested.

Max sighed. "Why would he do that? We've spent time with Martin, and he's a perfectly nice guy. I can't see him skulking around this house peering into windows."

"I, personally, find the idea of someone not only peering into windows but also having the nerve to come in, scary as hell," Kathy stated.

"I agree," Elise said. "Max, don't you have a security system?"

"No. I didn't feel it was necessary. Besides, how can you have a security system when you have guests who could be coming in and out at all hours?"

"I'm not going to sleep until we make sure there's no one hidden in this house," Elise said.

Kathy looked thoughtful. "Could we be getting upset over nothing? What if Cyrus or Virginia took the ore?"

Jack rose from his chair. "Okay, on that weird thought, I'm going to help Max check the house, and then I'm going to bed. Otherwise, we'll sit here all night speculating."

Max yawned. "I agree. If Cyrus or Virginia took it, maybe by morning they'll be done with their little joke and will have given it back."

Scowling, Cyrus materialized in front of the bookcase once the room was empty.

"Joke, indeed. Do they honestly believe I would have them find that ore only to take it away?"

Virginia, seated in the chair Jack had just vacated, sighed. "They're scared and confused. I'm just thankful they didn't encounter the thief."

"If you hadn't stopped me, I could have intervened and exposed the intruder."

Virginia shook her head. "That would have served no purpose. They still haven't unlocked the secret. It's enough they know the ore exists." She rose and went to stand by Cyrus. "They're getting close. We must be patient." Her eyes narrowed. "As for our thief, we'll be ready when the time is right."

The smell of cigar smoke filled the room seconds before Garrison appeared, leaning against the mantel.

"Ah, sweet sister, you and your murderous husband think you're so clever." He flicked imaginary ash into the fireplace and grinned. "But the ore is gone and there're others cleverer than your group of bumbling amateurs. With my help, they will succeed where yours fail."

Virginia cocked her head. "You've been acting quite the exhibitionist, Garrison, and your antics are becoming rather tiresome. Your theatrical displays have proven useless in dissuading Max and Elise from continuing their search and discovering the clues they'll need. So I suggest you resign in defeat."

The red tip of Garrison's cigar matched the glow in his eyes. "I've been stuck in this mausoleum with you and the man who murdered me for over a century." His voice rasped like a rusty hinge. "The day my revenge is complete will be my release. I will stop at nothing nor will I allow anyone to stop me from fulfilling my goal." He flung his arms into the air and fire shot from the candles on the mantel, igniting Virginia's portrait as Garrison vanished.

"Cyrus!" Virginia screamed. "Do something."

"My dear, calm down, it's not real. It's only an illusion. See?" He pointed to where the fire had disappeared. "But, I must say, it was very well done."

Silver tears pooled in Virginia's eyes and her voice quavered. "I swear I could feel the heat."

Cyrus put his arms around her and held her close. "I would never let him harm you, my love. You know that."

She rested her head on his shoulder. "Cyrus, I'm afraid."

He kissed the top of her head. "Don't be. Garrison's plans to outwit us are as illusory as his fire. Even with assistance, he cannot overpower us."

She looked into his face. "Oh, Cyrus, I do hope you are right."

Upstairs, Elise sighed gratefully and sank down into the whirlpool tub's steaming bubbles. She closed her eyes and laid her head back. Her disappointment at not discovering anything during their search and her unease over the missing ore had made her too tense to sleep. As she began to relax, she let her thoughts drift away.

"Here, I thought you could use this."

She opened her eyes to see Max handing her a glass of chilled white wine.

"Thanks. Just what I need. Is this the promised bottle from your wine cellar?"

"Yep. I had Oliver put it on ice before dinner. Do you mind if I join you?" Not waiting for a response, he began removing his clothes.

"I take it this means you didn't find an unwelcome guest lurking in the house?"

"No, all's quiet."

She watched appreciatively as he removed his shirt, revealing his muscular chest with its thatch of thick hair. Her eyes followed his hands as they unzipped his fly. As he shrugged out of his jeans, her mouth went a little dry at the sight of his already hard shaft.

"See what you do to me, sweetheart?" He grinned and stepped into the tub, sitting across from her. "And all you had to do was look at me."

She smiled and took a sip of her wine. "I doubt that's all it takes. I have a feeling your imagination has a lot to do with your, ah, problem."

"You might be partially right." A grin spread across his face as he reached for a bar of scented soap. "Would you like me to show you what I'm imagining right now?"

A thrill of anticipation danced across her skin. "I'm not sure. What do you have in mind?"

"You'll see." He picked up her foot and lathered it with sweet smelling soap as he gently massaged her arch.

"That feels so good."

"I'm glad you're enjoying it."

"*Mmmm*. I could lay here and let you do that for hours."

He chuckled and gave the same attention to her other foot.

As his fingers worked their magic, she closed her eyes and sighed with pure bliss. When she felt his hands sliding up the inside of her legs, coming to rest at the junction in between, she jumped. "Max?"

"What? Just lie back and enjoy what I'm doing. Let the jets and me massage your troubles away."

She did as he asked and soon her body reacted in a way she knew only Max could make her feel. She stared into his eyes. Her breath coming in shallow little gasps, she opened her legs to give his fingers better access.

Knowing her climax was almost upon her, he withdrew his hand and gently pulled her toward him.

"Max, don't stop."

"I want you to come here to me." He said softly. "Put one knee on either side of me. That's it." He guided her into position. "Raise up, sweet." He slid down a little in the water. "Now bring your sweet-tasting self to me."

"Max," she squeaked. "I can't do that."

"Oh, yes you can." With his hands on her bottom, he pressed her forward so his tongue could take over where his hands had left off.

She let out a moan of pure pleasure, letting go of any inhibitions. She gripped the side of the tub and let his skillful mouth bring her to exquisite surrender.

"See, sweetheart, I knew you could do it." He chuckled low as he pulled her gently downward, kissing his way up her stomach until he reached her breasts. "I love the taste of every inch of you." Suckling one taut nipple, then the other, he guided her down onto his shaft and filled her welcoming heat.

"Now, sweetheart," he said, grinning wickedly, "you're going to ride me."

She threw her head back and fell into rhythm with his hard, deep thrusts. She dug her fingers into his shoulders and rode him faster and faster, taking them both higher and higher until, as one, their bodies shuddered in sweet release.

Hunger for gold is made greater as more gold is acquired.
— Aurelius Clemens Prudentius

Chapter 24

Saturday morning following breakfast the group assembled in the library, eager and ready to begin.

"Okay, we have all of today to finish the rooms we started with yesterday, and if we don't find anything in those, we'll move on to the others," Max said.

Kathy looked over at Jack and frowned. "Having Jack work in the library was a bad idea. It's taking him forever because he's thumbing through every book as he goes along. Perhaps Elise should take over in here."

"I'm just being thorough," Jack replied. "We wouldn't want to miss a clue, would we? Don't worry; Oliver and I are moving right along."

"Okay, well, I still have a lot of space to cover in the basement," Max continued. "Elise, you've finished the wine cellar. How about working on the master bedroom?"

"Sure, where should I begin?"

"There's the large walk-in closet. Check around the walls, floor and ceiling. As long as you're up there, you might as well go ahead and check all of the closets on the second floor." He paused, knitting his brows. "You know, now that I think about it, when I was painting the linen closet for housekeeping to use, the dimensions seemed a little off. Jack, maybe you should take a look in there."

Jack nodded. "It would be a lot easier if you had the blueprints for this house."

"I know, but I don't. Maybe Cyrus has a set we could borrow."

"What would really help is if Cyrus or Virginia would just show us where the money is," Kathy said with annoyance.

"Watch it, sugar. Never criticize the demonic trio, or you might find yourself turned into a bat or something equally disgusting. What?" Oliver frowned. "Why are you all staring at me like that? I wouldn't put anything past those three."

Jack grinned. "No one can ever say you don't have a hell of an imagination."

"No kidding." Max shook his head. "Want to check out the linen closet first, Jack?

"Sure, let's go up now." Jack stood. "Oliver, can you handle working alone in here until I get back?"

"I'll stay and help Oliver while you're gone," Kathy offered. "I've already searched more than half of Max's office. It won't take me long to finish."

"I'll start on the master closet." Elise got to her feet. "Good luck, everyone. Somehow, I feel that today is going to be our lucky day."

$$\smile$$

"Well, Jack, what's your professional opinion?" Max asked.

Along two sides of the closet, shelves held stacks of folded sheets, towels, and blankets. On the third wall, soap, tissue, and miniature bottles of shampoo, conditioner, and lotion were lined up in neat rows.

"Constance did a nice job organizing all of this. As far as the proportions, I'm not sure. What's on either side of the closet walls?"

Max rubbed his chin. "Let me see. We're standing just off the central hall, so to our right would be a guest bath adjoining one of the rooms, and to our left must be the little sitting area for the master suite."

Jack stepped back, studying each wall. "This closet is wide, but not all that deep. What's behind it?"

Perplexed, Max glanced around.

"What I'm saying is the bathroom on the one side and the sitting room on the other must run from the center hall to the outside wall. Obviously, this closet doesn't. So what's behind that wall?" He pointed to the back of the closet.

Max nodded with understanding. "Hell, I don't know, but how do we find out?"

"Let's do it this way. You go into the sitting room and I'll go on the other side into the bathroom. We'll start from the corner of the outside wall and work our way back. Knock on the wall as you go along. Perhaps we'll be able to hear if there's an empty space."

"And if there is?"

"Then, buddy, we do major damage to your paint."

"Jack, come here," Max called a short while later. "I found something."

Jack hurried into the room to see Max kneeling on the floor pulling on a section of the baseboard. "What did you find?"

"This entire wall sounds hollow and this baseboard is loose. I noticed it when I painted this room, but put it on my list of things to be repaired." He gave one last tug and it came away in his hand. "Hand me that flashlight," he said as he slid onto his stomach. "Holy shit, Jack, there's something behind there. Look."

Jack flattened himself on the floor next to Max. "Damn, you're right. Christ, Max, I think it's a flight of stairs."

"Let me see."

Jack handed Max the flashlight and he peered into the hole. "Son of a bitch, you're right." He turned to Jack. "Now what?"

I hate to say it, but we need to make this hole bigger."

Max shook his head. "No way, that wall is lath and plaster."

Jack sat back on his heels. "Okay, if this wall is original to the house, is the wall on the bathroom side as well?"

Max nodded. "Cyrus must have had indoor plumbing installed when the house was built. I've been modernizing them as I go."

Jack smiled. "Well then, buddy, you'd better be prepared to pay Constance some overtime because we're about to mess up all her hard work."

"Shit," Max got to his feet and sighed. "We're going in through the linen closet?"

Jack nodded. "If that's the top of the stairs, it might be easier to repair."

"Let's tell Elise and you and she can begin removing all the linens while I go get my tools."

"What's going on?" Elise asked, coming into the room.

"Now, Elise, don't get too excited, but we may have found something."

"Seriously?"

Max pointed. "There's a staircase behind that wall. I'm going to go get some tools so we can get a better look, but we have to go in through the closet. So I need you and Jack to clear it out."

"Wow. This could be it." She clapped her hands. "Wait until I tell Oliver and Kathy."

"Max is right, Elise. Don't get too excited yet. I've seen old houses where, for one reason or another, people blocked staircases to either close off floors or make larger rooms. If I had to guess, I'd say that's what happened here. I'm sorry," Jack said, seeing the excitement leave her face.

He frowned. "You know what? Kathy's right, I am a killjoy."

"Now, what have you done?" Kathy asked when she and Oliver entered the room. "Max told us about the staircase on his way downstairs, so we came up to help."

"Jack doesn't think the stairs have anything to do with the missing money," Elise said as she carried sheets and laid them on one of the guestroom beds.

"I agree," Oliver said. "You're not going to find money behind that wall; you're going to find a body that's been closed up in there for God knows how long." His voice became shriller as he spoke. "And I'll bet one of the demonic trio had something to do with it."

"If you're right, Oliver, one of us had better know how to kill a zombie," Max said coming back down the hall, tools in hand.

Elise and Kathy, mounds of towels in their arms, gaped at Max.

"Not funny," Elise said.

Max knelt down in the closet, pulled out the bottom shelf, and pried at a plank in the back wall.

"I can't stand the suspense," Kathy said. "Hurry up."

"I'm not looking, I'm not looking," chanted Oliver, his hands covering his face. "You people are really going to piss them off by letting whatever's in there out."

"Hey, Max, that's cedar. Clever way to make it a cedar closet." said Jack as he took the board from Max.

The space was large enough for Max to stick his head through.

"Max, what do you see?"

"Well, it's awfully dark in here. Hand me that flashlight. Okay, that's better. It looks like Jack's right again. There's a staircase, but it curves and it's so dark I can't see past the turn."

Max pulled his head back through the hole. "Jack, if I pull off another board, I should be able to get in there.

"I don't know. Who knows how secure those stairs are. There could be places where they're weak from dry rot."

"Max, don't do it," Elise cried. "You might fall and get hurt, then how would we ever get you out?"

"If I had a stronger flashlight, I might be able to see more from here," Max said.

"What about that work light in the basement?" Elise asked.

"Good idea."

"I'll go get it," Elise said.

"I'll come with you," Kathy said.

"I'm making a pitcher of Bloody Marys," Oliver said. "I think that sounds like the appropriate beverage."

"What do you see?" Jack asked after Elise and Kathy returned with the light.

"This is incredible," Max said peering into the opening. As far as I can tell, it's nothing more than a staircase that someone walled off. I don't see any other way in, other than where we are now."

"Do the stairs seem secure?"

"I really can't tell. I'll bet they were used as the servants' stairs at one time."

"Probably. What do you think? Do you want to go in?"

Max pulled his head out. "I'm not sure there's any point. It's pretty narrow in there. I don't see where anything could be hidden." He saw Elise's disappointment and sighed. "If you want me to, I'll go in and search, but I don't want to get your hopes up."

She shook her head. "There probably isn't any reason to. And it's not worth you getting hurt if it isn't safe. Come on, Kathy, I could use one of Oliver's Bloody Marys."

"Damn it, Jack, I wish we'd never found the stairs," Max said after Elise and Kathy had left. "Did you see the look on Elise's face?

Jack nodded.

Max glared at the hole. "Jack, if the stairs begin up here, where do they end?"

"Good question."

I'm afraid the only way we're going to find out what's at the bottom is for me to go in."

"Now, wait a minute. We're not sure those stairs are safe. Maybe, judging by their location up here, we can figure it out. What's directly below us?"

Max sat back on his heels. "I'd say either the library or my office. But I don't recall any walls being out of proportion."

Jack smiled. "Well, that's where I'm the expert. So I suggest we go take a look."

"Who's ready?" Oliver asked, carrying the iced pitcher of Bloody Marys in to the library.

"I am," Kathy said.

Elise nodded. "Me, too."

"Now, don't you two look so glum," Max said as he and Jack joined them. "We've got another idea."

"Way to go, Jack," Kathy said after Max explained. "How can we help?"

"For now, we'll leave it up to Jack and his architect's eye." Max poured himself a drink. "If he finds something that's out of kilter, then we'll decide what to do—which will most likely involve cutting holes in my freshly painted walls."

"I'm sorry about all this." Elise sat next to Max and put her arms around his neck. "I promise, if we find the treasure, I'll hire someone to fix your walls and anything else you need repaired."

"Don't tell him that, sugar," Oliver said, "or he'll have you putting on a new roof."

Elise smiled. "Oliver, if we find the treasure, I'll be happy to put on a new roof and anything else he wants."

"You'll put on anything I want?" Max asked, a wicked gleam in his eyes as he pulled her close.

She gave him a quick kiss. "I suppose, as long as it's within reason." She chuckled as he whispered his request in her ear. Gently pushing him away, she rose. "We have to find the treasure first. Then, perhaps, I'll think about it. But for now, I can't just sit here. Let's go see if Jack's found anything."

Jack, tape measure in hand, was standing in the central hall frowning.

"Did you find something?" Max asked.

Jack hesitated. "I'm not sure. The built-in bookcases in your office and those in the library back up to this wall. If my calculations are correct, there's more space here than necessary."

"So the bottom of the staircase could be enclosed behind that wall," Kathy said. "Jack, you're a genius."

"Why, thank you, love. But before you lavish me with praise, let's find out if I'm right. Max, we have two choices. Either we cut a hole down here, or we go in through the closet. Considering this wall is lath and plaster, I'd suggest we use the opening upstairs. Although that means you'll have to go in on the top of the steps, and as we said, we're not sure they're safe."

Max looked up at the ceiling, then down the hall toward the back of the house, then at the wall in front of him.

"I think you might be right. The location would make sense. If the stairs came out here, they'd be close to the kitchen and the back of the house." He smiled. "So I guess I'm going in. And I agree with you, I don't want to have to cut out this lath if I don't have to."

"Max, those stairs could give way beneath you," Elise said. "I don't want you getting hurt."

"What if we put a rope around Maxwell?" Oliver suggested. "Then, if he falls, we can at least pull him back up."

"Good idea," Max said. "I've got some strong rope in the basement. We can tie one end to me and the other to a piece of furniture."

"I don't know about this," Elise said. "I have a bad feeling something is going to go wrong."

Max pulled her into his arms. "I'll be fine. You want to find the treasure, don't you?"

"Yes, but—"

"Hush now. No *buts*." He kissed her soundly. "I'll talk to you the entire time I'm in there, so you'll know I'm all right."

Elise took a deep breath. "Okay, just please be careful."

"How about Kathy and Oliver stay down here, so when Max makes it to the bottom he can knock on the other side of the wall and we'll know if we're right?" Jack said. "Elise, you and I can wait upstairs. I'll be able to help Max if there's a problem, and you can hear him. What does everyone think?"

"Sounds good to me," Max said. "I'll go get the rope and meet you upstairs."

As Max squeezed through the opening onto the staircase, Jack said, "Go easy and watch your footing. Test your weight on the stairs with one foot before putting down all your weight. When you're in, I'll hand you the flashlight."

"Be careful, Max," Elise called, peering around Jack.

"Okay, the stairs seem sturdy enough," Max said. "I'm heading down."

"I'm going to play out the rope as you descend," Jack said. "Let me know when you reach the turn in the stairs."

"Okay, I'm here. Nothing so far but a lot of dust, cobwebs and spiders."

"Eww." Elise grimaced. "I'm glad it's him and not me in there."

"I'm heading down the last few steps."

Cr-rack. B-b-bump.

"Shit . . . Damn . . . Ow . . . Fuck . . ."

"Max?" Elise dropped to her knees and crawled to the opening. "Are you hurt? The lights went out up here."

"Max, I can't hold onto the rope," Jack yelled as it slid faster and faster through his hands until it disappeared through the opening. "Damn it."

"Jack what's happening?" Elise cried.

"I don't know." He was on his knees next to Elise. "Max, can you hear us?"

There was no reply.

"Max!" Jack again called.

Elise's eyes brimmed with tears. "Oh, my god, Jack. He must be hurt. What do we do now?"

"If he doesn't answer soon, we'll have to knock out the downstairs wall." Jack stuck his head back into the opening. "Max, can you hear me?"

"I'm all right," Max softly replied.

"Max, I can hardly hear you. Are you hurt?" Elise asked.

"My foot went through a rotten step and I hit the back of my head on the wall."

"How far down are you?" Jack asked.

"I'm at the bottom. And I can hear Kathy knocking on the other side of the wall."

"Well, that answers one question. Now we just have to figure out how to get you out. Can you tell what happened to the rope?"

"It's lying here next to me."

"It was as if it was being pulled right through my hands," Jack said.

"I don't think there's any way I can toss it back up to you."

"Jack, if he's hurt, how are we going to get him out?" Elise asked.

"We'll get him. Don't worry. The first thing we need is to get the lights working." The words had no sooner left Jack's mouth when they flickered on. He stared at Elise.

She shrugged. "I don't know."

Jack sighed and stuck his head back into the opening. "Max, the lights up here are back on. Is there another rope in the basement?"

"Yes, over by the work area. I've managed to get my foot out."

"Can you put your weight on it?" Jack asked.

"It's pretty cramped down here. I have to maneuver myself around to stand. Ow, damn it. It's sore, but I think I can walk."

"Can you tell if there's anything beneath the stairs?" Jack asked.

"Hang on a minute. I'll have to knock out the back of the step to see."

"We heard Max on the other side of the wall," Kathy exclaimed, running into the room, Oliver on her heels. "The treasure has to be hidden in there somewhere."

"It could be," Elise agreed. "But Max is hurt and he's stuck down there."

"I knew it, I knew it," Oliver declared. "I told Maxwell not to go in there. Now those demons have him trapped."

"Everyone quiet down, I can't hear Max," Jack said with impatience.

"I've got the back of the stair knocked out and it looks like there might be a rather large opening behind the staircase, but it's so dark I can't be sure," Max called.

"Can you climb up on your own? Or do I need to get the other rope?" Jack asked.

"Let me try. Other than the rotten step the rest were pretty solid."

Moments later, Max emerged from the hole, covered in dust and cobwebs.

"Good God, Maxwell, you look like a living dust bunny."

"I feel like one." He let out a huge sneeze.

Elise ran to him and threw her hands around his neck. "Oh, I was so scared."

He held her tight. "I'm all right, sweet. It's only a little sprain."

She ran her hand over the back of his head finding a good sized lump. He winced.

"Damn, don't. That hurts."

"We need to get some ice on your head and on your foot," Elise said.

He gently pushed her away. "I'm fine. I just want to get cleaned up. I'll meet all of you back in the library."

"What's that chiming sound?" Kathy asked.

"What?" Max glanced around.

"Listen."

"That's the front doorbell," Max said. "Who in the hell could that be?"

Hell has three gates: lust, anger, and greed.
— Bhagavad-Gita

Chapter 25

Elise headed for the hall. "You go wash up, and I'll see who it is."

"Jack and I will wait in the library," Kathy said.

"I'm heading for the kitchen to make another pitcher of drinks," Oliver stated. "Tell whoever it is we're not buying anything and to go away."

Elise opened the front door to see Sandy standing on the porch. She plastered a smile on her face. "Well, hi. What brings you out this way?"

"I hope I'm not intruding, but I'm on my way to Ann Arbor and since I didn't get a chance to see Max's inn, I thought I'd drop by." She looked embarrassed. "If this isn't a good time, I can come back another day. I should have called first."

Unable to come up with a good excuse not to let her in, Elise stepped back. "No, it's fine. Come on in." Even though Sandy was a good friend, she didn't want anyone to know about the hidden staircase. "I do have to apologize, though, we're still in the process of organizing the upstairs, and it's quite a mess."

"No problem. I understand the first floor is gorgeous enough."

Elise glanced up as Max slowly came down the stairs. "Max, look, Sandy's dropped by." Before she could continue, Sandy spoke up.

"Hi, Max. I'm being totally rude, but I was hoping for a tour."

"I've already told her what a mess the upstairs is," Elise said.

Max hesitated for just a second before he smiled. "You're always welcome. Come on and I'll show you around." He limped slightly as he led the way into the front parlor.

"What happened to your foot?" Sandy asked.

Max shrugged. "Just a slight accident. I'm fine."

When they had concluded their tour of the lower rooms and were seated in the library, drinks in hand, Max introduced Sandy to the others.

"Every time I've entered this room, I've felt as if I've stepped back in time," Sandy said. The painting above the fireplace caught her eye. "I see Virginia's portrait is still here. She's beautiful and, at the same time, kind of eerie. She almost seems to be watching us." Sandy gave an involuntary shudder. "Did you know they say she can't be taken down?"

Oliver opened his mouth to speak, but a sharp glance from Max made him close it again.

"I didn't know that," Elise said. "How strange. Have you tried?"

Max shrugged. "I like her there, so I left her alone."

"So tell me, how's the treasure hunt going?" Sandy asked. "I couldn't believe it when Elise told me the story of the missing silver." She paused and looked around the surprised group. "Have I said something wrong?"

She turned to Elise. "I'm sorry. I just assumed everyone here knew I had heard."

Elise sat speechless. It was her fault for telling Sandy everything when she was so upset, but hadn't she realized it had been said in confidence? Now she had to wonder how many other people she might have told. Before Elise could come up with a coherent response, Max laughed.

"Sandy, if Cyrus had buried treasure in this house, trust me, I would have already found it. I had to practically strip this house from top to bottom, and all I found were some dead mice and dry rot." He shook his head. "If there ever was a treasure, it's long gone."

"Well, that's too bad. Elise was so sure it was here in Cedar Bend."

Finally able to find her voice, Elise said, "I always knew it was a long shot." She smiled. "But it was worth trying. Besides, if I hadn't come to Cedar Bend, I would have never met all of you."

"That's right," Max said. "If it weren't for Cyrus and his buried treasure, Elise and I would have never met."

Elise was suddenly aware of the drop in temperature. Gazing around, she realized the others had noticed as well. When she turned to see Sandy's reaction, she was surprised to see her calmly sitting sipping her drink. Elise watched in horror as the prisms hanging from the Tiffany lamp on the table next to Sandy began to spin wildly. Seeming oblivious to this, Sandy set down her drink and smiled at Oliver.

"That was a wonderful Bloody Mary. I'll have to get your recipe."

Bug-eyed, Oliver opened and closed his mouth, but nothing came out. To Elise's relief, Max spoke up.

"So, Sandy, you say you're on your way to Ann Arbor for an exhibit?"

Sandy nodded. "That's right. I've always been interested in stained glass, and they have a local artist's work on display. I'd better get on my way."

Bang.

Everyone jumped, except Sandy, who was just staring at them all.

"What's wrong?"

"Oh, Jesus, not again," Oliver muttered.

Elise laughed. "Nothing. I'll walk you to the door."

"I'll go with you," Max said, also rising.

When they stepped into the entry hall, they found the front door standing wide open.

"That's strange," Sandy said frowning. "Elise, I'm sure you closed it behind me."

"Maybe it didn't latch and the wind blew it open," Max suggested.

Sandy laughed. "Well, I'm glad it was only the door. I was afraid Cyrus's ghost was going to float past."

These words had no sooner left her mouth when a cloud of dark smoke appeared floating above her.

Stunned, Elise tried to gather her wits. Sandy still seemed unaware of what was happening.

"Max, thanks again for the tour. Your inn is fabulous." She hugged Elise. "I'll see you Monday at work."

As Sandy walked through the open front door, Elise grabbed Max's hand. The smoke hovered behind Sandy until she got into her car, then disappeared as she drove away.

Max closed the door. "Christ, what the hell was that about?"

Elise let out a shaky breath. "I don't know, but Max, she didn't know any of it was happening."

"I know." They walked back into the library.

"Perhaps whoever it is can't appear to anyone but us," Max said.

"That was the most bizarre thing I've ever seen," Kathy said. "She just sat there while that lamp practically spun around next to her."

"I think it was more of Ghosty's bullshit sense of humor," Oliver said.

Elise opened her mouth to tell them about the incident in the entry hall, but when she glanced at Max, he shook his head.

Instead, she collapsed into a chair and said, "I still can't believe Sandy asked about the silver. I told her not to say anything to anyone."

"Well, Elise, you know, a secret is something you tell one person at a time," Jack said.

Max snorted. "Isn't that the truth?"

"Hopefully she hasn't told too many people, but in case she has, we'd better find the treasure quickly," Kathy said.

"I may have another idea." Jack got up and stood in front of the tall bookcase.

"What?" Max asked.

"I've been sitting here thinking. The staircase runs between this bookcase and the one on the opposite wall in your office. If there is a hidden door to the space beneath the stairs, it would have to be in here or in your office. My first choice would be in here. The problem is finding the release switch. It could be anything from pulling out the right book to a small button or knob hidden in the wood."

"What if we each take a section to examine?" Max suggested. "The guys can take the higher shelves while Kathy and Elise begin on the lower ones."

Jack nodded. "Sounds like as good a plan as any. We're going to need a couple of stepladders to reach those top shelves."

"Sure, I keep them in the basement," Max said.

When Max and Jack returned with the ladders, Oliver was studying the top of the bookcase, wrinkling his nose in distaste.

"Sugar, don't tell me it was you who picked out that hideous sculpture."

"What are you talking about?" Kathy looked where Oliver pointed. "I never choose anything hideous."

"I've never noticed it before," Elise said. "But Oliver's right, it's atrocious. I wonder what it's supposed to be?"

"It looks like some kind of weird cactus," Jack said.

"Not a cactus," Kathy said, "more like a weird-shaped mountain. How about you, Max? Do you know what it's supposed to be?"

Max glanced toward the top of the bookcase. "I haven't a clue. It was probably here when I bought the house."

"Let's put up one of those ladders and get it down," Kathy said.

"Aren't we supposed to be trying to find the switch that opens the bookcase?" Jack asked. "Why are we wasting our time worrying about ugly pottery?"

"It's horrid. It needs to come down anyway," Kathy said. "We can't leave it up there."

"Can you tell what it is?" Elise asked when Oliver reached the top of the ladder.

"No, it's as grotesque from up here as it was from down there. Besides, it's covered in cobwebs and dust. I think one of Constance's relatives has been living up here. *Ackk*!"

Oliver yelped as the ladder tipped out from under him. He grabbed at the cornice, his legs kicking franticly as they scrambled for purchase.

"Hang on, Oliver," they all screamed at once.

Max picked up the overturned ladder and placed it back under his feet. "What the hell happened?" he asked when a shaken Oliver reached the bottom.

"Didn't you see it?"

"See what?" Max asked.

"The bookcase," Oliver exclaimed. "As soon as I tried to pick that ugly cactus thing up, I heard a click and felt the case to my left move. It nudged the ladder enough to make me lose my balance."

"Oh my God, Oliver," Elise cried. "You've found it. You've found the secret room."

Kathy jumped up and down. "Max, hurry up. Open it."

"Everyone step back," Jack said. "Let's get a closer look before we go rushing in."

"Jack's right," Max said. He set the ladder out of the way and examined the small opening, then eased the bookcase from the wall.

Elise couldn't contain her excitement. "Max, what's back there?"

"Whoa . . ."

"Max?"

"Be patient, Elise. This hasn't been moved in quite a while. It's not sliding as easily as it's supposed to."

Kathy grabbed Elise's hands and they twirled round and round laughing.

Jack had to shout to be heard over the girls. "Max, is there a light inside?"

"No, get a lamp. You can plug it in over there," Max shouted back.

Jack grinned as the girls dragged Oliver into their crazed dance.

"Who wants to be the first one to go in?" Max asked.

Kathy collapsed into a chair. "I think it should be Elise."

"Okay, here goes." Elise took a deep breath and walked to the bookcase. Pausing, she glanced back. "Max, now I'm scared to look."

He nudged her forward. "It'll be okay. Go on."

She crossed her fingers, then edged through the narrow opening—and stopped. Unable to speak, she went slowly into the room, bent down and picked up the only item there. She choked back a sob of disappointment as she read the piece of paper in her hand.

Max came up behind her. "Elise, what did you find?"

She handed him the paper, then let her tears fall.

"Well, sweetheart, I guess this is your proof that at one time there was a treasure hidden here." Max took her in his arms. "Don't cry like that."

"What is it?" Kathy whispered.

He held it out, showing them a single thousand-dollar silver certificate.

"Christ," Oliver murmured. "There actually was a treasure."

"Poor Elise. I can't handle listening to her cry like that." Kathy walked back into the library. "What a letdown. I hoped, for her sake, we'd find the money."

"I know," Jack said. "But now she knows for sure. She no longer has to wonder. She can put that part of her life to rest."

"Oh, Max," Elise wept. "I wanted to be the one to find the treasure for Grace, and I failed."

Still standing in the middle of the empty room, Max held her close. "Elise, sweetheart, you did your best. You're the only one in your family who even tried. You can write your own diary now, telling all about how you found the place where the silver was hidden."

"Yeah, right. I can just hear my descendants talking about 'Crazy Elise', and how she wrote about having a ghost that helped her find the missing treasure that wasn't there. Why do you think Cyrus even bothered showing us those silver crescents and the chunk of ore, knowing the money was gone?"

"Maybe he wanted you to discover this for yourself so you would stop searching."

"Perhaps, but if so, it wasn't very nice of him to build up my hopes only to let me down."

He brushed her lips with a soft kiss. "If he were alive, I'd punch him in the nose. Now, are you ready to get out of here?"

She smiled weakly. "I'd like to punch him in the nose myself." She sighed and glanced around. "Yes, let's leave. I hope you don't mind; I'd like to go upstairs. I'd like to be alone for a while."

"Sure, if that's what you want. I'll be up later."

He watched as Elise stopped to thank Kathy, Jack and Oliver for all their help. Then, shoulders slumped, she left the library.

Tears filled Kathy's eyes. "I wish Elise had never found those diaries."

Oliver's eyes were also wet. "I think I'll go bake something extremely fattening, and full of chocolate and whipped cream to cheer us all up."

"Good idea," Kathy said. "I'll help."

"This is quite amazing," Jack said, inspecting the bookcase. "I've read about hidden rooms, but I never expected to actually see one. I wonder if we're the first to find the opening."

"That sculpture, or whatever it is, didn't look as if it had been touched in decades," Oliver said. "And it's attached somehow to the bookcase. When I tried to pick it up, it wouldn't budge."

"Oliver, how did you make it open?" Kathy asked.

He shrugged. "I haven't the slightest idea. I just tried to pick that thing up and heard the click."

"Well, it's all over," Max said. "We just have to find a way to take Elise's mind off her disappointment."

Before Max could sit down, the phone rang.

"Hello, Inn on the Bluff."

"Max, it's Sandy. If Elise is in the room, don't say my name."

"She's not here. What's wrong?"

"Sorry, I didn't mean to sound so dramatic," she hurried to explain. "I couldn't say anything while I was there, but I didn't know if you knew that Tuesday is her twenty-fifth birthday. It might be fun to surprise her with a little party. What do you think?"

"That's a great idea. Where and what time?"

"I thought we could try that new Mexican restaurant that just opened."

"Sounds good. If we're going to surprise her, how am I to get her there?"

"Why don't you tell her the two of you are going out for dinner? She won't know we'll all be there as well. Make sure to tell everyone else to get to the restaurant early, say around six o'clock."

"Will do. Thanks again, Sandy."

"That's what friends are for. See you Tuesday."

Elise sat cross-legged on the bedroom floor staring at her own reflection in the cheval mirror.

"Virginia, why did Cyrus lead me on like that only to pull the rug out from under me?" she asked aloud, pausing as if waiting for an answer. "I thought when I met Max and saw Cyrus's tombstone I had to be on the right track. It turns out I was, but for what?"

She laughed hollowly. "All the ups and downs Max and I have been through for the past week were for nothing. If I'd known early on that there wasn't any treasure, I wouldn't have moved in here with him. I wouldn't be sitting here now, hopelessly in love with a man I'm not even sure loves me. Now what am I to do?"

The slightest breath of air brushed across her face—shimmering in the mirror was the ghost of Virginia. With a pleading look in her eyes, she was pointing her finger and shaking her head. Unnerved at actually seeing the apparition again, Elise steeled herself and took a calming breath.

"Virginia, I'm sorry. Why are you shaking your head? Are you trying to tell me not to do something? Is that it? I don't understand. What is it you don't want me to do? Cry? You want me to stop crying?"

The ghost looked wistful and nodded.

Elise sighed and wiped her face with the back of her hand. "Well, to be honest, considering the fact that my lifelong dream has just been crushed, and the man I love doesn't love me, I think I have a lot to cry about. Tell me, why did Cyrus lead us on?"

Virginia began violently shaking her head.

Elise was perplexed. "Are you telling me he didn't?"

The apparition smiled and faded away.

"Oh, Virginia, I'm sorry. Don't go. Oh, please come back." While she anxiously stared into the glass, it again began to shimmer, and to Elise's disbelief, Grace appeared.

"My dear, I told you to follow your heart. If you love him, you must be patient and trust him."

Shaken, Elise stammered, "I d-do love him, but d-does he love me?"

Grace smiled and disappeared.

"Wait a minute," Elise called. "Don't go. What about the missing silver? Damn." She was as confused now as she had been when she sat down.

There is something perverse about more than enough.
When we have more, we never have enough.
It is always somewhere out there, just out of reach.
The more we acquire, the more elusive enough becomes.
— Dot Jackson, Charlotte Observer, 1981

Chapter 26

"I, for one, don't feel like cooking, and I'm tired of sitting around here with everyone looking like doom and gloom," Oliver stated. "I say we go into town and drown our sorrows in a couple pitchers of beer and a super deluxe pizza from Pasquale's."

"Hear, hear," Max agreed.

"I know I've said this a hundred times, but I can't get over that room being empty," Kathy said with a shake of her head. "I feel so bad for Elise. She still looked as disappointed this morning as she did last night."

"I'm still amazed there was a hidden room and we found it," Jack said. "The fact that it was empty doesn't surprise me, but I agree. For Elise's sake, I wish the money had been there."

"The look on her face about broke my heart," Max said. "It was bad enough we found that staircase, which turned out to be nothing, but then to come upon the actual room where the money had been hidden only to find a single silver certificate left . . ."

"I wonder what that certificate's worth?" Jack asked. "I know Elise was hoping to find her family's share of the money, but a thousand dollars isn't small change, and who knows? The certificate might be worth even more than that."

"I thought the same thing," Max said. "Perhaps after Elise gets over her initial disappointment, she'll realize that as well. We could take it to a bank and see what they have to say."

Oliver stood, hands on hips. "What I'd like to know is what was the point of all that ghostly freak show bullshit if there wasn't any money?"

"Elise asked the same thing," Max said. "I think it was to show her, once and for all, that the majority of the money was gone."

"Perhaps, but I swear that rope was purposely pulled from my hands," Jack said. He turned to Max. "And you said all the stairs were solid except for the one you fell through."

"Are you thinking Cyrus was responsible?" Max asked questioningly.

Jack shook his head. "Not him. Every time we've discovered a clue it either disappears, or something weird happens to try and stop us."

Max gazed at him thoughtfully. "You know, you're right. I didn't want to say anything in front of Elise, but when that stair gave way and I hit my head, I could have sworn I was pushed."

Jack nodded. "So our search may not be through."

"Are you two saying there could still be hidden treasure?" Kathy asked.

Oliver rolled his eyes heavenward and threw up his hands. "I am so done with this. Haven't you three had enough? You keep this up and you'll really piss that demented demon off. Then someone is going to get seriously hurt."

"Oliver may be right," Kathy stated. "As much as I'd like to find the treasure for Elise, I don't want anyone harmed."

Max's attention was drawn to Virginia's portrait. As he stared into her eyes, they seemed to plead with him not to give up. "I say we keep looking. And I think we'll be safe." He got to his feet. "I'll go tell Elise."

"Are we still going into town for pizza?" Kathy asked.

Max nodded. "Sure. We all need a break from this."

"Hey Elise, we've all decided to get out of here and go into town for pizza," Max said as he came into the bedroom. "And we've decided—"

He stopped, stunned by what she was doing.

"Elise what's going on?"

"I'll be ready in a minute. Pizza sounds good."

He walked farther into the room, closing the door behind him. "Would you like to tell me why you're packing your clothes?"

She took a deep breath. "Because it's time for me to go back to my apartment. I'll just drive my car, then I can leave from the restaurant."

He narrowed his eyes. "What do you mean you're going back to your apartment?"

She sighed and turned to face him. "I'm leaving because it's time for me to go. The only reason I've been staying here is that you thought I'd be in danger from whoever was after the treasure. Well, there isn't any treasure, so there isn't any danger, so there isn't any reason for me to stay any longer."

"As I started to say, we've been discussing it, and we're not sure there still isn't treasure to be found."

She glanced up from placing the last item in her suitcase. "Max, what are you talking about?"

He explained his and Jack's thoughts. "So what if we're right, and that spirit, or whatever it is, has been trying to stop us? Why would it do that if there wasn't something to find?"

She zipped up her suitcase. "Will you carry this down for me?"

"No, I won't carry that damn suitcase down for you, because you're not leaving."

"Fine. I'll carry it myself."

"Are you listening to me? I think the treasure is still here."

When she faced him, her eyes filled with tears. "Max, it's over. I've been thinking about this all night, and no matter how badly I want it to be true, my dad was right and this has been nothing but a waste of time."

"What about Cyrus and all the things that have happened? You're the one who got me to believe his ghost is here and he's trying to lead us to the money. How can you suddenly just give up?"

She rubbed her temples. "Max, I don't know. Yes, I believe Cyrus is here." She let out a short laugh. "I even had a conversation with Virginia. But, if it's true, why the empty room?" She shook her head. "I was supposed to find that one silver certificate and that's all. Now I'm going back to my apartment to decide what to do next."

)

Before she could reach for the bag, she found herself in his arms. "Max, let me go."

"No. Not until we've talked about this."

"There's nothing to talk about. I'm going back to my apartment." She pushed on his chest. "Now, let me go."

He looked into her eyes. "There's more to this than just not finding the treasure, isn't there? Elise, tell me."

She took a step back. "I can't just live here with you. Staying for a few days while we looked for the treasure was one thing, but now there isn't anything to keep me here."

"What is that supposed to mean?" he demanded. "There's nothing to keep you here? What about me? Just where in the hell do I fit in? Or is it because you don't think there's a treasure hidden in my house, so you no longer have a use for me? Is that it, Elise? Have I fulfilled my usefulness, so now you can walk out of my life?"

Her face drained of color as his words pierced her heart. Hurt and anger filled her voice. "Max, I'm not Teresa. I'm not the one who hurt you. I'm not walking out of your life. But I won't stay with a man who can't bring himself to take a chance and love again."

Silence filled the room as they stared into each other's eyes; tears streaming from hers, confusion and fear filling his.

"Elise, sweetheart. Please, p-please don't give up on me," he stammered, his voice raw with emotion. "I can't lose you."

The anguish in his eyes had her resolve slipping. She'd tossed and turned for most of the night trying to decide what she should do. She enjoyed her job at the paper, and she liked living in Cedar Bend. But what about her love for Max? She knew he cared for her, but what if he could never truly trust her? What if he couldn't tell her he loved her? Could she stay, knowing he could never give her more than they had now?

She knew the longer she stayed the harder it would be to leave. The best thing for her to do was to go back to Standish. She silently prayed for the strength to do what she needed to do, but before she could speak, he reached for her and held her close, kissing her as if he were drowning and she was his last breath of life.

"You can't leave me," he murmured against her mouth. "Please, tell me you'll stay."

With her heart pounding, she tried to hold firm to her decision. "You're not going to lose me. I'm not saying I don't want to see you anymore." She turned away. "I just can't live with you any longer. I'm not sure I can stay in Cedar Bend. Standish isn't that far. Perhaps we could see each other on the weekends."

"Standish? What are you talking about? I thought you meant you couldn't stay in this house. Are you telling me you're leaving town?"

"Perhaps. I'm not sure."

"I thought we had something special between us."

"We do."

"Then, why in the hell are you talking about moving back to Standish?"

"Because, you idiot, I happen to love you and I can't wait around until you've decided whether or not you love me."

Damn the man. How could she have lost control and blurted out her feelings like that? Well, it was too late to take her words back now. As she tried to gather her thoughts, he went to her and tenderly kissed her.

"Elise, give me a little more time," he begged when their lips parted.

Her hesitation was her undoing. He picked her up and carried her the few steps to the bed.

"Sweetheart, stay with me," he whispered as they toppled onto the mattress.

"I love you," she gasped before his mouth claimed hers.

Oh, please, Max, say the words. Tell me you love me, she silently pleaded.

"I need you, sweetheart. I need you so much. You have to stay with me," he murmured, kissing his way down her neck, fumbling with the buttons on her shirt, unhooking her bra as his lips found her rose-tipped nipple.

She groaned and ran her fingers through his hair, pulling him closer.

Raw need filled his smoky eyes as he gazed into hers. "You're the most beautiful woman I've ever seen."

She smiled. "And you're the most handsome man I've ever known."

"I think we need to get out of these clothes."

"So do I."

This task quickly achieved, he lay down and gathered her in his arms. "I could stay like this forever."

She kissed him with all the love she felt. "I know. Me, too."

He ran his hands down her back and grabbed her bottom. "Bring yourself up to me."

"No, it's my turn." She pushed him onto his back and lay on top of him.

A slow smile spread across his face. "Your wish is my command. Do to me as you will."

She grinned. "I'm going to make you scream like you do me."

His eyes shone with amusement. "How do you plan on doing that?"

"Like this." She ran her tongue along his neck and kissed her way across his chest, wiggled her way down his torso past his rock-hard abs and ran his shaft between her breasts, not stopping until she knelt between his legs, clasping his manhood in both her hands. "I've never done this before."

He lay back and closed his eyes. "I have a feeling you'll do fine."

She tentatively slid her tongue slowly up and down his shaft. "You'll have to stop me if I do something wrong."

"Sweetheart, I sure as hell won't be stopping you," he said, his words coming in short gasps.

"I believe this is how it's done." She took him deep into her mouth.

"Oh, Christ." He gasped through gritted teeth, his hands clenched into fists.

She licked the tip of his shaft, before encircling it with her mouth.

"Elise, you're killing me."

"*Hmm.*"

"I can't hold back much longer, he rasped."

"Then don't."

"Elise, do you understand what I'm saying?"

"Yes, Max, let it go," she said, taking him deep into her mouth.

For the first time since they'd been making love, Max shouted with his release.

"Elise, come here to me."

Grinning with her triumph, she lay beside him.

"You're awfully proud of yourself, aren't you?"

She couldn't hold back a laugh. "I'd say I did okay."

"Oh, you did better than okay, but now, sweetheart, it's my turn." He rolled her onto her back, grabbed both her hands in his and pulled them over her head.

"Hold onto the bedpost and don't let go until I tell you to," he demanded.

"Max?"

"Elise, do it."

Her eyes gleaming with anticipation, she did as he asked.

He began his sweet torture by running his tongue slowly around one hard nipple. When he took it into his mouth and gently tugged, she arched her back and a low "oh" escaped from her lips.

"Like that, do you?"

"Oh, yes." She moved slightly to give him access to her other breast.

He obliged her by taking her other nipple between his teeth, lightly flicking his tongue over the tip.

"Max." She squirmed beneath him.

"What?"

"I want you."

"I want you, too, sweet. But first let's see if I can make you come by doing this." He took more of her nipple into his mouth.

Her breath was coming in shallow gasps. She frantically rubbed her pelvis against him.

"Maaax."

With every ounce of willpower he possessed, Max held back his desire to sink his shaft deep inside her. With his mouth still on her breast, he reached between her legs and began to stroke.

"Oh, sweet Jesus," she cried as Max felt her climax ripple through her body. "Now, Max."

His own body throbbing for release, Max gritted his teeth. "Not yet."

He placed tiny kisses along her stomach and through the damp curls at the junction of her thighs. When his tongue slid over the tiny bud nestled there, she screamed.

"Now it's time." He moved above her and thrust himself deep inside her before the last ripples of her climax had subsided. Still holding the bedpost, she met him thrust for thrust. As once again her climax built, she let go of the post, digging her nails into his back.

As he poured his seed into her, he covered her mouth with his, swallowing both their screams. Sweat-soaked and totally satiated, they lay in each other's arms.

Elise let out a long breath. "That was quite something."

Max grinned. "I'm glad you liked it."

"*Hmmm.*" She ran her fingers through his damp hair. "I certainly did."

He began to move inside her. "So did I."

"Max, we were supposed to go for pizza."

"Do you want me to stop?"

She wrapped her arms around his neck. "No."

"I can never get enough of you," Max said, his lips inches from hers.

She sighed. "Nor I you."

"Will you stay with me?"

"Not fair asking me that now."

"All's fair, sweetheart."

"Max."

"Tell me you'll stay, or I'll stop."

"You wouldn't."

"Tell me."

"Max."

"Elise, say it."

"Okay, I'll stay, I'll stay," she cried, as once again Max sent her flying.

The quest for riches darkens the sense of right and wrong.
— Antiphanes

Chapter 27

Elise awoke early the next morning. Deciding she needed to go by her apartment to get a few more clothes and check her mail before she went to work, she quietly showered, and without waking Max, picked up her suitcase and went downstairs.

To let Max know why she had left so early, she got her notebook from her purse.

> Max,
> I wanted to get fresh clothes and check on the apartment.
> I'll see you tonight.

She hesitated and then wrote,

> Love, Elise.

She folded the note, wrote Max's name on the front, and left it on the desk in the entry hall.

At her apartment, she unpacked the suitcase, threw a load of clothes in her small stackable washer, packed fresh clothes, watered her plants, and then, while the clothes were drying, sat down with a cup of coffee to go through her mail.

She smiled as she read the birthday cards from her parents and from her brother in Philadelphia, laughed at the ones from girlfriends back home, and then frowned when she saw another envelope with her parents' return address. Opening it, she withdrew a single sheet of paper. A smaller sealed envelope was also enclosed. She unfolded the letter and read:

Elise,

While going through your grandmother's papers, I came across this letter addressed to you. It probably has something to do with that crazy treasure nonsense, but I thought I should send it on to you anyway.

All my love,
Dad

With eager anticipation, Elise quickly opened the other envelope.

Elise my dear,

If you're reading this, I'm no longer with you. This also means I didn't have the chance to explain to you about Grace and her trunk in person. I'm so sorry to be telling you this way, but I had to wait until the time was right.

I told you when you were a little girl that you and Grace had a special bond. Now I'm going to tell you something I've never told anyone else. About a week after you were born, I was in the attic looking for the bassinet I used for your dad. I planned on bringing it down for you to use when you were here. Suddenly the attic became extremely cold, and I saw a glow coming from a back corner. I have to tell you I was rather frightened, but something drew me toward the glow. When I got close, I had to move other items out of the way, but at last I saw it. Hidden in the corner was an old trunk, and it was glowing with a bright silvery light.

Now, Elise, I'm sure you're thinking your grandmother was imagining this, but I swear to you it is true. I wanted to run away, but for some reason I couldn't move. Then, as I watched—in terror I might add—the glow seemed to shimmy and formed itself into the vision of a woman.

By now, you truly must think I had lost my mind, but I promise you everything I say is the truth. The woman who took shape in front of me was Grace, and she spoke to me. She told me I was to keep the trunk hidden until your twenty-fifth birthday. At that time, I was to bring you to the trunk and show you what was inside.

I actually found the courage to ask her why it was me she was telling and not your grandfather, since he was her descendant, not me. She said he wasn't a believer and it was vital her instructions were carried out. I agreed to do as she asked, and Grace thanked me and disappeared.

Therefore, my dear, if you haven't already done so, in the back right corner of my attic, hidden behind a mound of junk, is Grace's trunk. I did not look inside so I don't know what it holds, but I have a feeling it's going to lead you to Eli Wilkey's stolen silver.

Elise, always remember I love you and wish I could have been there in person to explain this to you. Good luck, my dear.

Love,
Grandma

Tears streaming down her cheeks, Elise carefully refolded her grandmother's letter and placed it back into the envelope.

"Well, Grandma, I tried, but the silver is gone." She reached for a tissue and thought about what Max had said the night before.

She'd been so upset and determined to leave, she had barely registered what he'd been saying. Frowning, she replayed the conversation in her mind. He and Jack were thinking the treasure might still be in the house. But where? And why wouldn't Cyrus just lead them to all of it, not just show them one silver certificate? What about Grace? Why would she appear to both her and her grandmother if there wasn't a reason? Could Max be right?

Once again, excitement began to bloom inside her. Anxious to tell Max about the letter, she quickly gathered her things and was reaching for her cell phone when it rang.

"Elise, where are you?" Sandy asked.

She glanced at the clock and grimaced. She'd been there longer than she thought. "Hi, Sandy, I'm sorry. I stopped by the apartment and lost track of time."

"No problem. I need you to go to Brighton. I want you to do a story on the new fire truck the Brighton Area Fire Authority purchased for the township."

Damn. Elise bit back her annoyance. She wanted to show Max the letter from her grandmother. She sighed. It would have to wait.

"Sure, Sandy, I'll head over there right now."

Sandy chuckled. "I know it's not an exciting assignment, but . . ."

"But someone has to do it," Elise finished Sandy's sentence.

"That's right. I'll see you later."

Elise disconnected from Sandy, and as she walked to her car, punched in Max's number.

"Inn on the Bluff. This is Constance. May I help you?"

Elise frowned. She must have called the number for the inn, not Max's cell.

"Hi, Constance, this is Elise. Is Max there?"

"I don't know, Elise. I just got here and haven't seen anyone."

That's strange, Elise thought. Where could everyone be? "I left a note for Max on the front desk. Is it still there?"

"Yes, it's right here."

"Would you please make sure Max gets it? And tell him I had to go to Brighton, and I'll call him later."

"Sure, Elise. I'd be happy to."

）

Max and Jack were examining the hole they'd made to expose the hidden staircase. "I've been debating whether to open it all the way so the stairs are usable or just close it back up," Max said.

"If you want my honest opinion, opening it up would be a lot of unnecessary work. Besides, you'd lose the closet space."

Max nodded "I agree. I just wanted someone else to say it. So I'd like to get this fixed as quickly as possible before Constance sees it."

Jack grinned. "You're lucky this wall isn't the old lath and plaster."

"No kidding. But I have to run out to the lumberyard to replace those boards. I ripped the ends up prying them out, and I don't want Constance wondering why I've torn up the closet."

"I plan on doing some work from my laptop, and Kathy said something about her and Oliver going in to Ann Arbor. I'll be happy to help you when you get back."

Max nodded. "Great."

As they headed for the stairs, Jack asked, "Where's Elise? We decided when neither of you came back down yesterday, you had other things on your mind besides pizza."

When he'd awoken to find Elise and her suitcase gone, Max had been more shaken than he wanted to admit. After their conversation the night before, he thought she'd agreed to stay. He frowned. He wasn't about to beg. If she wanted to leave, then let her.

"When I got up this morning she was gone." He could tell by the look of surprise on Jack's face his tone was more brusque than he intended, but, damn it, he was pissed.

They'd reached the bottom of the stairs and Constance smiled from behind her desk.

"Good morning, gentlemen. Max, if you have a minute I'd like to talk to you."

"I'll be in the kitchen getting coffee," Jack said.

"What's up?" Max asked, stopping in front of the desk.

"I was wondering if you have any plans this morning."

Max cocked his head. "Kind of. Why?"

"I was talking with my friend, Paula. You know Paula Reynolds?"

Max nodded.

"She was telling me about a listing of hers that will be holding an auction today, a turn of the century house in Brighton."

Max shook his head. "I have all the furniture I need."

She smiled. "Sorry, I'm not being clear. I'm not talking about furniture. It's for this painting." She turned a catalog for him to see. "I understand you want something for the wall behind this desk and I saw this and thought it would be perfect. It resembles the view from your back terrace."

Max studied the landscape of rolling hills, colorful trees and a crystal stream and had to agree. "You're right, I like it. What time is the auction?"

"It's this morning at ten."

Max glanced at his watch. Nine fifteen. "I do need to go to the lumberyard."

"And you have to go past Brighton to get there," she added.

Max smiled. "Yes, I do. Okay, thanks. I'll stop and take a look."

"Max, would you mind if I go along? There're a couple of small items I might be interested in. But if you need me here, I'll stay."

"If you don't mind going on to the lumber yard, sure you can come along."

She grinned. "That's fine."

"Great, let me grab some coffee and I'll be ready."

"Max, I did have one more thing to ask you about."

"What's that?"

"It's about publicity items for the inn."

Max frowned. "What publicity items?"

"That's my point, there aren't any. I found the registration forms, but there're no note pads to put in the rooms, no pocket calendars or brochures telling about the inn. Postcards with a nice color picture of the house would be great to send out and have on hand as well. And what about a website?"

Max rubbed his forehead. "Whoa, slow down. I do have someone working on a website, but I hadn't thought about those other things." He smiled. "Could you take care of that for me?"

She hesitated. "I could, but I'd like you to pick out the letterhead. You know, the lumberyard is almost to Ann Arbor. There's a nice print shop there that I use for Christmas cards. We could run by and Sheila, the owner, could show you what she has."

Max waved his hand. "Fine, we'll do that. Give me about ten minutes." He began to walk away, then paused and turned. "Constance, did Elise call?"

"Not since I've been here."

A couple of hours later, Max had made arrangements for the painting to be delivered the next day, and he and Constance were sitting in traffic on East Grand River trying to make their way out of Brighton.

Max tapped his fingers impatiently on the outside door of the convertible. "I wonder what's holding us up?"

Constance tried to see past the van in front of them. "It looks like there's a fire engine parked by the road and there are people standing around."

"Great, it's probably an accident and we'll be stuck here for who knows how long."

"I don't think so," Constance said. "Actually it's in front of a firehouse and someone's taking pictures."

"Good, we're moving." Max eased the Mustang forward. "I guess people just like to gawk at anything." He shook his head. "Figures. You know what? I'm hungry. Do you want to get lunch?"

Constance nodded eagerly. "I'd love to. I'm starving."

"Okay, where would you like to go?"

"Well, since we're going to Ann Arbor, why don't we eat there? Then we can stop at the lumberyard on the way back."

"Sounds good." They'd made their way to US 23 and Max gunned the engine.

Constance laid her head back and laughed. "Your car is great. I love convertibles."

Max grinned. "So do I. There are some CDs in a case behind my seat if you'd like to get one out. But I have to warn you, my parents were old hippies, so my music tends to be more classic rock."

"That's fine with me."

As she turned in her seat to reach for the case, her breast brushed against Max's arm. Thoughts of Elise's words instantly filled his mind, *"She's nothing more than a trouble-making little tramp whose goal is to land herself in your bed."* Max frowned and glanced to where Constance was thumbing through the case of CDs. He mentally shook his head. The car was small and he was sure it hadn't been intentional.

"Oh, you have Neil Diamond," she exclaimed. "I saw him in concert. He was wonderful."

Max smiled. "That one belongs to my sister, but go ahead and put it in."

They drove, singing along with the music, until they reached Ann Arbor.

Max asked, "Where now?"

"There's a nice restaurant called Afternoon Delight. Would you like to go there?"

Max couldn't help but grin. "Sounds interesting."

She gave him a slow smile. "Oh, it is. Everyone likes a little afternoon delight, don't they?"

Max looked into her sky blue eyes and tiny alarm bells went off in his head, which he promptly ignored. "I suppose they do."

Elise couldn't believe her eyes. She'd just finished photographing fire officials standing around the new engine when she'd turned to see Max drive by with that tramp Constance. Furious, she'd hurried to her car, which thankfully was parked nearby. She was able to catch up and follow a couple of car lengths behind. As she drew closer, her fury rose. Constance was laughing and leaning toward Max who was smiling back.

"Jerk." She hit the gas and pulled up behind the Mustang.

Now she could hear them singing. *What the hell?* She stayed right on his ass but controlled her desire to pound on her horn. She gritted her teeth. *He doesn't even know I'm back here.* When her fury turned to angry tears, she let up on the gas.

Damn it, Elise, what are you doing? If Max Holt wants to play around with that tramp, let him. She brushed away tears, took the first exit, and turned toward home.

When she arrived back at the newspaper office, her anger hadn't cooled in the least. She stomped her way up the stairs and into her cubical. She dropped her camera case on her desk and flopped down into her chair.

"I know photographing fire engines isn't the most exciting thing, but was it that bad?"

At the sound of Sandy's voice, Elise turned. She gave a slight smile and waved her into a chair. "It's what happened afterward that has me upset."

"Want to talk about it?" Sandy asked.

Elise shrugged and told her about Max and Constance. "I'm probably overreacting and it was all perfectly innocent."

Sandy nodded. "Probably. Constance is a slut, but I don't think Max would be interested."

Elise sighed. "I can't believe I actually followed them."

"Which direction were they going?"

"Toward Ann Arbor."

"*Hmm*."

Elise narrowed her eyes. "What's '*hmm*' supposed to mean?"

"Nothing. Ann Arbor is a big city. They could have a number of reasons for going there."

Elise picked up a pen and began tapping it on her desk. "Sandy, what are you not telling me?"

Sandy got to her feet. "It's nothing, honestly. I'm sure when you see Max he'll have a good explanation. Now, I have to run. I have a budget meeting with the boss." She made a face. "Talk about fun. Call me later and let me know what Max says."

$$\text{☽}$$

It was a little after five when Elise entered the inn. The house was quiet and there was no one to be seen.

"Hello, is anybody here?" she called.

"Back here." Kathy stuck her head out of the kitchen. "Come see our new toy."

"Wow, an espresso machine," Elise exclaimed.

"Not only that." Oliver beamed. "We can make cappuccino and all kinds of fun coffee drinks. Here try this." He handed her a tall thin mug. "It's café mocha."

Elise took a sip and smiled. "This is delicious."

"Maxwell is planning on serving wine and cheese to his guests and I thought we needed something extra."

Elise nodded. "I think this is a great idea. Speaking of Max, where is he?"

Oliver and Kathy looked at each other. Oliver began fooling with the espresso machine while Kathy busied herself wiping off the counter.

Elise frowned. "Okay, you two, what's up?"

Before they could reply, Jack walked into the room. "Hey, Elise."

"Hi, Jack. Perhaps you can tell me where Max is?"

Jack glanced around. "He's not back?"

Elise shook her head.

Jack shrugged. "He left this morning to go to an auction, then to the lumberyard. I can't imagine where he is. Although I've been in his office all day, and he could have come in and left again and I wouldn't have known."

Elise turned back to Oliver and Kathy who still looked like kids who'd been caught stealing cookies. "All right, you two, spill it. What do you know?"

Oliver placed his hands on his hips. "You might as well tell her, sugar. She'll find out anyway."

Jack opened a beer and leaned against the counter. "What's going on?"

Kathy sighed. "Oliver and I saw Max and Constance going into a café in Ann Arbor."

Jack rolled his eyes. "So? I imagine they were hungry."

Before Elise could respond, they heard the front door open and close and the sound of Constance's laughter.

Elise stood debating whether she should do the logical thing and remain calm and stay where she was, or be totally irrational and go confront Max.

Kathy placed a hand on her arm. "Don't let her see you're upset. She'll only gloat. Make him come to you."

Jack sighed. "Kathy, stay out of it."

Kathy shook her head. "At times like this, us girls have to stick together."

"Hey, where is everyone?" Max called. "Come see what I bought."

Oliver rolled his eyes. "If Miss Thang helped him pick it out, I can just imagine."

Kathy put her arm through Elise's. "Come on. Let's go see."

"Oh, dear God, no," Oliver cried, covering his eyes. "Maxwell, have you lost your mind?"

Elise bit her lip to keep from laughing, while Jack cleared his throat and Kathy gasped.

"It's a Victorian umbrella stand, and I think it's great," Max said with annoyance.

"It's a dusty, dried up elephant foot and it's disgusting. Where did you get it?" Kathy asked when she found her voice.

"We saw it at the auction today. Constance thought it would look great here in the entry, and it would be somewhere for guests to put their umbrellas."

"If you want an umbrella stand, I'll be happy to get you something that looks decent," Kathy said. "Some poor elephant had to die to make that monstrosity."

Max narrowed his eyes in defiance. "I like it and it stays."

Kathy threw up her hands, turned, and walked back toward the kitchen.

Oliver mumbled something about people with no taste and followed Kathy.

"Great conversation piece, Max," Jack said, smiling, and headed in the direction of the others.

"Max, I guess I'd better be going," Constance said. "I had a wonderful time today. Thanks."

"I appreciate all your help," Max said. "You're going to be a great asset to the inn."

Elise had her jaw clamped so tight she was in danger of cracking her teeth. The triumphant smirk Constance gave Elise when Max's back was turned had her palm itching to slap her face. What was wrong with him? Couldn't he see what was under his nose? When Constance finally left and he turned to face her, she was so angry she couldn't speak.

A few minutes passed in silence before Max said, "When you weren't here this morning, I didn't know if you were coming back."

Elise frowned. "Didn't you get my note?"

He shook his head.

"Max, I left you a note there on the desk." She pointed. "And I called and told Constance to make sure you got it."

It was Max's turn to frown. "I never saw any note."

Elise glanced over at the nice clean desktop. "Well, it was there. Constance must have done something with it."

Max let out a long sigh. "Why would she do that?"

Elise wanted to scream. "Because, you idiot, she's a scheming little bitch who's trying to come between us. Did she even tell you that I called?"

He opened his mouth, closed it, looked thoughtful, and threw up his hands. "Okay, I did ask her if you called and she said no."

Elise gave him a triumphant smile. "See, I was right."

Max shook his head. "I don't know. We were in a hurry this morning and perhaps she forgot."

"Yeah, forgot on purpose," she replied, unable to keep the irritation from her voice. "I saw you two in Brighton. What were you doing there?"

He looked surprised. "We went to an auction. That's where I bought the umbrella stand and a great painting for this wall." He pointed at the empty space over the desk. "Why were you there?"

She gave a dismissive wave. "I had to do a story on a new fire engine."

Max smiled. "That was you holding up traffic?"

She shrugged. "I suppose. So why did you have to spend the rest of the day with that woman?"

When his mouth formed a stubborn line, she folded her arms and held her ground. "So?"

"So nothing." He ran his hands through his hair. "You know I don't appreciate getting the third degree about how I spent my day. But if you have to know, we went to Ann Arbor where we had lunch, and then we went to a printer where I chose stationary and stuff for publicity items for the inn. Then we stopped at the lumberyard, and then we came home. Would you like to see the receipts? Or would you like to tell me why I woke up this morning to find you and your suitcase gone?"

Her anger somewhat appeased, Elise said, "I left to go to my apartment to get fresh clothes and do a few things. And I have something to show you. My purse is in the kitchen."

When she turned, Max caught her arm, pulled her into a warm embrace, and kissed her.

She held him tight, letting his masterful kisses ease all her earlier worries and doubts away. When he lifted his mouth from hers, she saw desire in his smoky eyes, but was there something else? Did she see love there as well?

He cupped her face in his hand. "Sweetheart, there's nothing going on between me and Constance. You have to believe me. You're the only one I care about."

Oh, please Max, tell me you love me. She silently pleaded.

When he said nothing, she swallowed back the tears that threatened and stepped from his arms. "Let me show you what I found."

When they entered the kitchen, the others were sitting around the center island eating cheese puffs Oliver had made. Max helped himself to one and patiently waited for Elise to get her purse.

"This was in my mail." She handed the envelope to Max. "Read it out loud so everyone can hear," she said.

"Oh, my God," Kathy exclaimed after Max concluded. "There have to be more silver certificates hidden somewhere in this house."

Elise nodded eagerly. "I agree. Otherwise why would Grace, Cyrus, and Virginia be helping us?"

Elise turned to Max. "What do you think?"

"I have to say I think you're right. But we're back at square one. Where do we look now?"

"We can begin by eliminating the places we've already searched," Jack said. "And now that we know the money was once in a secret room, perhaps Cyrus stayed with that pattern and we need to find somewhere similar."

"Well, I'm going to be ready for any ghostly bullshit," Oliver said. "I bought this book today while Sugar and I were in Ann Arbor." He held up a paperback. *Ghost Busters and Their Secrets* was written in red across the top. "Let them try and fuck with me now."

"Ahh, okay." Max tried to hold back a laugh. "I say day after tomorrow we begin searching. We can use the time to think of where to start."

"Why not begin tomorrow?" Elise asked.

"Because, sweet, it's your birthday and I'm taking you to dinner."

Such are the ways of everyone who is greedy for unjust gain;
it takes away the life of its possessors.

— Proverbs 1:19

Chapter 28

"Max, are you up here?" Constance called.

At the sound of her voice, Max swore. He thought she'd be busy going through the dining room linens so he'd have time to cut new boards for the opening to the hidden staircase. Before he could stop her, she halted outside the closet.

"There you are," she said. "Sorry to bother you, but Martin is downstairs and wants to talk to you about the outside steps." She paused. "Oh my, what happened?" She peered closer. "Max, is that a staircase I see?" She pointed at the hole.

"Sorry about messing up the closet." Max tried to think of a believable lie. "Weird, isn't it? There was a water leak behind the bathroom sink and I was afraid it got into the wall. When I pulled off the bottom board, I found the stairs. I thought about opening it all the way so the stairs could be used, but I don't want to lose the storage. So I'm closing it back up." Max hoped like hell he sounded convincing.

She knitted her brows. "But why would anyone wall up a staircase?"

Max shrugged. "I guess somebody wanted another closet." He took her arm and steered her out into the hall. "You say Martin is here?"

A few hours later, Max had finished putting the linen closet back together and had inspected the wooden form Martin had built prior to pouring the concrete steps. Now he was hot, dirty, and thirsty. He'd grab a bottle of water then hit the shower. He didn't want to be late picking Elise up for her birthday party.

"Hey, Max, come see how nice the painting is going to look," Constance called as he came through the kitchen door.

He was surprised to see Paula Reynolds standing next to Constance.

"Hi, Paula. Don't tell me you delivered the painting in person?"

Paula smiled. "I have the van and I had to pass right by. Besides, I wanted to see how it looked."

"It's going to be perfect," Constance said. "Paula and I will hold it up and you tell us what you think."

"Okay, but I don't have time to hang it now. I have to take a shower so I can go get Elise for her party." Max stepped back and nodded. "You're right, it looks great."

"What party?" Paula asked.

"It's her twenty-fifth birthday and her friend Sandy is giving her a surprise party. Everyone else has already gone and I'm supposed to pick her up at work. So, Constance, you might as well go ahead and go home." He turned to Paula. "Thanks for bringing the painting."

"Sure, no problem."

As Max climbed the stairs, a heady sensation of the air shifting around him came over him. *Shit, not again*, he thought, glancing back down into the entry hall, but all he saw was Paula and Constance in conversation. He shrugged and continued on to his bedroom, stripping off his shirt as he went.

$$\smile$$

Standing in the shower, Max let the hot spray wash away not only his sweat and dirt, but all his past trepidations as well. He was in love with Elise, and he'd decided that tonight, after they were alone, he was going to ask her to be his wife, giving her Virginia's diamond ring.

Finally being honest with himself, he knew he'd fallen in love with her the first time he'd kissed her; he knew then that she was the only one for him. He couldn't stand by and watch her walk out of his life. The thought of losing her had given him the courage to open his heart and let her in. Even if they never found the rest of the silver, they could make a good life together here in Cedar Bend.

He stuck his head under the pounding spray and thought he heard the shower door open.

When small hands caressed his back, he smiled. "What happened, sweet? Couldn't you wait for me to come and get you?"

The soapy hands slowly glided their way down his back, working their way around his waist to stroke his increasing arousal.

"If you keep that up, sweetheart, we may never make it to the restaurant."

As heavy breasts pressed against his back, Max knew instantly that something was terribly wrong. He shut off the shower and turned, wiping the soapy water from his eyes.

"What the hell?"

As his brain registered the naked woman standing in front of him, he heard Elise on the other side of the door. "Max, what are you still doing in the shower? I passed the inn on my way back to the office and saw your car was still here."

"Fuck," Max said through gritted teeth.

"Hurry up. I'm ready for my birthday dinner," Elise said as she opened the shower door. "Oh, my God." She turned on her heel and fled from the room.

"Elise, wait! Please . . . Paula, you fucking bitch, get the fuck out of my house," Max shouted, pushing her aside.

Grabbing his jeans, his body still soapy and wet, he tugged them on as he ran, hearing Paula's laughter behind him.

"Elise, for God's sake, it was a setup."

Blinded by her tears and shaking uncontrollably, Elise caught her heel on the rug at the top of the stairs. Not waiting to get it unhooked, she kicked off both shoes and ran down barefooted. Two steps from the front door, Max caught her.

"Elise, sweetheart, listen to me."

"Let me go you lying, cheating son of a bitch."

"It was a setup. She did that on purpose."

"You're a fucking liar. Let go."

"No, not until you listen."

For the second time in their relationship, he tossed her over his shoulder and headed for the library, neither seeming to notice the swirling silver mist above their heads or the ominous shift in the atmosphere.

"Damn it, Elise, stop kicking." Shouldering the library door open, Max pushed it closed behind them.

"Max, put me down," she screamed, pummeling his wet back with her fists.

Flopping her onto her back on the sofa, he followed her down.

"Stop fighting me." Grabbing both her hands in one of his, he held them above her head, placing one of his legs across her lap. "Damn it, Elise, stop it."

Bucking her hips, she managed to roll both of them off the sofa, landing them between the sofa and the trunk used as a coffee table. He was able to get on top of her, pinning her securely beneath him.

"Elise, I just want to explain. Stop fighting and I'll let you go."

Scowling, she nodded. "How could you have done this to me? I trusted you," she said as she sat up.

"I'm telling you, I had nothing to do with it. I thought it was you getting into the shower."

"What? You thought it was me? When you were supposed to be picking me up? Try again, Max."

"Damn it, it's true. I was getting ready to come and get you, to take you to your surprise birthday party. Why in the hell would I then decide to take a shower with Paula?"

"A surprise party? I was surprised, all right. What are you talking about?"

"I guess it doesn't matter now, but Sandy is giving you a party. That's where everyone is. I was supposed to take you to the restaurant."

"And you're telling me Paula Reynolds just happened by and walked naked into your shower?"

"Yes, well, no, she was already here."

"How convenient. God, here I was worried about Constance and all the time it was Paula."

"Damn it, I'm not involved with Paula or Constance. I don't know what Paula thought she was doing, but I had no part in it."

"Well, you certainly looked as if you had a part in it. In case you hadn't noticed, Max, you had a hard-on."

"Sweetheart, I'd been thinking about you, and well, when she, I just . . ."

"You just what, Max? Thought you'd take advantage of the situation? What would have happened if I hadn't shown up?"

"Not a fucking thing would have happened. Damn it, Elise, don't you understand? I love you."

"What?" Her body went still, hearing the words she never thought she'd hear him say. Looking into the eyes of the man she loved with every fiber of her being, heart pounding and barely able to speak, she asked, "What did you say?"

With his mouth inches from hers, he spoke in the soft, seductive voice she loved.

"I said, sweetheart, that I love you. I love you more than life itself. Please believe me. I don't need to find a treasure in silver. I found my treasure, and it's you." His mouth closed over hers, pouring his love for her into that one kiss.

Elise wrapped her arms around his neck and hungrily kissed him back.

When their lips parted, he traced kisses across her cheek and down her throat, whispering his love for her as he went.

With her head turned toward the fireplace, it was Elise who saw the streak of silver flash through the window, striking the brick hearth. As she watched in amazement, a glowing silver crescent began to form on the bricks.

"Max," she whispered.

"Yes, sweetheart? God, I love the taste of you."

"Max, look."

"I'm looking." He was busily unbuttoning her shirt. "And I love what I see."

"Stop that. It's Cyrus."

"What?" Turning his head, Max gaped as the silver crescent glowed brighter. A jagged trail of silver light flowed from its lowest point and pooled on the tile below.

"What is it?"

The crescent was now shining so brightly that for a second, they had to turn away.

"The light on the tile is forming something."

They sat side by side on the Oriental rug and watched in fascination as the silver light became something like a mirror, where shapes were beginning to take form. Three men wearing Victorian clothing were visible. They stood in what looked like Max's library, their faces not yet clear. Then, as from a great distance, Max and Elise heard voices.

"Is that Cyrus?" Elise whispered.

"Watch and we'll see."

"Who the hell are you?"

"I am the brother of the man you murdered. Did ya know he had a brother? You musta known he had a wife and baby girl back east. Since you seen to it they were left with nothin', I guess you didn't give a damn, did ya? I told his wife if it took me to my dyin' day to track down the no-account bastard who did this, that's just what I'd do. Now, by God's grace and the kindness of this young man, here I finally am."

The third, younger man spoke. "In recounting your story to me, my good man, didn't you state there were two bodies found in that Colorado mine?"

The old man growled. "That's right. Not only did this no-account bastard kill my brother, he killed his own along with him."

"I killed no one. If you've been searching for your brother's murderer for twenty years, I'm sorry to tell you that you've been looking for the wrong man. For your information, your brother's murderer also died that day in the mine."

"If you didn't kill them, why'd you run off with all their money?" asked the old man.

"You don't understand; I was given no choice. Any wealth that I gained from the sale of that accursed silver has been replaced. You are welcome to take it all."

The younger man leaned forward. "Wait a minute. I want to make sure I understand this correctly, Cyrus. You're admitting to having the missing silver from the mine?"

"Garrison, you're nothing but a worthless piece of horse dung. I don't know how you came to be a part of this, nor do I care. So let me be very clear. Whatever recompense I owe this gentleman and his brother's family is between us. This is none of your affair."

"Oh, but I'm going to make it my affair."

Horrified, Max and Elise watched as in one swift move Garrison snatched the deed from Cyrus's desk, whipped out a pocket revolver, and shot the old man dead.

"Max, that had to have been Hank," Elise softly cried as blood darkened the front of the old man's shirt.

"Elise, I know. Please, just listen."

As Cyrus rose to his feet, Garrison pointed the gun directly at him. "All right, let's you and me have a little talk about where you've hidden the money from the sale of that silver. You know I never trusted you. I always thought you were concealing something, and now, thanks to this gentleman here"—he kicked the prone figure with the toe of his shoe—"my suspicions have been confirmed."

"You rotten little bastard!" Cyrus cried, lunging at him.

Stepping out of his reach, Garrison laughed. "Temper, temper, I don't think you appreciate the position I have you in with this filth out of the way." He gave Hank's body a contemptuous look.

"Max."

"I know." He put his arms around her as the young man continued.

"I'm the one holding all the cards. So you see, because of this little piece of paper and all it implies, you're going to give me the stolen money you've been hiding all these years."

Cyrus began to walk slowly around his desk.

"You know nothing of the truth of what happened that dreadful day in that mine shaft, nor do I intend wasting my time trying to explain it to scum like you. One thing I will make perfectly clear," he said, pointing his finger in Garrison's face. "You will never get your greedy hands on a single coin of that money. That silver is cursed. It's brought me nothing but personal grief and heartache. I'm sure that until it's in the hands of the one who is truly worthy, it will remain cursed. So it will stay where I put it."

"You're crazy." He shoved the gun in Cyrus's chest. "I don't give a damn if it's blessed or cursed. Tell me where it is."

In a moment, it was over. Max and Elise watched as Garrison fell dead at Cyrus's feet, the smoking pistol now in Cyrus's hand.

For seconds, an expression of horror filled his face as he stood looking down, the gun slipping from his shaking hand. Cyrus raised his stricken face to the portrait above the fireplace and let out a gut-wrenching cry, "Forgive me, Virginia."

Elise sniffed back tears. "Oh, Max, that poor man."

"Look at Garrison's hand, it's moving."

"Oh, my God, Max, the gun!"

Cyrus, his body shaking with sobs, didn't see Garrison's fingers close around the gun. His breath labored, his hand trembling, he pointed it toward Cyrus's chest and fired.

"If I'm going to hell, you're coming with me, you bastard."

As Cyrus fell, his head slammed down upon the edge of the raised brick hearth. Blood pooled beneath his him and began to trickle slowly down the side of the hearth. For less than a heartbeat, a smoky figure looked down upon the tragic scene below, disgorging an unearthly wail of unending grief and despair. A streak of silver light struck the blood beneath Cyrus's head, illuminating the bricks below with a shimmering, silvery glow. The silver on the hearth tile began to swirl, and as they watched, the figures disappeared.

So what, ghosts can't hurt you. That's what I thought then.
— Stephen King

Chapter 29

"Max, did you see the younger man's face?"

"Yes." He was more shaken than he wanted her to know. "It was Martin Todd."

"Not me," came a voice from behind them. "Virginia's brother Garrison, and my great-great-uncle."

Elise and Max turned to see Martin and Paula standing behind the sofa. Martin was pointing a gun. Paula appeared calm and smug. Elise scooted closer to Max and took his hand.

"Although, I must say the resemblance is rather amazing," Martin continued. "He even had the same unusual eye color as his sister." He glanced at the portrait and gave her a nod.

Martin, turning from the portrait, didn't see Virginia's eyes flash in anger, but Max did.

"I guess I should have paid attention to Elise's warnings," Max said. "She told me not to trust you, Martin, but Paula, where you come into this is beyond me. I can't imagine what you thought you'd gain by your little shower stunt?"

Paula laughed. "I just wanted to prove to myself you weren't as indifferent to me as you acted." She smiled. "And considering your body's reaction, I'd say I was right. As for Elise, I had no idea she would stop by. That was just an extra bonus. To be honest, it was never you I was interested in, it was the treasure. Imagine my shock when you came in out of the blue and wanted to purchase the house. I tried to dissuade you with ghost stories, but there was no stopping you."

Martin spoke up. "That's right. No sooner had I saved enough to make an offer on this place than you came along and bought it out from under me."

Degree by degree the temperature in the room had been cooling. Max felt

Elise's body stiffen beside him. When she squeezed his hand, he gave hers a reassuring squeeze back. He didn't want to take his eyes off Paula or Martin, neither of whom seemed aware of the cold.

"When you asked Martin if he knew anyone for your manager position, we couldn't believe our luck." Paula said. "We knew Constance would make a perfect spy. Being my best friend, she'd tell me everything that was going on."

Max frowned, remembering that the last time he'd seen Constance, she'd been with Paula. "Where is Constance?"

Paula shrugged. "After she told me about the hidden staircase, she had fulfilled her usefulness, so I got rid of her."

Elise gasped and Max squeezed her hand tighter.

"So, Paula, was it you or Martin who knocked Elise down when she surprised you in her apartment trying to steal her diaries?"

Martin shook his head. "That was unfortunate. When I looked through the window and saw all of you sitting around in here, I thought I would have plenty of time to conduct a search. But thanks to a tire on my truck blowing out, I was delayed long enough that I was still there when Elise got home."

"How did you even know about the diaries?" Elise asked.

He smiled. "That was pure luck. Constance happened to be in the diner, sitting in the booth directly behind Max and Jack. They blabbed and she told Paula. So, Elise, you have your lover to thank, along with this." He held up the chunk of silver ore. "This was all the proof I needed that the story was true. Cyrus Mosby did hide a stash of money somewhere in this house."

"The newspaper article never mentioned the silver so how did you know what happened here that night?" Elise asked.

Martin gave her a smug smile. "You're forgetting who I am and how powerful my family was back then. The details of that night were kept out of the paper and never made public. But the story of how Garrison met an old bum in Finnegan's Tavern has been told in my family throughout the generations. It seems Garrison overheard a conversation between the tavern owner and an old guy who was asking questions about Cyrus Mosby. Now, Garrison thought Cyrus had a secret he'd been hiding for years, but as hard as he tried, he couldn't get Virginia, his sister, to tell him what it was. So when he heard Cyrus's name, he became curious. After buying the old guy a few drinks, he learned who he was and why he was here. Then Garrison set up a meeting between the old guy and Cyrus. Thanks to Cyrus giving us a ghostly look into the past, I now know what happened to Garrison that night."

"That money never belonged to Garrison Hale," Elise stated. "It belongs to my family. Garrison murdered my ancestor Hank Wilkey and then tried to murder Cyrus Mosby. As far as I'm concerned, he got what he deserved."

"Cyrus was a nobody who married a Hale," Martin shouted. "He should have been grateful my family accepted him. After Virginia died, her half of Cyrus's fortune should have gone to her family. Garrison went to Cyrus repeatedly asking for a loan, but Cyrus wouldn't give him a dime. When Garrison found out about the stolen silver, he thought he'd just take what he had coming. Now, since Garrison's long gone, it's my right to take the silver for myself."

"What makes you think the silver is still here?" Max asked. "We searched this entire house and didn't find anything but an empty, hidden room."

Martin's grin was pure evil. "Why, it's right here."

Paula looked confused. "Isn't it beneath that enclosed staircase Constance told me about?"

Martin shook his head. "That was nothing but a red herring. My problem now is what to do with these two. I want to get to the silver before those idiot friends of theirs come back."

Martin's back was to the French window, but Max had a clear view of flashes of silver light outside.

"Just shoot them and be done with it," Paula said.

Martin nodded. "I suppose I have no choice. Now, you two, get up."

"Max." Elise grabbed his arm.

"It's okay. Just do as he says."

"Stop whispering to each other," Martin commanded. "And let me see your hands. That's good." He turned to Paula. "Constance is dead, right?"

"I believe so. I hit her hard and she fell and cracked her head on the desk." She shrugged. "She was bleeding pretty badly and not moving."

Elise made a small whimpering sound.

"Okay, the story will be that Elise caught Max with Constance, and in a rage she shoots him then attacks Constance." Proud of his cleverness, he grinned. "Then poor Elise, beside herself with grief, takes her own life." He laughed. "Yes, yes, I like it."

Elise grabbed Max's hand and gave it a slight tug. From the corner of his eye he saw Constance, her hair matted with blood, slowly crawl through the library door and ease her way toward Paula.

In order to keep Martin and Paula's attention away from Constance, Max said, "You'll never get away with that. In order to make it look as if Elise shot me, you'll have to get Elise's hand around the gun while I just stand here, and I'm not about to do that."

The expression on Martin's face turned from smug amusement to crazed cunning. "Not if I do this first." Quicker than Max could react, Martin clipped him under the jaw, knocking him backward. As Max fell, Martin grabbed Elise, thrust the gun into her hand, and all hell broke loose.

The room lit with a brilliant silver light.

"Release her," Virginia demanded, appearing in front of Martin, who screamed and threw Elise to the floor where she landed on top of Max. The gun slid across the floor. Constance, blood dripping down her face, stood shakily, picked up a table lamp, and brought it down on the back of Paula's head before collapsing.

The floor began to shake. Books flew from the shelves. The windows blew open and furniture toppled as a swirling black mist transformed into a ghostly Garrison. Max, still flat on his back on the floor, held Elise tight as she buried her face in his chest.

Martin, who hadn't moved, his eyes blank, seemed to lose all color as Garrison's image became clearer.

"I will have what's mine," Garrison declared, his raspy voice growing louder as it vibrated off the walls. "Martin has proven to be weak, but I will flourish and succeed."

Unnerved, Max couldn't take his eyes from the scene before him.

Martin, now pale as chalk, began to crumple to the floor as a light mist covered him and Virginia reappeared. "Garrison, I will not allow you to take another life."

Garrison laughed. "You won't, dear sister? I don't see how you'll stop me."

"Perhaps she cannot do it on her own," another female voice said. A striking redhead in a dark green velvet dress and a wide-brimmed hat floated down from Virginia's portrait. "But I've waited too long to retrieve what belongs to my family to allow you to stand in the way."

Max nudged Elise and whispered, "Stop crying and look."

Elise turned and gasped. "Max, it's Grace."

When she began to sit up, Max pulled her back. "No, stay down, this isn't over."

Garrison laughed even harder. "You honestly think I'll be taken out by two women?"

Spears of silver light ricocheted off the walls as Cyrus appeared in front of the fireplace. "Garrison, enough!" he roared. As they did over a century ago, the two men faced off. "I destroyed you once, I can do it again."

Garrison glared at him. "We were both flesh and blood men then, and you were helped along by the use of my gun. You cannot kill what is already dead, Cyrus, so do your worst."

He was warned. And now he's paid.
Let him be buried with the other victims of human greed and folly.
— Forbidden Planet (1956)

Chapter 30

It was over in a flash. Simultaneously, Cyrus, Virginia and Grace hit Garrison with converging spears of silver light.

Elise screamed and covered her face.

Max thought he'd never forget the sound Garrison made as his image exploded in a gleaming burst then vanished.

When the room went silent, Max gently drew Elise's hands from her face and whispered, "Sweet, it's over."

Elise tentatively glanced around. "Max, the room is back to normal."

"Almost. Look." He pointed toward the fireplace where Grace stood.

"My father's fortune is finally where it belongs. My darling, Elise, enjoy. Watch and you will see the truth."

She blew Elise a kiss and disappeared. The silver crescent on the side of the hearth again shone brightly, liquid silver swirling at its tip, once again forming a shimmering window into the past.

As Elise and Max watched, two angry men in a Colorado silver mine appeared in the mist.

"Nathan, you've killed him."

"Damn it, Clayton, it was self-defense. Eli came after me. He planned on killing both of us, then taking all the money for himself."

"That's a damn lie," Clayton cried. "Eli Wilkey was a good and honest man. He would never have stolen from us. My God, Nathan, you've killed an innocent man."

The face of the man called Nathan turned hard. "Clayton, we're brothers. Why should we split the profits from The Silver Crescent among three, when splitting it two ways will give us both so much more?"

Shock and disbelief filled Clayton's face. "Nathan, you just committed cold-blooded murder. How do you expect to get away with this?"

Nathan grinned. "That's easy. I'll just tell Sheriff Ervis it was self-defense, and if that doesn't work, he's never been opposed to having a little extra money come his way."

"My God, Eli Wilkey was our friend. Are you so consumed with greed you can kill a man and then just calmly walk away?"

Nathan's face twisted with rage. "Clayton, you always were a little prig with no guts. We've been up in these goddamned mountains for years before finally hitting it big, and I'm not about to share what I worked so hard for with some outsider. You're either with me or you're not."

"Call me what you like, but Eli Wilkey worked just as hard in this mine as we did," Clayton shouted. "I'm not going to be a party to his murder."

Nathan sneered. "Is that right? Well, little brother, either you go along with my story to Sheriff Ervis or I'll tell him it was you who killed Eli, and not in self-defense. I'll say you killed him so you could take his share."

"He'll never believe you. Sheriff Ervis knows me too well."

"Is that so? Little brother, you are about as naïve as they come. I've already paid Ervis to say anything I tell him. He'd even go along with me if I told him you tried to kill me, as well as Eli, so you could have all the money for yourself."

Clayton shook his head. "That's not true. Ervis won't believe I'd kill anyone, any more than he'll believe Eli tried to kill you, and I'll prove it."

"Prove it? Prove it how?" Nathan snarled. "It will be my word against yours. Besides, in case you didn't understand me, I've already paid him off. He's not going to believe a damn word you say."

"Then, I'll find an honest sheriff who will." Clayton turned his back on his brother and walked away.

"Max," Elise cried as Nathan drew a pistol, aiming it at Clayton's back.

"Hush. It's Eli. He isn't dead."

"Clayton, behind you." Eli Wilkey's weak voice came a second before Nathan fired. Clayton dove as the bullet slammed into the mine's dirt wall, inches from where he had stood.

"You little son of a bitch," Nathan growled. "You'll not ruin this for me. I'll kill you first."

Clayton watched from the floor of the mine, as with the last of his strength, Eli threw a chunk of ore, hitting Nathan on the side of his head and taking him to his knees. Not wasting time, Clayton moved, knocking Nathan onto his back, seizing his gun and pinning him to the dirt.

"It's over Nathan. Give it up."

"God damn you," Nathan screamed, and with the strength of the crazed, flipped Clayton off him. "I'm far from being done. I won't be done until you're both dead."

Max and Elise watched in horror as the two brothers rolled on the floor of the mine, desperately fighting for their lives.

"Son of a bitch," Max exclaimed when they heard the shot.

Clayton Hamilton, the revolver in his hand, knelt beside his dying brother, tears running down his dirty cheeks.

"Oh, Nathan, look what your greed has brought us to."

Nathan spat blood. "You think you've won, little brother, don't you? Well, the joke's on you. You're now a wanted man, Clayton Hamilton," he rasped out weakly. "I told Sheriff Ervis if something went wrong and I ended up dead, he was to charge whichever man was left standing with both murders." He grinned cruelly. "So it looks like you're going to hang." He coughed up more blood. "I'll see you in Hell."

They were his last words, leaving Clayton sitting in the silent mine.

Before Max and Elise could move, the silver mist began to swirl, next showing them Clayton in a one-room log cabin, digging a large hole in the middle of the dirt floor.

He dragged over a heavy-looking trunk. Opening the lid, he lifted out several leather satchels, placing them into the pit. When the trunk was empty, he filled in the hole, packing and smoothing the dirt until the spot matched the rest of the floor. Gazing around the sparse room, Clayton choked back a sob as he lifted the two remaining satchels and headed for the door. As he stepped into the twilight he paused, looking up at the mountains.

In a voice raw with fear and despair, he declared: "I'm no murderer, nor a thief. I'm only taking my fair share and hopefully, somehow, someday, I can atone for the wrong that occurred this night." Tears still streaming down his cheeks, sorrow etched on his face, he turned and walked away.

When he had gone, Max and Elise were left staring at the empty cabin and the surrounding mountains.

"What the hell?" Max exclaimed, sitting up straight, mouth agape.

"What is it?" she asked. "What's wrong?"

Unable to speak, he just stared.

"Max?"

"Elise, that's my parents' house."

"What? What do you mean, Max? Where's your parents' house?"

"There." He pointed to the log cabin still visible in the silver mist.

"What, that old shack?"

He shook his head. "That cabin is sitting directly behind my folks' place in Leadville."

"What are you talking about?"

"I'm telling you that the miners' cabin is still there, behind my parents' inn. My mother uses it now to make and display her pottery."

"Max, are you telling me we just watched Clayton bury the silver under the floor of your mother's pottery shed?"

He grinned. "Well, yes, but it wasn't her pottery shed then."

"This isn't funny. Are you saying, when all this time we've believed the money was hidden here in this house, it's been in Leadville, and this is your connection to Cyrus?"

"When my parents bought the inn and restored it, that cabin was empty. Over the years, a hardwood floor was put in and the cabin converted into a small cottage. My mother decided it would be perfect for her pottery, so Dad fixed it up for her. How were we to know millions of dollars were buried under the floor?"

"How can you be sure the two cabins are the same?"

His grin grew wider. "Because, sweetheart, since I was old enough to stand and look out of my bedroom window, I've seen the exact cut in the mountain range, just where Clayton looked when he stood in the yard of the cabin."

She shook her head. "There have to be hundreds of cuts like that in the Rocky Mountains. How do you know that's the same one?"

Throwing his head back, he began to laugh.

Elise's lips formed a thin line. "Max."

"Oh, I'm sorry." He tried to control his laughter. "It's just so incredible. I can't believe I've been so stupid." Gathering her into his arms, he kissed her before he continued. "The cut in the mountain behind my house forms a sort of half-moon curve under the peak, a crescent shape. I'm assuming that's where they came up with the name for their mine. The connection never entered my mind."

"Max, I don't know whether to kiss you again or just knock your head off. There have been silver crescents appearing all over the place. Five of us have just spent an entire weekend searching every inch of this house looking for a hidden room and the whole time the money is buried in a cabin sitting in your parents' backyard in Leadville, which happens to sit under the shadow of a crescent-shaped mountain, and none of this ever occurred to you?"

He smiled. "I know. I'm an idiot. In my defense, we've never referred to the rock formation as a crescent. It's always been a half moon. And Leadville looks a lot different now than it did during Cyrus's time." He shrugged, and his smile widened. "But none of that matters now. We know where the rest of the money is hidden."

"What do you mean, 'the rest of the money'?" she asked. "Isn't it all in Leadville?"

"Didn't you see Cyrus pick up those last two satchels?"

Her eyes opened wide as the image replayed in her mind.

"Max, you're right." She smiled, only to have her elation dissolve as she recalled the empty, hidden room. "If Cyrus hid the money he took with him in that room Oliver found, well, it's gone. And who's to say the rest of the money buried under that cabin is still there?"

A triumphant smile lit his face. "But, Elise, the money wasn't in that room. Or, I should say, it isn't there now."

Before he could continue, Constance let out a painful whimper.

Jumping to his feet, he hurried to where she still lay. "Constance, it's Max. Can you hear me? Elise, her eyes are open. Call 911. Constance, just lie still. You've been hurt pretty badly. You may have a concussion."

"Max . . ." She feebly began to speak. "I didn't know what they planned. I never wanted to hurt anyone." She began to cry. "Max, I'm so sorry. I didn't know how evil they were."

"It's all right. Don't talk. No one will blame you."

"The ambulance is on its way," Elise said, coming to sit on Constance's other side.

Constance slowly turned her head. Tears still streaking her face, she pleaded. "Elise, I'm sorry. I didn't tell Max that you called and I took your note. Max isn't interested in anyone but you."

"I know, it's okay," Elise said.

Constance took a ragged breath. "I tried to stop Paula. Did I kill her?"

"Hush now, just lie there. I hear an ambulance. Max." Elise motioned with her head for him to follow her. "Are they dead?" She pointed to where Paula and Martin still lay.

Max walked to Martin and picked up the gun. Tentatively, he touched Martin's neck checking for a pulse, sighing with relief when he felt the steady beat.

"He's not." He quickly went to Paula. "She has a nasty bump on the side of her head, but she's still breathing."

"What are we going to tell the paramedics happened to Martin? He's just lying there with no visible injuries."

Max turned to Virginia who was serenely gazing down at him from her portrait. She smiled and a light mist covered Martin, disappearing as quickly as it had appeared, leaving him awake and blinking in confusion.

"I think we should tell as much of the truth as possible," Max said. "Martin and Paula thought we knew where the lost silver was and they held a gun on us. They injured Constance, who managed to hit Paula and I took

Martin out."

Elise frowned. "But shouldn't he look as if he's been hit?"

With a smile, Max walked over and hunkered down in front of Martin who had just sat up, still looking dazed. "Martin, this is for sucker punching me and for putting your fucking hands on Elise."

"Max!" Elise screamed as Max laid Martin out with a hard right to the jaw.

$$\)$$

In the wake of the departing ambulance carrying both Constance and Paula, and a police cruiser transporting a cursing Martin, their friends came running into the library.

"Thank God you're all right," Kathy cried, trying to hug both Elise and Max at the same time. "When you didn't show up at the restaurant, Oliver was convinced you had both been murdered by the ghosts and your bodies consumed in a flash of silver light."

Looking unabashed, Oliver grinned.

Jack shook his head. "I tried to tell them their imaginations were getting out of control, but obviously something's been going on. What happened? Who's in the ambulance? And why were the police here?"

"Let's all sit down," Max said. "I could use a drink. Then we'll tell you an incredible story."

$$\)$$

"The little bitch," Sandy exclaimed, once they'd been told how Elise had found Max and Paula. "And I thought it was Constance Max had to be leery of."

"No kidding," Oliver said.

"Should I move on with the story?" Max asked.

"Yes, please do," Kathy said. "I'm on pins and needles."

They sat in stunned silence as Max finished his tale. Kathy looked horrified.

"He actually held a gun on you? My God, Elise, you must have been scared out of your mind."

She nodded. "I was. I thought he was going to make me shoot Max."

Kathy visibly shuddered. "I can't imagine being saved by a bunch of ghosts."

"At least they did something right for a change," Oliver stated.

"I have to say that's the most incredible story I've ever heard," Jack said. "You mean to tell us, Max, that the entire time we've been turning this house upside down, the money has been buried in your parents' backyard in Leadville?" He began to laugh uncontrollably. "That's too much."

"Too much is right," Oliver agreed. "Maxwell, I love you like a brother, but are you sure you're capable of running this inn? I mean really, it wouldn't take someone of extraordinary intelligence to put together a crescent-shaped mountain located in what was once an old silver town where you happened to have grown up with, say, silver crescents appearing all over your house which had originally been built by the same man who had the silver mine in Leadville and who supposedly hid an enormous amount of money, not to mention—"

"Oliver, that's not fair," Kathy interrupted. "Max has had a lot on his mind. Besides, we've all been to Max's parents' house and none of us thought of the mountain either."

Max cleared his throat. "If all of you are done questioning my mental capacity . . ." He paused to make sure he had their attention. "Would you like to know where the rest of the money is hidden?"

He smirked, seeing the surprise on their faces. "That's right. Stupid Max knows where Cyrus hid the money he was carrying when he left the cabin."

"Max!" Elise exclaimed. "Stop being an ass. Tell us where it is."

"Why, sweetheart, it's right there." Standing, Max pointed to where the silver crescent still glowed brightly on the side of the brick hearth.

He is no fool who gives what he cannot keep to gain what he cannot lose.
— Jim Elliot

Epilogue

One Month Later

"Hurry up, you two. Elise is on the lawn getting ready to throw her bouquet," Kathy called, standing on the edge of the inn's terrace, motioning for Oliver and Jack. "Doesn't she look beautiful in Virginia's wedding dress?"

Oliver smiled. "Yes, sugar, she looks fabulous and Maxwell cleans up rather well himself."

Kathy sighed. "I have to say, I wasn't sure we'd ever see this day."

"Well, sugar, we all know that on occasion Maxwell can be stubborn and a real blockhead, but I was confident Elise could break through that wall he put up around his heart."

She nodded. "They sure had their challenges. But I knew the first time I met Elise they were perfect for each other."

"Speaking of challenging relationships, since Constance will still be working here, I suppose I'm going to have to try and like the black widow," Oliver said.

"It seems she was nothing more than Martin and Paula's pawn," Jack said. "By the way, I understand Martin is in jail and being held for psychiatric examination. After all, he claimed he was assaulted by a ghost from a painting."

Oliver laughed. "Yeah, he must be completely nuts to believe in ghosts."

Kathy shuddered. "It still makes me sick when I think of what might have happened to Max and Elise if the ghosts hadn't helped. Oh, look, Sandy caught the bouquet! I'm glad she didn't get mixed up with Martin. Maybe, now that he's out of the picture, catching the bouquet will bring her luck and she'll meet someone who appreciates her."

"I still can't get over actually finding those silver certificates stashed under the hearth," Jack said.

"I was more amazed at finding the rest of the treasure still buried under the floor of Max's mother's pottery shed," Kathy said. "I laugh every time I recall the consternation on his parents' faces when he explained all of this to them."

Jack grinned. "I know. They thought he'd lost his mind, telling them a ghost showed him where to look."

"Elise's parents didn't believe her either," Oliver said. "Her father told her to get home where she belonged and stop all of this nonsense. Well, they believe it now. Her father even visited the Cedar Bend newspaper office and said that for a rural paper it wasn't bad. I guess he told Elise's boss he was lucky to have her and he wouldn't be surprised if someday she wasn't running the paper."

"What I can't believe," Jack said, "is that Kathy convinced me to move to this small town and open my own architectural office."

She hugged his neck. "I love it here. We'll find a terrific house and I'll decorate it and we'll be close to our friends. And I think this is a wonderful place to raise our baby."

"What? Wh-what did you just say?" Jack stammered.

"Way to go, sugar," Oliver exclaimed. "I get to be an uncle!"

"What's all the excitement?" Max asked as he and Elise came up the terrace steps.

Oliver grinned. "Sugar's gone and got herself pregnant."

Kathy laughed. "Well, I didn't do it on my own."

"Kathy, that's great," Elise said, hugging her friend.

Max slapped Jack on the back. "Old buddy, you look as if you could use a drink."

"I'm so excited you two will be staying," Elise said. "We'll all help you find the perfect house. In the meantime, you'll stay here with us."

"At least now, since Maxwell found the money hidden here in Collinwood, we haven't had any more visits from the demonic duo. Good-bye and good riddance," Oliver declared. "Things will finally be normal around here."

Pop.

"Oliver!" they all cried, as the cork from a bottle of champagne sitting nearby popped and sent a fountain of chilled champagne directly toward Oliver, spraying him from head to toe.

Glancing up, Max smiled at the two shimmering shapes as they waved and disappeared.

Acknowledgments

I'd like to thank everyone at The Writer's Coffee Shop for their help and advice, especially my senior editor, Wendy Depperschmidt. You're the best!

I couldn't have done this without the love, support, and encouragement of the following people:

All the members of my extensive Paige family;

My cousin, Janis Dalton, with special thanks for her many hours of reading and critiquing my manuscripts;

The "Hilton Head Gang," in particular my friend, Mike Haley, who gave me the idea for this book. Cheers, Mikey;

All my friends from the Oregon Historic District;

And my husband and "editorial assistant," David, without whom I couldn't have written this book.

I love you all.

About the Author

Debby Grahl lives on Hilton Head Island, South Carolina, with her husband, David, and their cat, Tigger. Besides writing, she enjoys biking, walking on the beach and a glass of wine at sunset. Her favorite places to visit are New Orleans, New York City, Captiva Island in Florida, the Cotswolds of England, and her home state of Michigan. She is a history buff who also enjoys reading murder mysteries, time travel, and, of course, romance. Visually impaired since childhood by Retinitis Pigmentosa (RP), she uses screen-reading software to research and write her books. Debby belongs to RWA, Florida Romance Writers, Hearts Across History, and Lowcountry Romance Writers.